Amber Laura

Redesigning Her

Publisher: LitLiber

COPYRIGHT

Amber Laura's biography, also known as "Five Fun Facts about the Author":

1.   As a writer, Amber Laura does her best daydreaming as a window-gazing passenger on long car rides.
2.   If there's creamer, she's drinking coffee. When she edits, there's always creamer.
3.   A blogger, she also writes web fiction—(free stories updated chapter-by-chapter, week-by-week). Check it out at www.litliber.com.
4.   Psst! Her debut novel, *Topaz and Lace*, a contemporary romance set in a fictitious Texas town, got its start on that same blog.
5.   While she may physically reside in the beautiful country of Northern Idaho, in her imagination, Amber Laura lives all over the world. She considers it one of the best perks to being a writer: easy, cheap travel. That and the oddball characters she meets along the way....

Other Novels by Amber Laura:

Topaz and Lace
Twenty-Seven Tiered Almond Cake
After She Fell

To my best friend, Angela (Angie Pants) Little.

*Thanks for <u>always</u> reading, supporting, cheering me on…
and most importantly, thank you for falling in love
with the male protagonist in this novel.*

This one's for you—I love you, darling girl.

TABLE OF CONTENTS

COPYRIGHT

CHAPTER ONE

CHAPTER TWO

CHAPTER THREE

CHAPTER FOUR

CHAPTER FIVE

CHAPTER SIX

CHAPTER SEVEN

CHAPTER EIGHT

CHAPTER NINE

CHAPTER TEN

CHAPTER ELEVEN

CHAPTER TWELVE

CHAPTER THIRTEEN

CHAPTER FOURTEEN

CHAPTER FIFTEEN

CHAPTER SIXTEEN

AMBER LAURA

CHAPTER SEVENTEEN

CHAPTER EIGHTEEN

CHAPTER NINETEEN

CHAPTER TWENTY

CHAPTER TWENTY-ONE

CHAPTER TWENTY-TWO

CHAPTER TWENTY-THREE

CHAPTER TWENTY-FOUR

CHAPTER TWENTY-FIVE

CHAPTER TWENTY-SIX

CHAPTER TWENTY-SEVEN

CHAPTER TWENTY-EIGHT

CHAPTER TWENTY-NINE

CHAPTER ONE

Somedays, a girl needs the routine of a predicable evening at home.

Letting herself into her apartment, Catherine Cryer sighed. Juggling the long, thin strap of her leather purse over her shoulder and three paper bags of groceries against one hip, she just managed to wiggle through the doorway. Without bothering to kick off her shoes, she strode down the long narrow hallway. Reaching its end, she turned sharply to the left; her feet veering naturally at the arched doorway separating it from her living room, Cat entered her small kitchenette.

Dropping the bags unceremoniously down on one of the counters, she bit back a sigh of exhaustion. It wasn't quite five o'clock on Friday evening, and she was definitely in need of the looming weekend.

Pulling out a carton of milk and a stalk of celery from the paper bag, Cat opened her refrigerator door. "I'm going to slip into a pair of fleece pajamas, order in pizza and binge watch TV straight through to Sunday evening," she vowed, depositing the food items before reaching back into one of the bags and pulling out a couple of cans of soup and tomato paste.

Padding over to a cupboard door, she nodded firmly. "It's going to be utterly delightful. I don't want to set eyes on another human being until Monday morning."

Slamming the door shut, she smiled thinly.

"No more people will suit me just fine." Moving robotically, she emptied the last of her groceries.

"No more, 'Umm, excuse me, Miss Cryer,'" she muttered, replaying an unfortunate encounter she'd dealt with earlier that afternoon at work, her voice a caricature of a long-suffering client. "But I think there's a bit of a discrepancy with your interest calculation..."

That had come from the one and only, Mrs. Agnes Barnes.

Having looked up from her admittedly outdated computer system at the voice of a frail older woman standing—unannounced—in the doorway of her office, Cat had barely suppressed a shudder. From three years of experience at the Fireside Credit Union, Cat was well aware that if Agnes looked frail, her particular style of speaking was anything but.

"Agnes."

"That's Mrs. Barnes when I'm at the bank."

"The credit union."

Agnes had flipped one wrist dismissively in the air.

"Fair enough. Mrs. Barnes—"

"I got this statement in the mail." Without waiting for polite conversation, Mrs. Barnes galloped into the reason for her visit. "And, as I'm sure you'll see, it's wrong."

Nodding, hoping the quick action would disguise the impatience marring her forehead, Cat had reached across the desk to grab the offending item from Mrs. Barnes outstretched hand. Warily, she'd done as requested.

It's not that Mrs. Barnes didn't have a right to question her loan (of course she did!); it wasn't the fact that long before Cat even had a chance to read through the billing statement she'd known that there was no accounting error (and there hadn't been!), or that she'd have to find the right tact with which to convey this to Agnes; it wasn't even the fact she had to have this conversation at least twice a week with harried overworked and underpaid community members who couldn't afford the price of their car payment anymore...

At least, Cat didn't think it was any of those reasons. She wasn't entirely sure what it was, she only knew she'd suddenly experienced a sharp, searing discontent steal over her person at the interaction. She'd felt an irrational, underserved, but all the same, very real weariness settle upon her chest.

Or maybe it hadn't been *quite* so sudden. And that had been all the more disquieting. It hadn't been the first time she'd felt this feeling of late, this overwhelming, aggravating sort of fatigue. It'd been haunting her the past few weeks. A sort of merry-go-round of the same boring old everyday things. Nothing spectacular. Nothing new or different.

And it wasn't just work. Hell, if it were just work, well, she could have easily found a solution to that.

"Is that so?" Cat mocked herself, carefully folding up the empty grocery bags now and placing them on a shelf in her pantry. "And what would you do? Find a new job? Hah! How many times have I heard that before?"

Opening the refrigerator door again, she brought out a can of sparkling water.

"Whatever," Cat mumbled, popping the top off the citrus-flavored drink. Shuffling out of the kitchen, she crossed the narrow strip of laminated flooring dividing them and stalked into her living room. The bank of windows against two of the four walls flooded the room in early evening light. Normally, she would have found the pinkish glow warm and cozy. Today, it only seemed to highlight her staid existence—managing to underscore the large oval lamp standing in one corner of the room, a relic of the nineties, as well as the bulky coffee table her parents had given her when she'd first moved out, the light splaying across the utterly unremarkable oatmeal-colored carpet...

Sinking into her bamboo-framed couch, the cushions a magnificent splash of lime green and white geometric designs, Cat sighed. Setting her drink down, she scooped up the remote. With a push of the power button, the TV flickered to life.

What she needed was a distraction.

"Here's to the beginning of a weekend spent doing nothing." Her voice was almost

Three hours later, in the midst of one of those home renovations shows the networks seemingly aired on repeat, Cat felt her mind wandering. The television show buzzed on in the background as the hosts discussed the best, cheapest way to tear out the bathroom—

It started with a twitch of her finger against the wooden arm-rest, and then her foot was tap-tapping impatiently against the thin carpeting, and pretty soon Catherine could feel her thoughts taking over her attention.

Another Friday night.

Maybe—maybe she'd been wrong. Maybe predictability wasn't what Cat needed. Maybe she should have shaken up her routine: gone out partying instead, indulged in a few cocktails with friends.

Maybe she should have done something social. Done *something*, anything at all...

With a snap, hardly aware of her intentions, Cat leaned forward to grab her silent phone off the coffee table. Automatically, her fingers scrolled through her contacts, stopping when they landed on Ashley's name.

Without further thought, her finger tapped against the screen, dialing her number.

One ring.

Two.

Three.

Four.

"Hello, you've reached Ashley Sanders's voicemail. I'm not availabl—"

Frowning, Cat disconnected. Staring dejectedly at her phone, she was startled when, seconds later, it dinged with a text notification. Opening the message, Cat's frowned deepened.

FROM: Ashley Sanders
8:11 p.m.
MESSAGE: Hey girl. Sorry, can't talk. Out with some coworkers.

"Of course you are," Cat muttered darkly, staring down at her phone as if it had personally betrayed her. "You've still got friends."

And that was the *real* problem. Just another Friday night. Spent alone. A sort of merry-go-round of the same boring old everyday.

"New friends," Cat continued, her voice thickening with emotion. "To go with your new city life."

With lithe movements, she replied:

FROM: Cat Cryer
8:12 p.m.
MESSAGE: No worries. Just thought I'd check-in. Miss you!

Three seconds went by when she received another message:

FROM: Ashley Sanders
8:12 p.m.
MESSAGE: Me too. It's been ages—I want to hear all about that new promotion at work. How about Sunday evening? Girl chat.

Cat swallowed her disappointment. Sunday seemed a long way away. Still, being desperate and sounding desperate were two very different things. And really, begrudging her friend for having a life? How pathetic. How mean.

With these thoughts in mind, Cat pinned a smile on her face as she replied again:

FROM: Cat Cryer
8:13 p.m.
MESSAGE: Sure! Sunday works for me.

Chucking her phone onto the empty seat beside her, Cat knew the conversation, short as it had been, was now over. Ashley would read it with relief before getting back to her coworkers. Cat wondered momentarily what that would be like: if she were ever to go out with the people at the credit union. Not that she'd ever had the opportunity.

"And who's fault is that, Cat? You can't do one thing and then cry when it works."

It was true, Cat hadn't built close bonds with her coworkers but that had been a strategic move on her part. She'd had promotions in mind, not social gatherings. Besides that, most of the employees were either fifteen-plus years her senior or college kids picking up part-time jobs as tellers—stuck somewhere in the middle, Cat had found little incentive to bridge the gap.

And even if she'd wanted to join in the water cooler chit-chat, it was hard to find common ground when Cat spent the majority of her time in a private office down the hall. Away from the goings-on of everyone else. Which she'd desperately wanted when she started working there, which she'd spent grueling hours of overtime accomplishing....

Because, well, she'd never wanted to confuse the personal with the politics, with the bureaucracy. She'd bent her focus on her career. It had never even occurred to her to think otherwise. Then again, she'd also never intended to stay at the credit union for so long. She'd thought of it more as a resume-builder stopgap. When most of her high school friends had left to go to colleges out of state, Cat had preferred to stay home, had gone to the local university. It had been a practical decision, both financially and professionally, especially as her degree was so sought after in her chosen career field. So, she'd played it safe, played it smart.

Only Cat had never meant to *stay* Not at the credit union. Not in her apartment, not even that town. Not permanently. Except there'd been no reason to leave. Unlike her friend Carly, she hadn't been transferred to a company branch in Ohio; unlike Ashley, she hadn't needed to move to Spokane to find better job opportunities; unlike everyone else, who'd never come back, Cat had never found her exit.... Instead, she'd gotten the promotion she'd so desperately applied for at work, and after that, she'd gotten a couple more. The pay raises had been enough to afford this apartment as well as offering a generous benefits package and all the trimmings of a safe and secure future.

And while she'd been doing that, she'd let herself get left behind. Her friends had gone out and explored, and she'd—

Cat's eyes roamed around the peach-painted walls of her living room, her sight catching on the leafy peace lily by the window, the slightly ajar door against the opposite wall which opened to her bathroom, the television set, anything to distract her thoughts... At the scrutiny, she felt that newly familiar dragging weight claw at her stomach, as well as the nausea that frequently accompanied such self-analysis.

"This is dumb," she told herself. "You've got too much time on your hands. One bad week at work," or two or three, she silently corrected, "and you've grown completely maudlin."

The television screen flickered vaguely in front of her as a contracting crew knocked down a shower stall, one guy succinctly chipping away at yellowed tiling on the bathroom vanity.

Scrambling to her feet, Cat clambered back into her kitchen. Her weekend of relaxation was turning out to be anything but and she was only three hours into it!

"Maybe instead of romanticizing Ashley's life…" Cat huffed as she stomped toward the cupboard she reserved for snack food, "you should…" What? That was the whole problem. Cat didn't know what she should do with her feelings because she didn't know exactly where or what they stemmed from.

And, unfortunately, this wasn't the first time they'd reared their ugly heads of late. It wasn't the first time she'd felt herself wondering what might have been if she'd only done something different, something a bit more daring, something less staid.

Opening the cupboard door carefully, for it hung loosely and crookedly against its frame, ready to fall off its half-secured bottom hinge at any moment, Cat peered inside its depths. Reaching up, she grabbed down a packet of popcorn but she knew almost as quickly as she retrieved it that she didn't want it.

Tossing it down on the counter, Cat went to shut the cupboard door, her fingers guiding the handle cautiously as she pressed it closed against the magnetic latch on the frame. Letting go, she cringed in knowing expectation when the door immediately sagged, slanting a bit too one side, askance of the structure.

"Stupid damn door." She'd only asked her landlord to fix it about five times now. Looking at it, Cat squinted. It only needed a screw on the lower half of the hinge and it would be good as new.

"It's not like it's difficult," she muttered. "Even I could do that…"

When asked later what prompted her, Cat would never be quite sure she knew the answer. She only remembered a rush of something building inside her as the words escaped her mouth, as a perfectly reasonable distraction made its presence known. She wouldn't remember exactly what had compelled her to make that particular decision, on that particular matter. But she would remember vividly the thought that had shrieked inside her head. *She was done letting her life slowly fall apart.*

Which is exactly how she found herself walking into the local hardware store some twenty minutes later.

CHAPTER TWO

As the glass-fronted door, proudly displaying the name McBoy's Hardware Store, swung shut behind her, Cat felt a fissure of agitation, of self-consciousness roll across her stiff shoulders, settle in her chest. Trying to find her bearings, her eyes flicked dizzyingly across the long, wide aisles marching up and down the width of the building.

That quick glance was enough to confirm the fears which had steadily morphed as she'd parked her car on the street. Rows upon rows of wood, carpeting, plumbing supplies, gardening tools, and holy hell—craning her neck, Cat spied an entire wall made up of small drawers holding sundry nuts and bolts and other miscellaneous thingamabobs...

Her eyes widening in consternation, darting this way and that, Cat stumbled to an uncertain halt scant inches from the entrance. Swallowing thickly, she considered her next move. The dawning realization that she had no idea what she was doing stuck slickly to her skin.

"Anything I can help you with, ma'am?"

At the masculine question, Cat unfroze, her head shifting naturally, though perhaps a bit too quickly, toward the sound. To the right of the front door, and behind a long wood-hewn cashiers counter, stood a tall, broad-shouldered man. Most of his face was obscured by the brim of a black baseball cap pulled low over his brow, but what features Cat could make out weren't exactly unpleasant: a square jaw with more than a shadowing of a beard, thin lips, and the finest of lines creasing the skin of what she assumed were high cheekbones.

She felt her stomach clench defensively, almost aggressively. She'd never felt more conspicuously out of place in her life: her mid-length hair pulled back in a low, tight bun, her feet enclosed in ballet flats, the last remnants of pink lipstick still dusting her mouth. In sharp contrast, the man behind the counter was wearing a blue-and-black plaid flannel shirt. Her nose crinkled. It was almost too typical of a handyman ensemble. All he needed now was a tin of chewing tobacco outlined on one of his back pockets and he'd be the quintessential man's man.

But when that manly man's thin lips twitched with the beginnings of a telling grin Cat realized, too late, that she'd stared a little longer than was considered polite. And she still hadn't answered his question. Jerking her gaze down to the flooring, she cleared her throat noisily.

"Ah, no. No," she assured him, flicking one finger nervously against her nose. "I'm just, ah, browsing."

Which was obviously a flat-out lie. Who browses at a hardware store? Worse, she wasn't sure why she'd decided against the truth. Except. Well, sometimes that was the best and only option. Especially when it was lie or look like an absolute idiot. When you couldn't even articulate what help you needed, well, what was the use of even trying?

And so, securing her purse more firmly against her shoulder, Cat sent him a slightly cool smile before shifting back toward the aisles before her. Her eyes focused intently forward, her senses hyper-vigilant to his following gaze, Cat marched onward. She had no idea where she was headed.

"Seriously," she muttered, her eyes taking in the unfortunate fact that she'd traversed down the plumbing aisle, her feet tromping from one end of it to the other stubbornly. "The door only needs a screw...at least, I think that's what it needs. Well, whatever, even *I* can handle that by myself." Turning down the next aisle, she felt her cheeks heat up in temper. "I'm an intelligent, independent woman. I don't need Mountain Man Mike over there to help me out."

What was that saying: How do you get God to laugh? Make a plan.

Minutes later, as she rounded the back of yet another mistaken aisle, her face blossoming into a deep maroon of irritation, Cat finally, finally found what she was looking for, she finally found the aisle she'd spotted upon first walking into the building—the one housing the end-to-end bank of small drawers of bolts and nuts, nails and screws, and other fasteners; she'd have found it quicker but, well, in her haste to get away from the cashier's quietly mocking gaze, she'd sort of forgotten about it. And when she had remembered, she couldn't have hoped to remember its precise location, not when she'd only been offered one hurried glance upon entering the store.

For half a second, as her eyes widened at the impressive inventory twinkling back at her, Cat almost swallowed her pride. *Almost.* There must have been twenty different screws on display alone. Scrunching up her nose, she tried to picture the cabinets in her kitchen. The hinge was a burnished sort of brass, smallish...but not too small (although, what that meant, Cat hadn't a clue). Though she recognized the situation for what it was—entirely out of her realm of knowledge—Cat found her mouth unwilling to cooperate, unwilling to move, to surrender to the help she needed. She found her body stiffening instead of shifting, standing still instead of seeking assistance.

It was probably her imagination, but Cat could almost swear she felt the knowing gaze from the man behind the counter. She could practically see in her mind's eye those thin lips jerking up a little to one side. Her back tingled with an awareness of him...the walls of the aisles weren't tall enough to hide her from his sight, and it wasn't like there were any other customers to distract his attention. And really, what could be more entertaining than a mechanically-disinclined blonde nodding stupidly at drawer upon drawer of screws?

Probably very little.

What was more entertaining than watching a woman cut off her nose to spite her face? And in the manliest of stores?

Gritting her teeth, Cat could feel her chest constricting. She felt like an art exhibit. As the sensation spread over her person, her hand shot out quickly, rashly. Jerking one of the small drawers open, she grabbed the first screw her fingers brushed against. Holding it up to her eyes, she studied it—honestly, it looked pretty much like any other screw she'd seen before, though maybe a bit longer than usual. She squinted uselessly. Or maybe it was shorter? Fatter, perhaps?

Oh, holy hell.

"Don't overthink it. It's just a damn screw," she muttered, annoyed with herself, with her clumsiness, at the sheen of sweat she could feel breaking out on her forehead. With a determined clamp of her fingers, Cat pocketed it in the palm of her hand and turned around. Her back ramrod straight, she stalked back to the check-out counter.

"That it?" The man asked, his eyes flicking down to the solitary screw she placed on the counter.

To Cat's chagrin, he didn't appear interested in her selection. Okay. So maybe he hadn't been watching her, after all.

Cat felt a little of her defensiveness relax at the thought.

"Yeah."

Wait.

"Umm, no." Smiling tightly, for as her mother was so fond of saying, Cat had a tendency to take herself a bit too seriously, she added: "I guess I'll probably need a, um…screwdriver or a drill or something, huh?"

If the man's eyes widened a little at this statement, he managed to keep thoughts of his incredulity silent. For that, Cat was grateful. It was altogether possible she'd misjudged him. Perhaps, he hadn't been thoroughly enjoying her bumbling stops and jerks since walking into the building. "Uh. Yeah, probably."

She nodded. "Right."

Standing so close to him, Cat could see that his eyes were a whiskey brown—and, despite his best attempts otherwise, were quickly filling with subdued mirth. The laugh lines running down either side of his nose deepened, became a bit more pronounced now too.

Okay, maybe she hadn't *completely* misjudged him. In response, Cat lifted her chin a fraction of an inch. "And where would I find one?"

"Screwdrivers are down the second aisle. If you want a drill, then you're looking at aisle three."

Tossing her shoulders back so hard it hurt, Cat forced herself to speak—and with it an uncomfortable, unreasonable embarrassment flooded her system. Her eyes shifted a little to the right, avoiding eye contact. "And which would you, ah, recommend?"

He glanced down at the screw sitting on the counter. "For a screw of this size…I'd say a drill. We have two different sets in stock and both come with three of the most common bit sizes."

That sounded rational. And helpful.

Nodding, her eyes still avoiding his, Cat took herself down aisle four. At least, he'd been cool about her questions. There'd been no trace of mockery in his answer. No doubt, he still thought she was an idiot (she was starting to have some serious reservations about that too), but he'd been professional about it.

Easily locating the drill, Cat took her final purchase up to the counter. Within minutes, she was leaving the hardware store, her shoes beating a hasty retreat, her fingers gripping the plastic bag in her hand.

Okay, so she'd looked a bit…foolish in there. Biting down on her lip, Cat told herself it was silly to let that man bother her, silly to care one way or another what he'd thought of her. She knew it was ridiculous to let her discomfort and self-doubt swell now in the wake of her purchases. But some part of her refused to believe it wasn't an omen for what was to come.

On that score, she would prove to be correct.

In less than an hour, it all fell apart. Literally. Staring downward fixedly, Cat forbade herself from crying. Her eyes stung from the command, but by sheer determination she kept her rapidly expanding chest from exploding with the force of her feelings.

In her hands lay her kitchen cabinet—newly splintered and split into two separate, jagged pieces... For a moment, the moisture in her eyes gave way and Cat was temporarily blinded from the wrecked door in her grasp.

Cat still wasn't entirely sure how it happened. One minute, she'd been fitting the screw into the hinge, and okay, admittedly Cat had noticed it was something of a snug fit, and the next thing she knew a terrible crunch had rippled over the buzzing whirl of the drill—and before she'd had time to react, a thin crack had appeared. And then, just like that, it'd spread, and the wood had snapped.

But not quite in half.

That had come next.

Her chest shuddering with disgust, Cat would never admit to a single soul what had happened next—hell, she could barely admit the truth to herself. Glaring at the hairline crack, her lips had snarled as a warlike sort of fury had broken from her mouth. A fury as unexpected as it was uncontrollable.

"Stupid, mother-fu—" with a surge of strength which rather took her breath away in the remembering, Cat had managed, after three ruthless wrenching heaves, to rip the door completely free from the face frame, the other hinge snapping with the force of her grip. With a sharp and unthinking motion, she'd slammed the door down against her countertop. Hard. It had made the most satisfying whack. And then she'd done it again.

And again.

Breathing hard, she'd spat: "No good, rotten piece of—!"

And that's when things had gotten perhaps out of control. With one last vicious flick, the door had snapped in two, one half flying out of her hands to smash with a thud against her kitchen wall. It was only as the fractured piece fell to the floor that Cat came to realize the full extent of her actions.

Exhausted, her knees wobbling from the force of her thrashing, trying to catch her fast-releasing breath, Cat had allowed herself to slip down to the floor, her back resting against the doors to her pantry.

As her senses returned, she'd forced herself to stare at the remains of her temper-tantrum; the vile taste of humiliation and disgust had risen mercilessly in her throat. Mortified by the sight of her violent outburst, her unacceptable anger as the result of something so, so *minor*, Cat had gasped heavily for air.

It was just a goddamn door. What the hell had she freaked out about?

"Have you lost your damn mind?" she'd demanded, her eyes watering as she considered the mess on her floor. She was only glad no one had been there to see it. With deliberate movements, she'd picked up the ravaged pieces of the door—

All of which led to Cat's current state of unshed tears. As the present reasserted itself, as the wreckage in her hands resumed central focus, Cat winced. Forcing herself to move at last, her hands stiff against the splintered wood at her fingertips, she edged toward her garbage can. Gingerly now, she tossed the ruins inside. There was no point crying about it. Done was done.

She looked up at the now doorless cupboard.

"Grant will kill me if he finds out about this," she moaned. Grant was her apartment super, and he wasn't exactly what Cat would call friendly. Most of their conversations to date had consisted of her asking questions and him grunting half-structured responses in return. Not exactly the makings of great good friends.

Shivering a little, she wondered what his reaction would be if he were to see the door in question—hard to imagine it had snapped in two on its own. No, telling Grant was out of the question. Cat detested lying. Couldn't abide by it usually. But she had a feeling getting kicked out of her apartment would be worse.

And so, for the second time that evening, Cat found herself walking inside McBoy's Hardware Store.

CHAPTER THREE

It was nearing eight o'clock by the time Cat nosed her car into
a spot across the street from her destination. The drive over had
sent her fingers tightening on the steering wheel when she realized she had no idea when the place closed. Now, however,
peering over at the glass-fronted doors she spied the store's
OPEN sign glinting back at her.

Thank God.

Taking a deep breath, Cat unbuckled herself from her seatbelt before climbing out of her vehicle and into the chilly fall
evening air. When she reached the storefront, Cat yanked the
door open with unnecessary vigor before scurrying inside. It
was only then that she allowed herself to take a breath, to relax
the tense set of her shoulders. Still, keeping her eyes downcast,
she avoided looking toward the right, where the checkout counter stood.

It was mortifying enough, having to come back twice in a
matter of hours, but to have the same staff member ring her up
again… Biting down on her lip, Cat shook her head in resignation. It was altogether unlikely that the store had gone through
a staff change-over in the last hour.

Trudging down the first aisle she came upon, Cat's eyes narrowed, sharpened as she stalked her prey. Unlike earlier, she
found the object of her visit almost immediately. As Cat came
upon the wall, hung with an assortment of cabinetry, she felt an

instant rush of both relief and fear. She'd found what she was looking for, but what if they didn't have exactly what she needed? Her stomach knotted as her eyes roamed over the items on display. Taking out her phone, Cat glanced at the picture she'd taken before leaving her apartment: a close-up of one of her kitchen cupboard doors—a perfect, and intact, compliment to the one she needed to replace. Glancing at the photo earnestly, she tried to compare it to the cabinets facing her. She squinted. She glared...but no matter the scrutiny, she knew when she'd been beaten. Fact was, she'd been getting her butt kicked all day.

And she wasn't interested in another situation like the screw.

"And really, what are the odds that I would magically pick the exact replica of that door," she muttered to herself, her fingers feeling the wooden grain of one of the display doors before her. It had a rounded edge.

"After all, I thought the screw I bought earlier looked right and we see where that led—"

"Can I help you with something?"

At the question, Cat felt her shoulders stiffen. She'd been right. There had definitely not been a shift change. That voice, the cool masculine sound of it, belonged to the same guy who'd checked her out earlier. Bracing for the flicker of familiarity, she turned around, a grim smile marring her face.

His face registered neither surprise nor recognition. For that matter, it didn't even register much interest.

Cat felt her lips tug down the tiniest bit. All the same, her voice was even when she responded. She was not going to have a repeat of the screw situation. She would ask for help, take the guidance. "Yes. I'm actually, well, I'm not exactly sure what it is I'm looking for..." Cat could feel the tips of her fingers running across her collarbone as she faltered for the right words, the least humiliating words. "That is..."

Spit it out, Cat.

But other than a slight lift of one dark eyebrow, he didn't interrupt her babbling attempt at speech.

Urgently now, Cat flapped one wrist in the air. "That is, I'm looking for a door."

"I figured."

"For my kitchen."

The smallest of smiles played around his mouth. A tiny dimple formed on his left cheek.

Cat hated the jolt of awareness that shot through her system at the sight of it.

"Well, you're in the right place."

Despite herself, Cat smiled at the casual humor in his voice. "Yeah, I got that. It's just, I'm not sure exactly what door I'm looking for. I mean, I have a picture of it. Only I don't know..." Ugh. She was sounded stupider and stupider by the second.

Which was exactly what had held her back earlier that afternoon.

Thankfully, holding up a hand, the store employee warded her off. "I think I understand. Doing a remodel?"

Before Cat could clarify, he was already nodding down the length of the aisle. "This is everything we have in stock, but if you're looking for something else, we can pretty much order anything in, even custom specifications."

Cat blinked. "Well, umm...I was hoping you'd have one of these?" Rushing now, holding her breath, she held out her phone for his inspection.

Looking at the picture, the man smiled. Cat's stomach did another slow summersault in reaction. She frowned. The last thing she needed to do was admit to his attractions. That would only make her more tongue-tied and clumsier. With deliberation, Cat looked just over his shoulder. She figured it was safer.

"That's a basic free shaker," the man commented, studying the picture in question. "We have a couple of different options here in the store."

Cat's eyes snapped back to the right, back to his face but the man was already craning his neck, trying to locate them.

"You do? Oh, thank God. I wasn't sure..." Cat's hands tightened around her phone as she glanced down at it. "You know, a couple of doors look kind of like this one, but I wasn't sure they'd be exactly the same..." Peeking up at the man, the last of Cat's words died coldly at his expression.

"Exactly the same?" His eyes were wary now, a shuttered look falling over his face. "Do you mean...?" He flicked on his hand toward her phone.

Hefting up one shoulder, Cat confessed: "I need to replace *one* of the doors in my kitchen. But just the one."

"I see." That didn't sound promising. He cleared his throat. "What, eh, what are the dimensions of the door?"

This time, Cat was ready with an answer. Lifting her phone, she flipped through the photos until she located the one she needed. Turning the phone back toward the man, she announced: "I figured this was the safest way..." It was a picture of her front cabinet door (an unharmed one), with a tape measurer running horizontally from one end to the other. "I took length, depth, and width... swipe right to see the others."

With patent hesitation, he reached for her phone. His mouth turned down in a frown as he studied first one photo and then the next. "I see." That sounded even less promising.

Cat fidgeted impatiently while he looked. "And? Do you have any of *that* door?"

He blew out an exaggerated breath. "Yeah, no, I don't think so..." Still, to his credit, the man looked over his inventory, his eyes taking careful stock of the doors on the wall and shelving units in front of them. But alas: "No," he finally admitted. "No, I'm afraid we don't have that in stock."

Cat swallowed. "Oh."

"Not that I'm surprised," he admitted, giving her phone back. "It's an odd width."

Cat felt her teeth raze over her lip. "Right. Okay. Well..." Her shoulders slumped, her throat clogging. "Thanks for trying."

"Hold on," he said, reading her expression easily. "Let me check with some of our usual manufacturers. We may get lucky yet." With a wave of his fingers, he urged her forward. Cat didn't need to be told twice. Stepping beside him, they walked up to his check-out register.

For the first time since she'd walked in, Cat felt the knot in her stomach loosen. Appreciation spread across her chest at his easy assistance, his desire to help. "That would, that would be great. Thank you."

But five fruitless minutes later, she heard his fourth or fifth sigh as he surfed yet another company's website, as he offered another absent-minded goodbye to yet another representative from yet another manufacturer's shop...

"Do you know when these cabinets were originally put in?" he asked glancing up at her hopefully.

Cat shrugged. "No. I mean…I think the house was built in the forties."

There was another sigh. She wondered if he knew how loud, how telling, they were. "I'm going to guess they're original to the house."

"Right." Cat wasn't sure what that meant. When he didn't immediately respond, she ventured. "Is that a bad thing?"

He frowned down at the computer screen. "No, not necessarily. But it might explain the door's size, which is both a taller and narrower than today's typical standard designs."

Cat nodded emptily. "So, it's not a great thing."

He scanned at her set features. "Hey, we can always custom-order one. That's not out of the realm of possibilities here. But it's—"

"It's expensive," Cat guessed.

He shrugged. "Yeah. Usually." Upwards of three figures, but he didn't verbalize that.

"I see."

"But I'm not finding any stock cabinets in your size."

Cat tried to smile but her lips wouldn't cooperate. Luckily for her, at that moment the tinkling sound of the bell over the store's front door chimed, signaling the arrival of a new customer and stealing the man's attention as he lifted his head automatically in greeting. Taking the slight reprieve, Cat took a deep breath in and then out.

"Can I ask, does this door have anything to do with the single screw you bought earlier today?"

At the unexpected question, Cat blinked up at the man, whose gaze had settled back to her once more. Up to now, she'd been under the illusion he hadn't recognized her. He hadn't made any other reference up to this point.

"So you remember that."

He grinned slightly. "It was two hours ago, not two weeks ago."

Cat squirmed. "Right."

The man grinned a little wider. "What happened?"

Cat dropped her gaze down to the counter, where her fingers rested, clenched tightly together. "It broke. The door, I mean."

"Kind of figured that."

She shook her head. "It, ah, it snapped in two pieces."

Out of her peripheral vision, she saw his brown eyes round, watched his eyebrows raise incredulously. Worse, she heard the soft patter of footsteps, which belonged to the customer who'd just entered, pause at the wording. Good. Great. An audience.

"I see." But it was clear from his tone of voice that the man most definitely did not see anything.

Shrugging, Cat tried to explain. "The hinge was broken, and so I thought—"

"So you thought you'd buy a screw," he said, cutting her off. "But you bought the wrong size."

"The patronizing note in your voice is duly noted," Cat responded. "But yes, you happen to be correct."

"Well, don't let the shame eat you alive."

She gasped. "Excuse m—'

"It happens to everyone."

"What does?"

"Home improvement mistakes. It's part of the DIY gimmick."

Cat felt her lips stiffen with silent outrage.

"But...wait," he persisted, the hesitation in his voice echoing his gathering thoughts. "You said the cabinet door snapped in two? A screw wouldn't have done that much damage. Not by itself."

Cat felt her body react at his not-so-subtle intimation. Rounding her shoulders, she was searching for the most plausible answer when a third voice entered the conversation.

"Well, really Matthew! What kind of question is that anyway?" A woman asked, coming into view to stand beside Cat. "Is this an interrogation?"

He gave the woman, who must have been pushing seventy, an impatient glance. "No, I was merely..."

Cat held up her hands, heeding off any more interruptions. "Look, I'll pay whatever it takes. Custom-order it if you have to but I need another door. I need another of *that* door." With a sharp click of her fingernail, Cat tapped the picture still displayed on her phone.

At her insistent tone, the aggressive movement, all conversation died away. Leaning closer to the counter, the older woman looked down at the picture.

"Easy enough design," she murmured.

Bemused, not sure she even meant to respond, Cat found herself saying: "Odd dimensions though, I guess."

"Hmph."

Biting back the stem of rising hysteria, Cat tried again. Glancing up at the flannel-clad man, she had no idea how beseeching she looked. "The thing is, I'm a renter and, and if my landlord knew what happened, well…" She shrugged fatalistically.

"Oh dear," the older woman said, sending 'Matthew' a distressed look. "Of course, we have to help her."

"We're *trying*," he informed her through gritted teeth.

Turning a large blue-eyed gaze on Cat, the older woman's frightfully pink-painted lips smiled gently. "Do you know how much a custom-ordered door will cost?"

Cat tried to smile. "I'm guessing a lot."

"Plus some."

Cat nodded but her throat was too tight to allow for an answer.

"Unless…" Shifting a little, the woman planted one elbow on the counter, her gaze raking over the man standing so stiffly behind it.

"Unless what?" There was more than a hint of suspicion in his voice.

Instead of answering him, the woman shifted to speak to Cat, one hand coming to rest conspiratorially against the younger woman's shoulder. "Did you know that Matthew here actually does some woodworking?"

"No." Straightening, Matthew looked from one to the other. His voice was stiff now, hard. "No. That's a hobby."

"He's very good."

"He's also not a professional." There was no denying the hiss of irritation that had entered his voice.

"Which is why he won't charge like one, either."

Matthew's eyes narrowed. "Margaret—"

For the first time since she'd entered their conversation, the elderly woman directed her response to him personally. "That's Grandma to you," she retorted. "And I'll thank you not to sass me."

Cat smothered a bewildered grin.

"And I'll thank you not to—"

"Not to what?" she insisted. "Not to help a customer in need? That's what we do here. It's what we've always done."

"Grandpa used to design kitchen cabinetry for his customers?" Matthew smiled thinly. "I don't remember that."

"Well, really!" With a flick of her hand, Margaret gestured toward the rear of the store. "You're always back there in that workshop fiddling away with some new project."

"Not for commission. Not for something so…"

"So?"

Frowning, his hands balling into fists at his sides, Matthew stared at her. "This calls for an experienced craftsman."

"I know. That's why I thought of you." Without breaking stride, Margaret glanced at Cat. "Don't let him get all humble. He did my bathroom remodel last year. Stunning work."

In response, Cat smiled fleetingly. She wasn't sure what else to do. Matthew, on the other hand, closed his eyes, frustration lining his deep, even breaths.

"Well, really," the older woman continued, shaking her head at him. "What's the worst that could happen? It doesn't turn out and she has to buy a customized door anyway?" She turned back to Cat, who was watching all of this with her mouth agape. "What would you really lose? A couple of days."

Cat shook her head.

"But it won't come to that, anyway," Margaret assured her. "He's that good."

"I'm sure. But I-I don't think he *wants* to do it."

"Of course he does. He's just being bull-headed."

"I'm being bull-headed?" Thrusting his head forward, Matthew outright glared the other woman down. "Have you even asked what she wants?" he charged, waving a hand absently toward Cat.

"Well?" Hands on her hips, Margaret turned toward Cat.

Under that steady stare, Cat swallowed. Then she, in turn, looked toward Matt. "You seem to come highly recommended." Balking as the words left her mouth, Cat wasn't sure where they'd come from, what had enticed her to say them. Clearly, he didn't want to do the job, hadn't offered his services.

And yet….

Margaret clapped her hands together. "That's the spirit."

"Still." Taking a deep breath, Cat couldn't help but add: "The offer should come from him. And it didn't so it's rather—"

"Fine."

"Fine?" Margaret and Cat asked in unison, both pairs of eyes pinioning back around to Matthew at the hissed word.

His teeth clenched together, Matthew stared back at Cat. "If you want, I'll see what I can do. I can't promise anything. It might not turn out."

Cat rarely felt stupid. But she did at that moment. The conversation was progressing in such an unexpected way. "You mean, you'll make me a door?"

His lips thinned. "Yeah. I'll make you a door."

"Really?"

He sighed warily. "Yes. Really. But as I said, I'm not a professional."

"Oh, enough."

"Yeah, that's exactly how I feel about you too," Matthew returned, leveling a stony look at his Grandmother.

She didn't so much as bat an eye.

Jumping in, Cat felt herself scrambling. "Thank you. Thank you, thank you!"

He batted her words away. "Don't mention it."

Reaching for her purse, Cat was already digging for her wallet. "Ho-how much?"

Matthew sighed. "I don't know. I'll need to see the door first—"

"But, but I told you," Cat sputtered. "It's broken."

"No, not that one," he returned with a bite. He gestured toward her phone. "The one in the picture. Bring it in and I'll take a look at the material, create a mold, and cost everything out for you."

"Huh."

"That a problem?"

Cat blew out a breath. "No. Not really. I'm not exactly sure how I'll get the door off, that's all."

"What?"

"That's sort of what got me in this mess in the first place," she confessed. Cat could feel the heat rising on her cheeks with the admission. "Screws and drills and that sort of thing…"

Matthew grunted. "Yeah, well, a picture isn't going to cut it from here on out."

"No, I know but—"

"Go online. There's probably a million videos on how to un-screw a door hinge."

Cat felt her back stiffen again. It was the way he said it—unscrew a *door* hinge—that made her fingers flinch, that made her pulse skip in her throat. Matthew may have been gorgeous but he sure wasn't pleasant.

Smiling tightly, Cat reminded herself how much she needed him. How desperately her wallet needed him. Grouch or not, he was her last best chance. "I'll make sure to do that very thing. Thanks for the tip."

"Great." With a knock of his knuckles, he added: "Is there anything else I can do for you?"

"No, that'll be it. *Matthew*," Cat all but seethed.

"Fine. Bring the door here Monday afternoon. I'll see what I can do." And with that, he rounded the cashier stand and went to the front door where he unceremoniously switched the neon OPEN sign to CLOSED before turning down one of the long aisleways toward the back of the building.

Suddenly, he stopped, turned around and added: "Oh. And it's Matt."

"Huh?"

He nodded toward Margaret. "Only my grandmother calls me Matthew."

Cat nodded her head idiotically. "Matt then." Despite his lack of manners, she summoned forth a tepid smile. "And, ah, thanks. Again."

Other than the slight incline of his head, he offered no re-sponse, only turned on his heels once more and walked off.

And just like that, he was gone.

Still standing at the checkout stand, Cat blinked.

"Don't mind him, dear," Margaret said, bringing Cat's atten-tion back around. "He's cranky because it's the first Friday of the month."

"And what happens on the first Friday of the month?" Cat asked, playing along. After all, Margaret had more-or-less saved her sorry butt.

"It's our standing game of Bridge," Margaret informed her. Leaning toward Cat, she glanced over her shoulder, to make sure he was out of earshot. "And he's never been very good at the game."

Cat couldn't help herself. She laughed. It had a freeing effect on the knots in her stomach. This had been one of the worst nights in her recent memory. Then again, it had also been sort of...well, invigorating. Different to say the least. Yes, this Friday night had definitely been different.

"Umm..." Biting her lip, Cat tried for a look of nonchalance. "Thank you for, well, for helping me." Moving tentatively, she stuck out her hand. "My name's Cat Cryer, by the way."

"Pleased to meet you," Margaret returned, shaking her outstretched palm. "Margaret McBoy."

Cat pursed her lips. "As in, the owner of the hardware store?"

"Once upon a time. Well, me and my husband." She laughed richly. "I suppose I'll let him claim some credit in that too."

It was official. Margaret McBoy was delightful.

Cat grinned. "Good of you."

"We opened this place some forty years ago." A mistiness settled over Margaret's eyes at the statement, but only for a moment. "When he passed away, Matthew took over ownership."

Cat nodded.

"And," Margaret continued, a twinkle of mischief smoothing out her features, "if there are any two things that running a hardware store has taught me it's that us women have to stick together in this man's haven." With a wink, she added: "And two—never ask how something managed to get itself snapped in two."

Cat blushed, her eyes dropping down to the tops of her shoes. "Yeah..."

"Please, child, you think you're the first person to take a flimsy piece of wood over their knee? Think again."

Yes. It had definitely been a different Friday night. Walking out to her car moments later, Cat wasn't sure she could explain it, but there she was anyway, smiling.

CHAPTER FOUR

The next morning, the first thing Cat did after pouring herself a cup of coffee was to search the internet for videos on how to properly take off a cabinet door. Though she hated admitting, even to herself, that she couldn't do something as simple as that without guidance, she also wasn't interested in having two broken doors to replace. Grimacing as she opened her internet browser, Cat begrudgingly typed in her search request.

Turns out, Matthew had been right. There were scores of how-tos at her disposal. And much to her chagrin, they all made it seem rather easy. Still, Cat watched four of them before taking herself to task.

Sucking in a deep breath, her heart thudding at a distracting rate, Cat pulled out her drill once more. This time, however, she made sure to check her bits for the right size. Setting the point carefully into the pin, Cat pulled the trigger.

And just as in the videos, each screw slid effortlessly free.

"Aha!" Holding the newly-liberated door in both hands, Cat grinned. She threw her head back and shouted. Her feet pranced up and down as she danced a small jig on the laminate flooring.

"'Atta girl," she pronounced, setting the door down on her countertop. It stared back at her in all its undamaged glory. "See? That wasn't so hard. You've got the makings for house renos yet."

Cat smirked at the door for a couple more seconds—and if she looked a bit smug while she did it, so be it—before shuffling out of the kitchen and into the living room. One hand wrapped around her third cup of coffee, it wasn't until she arrived there that Cat realized…well, that she realized she was done. There was nothing else planned for her day. The only thing on her list of items to accomplish was complete. That was it. One project.

Plunking down on her couch, her eyes traveling toward the blank screen of her television, Cat winced. It was, as it had been the evening before, rather uninviting. Glancing furtively at her phone, she saw unsurprisingly that there were no notifications waiting for her—no calls, no texts, no social media comments.

Lame.

Taking a big gulp of coffee, Cat leaned back against her couch cushions as her gaze roamed to her laptop sitting beside her coffee table. She never reached for it. There was nothing she wanted to do with that, either.

And suddenly, she was right back in the same mental state of mind as the night prior. A whole lot of time alone doing nothing.

Drumming her fingers against the ribbed wood of her armchair, she frowned. Waking up that morning, she'd been unnervingly conscious of needing to get that door off. It'd been all she'd thought about as she'd clambered out of bed. And now…setting her cup down on her end table, Cat considered her options. "Now what?" she wondered to the empty apartment. "God, you really need a cat. Then at least you could pretend you were talking to it instead of yourself." Before she could help herself, Cat looked at her phone again.

Nothing. Her stomach knotted at the sight.

Letting her head drop back against the top of her cushion, Cat tried to shake away the crushing sensation settling on her abdomen. In a matter of fifteen or so hours the weekend she'd so been looking forward to now seemed endlessly boring. A bunch of hours to get through.

"Who are you trying to kid? It hadn't sounded that good yesterday," she scolded herself. "Mindless television so you could watch other people live fun, active lives?"

And really, with pep-talks like that, who wouldn't have a good start to their weekend?

… °•°• …

By Sunday afternoon, Cat was ready to go back to work. The four walls of her apartment were practically screaming at her. She itched to do something—go to a coffee shop or a restaurant, or hell, even just go shopping around the mall.

Except... going out alone held little appeal. It felt no different than making a solitary meal in her own kitchen and sitting down to eat it; only at home, she didn't have to see other patrons out with their family and friends, laughing and talking and generally feeling like they belonged. At home, she wasn't forced to feel so conspicuous about her aloneness; she could pretend she preferred it that way. At home, she was only bored.

And hostage to her thoughts.

So yeah, she was almost impatient to go back to work. To begin a new week. To welcome Monday. Which was probably the most depressing part of it all. Because Monday really meant McBoy's Hardware Store and as it currently stood, that was the most exciting thing going in her life. How telling was that? All of Saturday and Sunday, every time Cat walked into her kitchen a fissure of anticipation swept over her. She wasn't sure if it was fear or excitement, but she found herself inexplicably eager. If nothing else, it was something to shake the ordinary routine of a life that had grown stale.

Alone with her anxious thoughts, Cat couldn't quite bite back the merry-go-round of introspection. All through her college years, though she'd sometimes stopped and wondered what it would have been like if she'd gone away for school, she'd never quite found she regretted staying at home.

Her family was here.

Everything she knew was here.

She had friends here.

It was only recently, probably when Ashley had moved to Spokane that she'd realized, rather belatedly, that something was missing. And it wasn't just her friend. No, Ashely had merely been the catalyst, the presence (or lack thereof) which had thrust this acknowledgment to the forefront of Cat's mind.

Slowly, it seemed the life she'd always found so comfortable and easy had turned into a prison of isolation and sameness.

"I need a distraction," Cat mused. She was currently sitting on her bedroom floor, reorganizing her bookshelf. She just didn't know what kind of distraction she needed.

With these thoughts rolling aimlessly, mercilessly through her mind, by the time Ashley called her that evening, Cat clumsily raced for her phone, her fingers scabbing to answer it with a frenzied kind of desperation.

"Hello?" Cat's voice was high and breathy.

"Hey girl!"

Plopping down on her living room sofa, Cat forced her body to relax, forced her words to come out slowly, naturally. It was the weirdest thing, the attack of nerves sniping at her insides. "So. Tell me everything. How's the new job?"

Ashley didn't need to be told twice. "It's great. Hectic and I'm still training, but it's really amazing—"

"And obviously you're making friends." Cat winced at the bitterness edging the statement which had popped out unguardedly.

If Ashley heard the latent resentment in her friend's tone, however, she chose to ignore it. "Yeah, a couple of girls at the office are around my age. The first Friday of every month they go out for cocktails after work."

"That sounds nice."

"You know, it was a pretty good time." Ashley laughed cutely. "I mean, mostly it's a way to vent out some frustrations with people who get it, but the girls all seem nice. No cattiness or anything."

"Yeah? How's Tyler enjoying it down there?" Tyler was Ashley's long-term boyfriend.

Ashley sighed. "Well, he hasn't found a job yet…"

A terrible sort of glee filled Cat's person at the words. Well, well. So maybe Ashley's life wasn't perfect, after all. As soon as the thought materialized, Cat thrust it away, ashamed at the direction of her thoughts, the level of her spite and animosity.

"But there's loads of opportunities down here. I know he'll find something soon."

"I'm sure he will," Cat agreed with a little more generosity and conviction than was honest.

"But what about you?" Ashley asked. "How's life at home?"

"It's…" For a moment, Cat wasn't sure what to say. The same? Totally predictable and exactly what you'd imagine?

That felt way too close for comfort. For obvious reasons, Cat didn't want to admit that her life was something direly less than glamorous. Not when Ashley had just landed her dream job. "It's good."

"Yeah?"

"Yeah. I mean, nothing major…" without quite meaning to, Cat's eyes flickered toward her kitchen, where the edge of her newly disconnected door could just be spotted, laying on the countertop. Her stomach clenched. "I did a little redecorating this weekend."

Ashley snorted. "Whoa, hang on to your hat. Party animal."

Cat frowned, her fingers curling against the back of her phone. She knew Ashley hadn't meant to be insulting, only her words were uncannily close to Cat's own thoughts. For a moment she considered telling Ashley what had happened to her weekend; she wondered for a split second how her friend would react if Cat told her how she'd violently snapped her kitchen cupboard in half…

But, of course, Cat didn't admit to any of that. It was embarrassing. Mortifying and all together, well, childish.

In fact, Cat refrained from making any further mention of her disastrous kitchen fiasco. It probably would have made for a good story, even with some of the facts omitted. She could have smoothed over the broken door and plunged instead into the crazy turn of events—if nothing else, it would have given her a few talking points. But the words died on her lips.

"Yeah, honestly I didn't do much this weekend. Lazed around."

"Well, good for you. We all need weekends like that."

Cat's frown deepened. She knew Ashley was being supportive but her words were eerily close, far too close, to the lie that Cat had tried to tell herself the last two days.

"I guess." Regret circled low in Cat belly—regret that she'd set up this phone date with her best friend. Instead of cheering Cat up, it was only highlighting what she was becoming all too uncomfortably aware of.

Just how tragic her life was turning out to be.

For God's sake, she wasn't even thirty yet.

"And, did I mention—"

"Ashley, what kind of hobbies did I used to enjoy?" The words, tripping out of her mouth without deliberation, held an intensity, a pitched agitation of tone.

"What?"

Cat closed her eyes. Then she cast her pride to the side. "I can't seem to remember."

"What are you talking about?"

Cat could hear the thick cloud of confusion in her friend's voice at the abrupt change of topic. At the urgency of Cat's question. She shrugged. "My hobbies—what are they?"

"How should I know?"

"Well, what did we used to do together?"

"What?"

"Stop asking me that!" Cat was mildly surprised at the vehemence in her voice.

Silence filled the line for a moment, then the sound of a carefully drawn breath. "Okay. Well...let me think." That was hardly promising. "Oh, I know! Reading. You love to—"

"No."

"No?"

"Nothing solitary."

"Okay." Ashley cleared her throat. "Well then..."

Another bout of tense silence passed. Cat waited.

"What about volleyball? Remember we played on that indoor league for a couple winters. You loved that. Ace server."

Cat felt tears prick her eyes. Much like her violent outburst with the kitchen cabinet, the feel of them pulsing against her eyelids not only surprised Cat, they outright shocked her. But damned if she wasn't about to start crying again.

Great. Volleyball.

To be fair, Ashley had done what Cat asked. That particular sport was far from a solitary event. Only—it required *five* other people. Five seemed like an awfully high number. An unattainable number for a woman who'd spent the entire weekend without receiving a single text message, invitation or call. At which estimation, her stomach dropped. Totally pathetic.

"What else?" Cat didn't even care anymore that she sounded desperate.

Volleyball was out. For one thing, both Ashley and Carly used to be on the team, but as they'd moved away, Cat would have to find replacements for them... and really, the only other person she'd known well on their team was Mariah and she'd always been more of Carly's friend so....

"Do you want to tell me what's going on?" There was a softness, a gentleness to Ashely's question. She'd clearly heard past Cat's desperation.

"I'm just..." Cat swallowed hard. "I'm feeling a little...restless lately. That's all."

Ashley was quiet for a moment. "Why don't I come up next weekend for a visit?"

"Thanks, but that's kind of the problem."

"I'm the problem?"

"No!" Cat laughed. "God, no. It's—"

"Come on, Cat," Ashley prodded. "Don't hold out on me."

"I don't have any friends anymore."

A static, unnerved sort of silence answered her.

Cat laughed again. It had a shaky sound. "Please, don't think I'm some sad-sack loser—"

"Shut up. We've been friends since we were six years old," Ashley informed her. "I'm never going to think you're a loser."

"Yeah, right."

"I won't. I'm ...surprised, that's all."

"Me too."

"And I'm sorry."

"Because you left me?" Cat's attempt at a joke fell flat.

"Because I hate the hurt I heard in your voice just now."

"Oh, please."

"I'm serious."

"I'm not interested in your pity."

"Good, because I'm not giving it to you."

"I'm fine. Really, Ashley."

"Okay. So. Hobbies." Ashley's voice sounded determined now. Cat could almost see her pointed chin thrusting forward. If there was one thing Ashley had in spades it was stubbornness. "Yeah. Okay. Get a pen and paper. We're going to figure this out."

"You don't need to—"

"Shut up. Just get ready to write."

Cat nodded. "I'm ready."

CHAPTER FIVE

Getting out of her car on Monday morning, Cat took a deep breath of still morning air. The quiet chill of autumn swirled bracingly inside her lungs. There was an energizing quality to it, a promise of bonfire and scarf-wearing weather around the corner. The promise of something awakening.

Shouldering the thick strap of her messenger bag as she shook away the fanciful thought, Cat shut and locked her vehicle before hiking up to the front doors of the credit union. Only, unlike her usual brisk entrance, as she was on the verge of slipping through the small vestibule separating the main lobby from the parking lot, her eyes caught sight of the community board tacked up to a sidewall.

She'd seen it numerous times before. Or perhaps it was more apt to say, she'd seen through it, caught absent-minded glances of it before walking on, never giving it more thought than that. For years, she'd tromped in and out of these same doors, her eyes always in the same direction, boring straight ahead of her, her attention either already sorting through the applications awaiting her on her desk, or contemplating what she'd make herself for dinner as she locked up for the evening.

But today, Cat's eyes skipped toward it, taking in the papers stuck to the cork-board, the assortment of colors waving at her with the slight wafting breeze of the door. Her eyes narrowed and, almost without conscious decision, Cat felt her feet slant in its direction, bringing her closer.

Her eyes roamed over the announcements: a high school concert, a city council meeting, a few garage sales and—her eyes squinted. What was that? Running her fingertip along one of the pieces of paper, Cat read the headline:

Dance Classes at the Main Line Community Center—Couples or Singles Welcome!

Feeling the slight pressure of her teeth against her bottom lip, Cat's eyes anxiously raced toward the bottom of the sign, where the details seemed to be displayed. When—?

"Good morning, Catherine."

At the sound of the slightly nasal welcome coming from behind her, Cat jumped, her hand dropping from the paper as though she'd just been caught doing something naughty. Feeling the tips of her ears burning in a rise of prideful shame, she turned stiffly.

"Hello, Janice." Janice Beasley—one of the senior tellers at the credit union. She was fifty if she was a day, and though she outranked even the vice-president in terms of time served, she'd never seemed inclined to climb any higher in her career. Still, as far as Janice was concerned, no matter her title, pay grade, or responsibilities, she *was* the credit union, the face of the company, the employee the entire community knew—and every employee did best to remember that.

And if they didn't, she'd remind them of that fact. Empathically. Painfully.

Seeing that Cat was almost twenty-five years her junior, it wasn't such a wonder that the two women had never exactly bonded. Cat could feel the older woman's resentment like a heavy blanket, her stalwart resistance because, despite the age discrepancy, Cat was technically her superior. Likewise, proud of her success and ambitions, Cat refused to succumb to Janice's expectation that everyone would fall in line with her little "rules."

So, yeah, they weren't exactly close friends. They were strictly civil to one another. Tolerant and professional.

Which made it all the worse now—having Janice finding her desperately trying to think up a social life. Gritting her teeth, before she could think properly, before she could come up with an adequate reason for being found there, Cat already felt her mouth moving rabidly, idiotically as the overwhelming sense of transparency swamped her.

"I, uh, I usually don't stop to look at the board. Obviously," Cat insisted, waving toward it aggressively. "But, um...one of the papers looked like it was about to fall off its thumbtack—" Stalling, Cat could only lift one shoulder in a lame conclusion that was as rushed in ending as it'd been in start.

She hated lying. She also hated how easily the lie tripped off her tongue.

But Janice wasn't deceived. Ironically, had Cat not tried so hard to convince her otherwise, she probably wouldn't have noticed anything amiss about the younger woman looking at the announcement board. But that defensive stain on her cheeks, and her quick-fired, too animated, excuse was—how did that saying go? Cat had protested too much.

Holding the second set of doors open, Janice nodded, the action inviting Cat to walk in ahead of her. The lobby was still dark, but the sound of Melanie, another teller's, footsteps could be heard in the backroom, as well as the hiss of the coffee maker.

"That's how I found my knitting club," Janice said, surprising Cat with the note of sympathy in her voice. "I was walking in and I found one of the flyer's dangling crookedly—" at this, she sent Cat a knowing wink "—or so the story goes. Anyway, if you have any interest in knitting, we're always welcoming new members...?" Janice left the sentence dangling meaningfully.

Choking a little in surprise and something akin to gratitude, Cat still wasn't sure how to respond to that *very* unsolicited invitation. She couldn't think of anything she'd rather do less than sit around a table with a bunch of women like Janice, discussing different types of yarn.

Cat winced. That sounded harsh, even in her own ears.

Janice was being nice and all Cat wanted to do was duck and run for cover.

And really, could she afford to be choosy? After all, she and Ashley had come up with a big whopping nothing yesterday evening in their attempt to find her some hobbies. Try as they might, no matter how many suggestions they threw out, nothing had materialized. Nothing solid anyway.

Swimming would be difficult since Cat had never been formally taught how to. And that was almost as bad as reading. Too solitary unless she was on a team.

She didn't know how to play tennis or racquetball, both of which would only require one other player, and she didn't belong to a gym. Nor did she particularly relish the idea of running on a treadmill to beat back the rush of boredom engulfing her.

She was too impatient for painting. And unless she signed up for a class—well, there was that whole solitary business again.

Multi-player team sports were out since, well, since she didn't have a team to join.

So now, staring up at Janice's unusually kind expression, Cat hesitated. She'd rather bust another cabinet door over her knee than endure conversation over knitting needles with that woman, but then again, she wasn't sure she was in a position to turn away any kind of offers for friendship.

Opening her mouth guardedly, unsure what she intended to say to Janice's expectant face, Cat was saved from an answer when the overhead lights blinked to life. Furthermore, squinting against the harsh glare, Cat was duly spared from answering because, at that same moment, Melanie appeared, carrying a coffee air pot up to the small service station to one side of the entrance.

"Morning girls," she called out gaily.

"Morning."

"Say, Janice. I have a question about my morning cash count..."

And just like that, the moment was over. Slinking out of sight and down the long corridor leading off the main lobby, Cat took herself smartly to her private office. Shutting the door behind her, she leaned against it for a second, letting her eyes roam over the sparse room: two large, cheaply-made bookshelves stood on either side of her desk against the back wall—amongst the books on display, the top shelves housed her framed college degree and the miscellany certifications she'd received in the five years she'd work at the Fireside Credit Union. Opposite of this, welcoming clients for a sit-down visit, sat two wooden chairs, each covered with thin forest green padding. Other than that, the walls held an assortment of prints depicting nature scenes. It was all rather neutral.

It was all rather dull, dated. Unremarkable.

Dropping her eyes to the gray carpeting at her feet, Cat's shoulders sagged with sudden exhaustion. On her desk, beside her computer, she knew a pile of papers were neatly stacked, waiting for her attention. A large part of her job was spent loaning out money to the hard-working residents of Dupré, Washington. It was a good job. A job she used to love…excepting of course for those meetings when she was forced to admit that, unfortunately, the customer's request had been denied. She used to feel like she played an important part in some of the most special moments in people's lives: their first car, their home, their college tuition, their business dreams…

But then, face after face, application after application, she'd grown, not exactly cynical, just a bit indifferent to it all. Her smile had become more robotic, her responses more scripted, her interest waning as her fingertips tapped impatiently on the edge of her desk as she waited for her next appointment.

The thought was as lowering as it was aggravating. And one that she couldn't seem to help circling back to. Again and again. Her life had become as dull and unremarkable as the décor in her office.

"That's enough," Cat barked, the outrage in her voice shocking her into standing erect, pulling herself almost violently off the door. The whip in her voice jarred Cat effective out of her reverie. "This is becoming too much now. Grow up, pull yourself together. And while you're at it, shut the hell up. You've moped and moped all weekend. Get over it or change something." Shaking her head wearily, the smacking force of her words carried Cat across the floor as she flipped on the lights and stalked over to her desk.

Pulling out her chair, she turned on her computer. Her lips were stretched into a fine, hard line. "Even I'm getting sick of the pouting," she muttered as her fingers punched down on the keyboard.

If she felt like some of the enthusiasm in her job had waned, well, that was probably nothing out of the ordinary. And it wasn't unfixable. Like a relationship, the love and excitement sometimes required a bit of work, a little extra attention.

So fine, no big deal. Maybe that's what this was all about: Cat simply needed a reminder call. Maybe she'd actually

needed this past weekend—needed all the whining and pouting—to take stock of what she was letting fall apart in her life.

So, okay. She'd done that. Now, it was time to put a little
muscle behind all that complaining. A little conscious thought
and nourishment might bring back some of the love she'd once
felt for her job.

With that in mind, for the first time in months, when Cat
looked down at her appointment book the smallest glint of anticipation filled her person. She had a meeting that very afternoon to discuss the possibility of someone taking out a small
business loan. Cat felt her shoulders straighten. She felt her lips
pull up the slightest bit.

"Make it count. Make it good."

"Welcome to Fireside Credit Union, Ms. Amelia Kelley." Shifting her eyes to the application sitting on the desk, Cat smiled
nicely. Politely. A practiced look meant to diffuse the nervous
energy swelling around the room.

The woman who'd just walked into her office and taken a
seat across from her desk wasn't much older than Cat herself.
She was also stunningly gorgeous. Tall with long legs demurely
crossed at the ankles and a wealth of dark hair, Amelia Kelley
was a smooth blend of brains and beauty.

And at the moment, a bundle of nerves. Hands clutched
tightly in her lap, she didn't appear to have taken a full breath
since she'd sat down.

Cat wanted to put her at her ease. For one thing, it was only
too obvious from the paperwork she'd presented to Cat, the ex-
ecutive summary one of the most concise Cat had had the pleasure to read, that she possessed a great deal of not only intelli-
gence but professionalism and attention to detail.

At the thought, Cat spoke. "So, let's talk about this business
loan."

"Yes." Amelia nodded sharply. Her fingers pressed together
even more tightly, the knuckles turning white in the grip.

With a flick of her eyes, Cat again noted the stiff posture, the
tension in Ms. Kelley's unbelievably straight shoulders. Cat

remembered her conviction earlier. Shifting the papers to one side, she leaned across her desk.

"Ms. Kelley."

"Hmm."

"I fear that if you grip your hands together any tighter, you're going to cut off the circulation to your fingers."

"Huh?" Jerking a little, Amelia blinked.

Cat smiled. "Please relax. I promise it's not nearly as painful as, well..." Cat nodded toward Amelia's clenched hands. "As that."

Hearing the kindness in Cat's voice, the other woman laughed weakly, her finger springing apart nervously, almost guiltily. "Yeah. Sorry. I guess I'm a little nervous." She rolled her shoulders for good measure.

"Good."

Amelia's eyes widened.

Cat's smile lengthened. "It means you really want this."

"Oh, I do!"

Cat nodded before lowering her eyes to the loan application and presentation packet on her desk. She managed to do it without looking patronizing. It had taken years of practice to master, especially when most of the people sitting across from her tended to be twenty-plus years older than her and inclined to feel uncomfortable by her very lack of age. "It shows in your application. In fact," lowering her eyes to the paperwork before her, she whistled. "I'm impressed."

"You are?" Leaning forward, Amelia aimed a big-eyed glance Cat's way.

"Yes. I am. Your business plan is thorough, as are your credentials and analysis of the market..."

And slowly, as the words flowed from her mouth—words of a familiar and comfortable world in which Cat knew her business—she watched as Amelia transformed, her stiffness giving away to an affinity to talk with her hands, her laugh lowering to a normal octave, even a few jokes managing to pass between her lips.

It wasn't so strange, then, was it that Cat's premonition turned out to be correct? She enjoyed her conversation with Ms. Kelley, felt again that flicker of excitement when she informed Amelia that she would indeed be getting her loan. She hardly noticed the time passing as they sat and talked, Amelia pouring out her vision for her new studio to an unexpectedly apt audience.

Standing up at the end of their meeting, Cat held out her hand. "Welcome to Fireside Credit Union. I'm looking forward to doing business with you."

She was rewarded for her show of good faith by the sudden surge of Amelia's body bolting up and across Cat's desk, that woman's arms reaching forward to wind themselves around Cat's unsuspecting neck.

Bobbing up and down on the balls of her feet, Amelia promised: "You won't regret this. You won't! You absolutely will not."

"I believe you."

"I will work endlessly in my pursuit to be successful."

"Yes—"

Pulling away from her, Amelia brushed a quick finger under her eyes. Sniffling, she smiled. "Thank you. Thank you for taking a chance on me."

"Of course..."

"And I'm sorry for this," she said, gesturing between herself and Cat. "I promise I won't make this a habit."

"You mean, I can't expect a hug every time you make a payment on your loan?"

"Not every one." Twinkling now, Amelia smiled broadly. "But I make no guarantees when I hand over my final check."

Cat grinned back involuntarily, her professional mask slipping just the slightest bit. "Well, forewarned is forearmed, as they say."

Amelia managed to sneak out three or four more fervent thank-yous before finally making it out of Cat's office minutes later.

Alone once more, Cat nodded.

There it was. That warmth of satisfaction that she'd helped to change somebody's life. Maybe it wasn't as strong as a few years ago, but it felt a little bigger than it had last Friday when she'd barely acknowledged the triumph of Jenny Dean, who'd received her first ever car loan. Cat had offered her little more than an empty smile and a request for her signature.

So okay, the warmth of satisfaction invading her chest wasn't much. But it was something. And today, something was enough.

CHAPTER SIX

As the sun set that afternoon, Cat felt something sizzle down the center of her stomach—a frisson of emotion she wasn't sure she wanted to label. Sitting perfectly still in her car, she stared directly out her windshield, her eyes peering anxiously at the back entrance to McBoy's Hardware Store.

When she'd called the store that afternoon, her body a spewing pit of nerves—what if, at the last minute, Matt had changed his mind about the whole project—Matt had spared her just enough time to request that she drop off the cabinet door via the loading dock at the back of the store.

When she'd thought to raise the question as to why, he'd been gruff.

"You know we don't actually repair cabinetry here, right?"

Right.

"No, I know," she'd rushed to say, the fingers of one hand curling against the phone she'd held so hotly against her ear.

"So I don't want customers seeing you drop off a busted door."

Right. Right.

"Sure. Of course."

"There's an alley behind the shop. Between Second and Third Street."

So now here Cat sat, staring at the industrial vinyl siding of the mammoth building. On her passenger seat, wrapped in a towel to keep any prying eyes at bay, sat her kitchen doors. Intermittently throughout the day, she'd found herself wondering about this appointment, her thoughts at once worried —that he'd take one look at the door and tell her it wasn't going to work—and in the next, Cat found herself wanting, excited…impatient for the end of her day, for this moment. Which was so utterly tragic that she winced. There should be nothing interesting about this errand. It should have held little more intrigue than a trip to the post office to buy stamps. And yet, she'd never lost track of the time of day, her eyes itching to glance at the clock every few minutes as her afternoon crawled by.

And now, at last, the moment had arrived. And if she didn't get moving soon…. With a flick of her wrist, Cat turned off her car. Probably, it wasn't best to keep Matt waiting. Especially as he hadn't been particularly, well, thrilled about the whole arrangement to begin with. Nor had he been exactly subtle about his feelings on the matter. No need to piss him off any further.

Scurrying around the front of her car, Cat quickly reached the passenger door; yanking it open, her long arms stretched across the seat to grab the doors. Holding them in her grasp, she knocked the door shut with her hip before turning toward the building. Only. At the sight before her, her feet stumbled to a pause, her eyes wary as they lit upon three large garage doors in the loading dock bay. All were closed. Craning her neck, to the side of the building, Cat could just make out two separate service doors. She was momentarily struck unsure. Which door did she use? Hoisting her swaddled items a little closer to her chest, Cat felt her stomach tighten.

This is what she hated about new things, new places.

Not knowing what to do.

And feeling so damn conspicuous about it.

Rooted to the spot, she shook her head. "Okay, don't be stupid. Just try a door. If you don't find him, then try the next one."

The force of her voice, the frustration lining it, did the trick. No sooner had Cat started walking again then she resolved to try the nearest service door situated on the side of the building. Weirdly, a sense of calm stole over her person. She'd made a decision and if it were the wrong one…well, it wasn't like she was snooping or doing anything illegal. And really, if Matt had the gull to get irritated then perhaps he should have been more descriptive. These thoughts led her to the door where, juggling the items in her arms, she cautiously turned the knob. It twisted easily in her hand.

Pushing it open, Cat blinked as she crossed over the threshold. The ceiling was incredibly high, as were the thin, grimy windows marching across the building's impossibly tall walls. It had the effect of casting a rather dim light over the large space, even accounting for the rows of fluorescent bulbs flooding brightly against the cement flooring.

But at least Cat knew she was in the right spot. Standing directly across the way from her was Matt. Seeing him gave her serious pause as her ears accustomed to the whirling, whining spin of—what was that thing in his hands? Squinting, Cat shrugged as she watched a veritable shower of wood shavings twirl and fly around him, flecks and shavings of it sprinkling his clothes, the muscles of his arms bunching as he ran a block of wood across the side of what she recognized as a table saw of some kind.

Okay. Cat had located Matt…but it was obvious he had not yet realized she was in the building with him.

His head was bent down, his goggled eyes concentrating hard as he worked. Cat told herself that that was why she stilled at the edge of the door, her eyes watching his lithe, easy movements. After all, one wrong move, one surprised jerk and, well…

She told herself she stayed quiet, half-hidden in the shadows of the building because she didn't want to scare him, which could cause him to hurt himself. She was merely waiting until he shut off that deadly contraption.

But that was only partly true.

Stomach clenching as she watched him, Cat felt a tingle of awareness shoot through her body. She'd never thought to consider that a man might have sexy forearms. But by golly.

In her other, rather rushed run-ins with Matt McBoy, Cat had done her best to look at him as infrequently as she possibly could—a defense mechanism to keep him from seeing how mortified she'd been. If she couldn't see his eyes then he couldn't see into hers. She'd wanted to fade into the background, an unremembered, faceless customer. No distractions,

no advertisements as to her complete stupidity with home re-
pairs.

She shook her head amusedly. Well, now that they'd jumped
over that little hurdle, because there could be no doubt in his
mind about her inadequacies in that department now, she let
herself take stock of him, her gaze brushing over his broad
shoulders. He was wearing flannel again, this shirt white-and-
black, along with a pair of loose-fitting jeans and a tattered baseball cap, the bill of which was ripped and stained from what she
could only assume was the sun and sweat.

To say he was dressed casually was an understatement, and
yet there was something so, so…watching him work that ma-
chine, watching the bunching movements in those forearms, the
muscles and veins straining and stretching, Cat swallowed
thickly.

Her stomach seized in reaction again.

It had been a while since she'd had cause to notice a man
doing something so innocuously sexy. It'd been a while since
she'd found her attention unexpectedly stolen, drifting in that
direction. Pulled almost against her will. Hell, it'd been a while
since she'd so much as been on a date. Which likely explained
her rather sudden, unacceptable appreciation for the male body
so ruggedly on display before her now.

Her fingers curled sharply into the towel as she imagined—

"Hello? Hey, are you okay?"

At the words, Cat jerked, her eyes flicking quickly upward,
colliding with the questioning glint in the object of her current
fantasy's gaze. That's when she noticed the silence. The whining hum of the saw in front of him had been shut off. Matt was
no longer looking down at the wooden block on his work-table.
He was looking straight at her.

And judging by the tone of his voice, and the slight smirk
lining those thin lips, that had not been the first time he'd tried
to speak to her.

For the second time in as many minutes, Cat was grateful for
the dim lighting in the building. Clearing her throat, because
Matt was still looking at her, with one eyebrow raised now, she
sputtered: "Yes, hi." Advancing toward him, she prayed her
face wasn't as pink as she feared. She smiled brilliantly. "I,
umm…it's me, Cat. I mean, Catherine Cryer—"

"Yeah, I know who you are."

It was the way he said it that made an idiot of her and her statement.

To be fair, it had been a stupid thing to say. Of course, he'd recognize her. He was expecting her. Hardly a normal, everyday activity for him. He'd been more than clear on that front.

Clearing her throat again, Cat tried to laugh. It wasn't a terrible attempt. "Right, of course. I'm sorry. And, yeah, sorry for standing there all weird—" she cringed internally, wishing her damn mouth would just shut up already. Instead, it kept talking. "I didn't want to interrupt you earlier—"

He smirked.

That only spurred her on. "And I mean, yes, okay, I was kind of daydreaming at the end there..." Why? Why did she feel the need to explain herself?

Matt choked back a laugh.

Flicking her hair over one shoulder, Cat plowed ruthlessly, defensively ahead as her feet brought her ever nearer to his work station. "I, well, maybe daydreaming isn't the right word." Struggling to find a sense of casualness, she groped for the most readily available excuse. Her words held a frenzied quality. "Long day at the office. You know how it is, sometimes you just can't shut it off."

There. That sounded almost reasonable.

Matt's lips twitched again. Still, he didn't say anything. He didn't even bother to agree with her statement, which somehow made it all the more obvious. Instead, he nodded toward the wrapped package in her hands.

"That it?"

"What? Oh! Yes." Fetching up before him now, Cat held out her hands. "I also brought the broken piece," she informed him woodenly as he took the items. "I wasn't sure—you know, if you'd want it. Probably you don't, but just in case..."

"That's fine."

Snapping her mouth shut, Cat smiled tightly. She really needed to get the babbling under control. A rush of resentment coursed through her body. She was usually better than this. Clamping her lips together, she watched him set the bundle down on a nearby workbench before unwrapping the doors from the confines of her peach-colored towel. Tense, she waited as he inspected the unbroken piece, turning it this way and that, his fingers running down the curves. He did this for a few moments, but an eternity of nerves eddied their way up Cat's arms, closing around her throat.

"So?" Bouncing on the balls of her feet, Cat peered up at him hopefully. Though she despised the pleading note in her question, she found herself unable to hide it: "What do you think? Can you fix it?"

He set the cupboard door back down on the workbench. Then his eyes shifted to take in the pinched features of her face.

"As I said, I'll give it a try."

She supposed she'd have to accept that.

"Okay." Cat ran her tongue over her bottom lip. "But you'll do it?"

He sighed. "Yeah."

"How much?"

"Excuse me?"

She nodded impatiently. "How much will it cost?"

He shrugged, taking in the door again. "Well, this is a basic walnut veneer plywood door. It's a common material—in fact, I have some in stock at the store."

Cat nodded. "Well, that's lucky for me."

"It's also inexpensive. So yeah, lucky." Matt rubbed a hand against his chin as he studied the doors before him. "The fact that the doors are painted white will actually work in our favor. Hide any discrepancies."

Hearing him say it like that, another jolt of feeling zipped down Cat's stomach. There was something so scandalous in it all. They were pulling one over on her landlord. Though Cat was usually fastidious about her moral compass, for some reason, the thought gave her a kick.

Besides, her landlord was kind of a jerk anyway. So whatever. And in the grand scheme of things, it was hardly a speck of dust in criminal mastermind circles.

His head snapped back toward her suddenly. "Unless…that won't be a problem, will it? The fact that it'll need to be painted afterward?"

"Nope. I've got that part handled." After all, even she could manage to slap some paint on a door. She wasn't completely useless.

He nodded. "Okay. Good. I'll price the material out and get back to you tomorrow. Okay?"

Avoiding those brown eyes leveled so close to her own, Cat nodded airily. It felt somehow obvious, when she looked at him, what she was thinking. "Sure, no problem. And what about for you?"

"For me?"

"The cost for labor?"

Bringing one hand up to the back of his neck, those long-tapered fingers rubbed at the muscles there distractedly. "Well, how about we wait and see what the finished product looks like first."

"Okay. But I am going to pay you. Either way."

Matt shrugged again. "No one's fighting you on that."

"No discounts, either."

"Right. Okay."

"I'll pay the going rate."

Matt frowned. "I told you, I'm not a professional."

"And you also told me no one was fighting me on payments."

That stopped him momentarily. Then, with a weary shake of his head, Matt took a step back from the workbench. "Fine. That's up to you."

Cat bit back a smile. It felt good to finally be the one in control. "Good."

In response, Matt inclined his head toward the doors. "I should have it done by the end of the week."

"Really?" Cat's eyes widened. "That's fast."

"It's an easy design."

"Well, that's good," Cat mumbled inanely. She realized they'd reached the end of their conversation and she was assuaged with two diverging feelings: regret because that meant it was time for her to leave, and pure and utter relief that she could escape before she said yet another foolish thing.

As it was, Cat had a sinking feeling she'd replay her conversation with Matt over and over again until the early hours of the morning, her groans of mortification the only company she'd have as she berated herself as it was.

On that lowering thought, she took a pointed step backward. Raising her hand, Cat smiled. "Okay. Well." She nodded toward the table-saw. "I suppose I should let you get back to it." With those stilted words ringing in the dusty air, Cat took another step in retreat, trying hard to ignore the small voice in her head that hoped he'd call her back, give her a reason to step forward once again...

But of course, Matt didn't. "Sounds good. I'll call you tomorrow to talk about the material." And with that, he lowered the goggles back on his eyes again and, without bothering to watch her leave, turned back to what he'd been doing before she arrived.

"Right." With a whisper, Cat shifted, her feet beating a hasty exit.

CHAPTER SEVEN

Letting the warehouse door shut behind her, Cat moseyed into the falling evening, her feet in no particular hurry as she advanced toward her car. She had nothing left to do now but zip home and…and what, exactly? Cat considered her options: watch TV? Play solitaire? Darkly comedic as it was, her next thought tugged Cat's lips up the slightest fraction of an inch. She should take the opportunity to rearrange her snack and soup shelves, now that she didn't have doors covering either set of these scattered arrangements.

Whoop, whoop! Crazy Monday night happening at the Cryer residence.

"Good afternoon, Cat. It *is* Cat, isn't it? I tell you what, old age is nothing to envy…"

At the sudden onslaught of what appeared to be a one-sided conversation directed her way, Cat's head lifted, her neck twisting in time to see Margaret McBoy walking up toward her. Directly behind the older woman, parked in front of a carefully worded sign that read, *Reserved Parking. All Others Towed*, was a flashy red sports car. As Cat watched, bemused, Margaret hit a button on her key fob and the car in question flashed its lights as she locked it before pocketing the keys.

It was a car that screamed style, money, and youth. Yet, oddly, Cat had a feeling that Margaret rode it with an ease of elegance that belied her age.

She smiled at the notion. "Hello, Margaret. And yes, it is Cat."

Margaret shook her head. "I swear to it, I forget more than I remember now." She sent Cat a toothy smile; a smudge of her wild pink lipstick was smeared across one of her front teeth. "Speaking of that, did I tell you that no one calls me Margaret?"

Cat's thoughts stumbled, brought to a scattered end. "Uh, no."

"I didn't think so." Margaret's cheeks creased as she twinkled in amusement. Cat wasn't sure she'd ever met someone who infused so much happiness in the air simply by standing in it. "In fact, I think you're the first person to call me that in years. Well, except for Matthew, but he reserves that for times when I've truly annoyed him." The last sentence seemed to be said more-or-less for Margaret's own benefit.

"Oh." Cat wasn't sure what else to say. For one thing, Margaret had yet to tell her what everyone *did* call her. And for another, Cat had met this peppery woman only once before—and it wasn't as if this run-in had been scheduled.

"Birdie."

Cat felt her eyebrows rise in amusement. "Birdie?"

"That's what everyone calls me."

"Yeah, I know. I mean, I got that. But...why?" There was hardly any connection between the two names.

In some corner of her mind, Cat realized that she and "Birdie" were still standing outside on the dirt-packed parking lot at the back of the hardware store, blocking the path of any delivery drivers that may be en route...and all the while, having a nice little chat as though nothing were unusual about that.

But then again, there was always the chance that Matt would overhear them and come out...

Whoa. Where had that thought come from?

Still, Cat noticed that she was standing a little taller now, smiling a little brighter now. Just in case.

"You know, I can't remember!" Birdie giggled again. And that's what the sound was too. A girlish giggle about fifty years too young for her body. Still, like the car, somehow it fit. She brought a finger up to her chin, tap-tapping it there as she thought. Finally, Birdie turned her large eyes up to Cat, shrugging dismissively. "Been called Birdie almost my whole life."

Cat nodded, unsure what to say. There wasn't anywhere to go with that story.

"How about you?"

"Me?"

"Is Cat your actual name?"

Cat smiled instinctively. "Uh, no. It's Catherine."

"Umm, yes, I suppose that's what I figured."

"Disappointed?"

Birdie lifted one shoulder. "No. Only, well, I was hoping—"

"For something more exotic?" Leaning forward, Cat winked conspiratorially. "Caterina or Caterie?

Birdie giggled again. "Oh, goodness!"

Cat laughed too. She had a feeling it was the only natural reaction around Birdie. "No such luck. It's just Catherine."

"Nothing plain about that name."

Cat kicked at the loose gravel underfoot. "No, I suppose not."

Out of her peripheral vision, Cat watched Birdie's head shift, her gaze roaming over the industrial buildings hugging the hardware store on either side of them, as though she were struck by a new thought.

"What brings you out here?"

That wasn't quite the question Cat had been expecting. Still, not much about Birdie seemed to be predictable.

Hurriedly hitching her head over one shoulder, Cat gestured toward McBoy's rear entrance. "I had to drop off the doors for Matt."

"That's right." Birdie smiled. "Was he on good behavior?"

Cat blinked. Opened her mouth. Hesitated.

Birdie chuckled. "I'll take that as a no."

"I didn't—"

"Don't let that put you off. He's a good guy. A great one."

Cat nodded swiftly. "I'm sure."

Birdie lowered her voice. "And I know, despite his growling, he's tickled to be working on this project. He thinks I don't know it, but I do. This business," she waved dismissively toward the hardware store sharing her last name. "It's not his dream. Of course, he thinks it'd break my heart to hear that. But, as I said, I know."

Cat swallowed uncomfortably, her brain sluggish in the whirlwind of information she had no business hearing, her tongue struggling to find an appropriate, if neutral, response.

Thankfully, Birdie didn't make her come up with one. Instead, the older woman continued speaking: "This is good practice for him. You're good for him."

Cat nodded again, slowly, noncommittally (at least, she hoped it looked noncommittal). Desperate, she looked for another tract for conversation; oddly, it never occurred to her to simply end the dialogue. That would have meant going home. Alone.

"So...what brings *you* out here?" Cat figured turnabout was fair play.

Birdie started a little at the question, as if shaken out of her reverie. She looked back at her car as if the sight of it would remind her. "Well, it's Monday. Me and the girls always play Canasta down at Julie's Café on Mondays."

"Oh." That sort of made sense. Julie's Café was located about half a block away. But it had its own parking lot. Small, granted, but not likely to be filled at 4:45 p.m.

Birdie seemed to understand Cat's silent thoughts, seemed to perfectly read the question in Cat's eyes as her gaze shifted from Birdie's car toward the restaurant, the backside of which was just barely visible down the road. "I spent the better part of my marriage making sacrifices to my husband's business. Evening hours, weekends, double shifts and mountains of paperwork...sometimes, whole days would go by and I wouldn't even see him." She looked lovingly then at the bluish-gray exterior of the McBoy's Hardware Store. "He loved this place."

Cat smiled.

Shaking herself, Birdie looked back at Cat. "One of my only real recompenses for all those years was the coveted reserved parking spot I've secured for myself over here." With a flick of her head, she nodded toward that red flashy car. "It might not seem it, but it's prime. I'm within walking distance of just about anywhere in downtown."

Cat inclined her head. Now she understood. "It would be a shame not to use it at every available opportunity."

Birdie clicked her tongue. "That's exactly how I feel about it."

"Well." Much as she had with Matt, Cat felt the tugging realization that her and Birdie's conversation had reached a natural close. To continue it would only be to delay the older woman from her card game. And though Cat had enjoyed the exchange, she didn't want to intrude on Birdie's goodwill. "I don't want to keep you from your evening..."

And again, as she'd done with Matt, Cat took a telling step backward, her intentions clear. "Have a good day." Only, unlike Matt, Birdie reached out a hand, the action forestalling Cat's movements.

"Do you play?"

"Excuse me?"

Birdie smiled winningly. "It would be nice to have some fresh blood in the game." Pausing, she tilted her head to one side. "Unless, of course, you have other plans?"

It took Cat a moment to answer. "No," she finally admitted. It wasn't as humiliating as she'd feared. "No, I don't." She shrugged. "But I don't know how to play, uh, what did you call it?"

"Canasta."

"Yeah. That."

Grabbing Cat's arm, Birdie curled hers through the crook of Cat's elbow. "Well, that's no bother. We'll teach you."

"Isn't it supposed to be complicated?"

Birdie gave her a sidelong glance. "You seem pretty smart to me. I think you'll pick it up rather quickly."

Which is how Cat found herself being led not quite unwillingly up the alleyway to Café. Edging around the property line to the front of the diner, Cat blinked in bemusement. She wasn't entirely sure she even wanted to learn to play cards. Not for another forty or so years. A childish sort of embarrassment invaded Cat's person. So it had come to this. The only people she could get to hang out with her were people her grandparents' age. If her college friends could see her now.

God, if they could see her now, she'd probably have to duck under the table.

Opening the front door of the café, Cat found herself steered to a round table near the back of the short, squat building. Peeling, faded wallpaper and dusty overhead lights greeted her. As did four pairs of eyes of varying shades.

"Ladies." Birdie cleared her throat as if to make an important announcement. "I'd like to introduce you to my new friend, Cat—" Birdie blinked. She shot Cat a look. "I'm afraid I don't know your last name."

"Cryer."

"Well, there you have it. Meet Cat Cryer. She's graciously decided to play with us today." Then Birdie turned to Cat. "Cat, these are the ladies—" and one by one, she pointed them out. "Harriet, Eleanor, Mary, and Erna."

Cat waved a hesitant hand. "Hello."

"Hello."

"Good afternoon."

"You ever actually played before?"

"Mary!"

"What? The last person who joined—what was her name?"

"It was my granddaughter, as you well know," the one named Harriet informed Mary. "And her name is Elizabeth."

"Yeah? Well, Elizabeth stunk."

"Mary!" Birdie exclaimed.

"What?"

"Give the girl a chance."

Harriet glowered. "And shut your darn yapper while you're at it."

"I'm only saying—"

"Look," Birdie maintained with forced patience, "if we want to play teams, we need another person…"

Mary snorted. "Doesn't mean we need to get desperate."

Blinking, Cat wasn't sure if she should smile or turn and run. She wasn't given the chance to do either, as it turned out. Feeling the pull of Birdie's fingers on her arm, she looked over at the kindly woman.

"Pay Mary no attention. Here. Take a seat next to me and I'll give you a quick rundown of the rules."

"You'll be just fine, dearie." This encouragement was given by Eleanor. At least, Cat thought that was Eleanor. They all sort of looked alike: frail, permed, pale, and utterly content.

"Okay, so each card has a number value attached to it. And there are two wild cards…."

Concentrating, Cat tried to take in everything Birdie told her. Much as she'd suspected, the game *was* complicated. Listening to Birdie, Cat's heart rate shot-up, her nerves giving way to

Mary's rather ominous words: she feared that, much like Elizabeth, she'd probably stink.

"Does that make sense?" Birdie asked finally. It appeared she'd exhausted the list of rules and strategies and whatnot.

Cat swallowed thickly. "Uh. I think so?"

"Don't worry. You'll figure it out as we go." Shockingly enough, this boost of support came from Mary. Reaching for a ridiculously thick stack of cards, she started shuffling. "We'll play with partners, so that ought to help. Besides, I don't have all day here..."

"Okay." Cat prayed she wouldn't have to be on Mary's team.

An hour and a half later, Cat was stunned to note the time. More than that, she was surprised she was still there, sitting on the edge of a thinly-padded seat of Julie's Café, playing cards fanned out across her fingers, in front of her eyes, her left leg bop-bop-bopping impatiently while Erna considered her hand.

"Good God, while I'm still young here," Mary barked across the table at her partner. Not for the first time that evening, Cat found herself genuinely thankful that she'd been partnered with Birdie (for obvious reasons, or so Mary muttered when the teams were picked; that way, if Cat sucked it'd be Birdie's problem, since she was the one who invited her).

Only Cat wasn't terrible at the game. Turned out, she was actually kind of good.

Much as Mary had predicted, she'd picked up on the strategy of the game fairly quickly after they'd started. But even that wasn't the biggest surprise of Cat's evening. It was the fact that, despite it all—despite being forty years younger than her companions, besides playing a game she'd had little interest in only a couple hours prior, besides Mary's growling intensity—Cat was having fun.

She was having a great time.

Erna slapped a card down on the discard pile, giving Mary a long, dark scrutiny as she did so. Her nose lifted upward a little. "Too late for that, my dear."

Harriet snorted.

Birdie elbowed Cat.

"Careful," Mary said, but she wasn't wagging her finger at Erna. Her milky eyes were glaring straight across the table at Cat. "You won't always have that ass."

"Mary!"

"What? I saw her when she walked to the bathroom. She's got a nice tush."

"Goodness!" This came from Erna.

"You know it's true," Mary said, still talking to Cat.

Flushing, her bottom wiggling uncomfortably on her chair, Cat shrugged. "I...uh, I don't know. I've never really thought—"

"Stop it." Mary snapped the fingers of one hand in midair, the action quick, sharp, like a whip. "Of course you have. You've looked over your shoulder in the mirror. You've studied it. Don't lie to an old woman."

"What does your being old have to do with it?"

"And don't be impertinent, either!"

Cat smirked. She couldn't help it. "Sorry," she mumbled.

"Speaking of that, why are you here with us old cows anyway?" Mary winked. "*Especially* with an ass like that?"

"Cows? Speak for yourself," Harriet growled. "I'm no barn animal."

Erna chuckled. "I don't know, Har. We've all seen you eat..."

"Hush!"

Cat giggled at their antics. In the ninety minutes she'd spent with them, this style of conversation had become anything but unusual. It worked only because, through the biting sarcasm, there was open affection—and everyone felt it.

"Get ya another refill?"

At the introduction of a new voice to their laughter, Cat looked up. Standing just to the left of her seat was their server, a woman in her mid-forties wearing too much eye-liner and sporting a brown smudge on her otherwise white apron. Looking down at her coffee cup, Cat noted that it was, indeed, empty.

"Not for me," Erna said, covering the top of her mug with one fragile, crookedly-shaped hand.

"Me neither."

"I think we're good here, Beth. Thank you."

Mary looked up at the wall-clock that Cat had been subconsciously avoiding all evening. "Shoot. It's already after seven?"

She shook her head. "Somebody better win this hand already. I've got to get home."

Erna nodded. "Yeah. Me too."

Cat's smile tightened. Staring down at her hand, she waited for Mary to finish her turn. She waited for someone to go out. She waited for the fun to end....

CHAPTER EIGHT

Rinsing off the last of her dishes that evening, Cat yawned. By the time she'd left Julie's Café, a protracted affair of goodbyes, it had suddenly occurred to Cat that she was starving. She hadn't thought about dinner when she and Birdie had first arrived at the card table. After all, she hadn't planned to stay so late. And then, in the midst of learning the game, she'd forgotten all about her hunger. It was only after the group had disbanded and she'd reached her car that Cat had felt the first strong pangs of hunger clawing at the insides of her stomach.

Setting her plate on the drying rack now, Cat checked the time. It was a little after nine o'clock. Shutting out the lights of her kitchen, she bypassed her living room, turning down the short hallway until she reached the door to her bedroom.

Shuffling inside, Cat thrust away the dampening intrusion of her solitary meal, which had been deafeningly quiet in comparison to the liveliness of her chance encounter with a bunch of Canasta-playing grandmothers. Instead, smiling at the thought of them, Cat remembered the resounding sound of Mary's final whoop when she and Eleanor had gone out, winning the last game.

Birdie had tisked. "Mary's always been a bit of a poor sport."

"Spoken like a proper loser," Mary had retorted.

"Hey, at least this time she didn't stick her tongue out at you." This cheerful piece of advice had come for Harriet.

All the while, unable to help herself, Cat had giggled. Then she'd laughed.

"They can call me a poor sport if they want," Mary had told her, bending down conspiratorially. Then, loud enough to be heard, she'd hitched her thumb over one shoulder. "When you've got that as a partner...well, you take whatever success you can—ow! Hey now..."

"Oh, I'll give you something to *hey now!* about," Eleanor had muttered, dropping her right hand, the fingers of which had just flicked Mary behind her ear, back down to her side.

Flipping on her bedside lamp now, Cat moved around her room robotically, swapping her slacks for fleece, her button-down tunic for a cotton T-shirt before prattling into the adjoining bathroom. The yellow glare of her cheap light fixtures when she toggled them on blazed into the hallows of her cheeks washing out her already pale complexion.

If someone would have told her three days ago that she'd find herself playing Canasta on a Monday night with a group of women old enough to have forgotten more than she'd ever learn, she'd have told them...well, Cat would have been so shocked by the absurdity of it all she'd have been stunned silent.

And if that wasn't outrageous enough, Cat hadn't wanted the fun to end.

"Thank you so much for letting me join you ladies," she'd told them as they stacked up the cards into a neat pile at the end of the evening. Pushing her chair back, she'd made to stand up.

Eleanor. "It was a pleasure, my dear."

Erna. "You have a natural talent for it."

Birdie. "It's always lovely to introduce new players to the game."

"At least you didn't make a complete ass out of yourself."

Smiling, with a half-wave that made her feel more self-conscious—why was saying goodbye always such a production?—Cat had swung her purse over her shoulder. "Have a good night everyone."

"You too."

"See you soon."

"Anytime you want to play, you know where to find us!"

"We'd love to have you again!"

"It's great to play with partners—"

"Jesus!"

Birdie had turned then toward Mary's scowling expression. "What now?"

"Be cool. Play it coy. That's how you reel 'em in!"

On those words, Cat had laughingly made her exit, walking up to the antique cash register at Julie's to pay for the cups of coffee she'd consumed.

Smiling in her dinky vanity mirror at the memory, Cat rubbed lotion on her arms and neck before reaching for her toothbrush. Her movements were natural, soothing as only things of routine can become. Within minutes she'd returned to her bedroom. Pulling back her quilted covers, Cat clambered into bed. Settling against the pillows, she reached over to shut off the lights.

It was early but between the nerves that had attacked her all morning over her meeting with Matt and the mental taxation of learning Canasta, Cat found herself exhausted. She sighed tiredly. The ghost of a smile was still stamped across her mouth.

What happened next was the damnedest thing.

Amid the silver light managing to slink through the thick curtains covering her windows, through the wisps of sound as late-night travelers trekked down her side-street, Cat felt the soft, wet moisture of tears fall onto her cheeks.

Sniffing with something of a snort, she turned on her side. Curling her legs up close to her chest, Cat felt something explode inside her stomach. Her shoulders quaked, her breath burning, rending as she sobbed.

It was silly, really.

Thinking about that stupid dinner eaten alone.

She'd had a lovely night. A great night.

A great, lovely night. With someone else's friends.

Made all the more obvious by the solitary sandwich she'd eaten afterward.

... °•°• ...

Hunched over her computer screen the next afternoon, Cat's attention was roused by the sudden, loud ringing of her phone. Frowning, she turned toward the clunky piece of office equipment, her eyes narrowing at its clanging, insistent chirp. She was almost tempted to let it go to voicemail. She only had a few more pieces to review before signing off on the application form before her.

But at the last moment, instinct taking over, she felt her hand reach forward, taking the handset off the cradle. "Fireside Credit Union," she intoned, the words slipping thoughtlessly out of her mouth. How many phone calls had she started with those very words? So many that she didn't bother to switch her attention from the document on her computer screen, her eyes glancing left and right, down to the next line, then left again. "This is Catherine Cryer speaking."

"Hello, Catherine."

At the words, Cat started. With a fluster, she dropped her fingers from the keyboard to her lap. Her back straightened slightly. The voice on the other end of the receiver was masculine. Deep. And it did something funny to her stomach, just hearing it.

She hadn't spoken *that* many words to him, but Cat was left in no confusion as to who was on the other end of the line.

"Yes. Hello, Matt." Matthew McBoy. Cat was satisfied with the dignified control in her voice. The fact that her fingers shook the tiniest bit, she chalked up to surprise, clenching them into fists. And anyway, he couldn't see them.

It was just that she hadn't expected to hear from him.

Well, not so soon.

Cat frowned. Her conversation with him from yesterday floated across her consciousness: *"I'll price them out and get back to you tomorrow. Okay?"*

Well, whatever.

"I hope I'm not interrupting—?" Matt paused, waiting for her to assure him otherwise.

She didn't disappoint. "No, of course not," Cat assured him. And, just for effect, she minimized the document glaring out at her across the bluish-white light of her computer. Again, Matt couldn't see this action, but still... "What can I do for you?"

The moment the question came out of her mouth, Cat knew herself for a fool. She'd tried too hard in that instant to appear cool and collected. And, ironically, she'd only come out conspicuously flippant.

She knew why he was calling.

"Uh...you asked me to cost out the price of a new door?"

"Right. Of course." Cat laughed, groping wildly for an excuse, something to cover her blunder. "Please excuse me. It's been one of those mornings. Ten o'clock and it's already been an interminably long day. I'm afraid I've got zombie brain."

There. She was fairly impressed with the sincerity present in that lie.

Matt laughed quietly.

The band around her stomach clenched again. Tightened. Spasmed at the low rumble of sound.

"Don't zombies *eat* brains?"

"And now you've fully grasped how dire the situation is," Cat mumbled.

Matt chuckled again.

Cat grinned. But, sensing the end of this topic of conversation, she plunged forward. "Now, what have you got for me?"

"All right…"

Leaning back in her chair, a sense of calm finally stealing over her person, Cat reached for a piece of paper and a pen, ready to tally down his numbers.

… °●°● …

Walking over the greasy threshold of the Main Time Liquor Store that evening, Cat balked. A thin, stained carpet of what she supposed had once been light blue in color, stared up at her as she veered quickly to the right of the doors. Eyes downcast, she walked with seeming purpose but it was all a ruse. Cat had almost no idea what she was doing there.

Well, that wasn't quite true.

She knew *why* she was there.

To get beer.

The idea had come to her as she'd been preparing to leave work for the day but now…

Walking up to the back wall of glass display cases—marching side-by-side, one after another and housing every type of beer, from domestics to imports and even a few micro-breweries—she frowned, the finger of one hand moving along with her eyes as she considered the selection before her. When she'd reached the end of the line, she started back at the beginning, running through the selection again.

The only problem was, she had no idea what kind of beer she should get.

"Trouble making up your mind?"

At the question, Cat's head picked up. Turning at the sound of the voice, she felt her eyes widen the tiniest bit. Standing across from her, arms loaded down with assorted bottles of wine, was a vaguely familiar woman. Squinting, it took Cat a moment to place her.

Oh. There it was.

"Amelia." Amelia Kelley. The woman she'd approved for a business loan the other day. Cat gave herself a mental high-five. "How are you?"

Cat was treated with one of the largest smiles she'd ever seen. Amelia's brightly painted lips spread apart so wide that Cat wondered if it didn't hurt a little.

"I'm great." A dimple appeared on Amelia's left cheek. "Thanks in a large part to you."

Cat shook her head, a bit flustered by the words. "I didn't do all that much…"

But Amelia wasn't having that. "Without you, my dreams would still be paper fantasies. You made them a reality. Thank you. Again."

Cat felt her face heating up. She was used to a mild amount of gratitude from clients but Amelia's exuberance was nothing short of embarrassing. "I only approve of what I believe in. You created that."

"I got the keys to my studio today," Amelia said then, the words slipping out with an airy sort of quality. It was as if she were testing the weight and feel of them as they exited her mouth. She nodded down at the copious amount of alcohol in her arms. "That's actually why I'm here today."

Cat grinned, tilting her head a little to one side. "Because you decided to become a winery after all?"

Amelia laughed. "Just for tonight."

Cat grinned, eyeing up the mass quantity of wine. "That's a lot of celebrating."

Amelia grinned. "Especially for one person. But I'm up to the challenge."

Cat nodded uncertainly. She wasn't sure what to say to that—

Amelia, however, didn't seem the least disturbed by her singular status. Cat envied that. "I probably won't drink it all tonight."

"Probably for the best."

"But I couldn't figure out what I wanted. So I just grabbed a bit of everything."

Cat chuckled weakly. "I can see that."

Amelia nodded with her chin toward the beer cases. "How about you?"

"Me?"

"Looking for something in particular?"

Cat made a face. "I wish."

"Huh?"

"No, I mean..." Cat felt her hands open expressively. "I'm not buying the beer for myself." Truth be told, Cat wasn't sure why she admitted that. She wasn't sure why she hadn't just lied and let Amelia assume she was merely a picky connoisseur of beers and stuck with indecision.

"Oh?"

"I'm getting it for a friend. Well, no—he's not really a friend." Cat definitely wasn't sure why she'd admitted *that*.

Amelia blinked. "*No?*"

"No." Cat's voice was firm. Regardless of the reasons, she was already this far into the story. It would have been weird not to explain it all. "He's more of an acquaintance. And not one who's entirely pleased with even that slight arrangement."

Amelia tried to bit back a smile. She failed.

"But he's doing me this favor and I thought..."

"A little extra incentive?"

Cat sighed. "Yeah."

"But you don't know what he drinks," Amelia guessed, her voice conversational.

"It was a stupid idea."

"No way." Amelia juggled the bottles in her arms. "What's he like?"

"The guy?"

"Yeah."

"Right. Um." Cat considered the question for a moment. "Quiet."

"Okay."

"He's a man's man, you know... like a handyman."

"Okay."

"Sawdust, flannel shirts, mumbled replies. That kind of thing."

Amelia's eyes flickered over to the beers as she silently computed this information. Then with a definitive nod, she turned back to Cat. "Hops."

"Hops?"

"Yeah. The more the better. Get an IPA—maybe a slam."

"Are we still speaking English?"

"Not a beer fan?"

Cat grinned. "No. Wine and margaritas are pretty much my mainstays."

"Perfect."

Cat felt her eyebrows arch.

"I've thought about it. It would be irresponsible to drink this all alone." Amelia's eyes traveled tellingly over the wine in her arms. "Want to join me?"

Cat blinked in surprise. "Me?"

"Who else? Yeah. The more I think about it the more it makes sense." Amelia's smile was infectious, as was the ease of her conversation. "After all, without you—"

"Without me, another loan manager would have signed off on your application just as quickly."

Amelia wiggled her eyebrows suggestively. "Come on. Help a girl out. It's depressing, getting drunk alone. And honestly, you're the only person I know in this town."

Cat laughed as she was meant to, and then, oddly found herself nodding. Without her usual hesitation. Without any thought at all. "Yeah? Okay. Sure, I'm in."

Amelia squealed. "Yay!"

"I mean, us girls have to stick together, right?"

Amelia nodded with mock gravity. "Precisely. And it's imperative that I have someone to cheers."

Shaking her head bemusedly, Cat felt a smile stretch across her face, one to perhaps rival even that of Amelia. She supposed she should have reservations growing in the aftermath of her rather reckless acceptance to Amelia's invitation. After all, she didn't even know the woman. The night could turn out to be a total bust.

And yet.

There had been something surreal about the last couple of days. Something different. Some universal magic at play—giving her exactly what she'd asked for. She wasn't about to turn her back on it, even if it all felt wildly out of her comfort zone.

Grinning, Cat pushed the worrying thoughts away. "Still, I must insist that you have nothing to thank me for."

Amelia only inclined her head. "Meet at my studio? In an hour? Will that give you enough time to drop off the beers to your kind-of guy friend?"

Cat nodded. "Sounds good." She didn't have to ask where Amelia's studio was. She remembered from the loan application.

"Fab!" Amelia sang. "See you then!" With an ease of grace, she twirled on her heels and headed for the cash register.

Turning back to the stacks of beers ahead of her, Cat recognized the feeling fighting its way up her body.

Anticipation. Excitement.

With a tug, she jerked open one of the display doors ahead of her, her movements easy as she reached for and grabbed the first six-pack within reach. The letters IPA were splashed proudly across the label.

"I hope she was right," Cat said, but the anxiety of this purchase, which had flooded her person minutes earlier, was gone.

CHAPTER NINE

Of course, Cat being Cat, that sense of calm couldn't last. Within the three miles it took her to drive from the liquor store to the McBoy's loading docks, she felt her insides tightening again, her mind fussing, overthinking. Perhaps the beer hadn't been such a good idea. What if he thought it was a weird gesture? What if he thought she was being overly friendly, or that she was trying too hard?

What if he got the wrong impression: thought that she was trying to imply something else?

Another attack of nerves seized Cat. She should have told Matt that she was going to swing by the store after work. Frowning as she pulled into the backside of the hardware store, Cat felt her foot press down numbly on the brake pedal. It hadn't occurred to her to do so at the time. She'd only known, after their short phone call that morning, an almost overwhelming sense of indebtedness fall on her shoulders—an obligation to pay him back, post haste. Matt was doing so much for her, taking on all this extra work for her—a woman he didn't even know, on a project for which he hadn't volunteered. But he was doing it anyway, making it a priority. She'd felt an instinct too strong to resist that demanded she show good faith, that she offer some sort of reciprocity. Something to even the score.

It had seemed like a good idea at the time.

Fingers wrapped around her steering wheel, Cat glanced down at the six-pack on the floorboard of her passenger seat. "Well, screw it. You already bought them. It would be stupid to get this far only to chicken out."

With a crank of her wrist, Cat shut off her car, reached for the beer and alit from her vehicle. Walking determinedly up the long, rutted path, she forced herself to stop thinking. To just act. Unlike the last time she'd visited the store, now Cat's footing was sure as she stalked up to the service door on one side of the building.

Entering the warehouse, she took a moment to let her eyes adjust to the dim lighting, her gaze flicking once again to the wooden joists crisscrossing the ceiling, the small grimy windows overshadowed by the fluorescent bulbs scattered heavily throughout the space.

Same as before, standing against the far wall, bent over a table saw, was Matt McBoy. Only today, he wasn't wearing the usual flannel shirt. Instead, he was sporting a plain white long-sleeved shirt, liberally speckled with a fine yellow coating of what she could only suppose was wood shavings. Only today, Cat wasn't going to get caught gawking at him.

Straightening her shoulders, she was only too intent on making this visit different than the last one. No more overt anxiety. No more awkward bumbling. No more blushing. Keeping her attention focused on the task at hand, Cat's fingers curled more securely around the cardboard container holding the beer. Walking forward, she waited until Matt had turned off the whirling saw—his eyes focused as he leaned over the wood laid out on the table, his hands smoothing up and down one edge— and only then did Cat let her voice be heard.

"Hi, Matt."

With a snap, his head bobbed upward.

Hah. Cat reveled in the flash of the advantage stealing over her person. Yes, this time would be different. He could be the one disconcerted. It was only fair. Through the goggles he wore over his eyes, Cat caught a gleam of surprise, perhaps even confusion, pass across those lens.

"Catherine?"

"Please, call me Cat." Catherine sounded stiff, formal. For some reason, she didn't want that association when it came to him.

Pushing his goggles up on top of his head, Matt's gaze narrowed. Now Cat could clearly see the glint in those brown eyes. But unlike moments before, she didn't feel quite as cool about the growing perplexity echoed there—not when she watched that gaze flicker down to the alcohol she held at her side, back up to her, and then down to the beers again.

Making connections.

And probably a few misconceptions.

Dammit. She'd been right. Feeling conspicuous and guilty, even though she had nothing to feel guilty about—let him put any spin he wanted on her gift—Cat frowned. She hadn't stopped by because she'd misread his offer of help as some romantic overture. She wasn't there because she thought this project had made them buddies.

She wasn't being clingy.

Still, the idea that he might think that rankled. Rattled her.

His mouth thinned, his brows drawing together in consternation. "What, ah, what's up?"

It was a less than welcoming question.

Point made. He wasn't thrilled to see her.

Tilting her chin up a notch, though she'd promised herself she wouldn't overthink the situation, Cat found her body practically vibrating with discomfort and jittery nerve muscles. "I came to pay for the materials." Her voice was unusually high. Stilted.

At the words, his eyebrows wrinkled. "Oh. I thought…"

Cat waited for him to finish speaking.

Matt coughed. "You didn't need to come all the way down here to do that. I figured you'd pay me at the end."

Her skin itched. Still, Cat forged ahead. "For your labor, yes. But for the material? You shouldn't have had to pay for that yourself at all."

Matt grinned. "Well, technically I didn't pay for it. I just started a tab for you." The smallest hint of mockery skirted the edges of his mouth now. "Besides, that's usually how it goes, right? You pay for the job once it's complete. Parts *and* labor."

Cat wanted to sink through the floor at his perfectly reasonable and logical response. After all, you didn't pay your car mechanic in two-part increments. Hearing the words, Cat felt her body tense. Worse than sounding desperate, it was clear that he thought she *was* desperate. Furrowing her brows, Cat tried to regroup. "Yes. But as you've said to me on more than one occasion, this type of work is hardly regular for the store. As such... look, I didn't want to put you out any more than I obviously already have. Clearly, it was a stupid thought."

He chuckled. "Not stupid. Just unexpected." Walking around the edge of the table, his movements easy, Matt shrugged. "I don't have an invoice ready for you but I can go get one—"

"No, no," Cat assured him. Reaching for her purse, her movements jerky and ungainly by way of the beers she still held tightly in one hand, Cat fished clumsily inside the contents of her bag. "Please don't do that. One invoice—one *final* invoice will be fine." Struggling, Cat just managed to retrieve her wallet. But even as she shouldered it free, she realized...annoyance flared, licking at her brain.

She wouldn't be able to open her wallet single-handedly.

She'd have to put the beer down anyway.

With a weary sigh, hating the rushed, betrayed jostling of her body, Cat set the six-pack down at her feet. Snapping the clasp on her wallet viciously open, she rifled through it for her cash.

"Okay," Matt intoned, his hand reaching out to take the money Cat held out stiffly. "I'll make a note on it that you paid for the materials today."

"I'm not worried about that. I trust you." Her voice came out prim but there was sincerity within it. Because, inexplicably, Cat did trust him. Forcibly, she brought her gaze up to his. "And, I appreciate how quickly you're moving on this. That's why..." her voice petering out, Cat wasn't sure further explanation of her impromptu visit was necessary at that point. Or helpful.

Matt inclined his head. "No sweat."

"Is that it?" Cat nodded toward the rectangular piece of wood stretched out on the table saw.

Matt followed the motion of her gaze. Then he nodded. "Yup."

She whistled. "You're not wasting time."

One eyebrow lifted incredulously. "I thought you just said...?"

"No," she stuttered at his sardonic tone. "I meant—"

"Would you like me to wait on it?"

Cat knew he was teasing her, picking at her. It only made matters worse. Further tightened her shoulders, hardened her voice.

Cat made a sweeping motion with her hands, encompassing the workbench. "Please, don't let me keep you." Pivoting on her feet, she turned to walk away. As far as exits went, it was perhaps a bit brisk. Perhaps a bit quick.

And poorly executed.

She hadn't taken more than four steps when Matt called out to her.

"Hey. Cat?"

Half-turning toward him, she waited. "Yeah?"

"Don't forget your beer." With an amused flick of his wrist, Matt pointed toward the floor, where the six-pack of IPA's she'd so hastily set down moments ago remained.

"That?" Feeling her face flush, Cat nonetheless tried for nonchalance. "No, it's for you."

His eyebrows rose again, but she could see the sarcasm in the action. He'd known it was for him. He was teasing her again.

"You bought me beer?"

Cat sighed tiredly. Shrugging her shoulders, she studied the cement floor at her feet. "It's not like a big deal or anything," she assured him. "I just wanted to say thank you."

Out of her peripheral vision, she saw Matt's lips twitch. "So instead you said nothing at all?"

"You were kind of making it difficult."

"Sorry." He didn't sound the least repentant. He sounded downright amused.

Turning all the way around now, Cat spared him a dark look. Throwing her hands on her hips, she shook her head. "Look, I know you didn't want to do this. I know that Birdie all but forced the issue."

He inclined his head a little. She wasn't sure if it was in agreement or exception. She didn't want to find out.

"But I really *do* appreciate it. I wanted to…hell, I don't know." A new thought occurred to Cat. "God, do you even drink beer?"

Matt grinned. "Yes."

"Oh, good." Cutting her eyes back to the object at hand, Cat shrugged. "I wasn't sure what you'd like."

Following her lead, Matt glanced down at the six-pack. "This's good."

Cat rocked back on her heels, disproportionally pleased. "It is? Okay, good." Frowning, Cat realized the word good had probably been said too many times by now.

Matt remained silent.

"Well…" With a slight lift of her hand, Cat smiled. "Um, enjoy them. And *thank you*." At the emphatic words, Cat shifted back around, resuming her journey toward the dor.

Behind her, Matt chuckled again. "Are you always so dramatic?"

Cat almost tripped to a halt. Her head snapped around. And then—God, as if to prove his point—she spun back to face him. *Yet* again. "Excuse me?"

One side of his mouth pulled up. "I bet you are."

Cat felt her eyes widen. "What are you talking about?"

"How'd your kitchen door get snapped in half?"

She swallowed. "I told you…"

He waved away her answer. "A loose hinge wasn't good enough? Had to bust the damn thing?"

Her eyes narrowed. "I'm sure I don't—"

"I'm just saying—"

"Spare me, please."

Matt gestured toward the beers. "I'm just saying, you don't need to try so hard."

"I was being polite."

"Hmm. Okay." Then, suddenly, he asked: "You want one?"

Momentarily taken aback, Cat tried to piece together the random threads of conversation swirling around them. "A beer? Ah, no. Th-thanks, I can't." Still, she couldn't deny a spark of excitement at the invitation. He'd offered her a beer. Asked her to stay.

"No?" Bending down, he plucked one out of the cardboard holder.

"I actually have plans tonight." Cat felt a thrill of power in the response. She hadn't come schlepping all the way down there *just* to see him. Even if it sort of had looked that way. She had her own life to live. She wasn't some desperate woman, hanging on to whatever few minutes of his time he offered.

She got the feeling that a lot of the women in Matt's life fit into the latter category.

Straightening up, Matt pulled back the tab on the can. "Too bad."

Cat's eyes widened but before she was allowed to speak (or find the words to reply), Matt continued talking.

"Thanks for the beers. Hardly necessary, but *very* polite." With that, he moved back toward his workbench, the can wrapped around one hand. The dismissal was as easy as it was unignorable. He had work to do. Her time was up.

"You're welcome." It came out almost as a question. Tinged the tiniest bit with hope.

CHAPTER TEN

The drive from the hardware store and back into the center of town flew by in a blur. It was fortunate for Cat that she'd grown up in the small city, that she knew the geographical location so well that she could have more-or-less driven to Amelia's place of business blindly. Certainly, she hadn't been paying a lick of attention as she'd maneuvered her car down the roads separating it from McBoy's Hardware Store.

"So, he thinks I'm dramatic, does he?" she seethed as she passed city blocks, her incense only rising as she finally reached her destination. The man was too much. Mocking her one second and thanking her the next. And then, before she could wrap her head around the swift shake-up, he was mocking her again.

Cutting the engine and uncurling her fingers from the steering wheel, Cat took a deep breath. Shook away the offending thoughts crowding her head. They'd make her bad company if she allowed them to persist.

"For God's sake, stop giving him the power," she muttered. "Despite whatever he thought, it was obvious why I went there. To pay him. And I did that."

On those words, Cat scrambled out of her car. Rounding it, she forced a smile on her lips as she crossed the sidewalk and fetched up before the front door of Amelia Kelley's newly leased building. Glancing up at the painted sign on the front door that clearly labeled the building as a daycare facility, she shook her head. One of Amelia's first jobs would be getting that removed.

She was reaching for the door handle when Cat hesitated. She wasn't sure if she should just walk inside. That seemed a bit presumptuous. Peering through the glass-fronted door, she tried to make out Amelia's figure, but only a dim light shone through from somewhere in the back of the building. With a sigh, she raised her hand and knocked on the glass pane.

There was no answer.

No silhouette coming forward.

Knocking again, Cat waited, her eyes zipping up and down the street as a wave of foolishness washed over her. Maybe this hadn't been such a good idea after all. What if Amelia had changed her mind? What if, what if she was one of those flaky people who'd forgotten about Cat almost as quickly as she'd left her?

Still no answer.

"For fuck's sake." With a weary sigh, Cat pulled on the door handle. It wasn't locked. Poking her head inside the building, Cat called out a soft greeting. "Amelia? Amelia, it's Cat Cryer?"

Nothing.

Swiveling her head a little from side to side, Cat's eyes canvased the interior before her—a small rectangular room immediately greeted her sightline. Light green paint on the surrounding walls set off a soft glow. Straight across from the door a receptionist desk sat beside which ran a long, thin bench riding low to the ground. Farther down the narrow stretch of the front entrance were two bathrooms.

Slowly slipping inside, Cat called out Amelia's name again. Stretching her ears for any sound, feeling like an intruder, she waited. She decided to give Amelia officially fifteen seconds to respond.

And there it was.

A soft noise coming from the large arched doorway immediately to the left of the receptionist stand. Stepping hesitantly forward, her footfalls almost noiseless on the thin carpeting under her feet, Cat moved forward until she found herself in a large backroom. Sconces high up on the walls cast a gentle glow upon the large, open space.

Unwilling to step farther inside, her senses on high alert, Cat took stock of the area. Unlike the front entry, this room was large and square-shaped. Floor-to-ceiling mirrors took up an entire wall. Opposite of this was a bank of windows which Cat thought probably offered an amazing amount of sunlight into the barren space. The room was almost entirely empty, save for a handwashing station and a large, dented, incredibly bulky wardrobe pushed up against one corner of the room. The floor was polished wood. And that was it. It was a wide-open space.

And still, no Amelia.

Clearing her throat, her skin starting to itch at the lack of a greeting, the lack of a presence, Cat called out one final time: "Amelia?"

"Cat?"

The disembodied voice came from one of two small rooms at the very back of the studio—both of which were so unassuming, the shadowed doorways barely admitting the light from the main floor, that they'd escaped her initial inventory.

Following the sound, Cat took a tentative step forward. "Yeah, hey…sorry to just walk in…?"

"Nothing of the sort," Amelia said, and on the last words, that woman herself emerged from the muted depths of the room on the right and into the main studio. She was holding two very full glasses of wine in each hand. Holding them up in answer, she smiled. "You got here faster than I was expecting. I'm glad you made yourself to home."

Cat blushed. Looking down at her feet, she shrugged. "Yeah, it was a pretty quick errand."

"Am I to understand that the visit to your kind-of, not-really friend didn't go well, then?"

Cat shrugged again. Chancing a look up at Amelia, she managed a smile. "Got it on the first guess."

Amelia handed one of the two glasses to Cat. A small, almost sad smile lit upon her face. "Yeah, I know the look all too well. I've worn it myself, a time or two."

A moment of silence descended. Then, snapping back to attention, Amelia held out her glass. "Well, forget about him."

In response, Cat clinked her wine glass against Amelia's. "This is bound to help," she teased before bringing the wine to her lips and taking a sip.

"That's the spirit," Amelia returned, saluting her new friend.

And suddenly, Cat realized the truth of that notion. Amelia and Cat were friends. Just like that. That fast, that simple.

"And besides, we've better things to discuss…like your new digs."

"Yay!"

"I'd love a proper tour of the place."

"Fabulous." Linking her arm through Cat's, Amelia turned them smartly toward the front of the building. "That way I can describe what I envision it'll all look like after renovations." She sent Cat a sidelong glance as they passed underneath the arched doorway and back into the boxy little entrance. "And this room definitely needs the most TLC."

Pausing in the center of the squat space, Amelia frowned in concentration. Following her gaze, Cat waited.

"Well," Amelia finally said, one finger tapping against her chin, "the green paint is going. Too bland."

"Okay."

"And so's that bench," Amelia said with a flick toward the low, thin piece of furniture.

Cat tilted her head a little to one side. "It doesn't look very comfortable."

"Or welcoming."

Cat nodded.

"And you're right," Amelia admitted ruefully. "It's super un-comfortable. Terrible on the bum."

Cat snorted amusedly. Bringing the wine back up to her mouth, she took another drink. "What will you replace it with?"

Amelia wiggled her eyebrows. "I found these amazing chairs."

Cat bit the side of her lip. The room was long and narrow. "You don't think…?" she hesitated to say too much, but her eyes sized up the limited space rather tellingly.

It didn't matter, Amelia knew what Cat was unwilling to say. "They'll be too big? No, and that's the best part. These chairs are small, petite, and elegant. The cushions are a teal green. An-other reason the paint has to go."

"I see."

Amelia swung her gaze around the room. "And the pictures."

Cat inclined her head, following along with Amelia's change of topic. "Yeah," she admitted, her eyes tracing the motivational posters pinned up around them. "They're a bit…tacky?"

"Overdone."

"What will you put up instead?"

Amelia shrugged. "I was thinking images of different cameras over the ages."

"Cool."

"Stenciled work."

"Do you know someone?"

"Not yet."

Cat laughed. "But you will."

Amelia nodded absently, her mind still bent on the upcoming transformation of the room around her. "Other than that, I suppose it'll look pretty much the same in here. Throw in a few small plants, maybe succulents, and some pillows and whatnot…" Her eyes swung from the left to the right. "Well, I may get a new receptionist desk. But that'd be saved for a later date."

Cat shifted her attention to where Amelia referred. The receptionist desk was indeed a bit dated, curved in a crescent shape with white plastic paneling down the front and a cream Formica counter on top. But Amelia was right. It could wait for another day.

"Okay."

"And in here…" Circling abruptly, Amelia brought them back into the main studio floor. She shrugged. "Well. Not much will change here either."

"You'll keep the mirrors?"

"Those?" Amelia made a face. "God, no. Those'll be the first things out of here."

"It's a bit ballet class."

"It's a bit jazzercise."

"Yeah."

"But other than that—" Amelia turned them in a tight loop, her eyes gazing out at the room as though it were the first time, as though she hadn't already noted every crack, every chip, every line and angle… "It's perfect."

"What about that?" Cat nodded with her chin toward the mammoth wardrobe shoved against one corner. It looked like something straight out of the seventies. The grain of the wood was a bit rough and the stain unnatural.

"What about it?"

"Keeping it?" Trying to infuse an element of neutrality in her voice, Cat didn't want to offend Amelia. But honestly, the thing was an eyesore.

Patting the heavily lined wood, Amelia smiled. "Yes."

"What'll you do with it?"

"Costumes."

"Costumes?"

"And props."

"I thought you were a photographer?"

Amelia laughed. "I am."

"What do you need costumes for?"

"Style. Mood. Setting," Amelia said, her fingers splaying dramatically with the words.

Cat considered that for a moment. "Okay."

Amelia gave her an amused look. "You don't sound convinced."

"To be fair, the only photography I know is headshots, school pictures, and weddings."

"Of which I'll only do one."

"School pictures?"

"Funny girl."

"Portrait photography," Cat murmured. She remembered the phrase from Amelia's application.

"A fancy way of saying, whatever the client wants."

"And the costumes?"

"Again. Whatever the client wants."

"And some of them want to dress up?"

"You'd be surprised."

Cat took another drink of wine. "Still, I've got to be honest. The wardrobe is hideous." There went her sense of delicacy.

Amelia grimaced, glancing back up at the honey-blonde wood. "Well, yeah it is." She sighed, as though admitting that had been difficult. "But it's so damn convenient."

"Yeah."

"Like the receptionist desk, it'll go on the *maybe-someday* replace list."

Cat squinted at the door, unwilling to let her thoughts roam too freely. There was something about that closet that kept click-clicking in her mind...

But Amelia had already told Cat to forget about Matt for the night.

Cat swirled her wine glass. "And in those rooms?" She pointed to the backrooms.

"Ah. My extra-curriculars."

Cat laughed at the phrasing. "Your what?"

Beckoning Cat to follow, Amelia marched forward, slipping easily inside the room located on the left. Fetching up beside her, Cat waited as Amelia hit the light switch. A small, square room blinked back at the women. It, like the front, was painted in that pale green color. Small windows lined two of the four walls. There was no furniture, no other fixtures. It was a green box.

When she was taken into the next room, Cat was treated to a similar image. Other than the wine bottles that Amelia had purchased that evening and left lined up on the floor beside the door, she found the room to resemble a mirror image of its counterpart. Small, square. Boring.

Leaning against the door, Amelia waved her hand around the room, her gaze shining with excitement as she took in the same unexceptional sight. "When I found this place, these rooms were like little bonus features."

"Yeah?"

"For most of my indoor work, I'll use the main studio. It has the room, the lighting, and the airiness necessary for scene and staging. But these..." Amelia nodded with satisfaction. "Well, the possibilities are rather endless, aren't they? Special photoshoots. Classes. Showings. Discussion groups. Maybe an office. I don't know. But that's the point. They're limitless."

Cat nodded.

"Don't be deceived. It's their very nondescript nature that makes them so perfect. They're transformative."

Cat grinned. "You know, when I very first saw the address on your application, my heart skipped."

Amelia raised one eyebrow before taking a drink from her glass, silently inviting Cat to go on.

"This building. It's not had the best track record," Cat said, choosing her words carefully.

"I sort of figured that out myself."

"You did?"

"The price was kind of a steal."

Cat sighed. "Yeah."

"It was a ballet studio at one time."

"And a daycare center." Cat frowned. "And I think it was even a clothing boutique a few years back."

"Worried I won't stick?" But there was no defensiveness in Amelia's question. Only curiosity.

Cat grinned. "No. That's my point. I think this space finally found its home."

Amelia held out her glass. "Here's to something new."

Cat clinked glasses. Something new, indeed.

The next morning, slightly more hungover then she wanted to admit, Cat drug her half-protesting body out of bed. Standing under the hot spray of the shower, her thoughts went back to the night before—her and Amelia sitting on the floor of that woman's studio, candles lit on the polished wooden floors, their flames sparkling against the mirrored glass wall; Amelia confiding in Cat about the reason she'd moved away from home, moved to a new area to start-up a brand new business so far from her friends and family.

"...we'd talked about getting married," Amelia said, shaking her head sadly. "And then, one day, it all fell apart. I never saw it coming, just walked into a half-empty house."

"I'm sorry." Cat felt the impotence of those words sharply, but they were all she had to offer the other woman.

"I couldn't stay. There were too many memories of us, too much hurt. So I packed up too. Sold the house and came here."

Wine had a way, after all, of making best friends out of new acquaintances. Neither woman had found anything unusual in Amelia's tell-all of her failed romance.

Amelia shrugged. "But this place. This place is going to be good for me. A fresh start. And you know, I always wanted to have my own business."

"It'll keep you occupied."

Groaning under the spray of her shower, Cat considered that comment might have been a bit insensitive.

Then again, Amelia had only laughed in response.

"Tell me about it. I still have to get a website started." Making a face, she'd sighed disgustedly. "I know, I know, as a millennial I should be tech-savvy but...I'm just not."

"As it happens, I know a guy who builds websites professionally."

Amelia had leaned closer. Her large eyes had grown wider in excitement. "You do?"

Holding up her hand, Cat had felt obligated to explain. "He's a client of the credit union so you may want to take my suggestion with a grain of salt. I, ah, I actually helped him get a loan when he started up his *own* business, but I can honestly tell you that he's good. He worked with my mom when she started up a blog for the local gardeners club."

"Hey, if you vouch for him, I would love his contact information."

But even as the smiling thought floated across Cat's mind, other memories bombarded her. Memories that were a bit more...personal in nature. Pressing her forehead against the porcelain tile, Cat winced as she remembered the other things.

Like when she'd admitted to Amelia how lonely she'd been of recent.

"...you know, I'm not sure but maybe Matt was right. Maybe I did snap that door in two pieces for a reason."

Yup. She'd told Amelia about her kitchen cabinet fiasco.

"Fuck." Twisting off the water, Cat threw back her stall door, reaching blindly for her towel.

"And why would that be?" Amelia had wondered. They were on the second or third bottle of wine by that point. It was that time in the drinking conversation when everything became bloated, emotional, a whispered sort of confidence...

"Maybe I was forcing myself to get out of the rut I'd found myself in."

Amelia's forehead crinkled as she waited for Cat to expand on that.

"Everything had become so banal, so boring. My job, my apartment. Everything was so...gray and tired."

"Really? That's funny."

Cat felt her head tilt backward. "Why's that?"

"Because that's not how you appeared when I sat in your office the other day. You were..." Amelia flapped one hand, searching for the right words: "kind, determined. Invested. You were a breath of fresh air in the business start-up world. And I should know. You were hardly the first person I spoke to since I began this career move."

Cat felt the warmth of those words to the tips of her fingers. Still, she felt obligated to confess, "Yeah but, I hadn't been like that even a day earlier. It'd been a long time since I'd felt that kind of presence in my work."

"What changed?"

Cat gave her a level look. "I broke that damn door."

"Maybe it's the wine, but I'm not seeing the connection."

"Symbolism."

"Still lost."

"No." Cat laughed. It felt good. "I mean, it made me realize how angry I was, how unsettled. And, I don't know how to explain it, but I felt sort of invigorated when I broke that door. Like it woke me up or something."

Amelia was silent for a moment and then she nodded slowly. "Broke you out of the humdrum."

"Something like that."

"Left you analyzing your feelings."

Cat had smiled ruefully. "I guess that sounds kind of stupid."

"Not at all."

"Stupid fucking door."

Amelia had raised her glass then. "Maybe not so fucking stupid."

Cat had considered those words for a moment. "Yeah, maybe not."

"And I'll cheers to that."

Wiping the moisture off her bathroom mirror now, Cat felt a little of the anxiety churning at her stomach loosen. So she'd said a little more than she wanted to, then she'd meant to share. So she'd spilled her guts to a woman who, five days ago, she'd never met. So what.

She hadn't said anything that wasn't real. Wasn't true.

And she liked Amelia—liquor notwithstanding.

"Well, here's to stupid fucking doors," she said, repeating herself from the night before, a smile forming on her lips.

Walking back into her bedroom, she was just in time to hear her phone buzzing on her nightstand. Reaching down, Cat saw a text message pop up on the screen.

FROM: Amelia K.
6:48 a.m.
MESSAGE: I hate you for making me drink that much. ☺

And then, as if a sign of validation, Cat felt herself fully exhale at the words. Typing as she walked to her closet, Cat responded:

FROM: Catherine Cryer
6:49 a.m.
MESSAGE: The feeling is mutual

She'd only just slid one of the doors open when her phone buzzed again.

FROM: Amelia K.
6:52 a.m.
MESSAGE: When can we do it again? ☺

Cat bit her lip but it did nothing to mar the smile breaking out across her face. There was something so satisfying in having someone reach out to her, to contact her...

FROM: Catherine Cryer
6:53 a.m.
MESSAGE: You're incorrigible! (I like that about you.)

FROM: Amelia K.
6:55 a.m.
MESSAGE: Obviously one of my better qualities. Okay girl. Chin up at work today. Don't be jealous that I'm contemplating a little hair of the dog right now, either.

FROM: Catherine Cryer
6:59 a.m.
MESSAGE: Don't worry. Your day will come.

FROM: Amelia K.
7:01 a.m.
MESSAGE: I'm counting on it!

Shaking her head, Cat reached into her closet, rifling through her clothes. Ten minutes later, dressed and walking out the door, she forced back a yawn. Today was going to be grueling at work. She felt exhausted; her skin looked washed out and pale; she was already desperately looking forward to the evening ahead of her.

Pajamas the moment she walked in the door.

Maybe a movie.

Maybe a bath.

Definitely an early bedtime.

Walking toward the front entrance of her apartment building, it took Cat a moment before she realized the simple enormity of her thoughts.

It had been a long time, a truly long time since she'd *sincerely* looked forward to a quiet evening at home.

CHAPTER ELEVEN

Shuffling from the confines of her office and into the main
lobby of the credit union that afternoon, the mild headache
which had accosted Cat all morning rapidly intensified.
Boomed warningly against the edges of her temples when she
caught movement out of the corner of her eye. Empty coffee
cup in hand, Cat had been on the verge of refilling her mug
when she'd been spotted.

By none other than Janice.

Groaning inwardly as she watched that woman skirt around
the teller station, her slacks whipping crisply as she made a bee-
line for the coffee cart, Cat pretended not to notice Janice's intent stare, her purposeful approach.

"Hello, Catherine."

"Afternoon." Cat smiled politely as she reached for the coffee air pot.

"I've been meaning to catch you. I don't think we ever got to
finish our conversation the other day...." Janice raised both eyebrows expectantly.

For her part, Cat tried to look blank. It was only delaying the
inevitable she knew. But still...

Janice smiled meaningfully. "You were looking for a club to
join?"

Cat felt her face flush. Janice hadn't bothered to lower her
voice. Indeed, Cat thought she might have actually raised her

voice louder with the words. In the background, she heard the unmistakable chime of the credit union's door buzzer, announcing the entrance of a new customer, the ping of keyboards as tellers quickly tallied up deposits…. She was thankful that, standing in front of the coffee cart, at least no one could *see* her expression. The pink rising in her cheeks couldn't be ignored.

Cat's smile stiffened. As if Janice's words weren't humiliating enough, now she'd have the benefit of the audience of her peers to overhear it. Just what she needed.

Oh, get over yourself. No one cares about your private life. And it's not lame to join a club.

"Did you give any thought to joining my knitting group?"

Cat stilled, unsure how to respond. Janice thrived in uncomfortable atmospheres. Cat wasn't sure if that was a byproduct of her social awkwardness, or if it was a deliberate attack strategy. Either way, Cat scrambled for something to say. She wasn't a knitter. Possibly, it could be something fun to learn. Not her kind of fun. But someone's, surely. Maybe. She guessed.

But to do it alongside Janice?

God no.

It's not that Janice was so completely unlikeable—although Cat certainly didn't seek out her company. It's just, Janice could be…a bit much. Overbearing, manipulative, and a little rude. Kind of like right now. She looked sympathetic but her voice was a fog-horn and her implication was only too clear. *Someone needed to help out poor, pathetic Cat. And everyone should hear about how good a person Janice was, for being the one kind enough to do it.*

It was mortifying.

That or Janice was utterly oblivious.

Neither option improved that woman in Cat's opinion.

"Yes, well." Cat made a face. "I may have mentioned it, but I don't knit…"

"That's all right," Janice said, waving away Cat's words aggressively. "It's super easy. I could teach you."

"Oh, no. I wouldn't want to keep you from your work." Cat couldn't quite meet Janice's eyes.

"Nonsense. I love teaching people the craft!"

And again, this is where Janice could get a little difficult. For as long as Cat had known her, the woman just wouldn't let something go until she got her own way. She'd keep politely (irrefutably politely) barreling her way past protests and arguments to the contrary until she simply wore people down.

"Thank you for that, but really, I'm not sure I have the time needed to invest in learning a brand-new hobby..." Or the interest.

"It's only once a week. There's no pressure to work outside of the group."

"She can't."

At the introduction of a new voice to the conversation, both Janice and Cat turned to see a frail, short woman clomping up to them, her rheumy blue eyes staring directly at Janice's arched expression.

Cat blinked. It was Mary. From Canasta. Mean Mary.

"Excuse me?"

"She can't join your knitting group," Mary said, tossing her head dismissively toward Cat.

Janice blinked, confused. "Uh, do you two know each other?"

Mary scowled, one arthritic hand curling around her plastic purse. "Why would I be talking to you now if we didn't know each other?" she asked, one gnarled finger pointing between herself and Cat.

Janice nodded slowly. "Right. Of course." She looked to Cat for an explanation.

Cat wasn't sure she had one—and anyway, she wasn't about to look a gift horse in the mouth. (And...Mary sort of scared her.)

Still, Janice being Janice, she wasn't about to be fobbed off so easily. Not even if it meant squaring off with Mary. "And why can't she?"

Mary sighed. "Because. She's on our Canasta team."

"Your Canasta team?"

"If you'd given her the chance to finish one statement, I'm sure she'd have told you that."

Cat nodded eagerly. "Yeah..."

Janice nodded. "I see. Well..." Then she brightened. "Well, maybe she'd be able to do bo—"

"What day of the week is your knitting group?" It wasn't a question, more an accusation.

"Tuesdays."

"Yup," Mary said, almost before Janice had finished speaking. "Nope. It wouldn't work."

It was official. Cat loved Mary.

Seeing no other way around the situation, Janice relented. Cat wasn't sure she'd ever been witness to such an event. Someone getting the better of Janice. Conceding the point, she turned back to Cat, who was now leaning against the coffee station, her cup of coffee half-obscuring her trembling mouth.

"Well, I'm sure we're disappointed but...but Canasta sounds fun too."

Mary harrumphed.

Janice looked vaguely harassed. "But, uh, I suppose I should get back to work..."

"Yeah. Me too." Pushing off the coffee cart, Cat nodded towards Janice's quickly back-pedaling figure. Then she glanced at the older woman still standing between them. "Nice to see you, Mary." Lowering her voice, she added as she made to walk by: "and thank you."

"Yeah, yeah," Mary muttered. "Just remember not to stink."

Cat wasn't sure what surprised her the most: the fact that Mary seemed to be sincere in her invitation to let Cat continue to play, or the fact that Cat was so eager to accept it. Smiling gamely, she winked. "I'll do my best."

"See you Monday. Don't be late. Maybe I'll even let you be my partner."

"Monday?" Hearing the words, Janice, ever-hopeful, stopped, called back to them. "But I thought you said you played on Tuesday?"

"And what?" Mary asked, placing her hands on her hips. "Is there some law in town saying we can only play one night of the week?"

No, scratch that, Cat *adored* Mary. The ladies didn't play Canasta on Tuesdays (at least, Cat didn't think so), but Mary's words, while not technically a lie, effectively left that assumption open to interpretation.

Janice recoiled. "Uh, no..."

"I didn't think so." And with that, head held at an almost regal angle, Mary marched forward, toward the waiting, and quietly amused, bank teller who'd heard every word.

Walking back to her office, Cat considered that by now every member of the credit union probably knew that she belonged on a Canasta team, made up of entirely retired women...and one lone girl in her late twenties.

Opening her office door, Cat smiled.

She'd made the team.

She'd made the fucking team.

"Yes!"

... °•°• ...

It was Friday afternoon the next time Cat heard from Matt. After his initial call to the credit union to discuss materials, Cat had given him her cell phone number—considering the fact she'd almost ignored that first call, due to a lack of proper caller ID, she hadn't wanted to take the chance again. Plus, if he'd needed her after hours...well, it had seemed perfectly reasonable.

So when she heard the muffled but still telltale ping of a text message notification, the sound muted from within the depths of her purse, as she opened the door to her apartment that evening, Cat had cause to be grateful for that decision.

Digging her phone out of the front pocket of her handbag, Cat automatically swiped her finger across the screen, her eyes following the action as she checked the message.

Her heart sped up at the sight of his name.

Her hands shook just slightly.

> *FROM: Matt McBoy*
> ***5:11 p.m.***
> *MESSAGE: Door is done.*

That was it. That was all the message said. Closing her eyes, Cat felt an excited nausea rasp up her throat. Without thinking, she pressed the CALL button before bringing the phone up to her ear.

"Hello."

"Matt?"

"Yup."

"Hi, it's Cat—"

"I know."

Cringing, Cat made a face. Of course he knew. He just texted her! "Right." Stalking up and down her narrow hallway, Cat tried to exercise the energy exploding inside her. "So? It's done? How's it look?"

There was a slight hesitation on the other end of the phone.

"Look, this is no time for modesty—!" Clamping down on the words, Cat grimaced. Okay, even she heard the dramatics in *that* statement.

"It looks good."

"Yeah?"

"It wasn't exactly a difficult design." His tone couldn't have been drier, more dismissive.

Cat didn't have the presence of mind to disguise her anxiety. "But do you think…? Will it, you know…?"

"They'll never suspect a thing."

"Thank God." Even though she knew Matt was mocking her, could, in fact, hear his muffled amusement over the phone line, Cat didn't care. The first real wave of relief settled across her shoulders since this whole ordeal had begun. It was done. And it was good.

"It only needs to be painted."

Right. Of course. The cabinets in her kitchen all wore a coating of white paint on their exterior surface. "Oh. Sure. But I mean, that should be pretty easy, right?"

"Painting a single door?" Matt didn't even bother to cover his sarcasm.

Cat's smile stiffened. "Never mind. I'll, ah, I'll pick some up when I swing by the store."

"Some what? Paint?"

"Presumably you do sell that?"

"Well, yeah." Matt's voice turned hesitant. "And you know the exact paint that was used—brand, color, finish?"

"Ah. I mean, no…"

"That's kind of important."

"Right."

"I thought you said…" Matt sighed. "Anything but a perfect match will be pretty noticeable—kitchen cabinets are a high-traffic, monochromic area after all. I guess I should have been clearer on that point when I first brought it up to you." Because he *had* asked her about paint. If she had that part covered.

Though he refrained from outright reminding her of this fact the very pointedness of his words said enough.

"B-but can't you just compare the paint from the sample door? Or what about the broken one?" Cat was speaking quickly now. "Chip some paint off of that and, um, maybe..."

"Look, I can try. It's not a perfect science. Paint fades and different companies have different color gradients..." Cat could practically see him shrug on the other end of the phone. "In all probability, they'll be a close match."

"Right. *Right.*" Biting down on her fingernail, Cat thought for a moment. Her mind spun frantically as she tried to create and connect dots. "If the landlord had extra paint lying around where would he keep it?"

"I don't know. Maybe a spare closet?"

Smiling, because she hadn't expected him to actually offer up a suggestion, Cat considered the words. "No," she was forced to admit. "Those were all empty when I moved in."

"Basement storage?"

Cat stilled. Then she nodded. "Yes. Yeah, I almost forgot about that..."

If Matt found this part of the conversation odd or tedious, he was kind enough not to let on. "Haven't been down there in a while, huh?"

She shook her head. "It's not exactly welcoming."

"Might want to make an exception this time."

Unsaid, both of them were undeniably thinking the same thing—especially considering the amount of work Matt had already done for her.

"Yes. Okay. I'll do that. I'll call you with what I find."

"There's no rush."

And again, with that flick of casual indifference, Matt somehow managed to make Cat sound equal parts over-eager and pathetic.

Ugh. He made her *feel* dramatic.

"Of course. Whatever. Talk later then." And then, because of it, she said even more ridiculous things like that. Could she have made her offense more obvious?

Before she could further humiliate herself, Cat ended the call, shoving her phone mutinously into the front pocket of her slacks. With a low growl, she turned on her heel once more, only this time she was headed straight for her bedroom.

She'd need to change before she went trekking into the basement of the building.

She hadn't been exaggerating when she'd told Matt it wasn't the most inviting part of the building. The one and only time she'd made the voyage down there, she'd labeled it creepy and never returned.

Dangerously steep stairs led down to a musky, low-ceiled rock-walled enclosure. Advertised as extra storage for the first-floor tenants, wooden pallets lined most of the cement floor which grew damp with the spring frost. Stacked on top of the pallets, a cheap fix to keep any mold at bay, sat the storage boxes of any willing renters. It was dark, shadowy, with barely enough light to navigate the short, narrow room undoubtedly loaded with spiders.

When Cat had first moved in she'd gone down there with the expectation to do just that: stow some excess household items. She'd never made it down from the last step, however. The site of the musty, claustrophobic space had convinced her that whatever she couldn't manage to squeeze inside of her apartment was better left given to secondhand stores.

Exiting her apartment a few minutes later, her work attire exchanged for a blue pullover sweater and a pair of tattered jeans, Cat traversed down the hallway. If memory served, the storage room was the last door down on the left. As she walked, Cat couldn't help but notice the slight shine of grease coating the sandy-colored walls of the long corridor enclosing her on either side. It was probably due to the painting that she was about to embark on, the realization that nothing in this apartment complex was proving worthy of the effort she was exerting, her eyes holding tight to the faint scuff marks and fingerprints marring the walls—smudges she'd never thought to look at before. Nor could she deny the soft scent of mildew, feet, and carpet shampoo which permeated the air around her.

But whatever. So her apartment was a little dumpy. So she was putting forth a lot of work for little payoff. Still, she wanted that damned security deposit back.

These thoughts took Cat to her destination. At the sight of the smaller-than-average door of the basement storage, Cat took a deep breath. Like all the other doors on the first floor, its front was painted in a complimentary brown to the carpet, a soft pairing against the caramelized-coloring on the walls. It gave the space an almost nauseating sort of neutrality.

Reaching forward, Cat grasped the doorknob in her hand. With a wrench, she twisted it open. Letting it swing free from her hand, she leaned forward, her fingers searching for the light switch. When she found it, Cat was both annoyed and utterly unsurprised when the overhead bulb appeared to be burned out.

ON and OFF.

OFF and ON.

It didn't matter how many times she hit the toggle; no light was forthcoming.

"Typical," she muttered. If that wasn't an omen, Cat wasn't sure what was. Fuming, she turned sharply on her heel and headed back for her apartment. Within minutes, she'd returned, this time with a large metal flashlight held firmly in her grip; the sheer weight and bulk of it had been oddly comforting.

Flicking it on, she shone it down the basement staircase. The yellow glow only seemed to accentuate the paint-chipped, warped and steep steps before her. Grabbing for the railing on the left-hand side, Cat trudged downward. A damp sort of musk soon enveloped her. At the landing, Cat found the darkness swirling about her even more oppressive, swallowing her in its dense air...

Okay, so maybe Matt had another point: maybe she could be a bit dramatic.

Swinging the light toward the wall, Cat hoped to locate another light switch, but to no avail.

"Of course not," she muttered darkly to herself.

Aiming her light first low to the ground, the better to watch her steps, Cat slowly advanced into the dreary space. After a few paces, she paused. Letting her feet slide in a slow circle, Cat gradually lifted and lowered the flashlight up and down as she swept around the small room, casting its beam across the sundry items and boxes clumsily stacked within the cramped confines. She'd almost made a complete turn, her light catching the edges of cardboard boxes, plastic and rubber bins, one hideously fake Christmas tree, and a pile of fishing rods when Cat's beam landed on a pair of sneakers. A pair of ankles...

Breathlessly, she shifted the flashlight higher, illuminating a length of very-human legs attached to those shoes.

Cat was not alone down there.

CHAPTER TWELVE

"ARHH!" The scream which erupted up and out of Cat's throat was as involuntary as it was deafening. With a jerking motion, the flashlight swung over a feminine face, the glare highlighting gaunt, high cheekbones and short, chin-length blonde hair.

But the beam of illumination only lasted for a moment.

Nerveless in her fright, Cat dropped the flashlight almost as quickly as she identified the unexpected stranger lurking down there with her. The heavy tool hit the floor with a clunk, the light swerving drunkenly, veering crazily against the walls as it slowly spun to a stop.

"Sorry! So sorry!"

Stumbling backward instinctively, retreating away, Cat brought both hands up to her mouth, stemming the loud, piercing cry still shooting out of her mouth as the now disembodied, but distinctly female voice, blubbered out.

"I didn't mean startle you!" The voice continued. Through the dark shadows, Cat thought she saw the girl's arms reach forward.

Breathing heavily, Cat swallowed twice at the gentle, though intense, sincerity of the words. "Jesus," she yelped through her hands, her voice wobbling but calming a little now. "Startle me? You scared the shit out of me!" Forcibly dropping her hands back down to her sides, her fingers locked into fists, Cat felt a prick of suspicion swell inside her. "Why didn't you say anything when I came down here?"

"Honestly? I was trying *not* to scare you." Bending down, her voice dropping with the action, the girl, who appeared to be somewhere around Cat's own age, picked up the flashlight. Straightening, she handed it over. "At first, when I heard you coming down the stairs, I thought you were my boyfriend and then," she laughed weakly, "when I realized you weren't, I wasn't sure how to alert you to my presence without...well, without terrifying you."

Cat wasn't sure how to respond to that. Expelling a deep breath as her fright passed, she unclenched her fingers as she took back the flashlight.

"Clearly though, saying nothing was not my smartest move," the girl continued when Cat remained silent.

"No, it's fine...I just, I didn't realize anyone else was down here."

"And then you thought you stumbled upon the great cat-burglar of Dowsley Apartments, huh?" The stranger laughed and then, just as abruptly, stopped. "God, I swear I'm not robbing the place."

"No, of course not..." But still, Cat wasn't quite sure.

"I didn't trip the breaker. Swear it." Seemingly amused by her own joke, the girl giggled again. "The lights haven't worked down here in weeks. Something with the wiring, I guess." As if to further prove her innocence, she retrieved her phone from where it had been hiding inside one of the large rubber bins Cat now noticed beside her. A bright white light radiated from the screen; she was using a flashlight app. As quickly as she'd held it up, the young woman put it back down.

Feeling as though she ought to do the same—for fear she'd blind the poor girl across from her—Cat set her flashlight down on a nearby box, shifting it so the beam wasn't shining directly in anyone's eyesight. It had the effect of casting a general, though still shadowy view. "Well, that's reassuring."

"Which part?"

Cat chuckled then, a reluctant smile breaking across her mouth. "Both?"

"And you?"

"Huh?"

The girl grinned. "I mean, you aren't the great cat-burglar of the Dowsley Apartments, are you?"

"Uh, no," Cat admitted ruefully, shaking her head at the inanity of where this conversation had led. "But fair point." Cat held up one hand in mock solemnity. "While I've never actually made it all the way down here before, I assure you that I'm a tenant within the building."

"Looking for some extra storage space?" she asked, her swift redirection making Cat blink in momentary confusion. "There's technically no 'assigned' areas, but each tenant gets two side-by-side pallets so…" turning her head, the girl pointed helpfully a few spaces down. "There's room over there."

"Oh. No, actually…" Cat bit her lip. She wasn't sure how much to say.

But it was too late. The girl in front of her, who Cat could now make out more clearly—unbelievably thin, unbelievably tall with sunk-in eyes and large hands—was already tilting her head.

"Actually?" she returned.

Taking a deep breath, Cat figured she had little to lose. She hadn't told the girl who she was, or what apartment she lived in… "Do you know if Grant keeps any extra paint down here?"

"Extra paint?" But it was clear the other woman was only repeating this to herself in thought, not question. "For the walls?"

"Umm…actually for the cupboard doors. In the kitchen."

The stranger's thick, straight eyebrows rose a little.

"I just noticed…well, the paints starting to fade a little. And there are a couple of chips. And, I don't know, it's started to bug me and I've got little going on—" eyes bulging wide, Cat could hear the words fighting to get out of her mouth. She was talking too much. That was usually a dead-giveaway to a lie.

Over-explaining.

Forcing her lips together, Cat nodded. She regrouped.

If the girl noticed Cat's blast of information sharing, she didn't comment on it. Instead, Cat saw her forehead crinkle, one hand coming up to her chin, a finger tapping against her upper lip in concentration. Her eyes, much like Cat's had moments before, swept the room.

"I don't think so…" Leaning forward, the girl seemed to be doing a quick inventory of the stacks of boxes meeting her stare. "I'm not sure Grant keeps anything down here."

"Ah."

Suck.

"Okay," Cat continued, her voice overly bright. "No big deal. I just thought I'd check…"

"Yeah, I'm sorry." The girl made to turn back to her box. Then, on second thought, she glanced back over at Cat. "But if you find any spare cans laying around will you let me know?" A glint of mischief entered her look. "Heads up: don't write on walls with lipstick. It stains."

Smothering a laugh, Cat nodded. "Good to know."

"I'm Sam, by the way."

"Cat."

"Well," with a polite shrug, Sam gestured around. "Good luck with the paint hunt." Turning back to her box then, Cat watched her arms shifting through the contents inside.

"Thanks. You too," she said, shifting back toward the stairs. Only, as her foot landed on the bottom tread, Cat paused. The cavernous darkness had all but swallowed Sam in its depths.

"Dammit."

"What's that?" Sam's voice called out, breaking easily through the blanket of blackness.

Forcing the invitation past her mouth—on other people she noticed they came easy, natural, but she wasn't so sure… "Do you, ah, do you need any help down here?"

"Huh?" She wasn't sure but Cat thought Sam's head tilted momentarily to one side. "No. No, I'm good."

Cat sighed. But still, she didn't climb the stairs.

"Cat?"

"See that's the problem."

"There's a problem?"

"You can't even see me. You have no idea if there's someone else down here."

"Ah. I'm pretty sure it's just us."

"It's, after being down here…It's creepy."

Laughter bubbled up from Sam's general direction. "Yeah."

"And—" Cat felt her arms splaying out to the sides "—I'd feel like a real ass, leaving you down here, all alone. Practically lightless."

"Ahh."

"Unless, I mean, I don't want to overstep or, or invade your privacy or anything. I just thought..." Cat was babbling again.

"Yeah. Now that you mention it, I could probably use an extra flashlight."

... °•°• ...

Twenty minutes later, Cat found herself carefully ascending the rickety basement stairs, her arms weighed down, balancing three mason jars stocked full of brushes and a bin of acrylic paints, her flashlight placed precariously atop the latter of these so she could see where she was going. Directly ahead of her was Sam, that girl's arms juggling copious canvases, in assorted sizes, hugged tight to her body as she climbed upward.

Finally mounting the last step and regaining the main hallway, Cat cast one long last glance down at the storage door before kicking it shut with the toe of her shoe. She, for one, was glad to be gone of the place. The measly amount of time spent down there had only reaffirmed all her suspicions. The storage unit was a flat bust of a deal.

"Thanks again for your help," Sam huffed over her shoulder as she began leading them down the hall.

Following close behind, Cat grunted in acknowledgment of this. Sam had been outspoken in her appreciation of Cat's insistence to stay and help her sort through the sundry boxes splayed around her in the basement.

"Really, it was no problem," Cat repeated. Her steps matching Sam's, she glanced between the items held between them. "So, what are you painting, can I ask?"

Sam inclined her head quizzically, as though the thought hadn't occurred to her. "You know, I don't know yet."

"Just got the sudden inspiration to do it again?" Because it was obvious that Sam hadn't partaken in the hobby for some time. Shoved at the bottom of a bin and covered beneath a variety of random household objects, they'd clearly been neglected for some time. But also, just as obvious, from the vast collection of supplies, they had been, at least once, a beloved part of her daily life.

"Yeah, I guess you could say that," Sam muttered as she sped down the corridor, her arms no doubt aching from the heavy, awkward bundle in her grip.

As they passed by her own apartment door, their steps headed ever nearer the front entrance of the building, a new thought struck Cat. When they'd been in the basement, Sam had volunteered the information that she'd lived in the apartment for a little over six months. Now, as they trekked steadily forward, Cat wondered how often she'd walked by Sam's apartment on her way to and from the complex. Without having to be told, Cat knew that Sam lived on the first floor. Only those who did were allowed to use the basement storage (the second-floor tenants had access to the attic—Cat shivered at the thought of what those poor people had to endure…bats more than likely). Added to that, Cat couldn't help but wonder if she'd ever walked right by Sam herself, her thoughts so wrapped up in her own life that Cat would have offered the other woman little more than an absent-minded nod and half-smile before moving past, dismissing the moment even as it was happening.

"Well, maybe that's a lie." The sound of Sam's voice, the wobble of guilt within it, pulled Cat's thoughts up short. "At least by omission."

"What's a lie?"

"My artistic inspiration."

"Oh?" Cat heard herself say when Sam stopped before a door marked A3. Fetching up beside her, out of her peripheral vision Cat could just see the edge of her own apartment door—A7. Four doors. Four doors separated her and Sam for all she'd ever noticed another woman her same age living in the complex.

"And I guess, I lied to you earlier too…" Avoiding Cat's gaze, Sam twisted the knob of her obviously unlocked door, her knee pushing against the structure as she swept it open.

Though Sam's words should have unnerved Cat, instead, that woman found herself more curious than skeptical. "Yeah?"

Crossing the threshold, Sam motioned for Cat to follow her inside. Cat was relatively unsurprised to see that Sam's apartment was more-or-less a mirror image of her own, only Sam's front hallway was shorter. And her walls weren't peach-colored. They were a soft oatmeal color.

Shuffling into her living room, Sam stacked the canvases against the side of her couch. Following suit, Cat settle her burden down beside them. "When you came into the basement...I didn't actually think you were my boyfriend."

Cat raised one eyebrow expectantly.

"Fact is, I don't have a boyfriend." Sam's lips thinned now. "Not anymore. Tony and I, we, ah, we broke up a couple of weeks ago."

"I'm sorry," Cat mumbled, unsure what to say.

Sam grinned, her eyes raking over her sparsely furnished living room. "I'm not sure who was more surprised when I decided to keep the apartment, him or my family."

Cat wasn't sure how to respond, but it turned out that it didn't matter. Sam kept talking.

"Everyone thought I'd leave. After all, they'd been outspoken in their opinions that we were making a mistake."

"Moving in together?"

"Moving at all." At Cat's blank look, Sam grinned. "Neither Tony or I are originally from here. We moved when he got a transfer from work."

"Right."

"But I mean, it's not like...we'd been dating for over a year. It wasn't like we weren't in a committed relationship when I offered to go with him."

Cat nodded mutely. The conversation had made a drastic left-hand turn and she wasn't sure how to proceed.

Sam shrugged again. "And I guess I wasn't *really* lying to you. But to myself. I'd *hoped* you were Tony, coming down the stairs...coming back to me." The last part was said softly, almost privately.

"Is that why you stayed?" Cat wasn't sure what prompted her to ask the question. It was none of her business and patently sensitive material. Then again, Sam had opened up the line of dialogue.

"No. No, it wasn't because of him."

"To prove to your family that they were wrong?"

Sam shook her head slowly. "No. I...I like it here."

"Dowsley Apartments?" Cat heard the incredulity in her voice and tried to tamper it with a cajoling smile.

"Yeah. And this city."

"Really?" There was no denying the surprise in Cat's voice now.

"It's beautiful. The old architecture of the downtown, the small-town feel, the nature and gorgeous scenery."

Cat shrugged. She supposed. She'd seen the cobbled streets and street lamps, modern replications of old-fashioned gas-fixtured lights, the exposed brick and marquee lights of the movie theatre, the stained-glass windows marching down the revitalization part of the commerce streets probably too often to fully notice them anymore. Same with the small botanical garden weaving throughout the middle of the town—she hardly looked at the display of flowers the master gardeners worked so hard to display. The fact that the city, which held a population of nearly fifty-thousand people, rolled up the sidewalks after nightfall, reminiscent of a much smaller, sleepier town, frequently infuriated her. But, yes, she supposed it was something that kept their town clean and safe. Perhaps unique.

"It's hard to explain. I moved for him but then *I* ended up falling in love with this area." Sam grinned mischievously. "That ticked him off. So I lost the guy, but I found a home."

Cat nodded. Once again, she wasn't sure what to say. Once again, it seemed it wasn't necessary for her to articulate this fact.

"God, listen to me." Shaking her head, Sam laughed. "I'm sorry, when'd we meet, half an hour ago? No need to run you off with my emotional baggage. You're probably terrified right about now."

"No, of course not." Well, maybe just a little but Cat squashed the thought.

Sam jerked her chin toward the canvasses. "Hence my decision to start painting again."

Cat smiled in understanding. "Ah. The second lie?"

"Yeah. I mean, I guess the inspiration to do it again was sudden, but not random." Sam splayed her fingers out wide, expressively. "I'm exercising my feelings. I have a lot of them right now."

"I see." Taking in the canvases and supplies dotting Sam's living room, Cat nodded thoughtfully. "I get that."

"It's very cathartic."

"Going to do an exhibit on Tony?"

Sam laughed. It had a deep, resonating echo. "You know, it's not a bad idea. I could call it, Small Man."

"Oh, I like that."

"Or maybe: Fuck Off Tony."

Cat tilted her head to one side. "I wonder if that'll be too subtle."

Tapping her fingers on her head, Sam nodded. "Always my problem."

Cat tilted her head to one side. "Maybe you should do a landscape."

"Of our spooky basement?"

"Of your new home here. I'd love to see it through your eyes." The words were bald but Cat found she genuinely meant them.

"Yeah?"

"I've lived here so long I think I've forgotten how to see it." The truth in those words was further punctuated by the sincerity in her tone.

Sam gave her a quick look. "You know what?"

"What?"

"I'm glad that our basement is, what did you say, creepy as fuck?"

Cat laughed. "Something like that."

"And I'm glad that it was you who came down those stairs."

"Yeah. Me too."

... °•°• ...

Ten minutes later, back in her own apartment, having left Sam practically salivating at the mouth, her fingers itching to put up her easel, Cat prowled restlessly across her kitchen, her thoughts scrambling.

She almost wished now that she'd taken Sam up on her offer of a beer—the invitation had been as unexpected as it had been kind, especially considering how eager Cat could see Sam was to get to her art. Though Cat had been tempted, she'd smiled nicely, regretfully as she'd declined. Unfortunately, she'd informed Sam, she had an errand she needed to run yet that evening. And if she was going to have the guts to follow through with it, Cat knew she was going to need a clear head.

"Rain check?" Sam asked.

"Without a doubt." And Cat meant it. With lithe movements, she'd walked to the door. Once there, she paused. "Oh, and Sam?"

"Yeah?"

"I'm in A7. In case you need anything."

"A7." Sam smiled. "Got it."

Now, standing in her kitchen, staring at the doors that should have been covering two of her cupboards, Cat considered her options. There was no paint. Matt could try to match the color based on the sample alone, but it was unlikely he'd be able to match the colors perfectly.

She titled her head a little to one side.

Her lips pulled down in a frown.

She knew what she needed to do. And it was all to do with Sam. Squatting in that basement beside her, their hands rummaging through boxes as one tube of paint after another was unearthed, a tiny idea had planted itself in Cat's head. A tiny, entirely unattractive idea. But regrettably, it was also the only workable idea that had presented itself. It was the only one that would effectively, comprehensively, fix the problem at hand.

She knew what she had to do. She just really, really didn't want to do it.

With a resigned sort of expectation, Cat reached in her back pocket for her phone. She might have known it would go this way. Everything else had, after all....

CHAPTER THIRTEEN

"Did you find the paint?"

Smothering back a telling grin, Cat turned toward the sound of Matt's voice. She couldn't deny the sensation pulling at the edges of her stomach at the question. When she'd sailed into the building minutes earlier, he'd been the first thing her anxious eyes had latched on to—only he'd been standing beside an elderly man, apparently deep in conversation about carpentry. She'd doubted he'd even heard the quiet jingle of the doorchimes announcing her arrival.

Well, no matter.

Ducking down the first aisle she came to, lest he should think that she was in want of his attention—she wasn't! Cat hadn't come here specifically to see Matt, regardless of the slight letdown at his distracted presence. She was a capable woman and it wasn't like she didn't know what she was purchasing this time.

Besides, a small victorious voice had chirped in the back of her mind, he'd figure out she was there at some point, even if it was only when she checked-out. He'd be the one to ring up her purchases, after all. Smiling almost clandestinely, she'd traversed composedly down the long aisle. That would almost be an edge. The element of surprise. The delayed pleasure principle. Besides, it might come as a bit of a difference, her *not* searching him out.

And maybe she'd been hoping for this very moment: when he sought *her* out.

Looking up at his half-smiling face now, Cat ignored the surge of satisfaction at the realization that not only had he noticed her but he'd come to find her. For Matt, that seemed telling.

"'Fraid not," she replied, twisting her lips playfully. Then she shrugged, turning back to the paint samples in front of her. The paint samples she'd spent the last few minutes somberly studying.

"Yeah," he sighed, sticking his hands in his pants pockets. He angled his body toward the display of paint samples as well. "I suppose that would've been too easy."

"My thoughts exactly."

"Well, I did look at the paint on the doors and I think I can come up with something close."

Cat nodded absently, her eyes scanning an array of white paint options. "I don't know."

"Excuse me?"

At the slightly defensive tone of his voice, Cat turned back toward Matt with an apologetic shrug. "I don't mean…" she paused, taking a breath to find her words. "You've worked so hard and I don't think close is going to cut it."

His eyes gleamed in abject amusement. "I see."

"No, probably not."

"Yeah. Probably not." His eyes skipped over to hers. "Nothing unusual there."

Cat laughed. It held a throaty quality that she hadn't meant to achieve, but then, neither was she upset with the sound.

Rounding her shoulders, her gaze returned to the paint sample cards. "Do you ever do something and it has a ripple effect, but instead of ripples they turn out to be mammoth waves?"

Out of her peripheral vision, she saw Matt's lips compress with curbed amusement. "Uh…"

"I know, I know," Cat said, holding up a hand and beating him to the punch. "I'm probably being dramatic. But…"

Pausing at the sound of the front door opening and closing, Cat's head shifted, watching as a large man walked through the door. Turning back to Matt, she saw that his eyes had also followed the sound.

And then, as quick as that, he pivoted his gaze back to Cat. Another tingle of delight settled upon her stomach when he leaned one elbow against the shelving unit beside him, as though he had nothing else to do with his time. He grinned at her gamely. "But?" he prompted.

Still, despite the thrill that he hadn't made an excuse and walked away at the entrance of another customer, Cat felt some of her courage grow stale. She did not want to look needy. She didn't want to appear as though she came to monopolize his time. She didn't want him to feel obligated to help her simply because it was his *job*. And really, she felt pretty confident that she could tackle this end of the project by herself.

"Um…" biting her lip, Cat stalled out. Waving in the general direction of the front of the building, she hesitated. "If you need to help that customer, go ahead…"

"Nah," Matt said, dismissing this offer obliviously. "It's just Jim."

"Oh." Like that was supposed to mean something to her.

"Jim!" Matt yelled then, startling Cat. "I'm by the paints if you need me." Then he turned back to her. "You were saying? Something about ripples?"

Cat sighed. "I'm going to have to start from scratch."

Out of the corner of her eye, Cat saw Matt's frown of confusion. "Huh?"

"The whole shebang."

Rocking back on his heels, Matt waited.

Cat let out a deep breath. Saying the words out loud brought a sense of overwhelming reality that she wasn't excited to experience. "I'm going to repaint the entire kitchen."

He whistled. It wasn't exactly encouraging.

Facing him squarely now, Cat held out her hands. "What else could I do? After everything—all that time and work, to throw it away at the last minute?"

Matt lifted his eyebrows. "And this is somehow supposed to pass by your landlord unnoticed too?" He pursed his lips. "Must be a hell of a landlord."

"He is," Cat assured him dryly. "But no—I, ah, I called him." And that moment had sealed the deal, hadn't it? There was no turning back now, despite the knot of regret forming in her stomach at Matt's obvious incredulity.

"You confessed all?"

She rolled her eyes. "Hardly."

Matt waited again. He was good at that.

"Look, there was no leftover paint at the apartment. Zippo, zilch."

"Yeah, I got that."

Cat shrugged, dropping her gaze. Now that she'd made her decision, now that she'd already called Grant and settled her future, she worried she'd made a mistake. Another mistake. "Even if by some miracle, we found the perfect match, you were right earlier. The other doors, they're faded, chipped. The new paint would be glaringly obvious."

Matt inclined his head in quiet agreement.

"So—well, it's for the best this way."

"Sorry to interrupt, Matt. But have you got any of those LUX lights?" This came from the man who'd been identified as Jim moments ago. Standing at one end of the aisle, (Cat hadn't even heard him come up to them) he looked over at Matt expectantly.

Matt shook his head. He didn't look the least disoriented by the quick intrusion of another voice, the quick redirection of conversation. "Not in the store, I'm afraid. But I can order some for you."

Jim held out a slip of paper. "Sharon wrote down the kind. It's special, apparently," he said with a long-suffering sigh.

"Yeah. No problem. Can you leave that for me at the front counter? I'll get 'em ordered for you tonight."

Jim nodded. "Sounds good." His gaze switching to Cat, the older gentlemen tipped his ballcap in her direction. "Pardon me. Ma'am."

"No worries," Cat offered weakly, but Jim had already turned away, his lumbering steps taking him in the direction Matt had suggested.

"Sorry about that." Matt's attention returned once more to Cat.

"Not at all. So, um, do you have any recommendations?

Matt stared down at her for a moment. His brown eyes were steady on her face. "You're sure about this? Repainting your entire kitchen?"

"Well, not the walls," Cat joked lamely.

"Right. Because *that* would be weird."

She blushed. "Shut up."

"Doesn't this all seem a bit extreme?"

Cat bit down on one side of her lip, her gaze sliding away from his. "Sort of the story of my life when it concerns home improvement."

He chuckled. "So, what did you tell your landlord?"

Cat shook her head. "God. Whatever I needed."

"Are you being elusive deliberately?"

Picking up a paint sample card at random, Cat gazed down at it intensely. "No, I just feel kind of rotten about it."

Taking the card out of her hand, Matt's lips twitched as he glanced at it. "While I like the color yellow, I'm not sure it belongs on a cabinet door."

Cat sighed, hardly listening to him. "When I was merely re-creating the truth... hoping he'd never notice a new, but identical, door, that was different. But today I actively *lied*."

"What'd you say?"

"You're laughing at me," Cat accused, nabbing the sample card back out of his hands. She tried not to notice the slight feel of his skin against her own, the tingle of awareness that shot up her arm at the mild contact.

"Only a little."

"I convinced Grant that I wanted to repaint the kitchen. You know, to brighten it up or something."

"Or something."

Cat smiled in a self-deprecating manner. "Yeah."

"And he didn't think that was strange?"

"Honestly," Cat blew out a breath before the smallest of chuckles escaped her mouth. "I don't think strange entered into it. Money did."

"Ah."

"I think most of what he heard was 'free labor.'" Cat made a face. "Grant isn't what you'd call a very *involved* superinten-dent. Or hands on. I can't remember the last time I even saw him at the apartment complex. If he can get away with doing nothing..." she shrugged significantly, "then he's pretty easy to get along with."

"Ideal for this situation."

"For this one, yes."

Certainly, it had worked out for her in this instance. Cat had barely gotten through her proposed project when Grant had of-ficially signed-off on it. As it turned out, he'd offered the closing argument in her defense without any help from Cat. She'd had little issue picturing him in her mind's eye at that moment—a fat man with shirts that frequently didn't quite cover his belly, a scrabble of facial hair on his red cheeks, and deliberately unruly hair which utterly failed to cover the bald spot on the crown of his head. She'd practically been able to see the spittle that always formed at the edges of his mouth when he told her: "Hey, that works for me. As long as you don't pick a crazy color." He'd even guffawed over the line, "That way, if you decide to move out, I won't have to touch up the kitchen at all."

"Of cours—"

"And you're paying for this, right?" That had been the only note of suspicion in his voice, which she'd quickly and effusively quieted with her promise that he'd never see an invoice for the paint.

Mentally shrugging the thought away, Cat said now: "Anyway, he agreed so fast I didn't even need to finish pleading my case before he hung up the phone."

"So not a big lie then."

"I guess not. But the intent was there."

Cat wasn't sure if it was her imagination, but she thought she detected that tell-tale note of approaching indifference entering at the edges of Matt's words. To be fair, she was surprised by the level and amount of interest he'd shown up to this point.

"So here I am," Cat concluded. "I told him I'd pick out a neutral color and..." she waved meaningfully toward the display rack.

Turning at her pointedness, Matt pursed his lips as his eyes ran down the sample paint cards at his disposal. Cocking his head a little to one side, he seemed in deep concentration.

Another point of victory Cat tried, and failed, to suppress. So maybe he wasn't quite so ready to leave her to her own devices.

"Sticking with white, then?"

She nodded. "Figured so."

"Okay."

Silence descended while Matt looked over the options and Cat pretended not to look at him. Though she told herself he probably did this for every customer who walked through the door, she couldn't help but feel special as he carefully ran through the list of possibilities, took his time to invest in a decision that had no bearing on his actual life.

"Do you get a lot of natural light in the kitchen?"

"No." Cat grimaced. "None actually."

He nodded absently, his thoughts clearly on the topic at hand. Which only made her feel more ridiculous—here she was, surreptitiously checking him out and there he was practically unaware that she was a female.

"But it's not dark, either," she added for something to say. "The living room is across the hall and *that* room does get a lot of natural light."

"Okay." Rifling through the options, his fingers paused momentarily over one particular piece of cardstock, the color splashed across it aptly named, *Pearly Antique.*

"That's pretty."

"Yeah—"

"Thanks, Matt!" Jim called out then, his booming voice coming from the direction of the front door. "Let me know when they come in, will ya?"

"Of course! Talk soon!" Matt returned at the sound of the door chimes ringing once more, this time announcing Jim's departure.

Plucking a card out of the holder, Matt set it down on a nearby shelf. Returning to the display he scoured the selections before grabbing another one—this one had a creamier look to it and was called, *Soft White.* Then, before Cat could open her mouth to so much as comment on the choice, he'd grabbed one more, *Farmland White.*

Taking up all three samples, he fanned them out in his hands as he turned to Cat. "These are popular choices for creating lighter, brighter kitchens." Watching her, Matt said no more, apparently waiting for her reaction.

Cat looked down at them. "Okay. So, how do I choose?"

"Well, I can give you sample paints in each color and you can try them out, see which one you like best."

Cat frowned. "That sounds time-consuming."

A sardonic smile tilted the edges of Matt's lips at the unwise wording. His eyebrows rose. "Do you have any idea how long it takes to paint an entire kitchen?"

Fighting a blush, Cat played for indifference. "No. But I figure it'll take my entire weekend."

Matt nodded. "And if you pick the wrong color…" he let the sentence dangle implicitly.

Cat caught on quickly. "Then I start from scratch. Again."

"Yup."

"Well, it's not like I'm emotionally invested in the color."

Matt inclined his head, the look on his face reading both amusement and agreement. "True."

"And do you really want me tromping in and out of here every few days?" she teased him, glancing up with a sidelong look.

His lips quirked up at the edges. "As opposed to now, you mean?"

"Oh, shut it," Cat said, swiping at his arm again. Still a small pang of embarrassment laced through her at his comment.

"I never said I minded it."

And just like that, Cat felt her mouth slipping upward, that swell of unease disappearing almost as though it'd never been. Unfortunately, it was the type of comment she'd come to expect from Matt. Just flirty enough to make her wonder, but just un-assuming enough to keep her from responding in kind. He could have been being friendly or that of a shrewd businessman. She didn't know.

Clearing her throat, Cat returned her gaze to the paint samples. "Do you think any of these options are risky?"

Matt chuckled, his shoulders moving a little with the sound. "Uh, no. Definitely not."

"Okay. Then, that one," Cat decided, pointing out at random. Her finger landed on *Pearly White*.

"Yeah?"

She shrugged. "Yup."

Matt slipped the other two cards back in their slots. "Okay. I'll get that mixed up. Shouldn't take me more than a few minutes."

"Um," biting down on the inside of her cheek, before Matt could take himself off to that task, Cat forced herself to ask, "Are there any other things I should know about painting? Any tricks of the trade or supplies I'll need?"

"No experience in that, either?"

"Not really."

Matt shook his head. "Well, I suppose that depends on a few things."

"Like what?"

"How big the kitchen is—"

"Not big."

"What supplies you already have—"

"Probably none of them," Cat murmured dryly.

"—how many people you've got helping you out."

Cat cringed. "That would be me."

"Just you?"

Matt's words were hardly encouraging, but then again, she'd also come to expect that from his remarks as well. "Yup. Just me."

At the verification, Matt stalled-out. Raising his eyebrows—which she sometimes felt sure was his favorite pastime when it came to her—he clicked his tongue against the roof of his mouth. "You're going to do it all alone?"

"I believe we've covered that," Cat said lightly. Wanting to end this track conversation, to remove the stamp of disbelief on his face, she nudged him with her elbow. "Unless, of course, that's an offer?" Smiling cheekily, she winked. Not bothering to wait for a response, she started to ask: "Okay. What size brus—"

But she was cut off before she could finish her question.

"Of course, it's an offer! Matthew, tell her!"

In startled unison, both Matt and Cat whipped around at the sudden inclusion of a new voice in the conversation. There, standing a few feet away from them, was none other than Birdie.

"Jesus! Where did you come from?" Matt grumbled.

"What a lovely welcome," Birdie told him through narrowed eyes. "Is that what customers can expect when they come in here? Your grandfather would have something to say about that."

Matt glowered at her but didn't bother raising to the bait.

Waving behind her impatiently, Birdie gestured toward the front entrance. "That lovely gentleman, Jim Harries, was on the point of leaving when I arrived. He held the door open for me." Without further explanation, Birdie turned to a bemused Cat. "You know, Matt could probably use some lessons in manners like that. A lost art." Tisking quietly, she shook her despondently.

Cat grinned. Then she shifted her gaze back to Matt's darkening eyes. "Oh," she said, wiping the smile off her mouth. "I'm sure that's not true."

"Hmm," Birdie murmured, her eyes taking the cardstock paint sample still held, half-forgotten, in Matt's grip. "For the door, I assume?" she asked.

Following her gaze, Cat sighed for dramatic effect. "The one and the same."

Matt looked from Birdie to Cat and back again, his already narrow eyes narrowing further. "Hah! I should have known." The look he leveled their way was full of suspicion and disgust.

Cat blinked in confusion. "Known?"

"An ambush, ladies?" But he didn't actually seem that upset.

Cat's mouth dropped open wide.

Birdie let out a loud cackling laugh.

"What? No! Of course not!" Cat insisted. Looking over at Birdie, she mouthed silently, inviting Birdie to back her up.

"Matthew, don't be ridiculous," Birdie implored. She shook her head regally, almost pityingly.

Matt wasn't buying it, his eyes swiveling untrustingly between the women. "So it's pure coincidence that you happen to be here right now?"

"Absolutely." Birdie pulled herself up to her full height. Her own eyes began to narrow.

He opened his mouth in rebuttal but Birdie stopped him with a look.

"Really, Matthew," she pleaded, "don't ruin it now."

"Ruin what?" Exasperation didn't quite cover the harassed tone of his voice.

"When I came in here you were on the verge of volunteering to help Cat paint her kitchen."

CHAPTER FOURTEEN

In answer to this not-quite-true statement, Matt's lips twitched. "Eavesdropping?" His voice held a silky quality that even Cat interpreted to mean that he was hardly amused. "I would suggest watching soap operas if you need some extra amusement in your life."

"All those years I spent teaching you how to be a good man," Birdie admonished, even stooping to wag a finger in his face. "Don't disappoint me now."

Cat's eyes widened. Birdie was laying it on thick.

Feeling the need to intrude (because, dammit, this was her conversation), Cat reached forward with her right hand, letting it come to rest against Matt's forearm. When his eyes swung back to her, she smiled. "Honestly, I couldn't ask you to do that."

Birdie snorted. "You didn't ask…"

"Actually, I kind of did," Cat returned, her gaze including Birdie now too. "But I was teasing. I never expected Matt to help me paint my kitchen."

"But doesn't that make it all the sweeter when he takes you up on it—?"

"Grandma," there was a warning note in that word. One which Birdie did not heed.

"Matthew," she returned. Standing between their clashing eyes, Cat felt itchy.

"Really," Cat insisted then, looking from Birdie's expectant face to Matt's hunted one. She held his eyes. "I simply cannot, *could not*, accept your help. You've already done enough for me. Too much."

His lips twitched.

Cat realized, belatedly, she was still touching his arm. With a jerk, she let her hand fall back down at her side. Unexpectedly, his eyes followed the conspicuous movement. Something flashed in his gaze.

"Do you have drop cloths?"

At Matt's abrupt change of topic, Cat's eyes widened. "Huh?"

"Hell." Breathing in roughly, Matt raised his gaze back up to her eyes.

"Take his help, dearie," Birdie advised, giving Cat a sympathetic look. "You're in way over your head."

"Thanks, Birdie," Cat mumbled, feeling her cheeks warm at the intimation that she wasn't up to the task of something as simple as painting a door, never mind the fact that she'd all but admitted as much to Matt only minutes earlier. It was one thing to say it, another to have it validated by the opinion of someone else. "Besides, *he* didn't offer to help me. You offered his help to me," she hissed under her breath. "There's a difference."

"Semantics."

Unable to help herself, Cat laughed. There was something so energizing about Birdie, something so…lovable about her bossiness and stubborn will. "No, not semantics. Facts."

Birdie waved this statement away as though of little substance.

Cat looked back up at Matt. Much as he'd done moments ago, she decided to end the conversation in the most direct and blunt way possible. By ignoring its existence and drastically changing topics. "You know what, I think I've changed my mind. Let's go with *Antique Pearl*." For added effect, she plucked the paint card triumphantly out of the display slot. "It'll pick up the light from the living room." She said this as though it were an obvious actuality. She had absolutely no idea.

Matt nodded.

"What kind of finish should I use?"

"I'd suggest satin."

Cat's gaze focused on him, deliberately avoiding Birdie. "Is that the best?"

"No. But then, this isn't for your house. But it's good."

Birdie opened her mouth to interject once more, but neither Matt or Cat gave her the option to speak:

"Sounds good."

"Half gallon?"

Cat nodded confidently, but again, she had no clue. "I think that should cover it."

Wrapping his knuckles against the shelving unit beside him, Matt stuck the chosen cardstock into his back pocket. "I'll go and mix it up now."

"Great," she returned tightly. "I'll meet you up at the front." Thanks to Birdie and her insistence to peer-pressure Matt into something he didn't want to do, her inadvertent insistence of once again thrusting Cat into the limelight of a problem that Matt needed to fix, the friendly banter of earlier was gone, replaced by his silent anger and her equally quiet resentment.

With those words settling in the air, Cat watched Matt turn on his heel, his body retreating under the heavy tattoo of his long-legged stride.

Cat winced, but before she could think of what to say, what to do to fix this situation, she felt the weight of Birdie's arm slipping around Cat's, forestalling any idea before it could gain fruition.

"I'll come up there with you." Without waiting for Cat's response, Birdie firmly led the younger woman up the aisle. "So, how does the door look?"

Cat jerked to a halt at the question. Incredulity assaulted her person. In the midst of everything that had transpired that afternoon, she'd completely forgotten about that. Hadn't even thought to ask about it, check it over.

Stuttering as she came to halt beside the checkout counter, Cat admitted ruefully, "I don't, I don't know actually."

"Blind faith?"

Cat laughed. "Hardly. I just got distracted." She sighed. Again. "But then, that's sort of been the theme with this project."

"Well, that's choice, dear."

Shifting her eyes over to Birdie, Cat caught the look of shrewd appraisal shining out of those blue eyes. "It doesn't feel like it."

"Well, no matter," Birdie assured her, patting her wrist as she let go of her hold on Cat. "Besides, I was rather hoping things would transpire in this direction."

Cat frowned at the wording. "I'm not following you."

Birdie winked. "That's choice too."

"What does that mean?"

But in this, Cat was again destined to be thwarted.

"You'll figure it out" was all that Bridie was willing to offer in response. Patting the counter, she nodded dismissively. Figuring it might better to play ignorant and let the curious, if loaded, comments pass, Cat only smiled vaguely. And anyway, Birdie wasn't waiting for a response, her voice ringing out as she moved away from the check-out counter and toward the front door. "But until then, I'd best get out of here before Matthew returns." She wiggled her eyebrows. "I have a feeling I'm not his favorite family member at the moment." She didn't look the least bit contrite or worried though.

Cat laughed. "Oh, I doubt that."

Bridie twinkled. "I was going to talk to him about finding me a mechanic." She sighed. "That's the trouble with getting older. Everyone you know is either retired or dead—"

Cat gaped at the older woman's nonchalance.

"But I think I'll wait on that consultation," Birdie continued conversationally. "The way Matthew looked when he left just now, I'd probably find myself on the receiving end of broken brake lines." She laughed delightedly at her little joke.

Cat smiled. "What do you need fixed?"

Birdie flipped one wrist dismissively. "My dashboard lights have been acting up."

"Jerry Briggs."

"Hmm?" That caught Birdie's straying attention.

"Jerry Briggs," Cat repeated. "He has a shop down on Hamline Street." Leaning closer, Cat lowered her voice. "He doesn't advertise it because he doesn't want to specialize, but he has experience with electrical issues on cars. And he's good."

"Jerry Briggs? Never heard of him. Friend of yours?"

Cat shook her head. "More an acquaintance. He took over Fred's garage a year or so ago. Like I said, he's good. His reputation is gaining serious traction. Schedule fills up fast."

"Well, I may have to look him up." Patting Cat's arm, Bridie winked. "Thanks for the tip."

"No problem," Cat returned. "As it happens, you're *my* favorite family member of Matt's."

"Well now, on that high note of praise, I'll take my leave," Birdie said, reaching for the door handle. "Will I see on Monday for Canasta? Mary said you were on the team now?"

Cat smiled. Mary had told the others. It was official. "If Mary said that, who am I to disagree?"

Birdie giggled in that girlish way of hers. Cat found herself wondering about that woman's marriage to the late Mr. McBoy. He must have cherished her to have left her so youthful. "Disagreeing with *Mary*? It wouldn't be your smartest move!" Pulling the door open, Birdie gave Cat a mischievous glance. "All right, love, I'll see you then."

Cat nodded. "See you Monday." Then she watched as Birdie, with a half-wave in goodbye, headed out into the early evening.

"She gone?"

At the question, coming from halfway down one of the aisles, Cat rolled her eyes. "Yes. It's safe to come out of hiding."

Matt grunted as he came into view, a can of paint held in one hand. "Not likely." Marching up to the counter, he set the can down beside the register before ringing up the purchase.

"But seriously, you know you don't have to come over and help me paint, right?" Cat felt obligated to say as she handed him the requested amount of money.

Closing out the order, Matt glanced up at her, a cutting expression playing out over his face. "Yeah, I know."

At the words, the patent indifference, Cat swallowed vague disappointment. Hell, who was she trying to kid? There was nothing vague about it. At Birdie's offer, she'd felt a surge of excitement at the idea of Matt inside her home. Well, never mind that now. Reaching for the handle on the paint, she pulled it toward her.

"This'll be enough?"

Matt hitched up one shoulder. "Depends on the size of your kitchen. Better to need more than to spend a bunch on unnecessary paint."

Ignoring the weight in her stomach that told her that the play-ful, teasing Matt had fully retired at the sight of his grand-mother, Cat nodded. "Okay."

"Well," hefting up the paint can, she smiled down at the counter uncertainly. She'd never been much good at small talk. She was always worried she'd either bore the listener with her banal stories or that she'd miss the signal that it was time to say goodbye. Her coping mechanism was easy. Avoid it all costs. At this particular moment, however, she mourned the lacking societal skill set. "Thanks for the help. Again." Wrinkling her nose for emphasis, she turned toward the front entrance.

"Hey Cat?"

Half-turning, she tilted her head. "Yeah?"

"Did you want to see the cabinet door?"

Feeling her cheeks pucker at the words, at the slight conde-scension in the question, Cat took a deep breath. Dammit! How could she have forgotten about the door? Again?!

"Yes. Of course. I just thought…you know, I didn't call and tell you I was coming down and I didn't want to distract you from—" Petering to a stop, Cat refused to meet Matt's mocking expression. "Besides," she added flippantly. "I didn't know if it was a silly thing to ask. I mean, it'll look like all the other doors, right?" Finally, thankfully, Cat stamped her lips together, stem-ming any more useless blabbering. God, would she never learn to shut the hell up?

"You can leave that here if you want," Matt said, coming around the counter, his gaze taking in the heavy paint in her hands.

In silent agreement to this, Cat plopped the can back on the check-out counter while Matt moved to the front entrance and flipped the lock on the door with one hand and turned off the OPEN sign with the other. Signaling for her follow him, Matt took himself swiftly to the very back of the building. Bustling to match his stride, Cat watched his steady gait lead them to-ward a door which would have been almost unnoticeable except for the sign overhead that read, *Employees Only.*

Crossing over the threshold, blinking as her eyes adjusted to the dim lighting, Cat found herself once again inside the shop's warehouse—only she'd never seen it from this angle before. As Matt progressed forward, Cat's eyes swiveled around the workspace, taking it all in. The first half of the immense space was crowded with supplies, stacks and stacks of cut, raw wood, boxes containing washing machines and cabinets and various other household appliances. Farther ahead were slabs of marble and quartz and yet more shipping crates and boxes.

It was only as they passed a couple of forklifts that Cat saw the loading dock at the far end of the building and to the left of that, Matt's workbench. This, at last, was familiar territory.

As they neared the makeshift woodworking station, Cat smiled impishly over at Matt. "Should I close my eyes?"

Chuckling softly, the sound a nice return to their earlier rapport, Matt shot her a teasing glance. "Uh, no. I don't think that'll be necessary."

"Spoilsport."

Without bothering to respond, Matt walked over to the workbench and plucked a rectangular piece of wood off its surface. Bending down to a shelf below that, he grabbed another one. Holding them out in each hand, he looked at Cat. "Here you go."

Stepping forward hesitantly, she let eyes take in their fill as she compared the pieces. In Matt's left hand was the new door, the walnut a whiskey brown shade. In his right was the sample door she'd supplied, its white paint currently coated with sawdust.

Her eyes flicked frantically from the one to the other, processing, matching… But, besides the color, which only required a new coat of paint it was… "Perfect," Cat breathed, leaning forward to trace one finger over the lined edges on the new door.

Lifting her eyes to Matt's, Cat surprised a look of pride etched on his high cheekbones, slivered through those brown eyes. "It's beautiful, Matt." Her voice was low, almost reverent.

"It was an easy design," he reminded her gruffly.

But Cat refused to be put off, refused to let him shrug it off. Shaking her head, she said, "No, it's more than that." Looking at the pieces again, she let her eyes shift back and forth again between the doors. "You're a real craftsman."

"Okay," he droned dryly. "Don't overdo it." Placing them back down on the workbench, he brushed his hands together, sending sprinkles of wood shavings spraying in the air around them.

Cat had a feeling she'd embarrassed him. Stifling back a smile, for some reason she was sort of satisfied with the possibility. She doubted Matt allowed a lot of people that much power of influence.

Stalking up to the workbench, Cat's gaze was riveted to the pieces. "I mean," she whistled, "I can't believe it."

Turning back to him, Cat felt moisture hit the backs of her eyes. Blinking rapidly, she tried to stem the unexpected reaction. "It's an exact match. Absolutely perfect. No one will ever know."

Leaning back a little, his hands shoved now in the front pockets of his jeans, Matt gave her a sardonic look. "I'm glad you're not being overdramatic about it."

"Shush," Cat said, batting away his words. Then, unable to help herself, she peeked back up at him. "Really though, thanks."

He rocked back on the heels of his feet, his eyes dipping away from her steady gaze. "Yeah, no big deal."

"It is to me." Swallowing, Cat attempted to gather her composure. Her voice was thready, her eyes still wet with unshed emotion. The last thing she needed to do right now was break down and cry. Matt had already accused her of being overdramatic. He'd probably faint if she started bawling.

"Yeah, I can see that."

Shaking her head, Cat didn't respond to Matt's quiet mockery. How could she explain to him what this meant? Especially as she wasn't entirely sure she understood it herself. How could she explain to him that her life felt a little like that broken door she'd brought in last week? At first, a little worn out, fragile, easily wrecked. How could she explain that, by breaking that door, she could almost feel a part of her own self healing? And looking at the finished piece, so much stronger and better than the original, that she felt hope?

"How much?" Her voice came out rough, uneven. She didn't bother lifting her eyes. She wasn't willing to meet the challenge she knew she'd find in his.

Out of her peripheral vision, Cat caught his shoulders lift in an empty gesture. Then one of his hands went to play with the bill of his ever-present baseball hat. "I don't know. As I suspected, it wasn't a difficult project."

"But it's beautiful."

"Thanks."

"How much?" Feeling a bit steadier now, Cat lifted her head, turning toward him expectantly.

"Ah. Well, I guess…" but the number he reluctantly shot out only made Cat purse her lips.

In disapproval. "I think it's worth more than that."

"I don't have that many hours into it."

"But I looked up the price of having it customized," Cat informed him. "Your cost is low."

"And I'm no—"

"Professional?" Cat said, predicting his next word. Scoffing, her hands waved toward the door. "I'm not buying that line anymore."

Matt scoffed. "You're not going to start crying again, are you?"

She glared at him, her hands come to rest against her hips. "I was not crying."

"Could have fooled me."

Forging ahead, Cat ignored him. "I insist. This is—"

"Look," with a mild flash of annoyance, Matt interrupted her. A slight ruddy color slashed across his high cheekbones. "It's been a long day. It's been a long week." Without further ado, he walked toward the small refrigerator crouched underneath a microwave and beside an industrial counter set-up against the back wall. Bending down, he opened the door and pulled out a beer.

"Want one?"

"Ah," Cat stuttered, unprepared for the direction of his thoughts. "Sure?"

Nabbing out another beer, Matt lost no time snapping the tops off both before he handed one over to her. "Okay," he said then. "Proceed."

Bringing the bottle up to her lips, Cat grinned. "Price negotiation over beers?"

"Is there any other way?"

Cat laughed before taking a swig. Matt was right about one thing. It had been a long week. On that thought, Cat cringed as she lowered her beer. "Shit. Are you closed?"

Matt raised an eyebrow. "I don't usually condone drinking on the job."

"Right," Cat said, shaking her head. "Obviously."

He gave her a long look. "What do you need?"

"Paintbrushes. I almost forgot."

Matt grinned. "Yeah, I wondered about that."

"Thanks for speaking up," Cat glowered as she brought the beer up to her lips again. The cold rush against her throat was refreshing.

Shrugging, Matt didn't look overly concerned. "I figured I'd just bring them over myself. With drop cloths."

Cat felt her stomach spasm at the words. "What?"

Matt sighed. "It's not a good business move, of course."

"Excuse me?" He was becoming as cagey as his grandmother.

"Left to your own devices, you'd probably pay the yearly mortgage on this place alone." A white slash of teeth followed this piece of cheek. "In less than a month at this rate.

"Gee, thanks." And probably, he wanted to see the back of her much sooner than that. Cat frowned at the realization.

In response, Matt only took another long pull off his beer. Leaning against the countertop of the makeshift—Cat wasn't sure what that was, employee break room? —he didn't seem the least bit worried about offending her.

"You realize how big a job it is, taking apart your entire kitchen to paint some cabinets?"

"I have an idea, thank you." Cat's voice couldn't have been primmer. "And even if I had, you'd have sufficiently cured me of that delusion by now."

"It's not just slapping paint around. You'll have to take down each door—"

Cat could feel her fingers pressing against the brown bottle of her beer. Her right eye narrowed. "Are you trying to be patronizing?"

"No."

"Good. Because I'm not an idiot."

Matt either didn't hear or didn't care about the warning note in her voice. "But you are a little rash."

"Excuse me?" Cat felt the slap of those words.

Matt frowned the way men do when they feel threatened by the emotions of a well-adjusted female. "Don't get your feelings hurt."

Cat's lips pulled into a snarl as she lowered her beer down to her side, her fingers gripping it with the force of her antagonism. She took a step toward him, her whole expression a threat. "Don't tell me what to do with my feelings."

He nodded toward the cabinet door. "The evidence sort of speaks for itself."

"Oh, hell," Cat swore, following his eyes. "How long are you going to hold that over my head?"

Matt pursed his lips in silent agreement of that. "Fine. Okay. How about today, coming in here to inform me that instead of painting one kitchen door, you're now painting *all* of them."

A fissure of silence descended.

And then, unbelievably, Cat smiled as a small chuckle bubbled up her throat. Said that way, well... "Yeah, okay. That *was* a bit rash," she admitted. Still, she bristled. "But I don't need my nose rubbed in it repeatedly."

Lips twitching amusedly, Matt nonetheless tipped his head in acceptance. "Fair enough."

"I'm not saying I don't suck at this type of stuff," Cat said with difficulty, her voice rushed and low. "But at least I'm willing to fix my mistakes. I want to learn. But I don't want to be judged."

Matt seemed to consider her words. "Okay."

"Okay?"

"I won't tease you anymore." At her raised eyebrows, he smiled gamely. "I'm sorry."

"Okay." Taking a breath, Cat's cheeks blew out with the action. "And fair being fair, I'll try not to hyperventilate when I screw up."

Matt tried to swallow a laugh. It came out as a muffled grunt. "So, what time are you getting started tomorrow?"

"Well, I was going to do it early. Nine?" She thought about it for a moment. "Is that too early?"

"Nine is fine."

"I could probably take down all the doors this evening though. Save us some time..."

Matt nodded.

Lifting the half-forgotten beer back up to her mouth for something to do, Cat was surprised to find that it was empty. "Should I, ah, should I take those with me?" she asked, pointing with the empty glass bottle toward the cabinet doors.

"I'll bring 'em with me tomorrow."

"Okay." Spying a small plastic garbage bin beside the mini-fridge, Cat threw her bottle inside it. Wiping her hands nervously against her jeans, she waited for Matt to speak, to say something. When he didn't, she forced herself to say the words itching up her throat: "I feel that I should offer you one last chance to get out of painting. You really don't have to." And she really, really didn't want to force his hand.

"I'm aware."

Cat chocked her head a little to one side. "Masochist then?"

A wolfish grinned crossed Matt's face. She wondered fleetingly if he had any idea how attractive it made him. He had the most devastating smile. "I could think of worse ways to spend my Saturday."

"And probably better ones too."

Matt's head tilted back a little. "Would you rather I didn't come over?"

"What?" Cat's eyes widened in dismay. The last thing she wanted to do was insult the man! "No, no that's not it at all."

"Okay, calm down—"

"I definitely want the help," Cat felt the need to explain. "I'm just not sure I should take it."

"Birdie would never let either one of us live it down otherwise."

"Ah." Cat nodding in sudden understanding. "So that's why."

"No, I didn't say that."

"Then you love painting?"

"I didn't say that, either."

Cat felt exposed, unprepared for what wasn't being said. "Then what?"

But Matt wasn't going to rise to the bait. All he offered her was a wink as he said: "I'll see you tomorrow, Cat."

With that, he tossed his bottle into the garbage beside hers before leading Cat once again back up to the front of the building where her can of paint still sat on the counter, where her car still sat parked out on the main street.

He didn't linger over his goodbye either, pausing only long enough to remind her that she'd need to text him her address.

Cat responded in kind, her answer a brief "Will do."

Small talk was over.

The purpose of the visit had concluded itself.

Over and done.

Frowning as Matt unlocked the store's door for her, Cat refused to acknowledge even the slightest sting of disappointment.

... °•°• ...

Cat was pushing the door to her apartment closed, her jacket only half-shrugged off one shoulder, when her phone buzzed. Hastily discarding her coat, she glanced down at it, assuring herself briskly that, of course she wasn't disappointed that it wasn't from Matt. It wasn't like she'd been expecting a text message from him anyway.

> FROM: Amelia K.
> **8:37 p.m.**
> MESSAGE: Drinks tonight?

> FROM: Cat
> **8:38 p.m.**
> MESSAGE: No can do. Sorry! I'm starting on a small reno project tomorrow and I need to get everything ready for that tonight.

> FROM: Amelia K.
> **8:41 p.m.**
> MESSAGE: Need help? Have wine can travel.

At the offer, Cat blinked. A warmth of feeling spread throughout her body and, in reaction, Cat's fingers closed tightly around her phone for a moment. It was amazing how that felt—to have a friend again.

Still, looking around her apartment, Cat frowned. Besides taking down the cupboard doors and scrubbing them clean, she had a sudden, and not altogether unsurprising, desire to tidy up the house before Matt came over. The carpet needed a good vacuuming and the windows could stand a little attention, not to mention the fine layer of dust coating the entertainment stand

and potted plant. She needed to get the dishes done, not to mention sweep and mop and...

> *FROM: Cat.*
> *8:43 p.m.*
> *MESSAGE: It would be cruel and unusual punishment. But thanks for the offer. Raincheck?*
>
> *FROM: Amelia K.*
> *8:44 p.m.*
> *MESSAGE: Fair enough. I have a couple of sessions this weekend but if they wrap early I'll see what you're up to.*
>
> *FROM: Cat*
> *8:43 p.m.*
> *MESSAGE: Do that! If I'm free, I'm yours!*

(Then again, if there was even a chance that her and Matt's time together should evolve over the weekend, well, she wasn't about to jinx it by making hard and fast plans with someone else. But Cat didn't feel the need to expand on that small hope.) Instead, pocketing her phone, she walked resolutely into her kitchen. Opening the cupboard door underneath her sink, she allowed the small groan to escape her mouth. Reaching inside, she grabbed out a bottle of cleaner.

Did she realize it was stupid to clean her apartment from top to bottom before tearing it all apart tomorrow? Well, of course she did.

But she needed something to distract her from the realization that Matt would be in her apartment tomorrow. Just her and him. (And, she also didn't want him to walk and think she was a slob or anything.)

"Just get it done," she muttered to herself as she slapped on a pair of rubber gloves.

Two hours later, sweaty in the aftermath of her self-imposed deep-clean, Cat put her mop away. Her hands and fingers ached from the level of scrubbing and grubbing, and her muscles protested even that mild action. Her face was flushed and her hair was sticking out at all angles from her ponytail. But, turning in a small circle, she nodded, satisfied at last.

It had been worth it.

The floors sparkled; the pictures gleamed in their frames. Her couch had never looked fluffier.

Ripping off those same rubber gloves now, Cat brushed the sweat off her forehead with one arm. "Okay," she said to the quiet house, "now it's time to get the real work started." Setting the gloves in her sink to dry out, Cat went to retrieve the screwdriver from her junk drawer.

"You got this. Remember that," she told herself as she cautiously moved toward a cabinet door. She was right. Within minutes she'd taken the hinges off the first set of doors, the evidence of her success laying, one on top of the other, on her kitchen table. Slowly, methodically, she continued until every last one was stripped from the cupboard frames.

Surveying her work, Cat grimaced. Every can of soup and packet of rice, every kitchen appliance and jar of preserves she usually kept hidden behind closed doors were on loud display. "Yikes," she muttered, her hands twisting and righting the objects on their shelves until they all stared back at her, labels neatly facing out and lined-up in perfect formation, side-by-side. Then she got busy with her next project, scrubbing each cabinet door clean of any residual smidges of dirt or grim.

It was a little after eleven o'clock by the time she finished. Yawning protractedly, Cat nodded. "Done," she claimed. Lest she should find yet one more item to clean or organize, she turned on her heels and headed smartly out of the room, her feet taking her directly to her bedroom.

Pausing only long enough to strip out of her clothes, she landed with a plop on her bed. Within minutes she was a sleep…still on top of her comforter.

When her alarm clock sounded the next morning, Cat groaned groggily at the watery light filtering in through her window curtains. Pulling herself up and off the bed, she tumbled toward her bathroom.

"Welcome to the great weekend waste," she muttered to herself, determinedly ignoring the flip-flop in her stomach at the expectation, the imagined vision of Matt standing beside her in the tight quarters of her kitchen. Striding to her shower, she flicked on the water.

By eight o'clock, carefully dressed in a pair of tight lycra capri yoga pants and a plain white t-shirt (that, okay, yes, was slightly form-fitting), Cat was just pouring her first cup of coffee when her apartment intercom buzzed.

Jerking the pot, she splashed a little of the hot liquid on her hand. "Shit," Cat cried as she plopped it hurriedly down on the holder. Sucking on her hand as she raced out of the kitchen and down the L-shaped curve of her hallway, Cat cursed her lack of preparedness. She'd meant to be standing right beside her intercom system when Matt arrived—the last thing she'd wanted was for him to wait outside.

Reaching the small door station, Cat was already reaching for the ADMIT button before she'd come to a complete stop. "Hi, Matt," she called through the loudspeaker. "Come on in!"

Without waiting for a response, Cat threw open her apartment door, her head poking out into the hallway just as she heard the sound of the front door opening. Rising one hand, she waved frantically as his lumbering frame came into view.

"Morning!" she called out, her voice a caricature of its normal pitch.

In an incredibly more casual tone of voice, Matt responded as he neared. "Hey, Cat." Hoisting a large backpack over one shoulder and a toolkit over the other, Matt looked earthy and masculine.

Swallowing thickly, Cat moved out into the hall to allow him easier entrance as he reached her door. "Need help carrying anything?" And then, before he could answer, she called after him: "Kitchens at the end of the hall on the left."

"Thanks. I'm good. Gonna check out the work station before I decide what else I need."

Nodding idiotically, Cat realized how stupid she probably looked, just standing in her building hallway. Rushing after him, her stockinged feet padded hastily in his wake. "Okay," she said. "Well, what can I do to help set up?" Slowing her pace as she entered the kitchen, Cat took a much-needed breath. The brightness in her voice had only increased since Matt's arrival. When she got nervous, Cat tended to get chirper. To chirper.

Dumping the backpack anyhow on the floor, Matt thankfully didn't seem to notice her sharp timbre. Instead, his hands coming to rest on his hips, his focus seemed intent on the room at large. "There's not a lot of space. We'll want to push the table into the hall. Or the living room. Give me a hand?"

Cat nodded eagerly. "Sure." Once it and the two accompanying chairs were successfully out of the way, Matt returned to the kitchen. "Hmm. Yeah, sawhorses still won't fit. I guess I can lay out two-by-fours though."

"Sure," Cat offered feebly.

"I'll be right back. While I'm gone want to spread out the drop cloths? They're in there." He indicated the bag he'd recently discarded, which was laying on the floor by the kitchen entryway.

"Any particular way you'd like me to lay them out?"

Matt gave her a level look. "No. Just cover the floor and anything else you don't want splattered with paint."

Okay. Point taken. It had been a stupid question. Feeling her face flush, Cat lowered her gaze as she walked over to retrieve the materials. Ignoring him, she didn't say another word as she unearthed the cotton fabric.

She'd almost completely covered the floor by the time Matt returned with the last of the items. Glancing up from where she was tucking a last fold into one corner, Cat avoided looking directly at him. "So, uh, not to sound like a total newb or anything—"

"Never."

Ignoring his overt sarcasm, Cat continued. "But, um, what should we do first?"

Matt gave her a hopeful glance. "Coffee?"

"Oh!" Jumping to her feet at the question, the drop cloth slip-sliding loosely underneath her, Cat felt her legs shifting at the sudden tilt in her equilibrium. Reaching out, her fingers scrabbling for the edge of the countertop before her, she just managed to stay on her feet.

"Easy there." Instinctively, Matt reached out to grab her upper arm. The weight of those long, lean fingers brought her gaze skipping up to his brown eyes. She surprised a look of concern and something else...something darker in his expression, but before she could identify what it was, it changed again, replaced by a look of wry amusement.

"Yeah. I, uh..." but his hand, still wrapped around her arm, was distracting. Slowly pulling herself completely upright, her legs firm underneath her once more, Cat shot him a teasing glance. "No sudden movements. Got it."

The fine lines around Matt's eyes crinkled in response. When he spoke, his voice seemed lower, gruffer than normal. "All good now?"

There was something in the quality of his voice that sent a shiver down her spine, a tingle up her stomach—but all the same, Cat managed a jerky nod. "Yeah. I'm, ah, I'm good." Her breathing seemed scratchy, rattling loudly in her ears, and she feared the telling sound was filling up the small space in the kitchen.

But Matt's only reaction was a wink as he let go of her arm.

"Right then," Cat said, clearing her throat. "Coffee. Let me get you a cup." Turning with exaggerated care, she fetched him a mug. "Cream or sugar?"

"No. Black is fine."

As she poured the coffee, the rich aroma of the hazelnut flavor filling the room, Cat watched Matt sling the leather toolbelt across his hips. God, as if the man needed an accessory to make him even hotter?

Putting the pot back on the warmer, she held out the mug. "Okay. What's next?"

"First, I drink this."

Glancing down at her feet, mostly because she wasn't sure where else to look, Cat laughed weakly. "Right."

"Then we tape. Or more precisely, then you tape."

She scrunched her nose. "Ugh. I hate that part. I was hoping you'd have some professional trick up your sleeve to avoid—"

"Everyone hates that part. Cutting corners isn't advised, that's my professional tip."

Blowing out a resigned breath, Cat conceded. "Okay. But I didn't actually—"

"I know," Matt said, apparently sensing what she was about to say. "I brought the tape with me." He hooked a thumb over his shoulder. "They're in the canvas bag. Front pouch. Along with the brushes."

Scooting over to it, Cat unearthed the necessary supplies, laying them out on her kitchen table. When her hand curled around a roll of universal blue tape, a hallmark symbol of a day spent painting, she cringed. "All right. Any strategy to this?"

Leaning back against her counter, Matt grinned at her over the pottery-mug in his hand. "Have you ever painted before? Anything?"

Pouting, Cat held out the tape. "No teasing, remember?"

He held up the hand not clasping the coffee. "No mockery. Just incredulity."

She narrowed her gaze. "I feel like we're splitting hairs here."

Straightening up, setting his cup absently on the counter, Matt approached her. There was something almost predatory in the silent way he moved, in how close he came to her before finally coming to a stop; Cat's head was forced to tip backward as she looked up at him.

When his hand reached out, she found herself holding her breath. His fingers just grazed over hers before sliding the tape out of her grasp.

Had it been her imagination, or had there been something slightly suggestive in the motion?

Feeling her chest constrict, her eyes guarded now, Cat watched as Matt meticulously ripped a long piece off the roll. "It's pretty easy," Matt instructed, his voice low as he looked down at her. He was so close that Cat could make out the individual flecks of gold in his brown eyes. "Stick it to the border of the area to be painted and stretch it taut before pressing down."

Forcing her eyes onto the tape he held out for her, Cat's fingers carefully took hold of the offered item. Sliding a little to one side of Matt, she positioned herself before the backsplash above her stove. Forcing her thoughts clear, even as she felt those eyes watching her movements, felt the slight shifting in his position as he studied her, Cat pressed one side of the tape down securely before stretching the rest of it tightly across the upper edge of the tiling.

"You're right," she agreed, keeping her voice neutral. "Pretty simpl—"

Gaping to a shocked silence, Cat froze mid-word when she felt Matt's hand close over hers. Pressing his thumb against hers, he guided her movements, firmly running the pad of her fingertip back and forth over the seam of the blue line of tape.

Her stomach tightened, seized as she let him lead her min-istrations, the calloused feel of his skin against hers sending quivers of sensation up and down her arm.

"The tape needs to be flat. Paint will find its way inside it, otherwise," Matt said, his voice quiet as he leaned forward.

She didn't hear a damn word.

It was only seconds later, when she felt the sudden loss of his hand that Cat remembered to blink, to take in a breath. Letting her hand fall limply down to the countertop, she stared vaguely ahead at the wall in front of her. It offered little comfort to her outrageous heartbeat.

She wasn't sure what was happening.

She didn't feel prepared for this level of...closeness.

Stealing a sideways glance at his profile, however, snapped Cat out of her reverie.

Matt looked much the same as usual. Not an ounce of expres-sion marred his face. Frowning, Cat skirted her gaze just as quickly away from him, schooling her expression to one of de-tachment as well. Had she merely imagined the sizzle of sexual tension in the air? Had it meant nothing more to Matt than sim-ple instruction?

Squirming under the humiliating thought of unrequited at-traction, Cat absently tucked a stray strand of hair behind her ear. Not for the world would she admit how much the thought bothered her.

"Okay," Matt said, the sound of his voice forcing her gaze back to his. The coffee cup was back in his hands. Using it to gesture toward the wall behind her, he continued: "If you want to get started on that, I'll get to work painting the doors."

Nodding briskly, Cat reached blindly for the tape once more. Ripping off a piece, her stomach morphing into a tight, hard knot, she leaned forward as she stuck it against the cool tiling. She was moderately pleased with the straight line. "Do you, uh, do you think we'll get it all done today?" She wasn't sure which way she'd hope he'd answer. While she didn't relish the idea of spending her whole weekend painting, she also didn't welcome the idea of Matt's mass exodus.

Either way, it seemed like a safe enough topic of conversa-tion. Nothing to get her overly excited. Nothing to alert him to her sweaty palms and complete overreaction to his mere presence. The latter was paramount of all.

As she waited for his response, Cat repeated her sweeping motion, her fingers pushing firmly back over the tape once more. Though they shook the tiniest bit, she found her nerves steadying with the mundane action.

At his continued silence, Cat glanced back over her shoulder. Leaning against the counter, at her look Matt lifted his eyes up and away from doors laying in neat stacks on the chairs flanking her dinner table out in the hallway.

"What was that?" he asked. "Uh, I don't know. Maybe."

"Those doors hold the mysteries of life or something?" Cat couldn't resist teasing.

Matt smirked. "Trying to figure out the best game plan here."

"Usually, it starts with opening the paint can…"

He shot her a dark look. "Speaking like an amateur."

She laughed. "Yeah, yeah."

"Keep your lines straight."

At the command, Cat snapped her head back around, her face contracting. Dammit. Did the man have to, just have to point out—

With a vicious snap, Cat yanked the tape back. Then, leaning closer to the wall again, her hipbones jutting into the countertop, Cat laid the tape back down. Heeding his advice, she felt her fingers press down on the tape—only a remnant of her earlier twitchiness remained. Sliding down the line, her contraction bending to the task at hand, she couldn't help but wonder at her current position, her butt slightly raised in the air, her back arched as she bent over the counter…

But when she flicked a surreptitious glance over her shoulder, she was forced to acknowledge that Matt wasn't even looking her way.

Well, of course he wasn't.

"Okay," Matt announced, his eyes shifting from the doors to the stack of two-by-fours he'd brought in earlier. Piled against one wall of her kitchen, Matt walked toward them determinedly. "There's no way around it." Grabbing one in each hand, Cat watched Matt place them on the floor. This was followed by another set of planks. "I'm going to have to lay the cabinets down on these. It's not an ideal situation, but then," he sighed, "there really isn't a lot of room."

"I guess it's better than putting them directly on the floor," Cat mused.

Matt chuckled. "Undoubtedly."

Turning away as Matt finished setting up, Cat resumed taping. Edging along the perimeter of her kitchen, she found something of a rhythm after a while, her fingers soon moving by memory as she stuck and lined the tape. For a few minutes, the only sounds came in the form of a soft ripping from her hands and the slight shifting of wood as Matt prepped to paint.

"Heads up," Matt said, his voice pulling Cat out of the momentum she'd been riding. "It's going to get a bit...crowded." He motioned to the floor. So be careful. The doors will be wet and a tripping hazard."

"Roger that."

Which was all good and fine in theory but when, ten minutes later, Cat could literally feel Matt crouched down on the floor behind her, her legs brushing up against his back as she reached up to get the bottom half of an upper cupboard door, things became...trickier.

He hadn't been kidding when he said there wasn't a lot of room.

"Oops. Sorry," she called out over her shoulder when she stumbled on his foot.

"You're fine."

Cat laughed, letting her sore arms drop down to her sides as she glanced over at him. "I always knew my kitchen was small but this..."

"I think a realtor would describe this as cozy."

"It's definitely that," Cat agreed lamely. Racking her brain, she searched for something else to say, something to carry the conversation forward but they'd more-or-less exhausted that particular topic, which had hardly been scintillating in the first place.

With a silent sigh, she turned back to taping. It was so quiet in the kitchen. It was too quiet...too focused. Which was fine, they were getting things done only, well, it wasn't exactly how she'd planned this morning would go.

It wasn't how she'd hoped it would go.

"Hold still."

"Huh?" Tugged out of her musings, Cat had no sooner asked this then she felt Matt standing up behind her. Too late, however, she'd already half-turned toward him in question so that she found herself suddenly pinned between his body and the kitchen counter.

"Oh," she breathed as his right hand reached around her for the lip of the counter on her other side.

Blinking up at his brown eyes, Cat sucked in her breath as his right leg swung around her. With the doors scattered at their feet, he was fully brushed up against her half-turned body—not a spare breath of space between them. She could feel the soft material of his flannel shirt as it grazed against her forearm.

"Sorry," he muttered. "I need to grab the paint."

CHAPTER FIFTEEN

Nodding mutely, Cat was woefully distracted by the hints of sandalwood and spice in the cologne that clung to his shirt. Or maybe that was just the natural scent of a woodsman.

Heart thudding, Cat reacted on instinct, her movements rushed, frenzied as she twisted back around to face the counter-top. Bringing her body up as tight as she could to the hard surface, she waited as she felt him shift behind her, his toolbelt skimming past her lower back. Both of his hands were cocooned around her as he stepped over the doors and around her.

Swallowing, Cat felt frozen in place, her body tense with the sudden feel and weight of him.

And then, just like that, he was gone, his body drifting past hers to the other end of the kitchen.

Staring with intent at the wall, Cat focused on her breathing. It wouldn't do to hyperventilate now. Then again, a small voice chimed at the back of her head, wasn't this perhaps how she *had* hoped this morning would conduct itself?

A little breathlessly?

"Here," at the sound of Matt's voice, carrying with it a husk-ier quality then she felt sure had been in it moments before, Cat's head rotated in his direction.

He was holding out the can of paint. "Will you put this down for me?"

"Sure." Hating the quiver in her voice, Cat reached for the can. Her fingers trembled slightly as she took it from him, her hand brushing against his as she lifted the thin metal handle. Swinging around, she placed it down where he'd been kneeling earlier.

When she straightened back up it was to see that Matt was tucking a couple of brushes in his back pocket. Smiling gamely, she made an empty gesture. "Maybe I should just...?" Scrambling, Cat moved forward, closer to where he was standing by the kitchen doorway. "Just clear the way a little," she rambled as she stepped into the hallway and toward the table which was laden with sandpaper and paintbrushes and rags.

She waved him forward earnestly. "There," she said, indicating the now relatively clear path back to the cabinets. "That should make things a bit easier."

Toying with her ponytail, Cat heard herself murmuring. "You know," she said, her hand reaching out to run absently against the bristles of a paintbrush, "I used to think about getting a dog or a cat. You know just to have a little company. Someone who'd force me to get a little exercise." Cat laughed weakly. "But now maybe I'm glad I didn't. I doubt there'd even been enough room in here for that—"

"Cat."

"Yeah?"

"Thanks. You can take your spot back."

Cat's eyes snapped back toward her kitchen. Sure enough, during her little monologue of nonsense, Matt had resumed his position on the floor. The walkway was open once more. Biting down on the feeling in the pit of her stomach warning her that, yet again, she'd made a fool of herself, Cat sighed silently. With a sense of disquiet, she returned to her post.

Sooner than she'd expected, Cat was finished taping.

Wiping her hands together, she looked down at Matt. Much like her, he'd finished painting the front of most of the doors by now. A glance at the clock assured her it was only a little after noon. At this rate, they would be finished within the day.

She frowned at the thought.

"All right, what's next, Captain?" Pointing with the toe of her shoe toward the remaining doors, Cat asked, "Should I help you with this?"

"Ah, no." Lifting his head, Matt seemed to be inspecting her taping job. "Let's get you started on the framing."

"Sounds good."

Gaining his feet, Matt motioned her out and into the hallway beside the table. "Here," he said, reaching down to grab a brush from the selection of options. "I would start with this one."

Cat eyed it. It was small. Slender. She sighed. "Okay."

As though he'd read her thoughts, Matt grinned. "It won't take as long as this might imply. And remember, the framing itself is thin."

Cat took hold of the brush. "I'm sorry," she said. "Here you are being my white knight and all and I'm—"

Matt made a low sound in his throat. "That might be pushing it."

Cat looked at him."

"White knight?" There was no denying the heavy dose of mockery.

"God," Cat muttered, rolling her eyes. "Do you always have to make it so difficult."

Matt tilted his head.

"I'm just trying to compliment you."

"Do you always have to make it so overdone?" Matt parried before swiping up a plastic cup from the kitchen table, one of the miscellaneous items he'd brought with him that morning.

Watching as he took the empty cup over to the paint can, which was still sitting in the middle of the kitchen floor, his movements lithe as he poured a small amount of liquid from the one and into the other, Cat felt her lips pull into a straight line. "Right. Of course. My apologies."

Nabbing up the stepstool she'd had the foresight to bring out of her broom closet earlier that morning, Cat struck it down forcefully before one end of a line of cupboards. "But then again, according to you, everything I do is dramatic to the extreme so this is just par for the course, huh?"

She'd managed to climb the first couple of steps before Matt's voice halted her progress.

"Don't forget the paint," he said, holding the cup up for her.

Glowering, Cat quickly descended from the stepstool and took the proffered item mulishly before retracing her steps.

Seemingly unperturbed by her snappishness, Matt reoccupied his position on the floor, his attention already returning to the doors, his brushstrokes confident, his attention absorbed with the undertaking.

This went on for some time, the room awash with the swishing sound of paint being meticulously applied to wood. Cat's nerves stretched, her stomach churning as the quiet ebbed on and on…

"So, uh, how's it going down there?" she asked, peering over her shoulder to catch sight of Matt's progress.

Bent over a door, he didn't bother to raise his head. "Good."

"Yeah. I'm almost finished with this section," Cat returned inanely. She nodded at the cabinetry in confirmation of this.

"Great."

Cat dipped her brush in the small cup. "You know, you're in a pretty good position here."

That got his attention, at least. Lifting his head, Matt glanced toward her. "Excuse me?"

"Well, after this," Cat mused, letting her brush stroke down the frame in a smooth line. "I'll owe you for, like, ever."

"I think you already did anyway."

Smiling cheekily over her shoulder, she conceded the point. "True. So, if you need anything painted at the store…?"

"I'll keep it in mind." And that, apparently, would be that. Matt returned to his door.

Biting her lip, Cat pressed on. "Or, you know, whatever. I'm pretty good at stocking or…you know, if you need a display design…"

"Hmm," he murmured noncommittally.

"Or I could just assure Birdie that I should have been lost without you," she considered, the sound of her voice soothing in the otherwise oppressive silence.

Matt sighed, his head drooping a little with the action. "There you go again, making me out to be some saint."

"Well, really," Cat insisted, "we hardly know one another and yet, here you are," she said, spreading her arms out wide to indicate the mess of her kitchen. A blob of paint dribbled off the end of the brush in her hands, landing with a smack on the drop cloth at her feet. "Wasting a Saturday to paint. I mean…"

Matt set his paintbrush down. "I don't mind painting."

"No?"

"No," he insisted. "It's easy. I can just, think."

And if that wasn't a subtle snub, Cat wasn't sure what was.

Swirling her brush in the cup of paint, Cat heard the bubbles blobbing around the plastic edges. Swish, swish—she thinned the excess paint off the brush. The melodic stroke of the brush against the grain of the cupboard filled her ears—making her almost want to scream. She tried biting her lip. She tried singing silently to herself. She thought up imaginary conversations.

"When did you realize you liked doing woodwork?" The question popped out of her mouth almost involuntarily.

There was an exaggerated sigh from down below. "I don't know."

"Just found yourself building a chair one morning?"

"What?" Cranking his head upward, Matt frowned at Cat's coy expression. "No, of course not."

"Well then?"

"My grandfather. He showed me."

"Yeah?"

"Yup."

Cat took her brush away from the door. It gleamed back at her wetly.

"I would have loved that." She knew she was annoying him, that she was probably being rude by not giving him the silence he'd all but demanded, but Cat couldn't seem to help herself. The silence made her itchy. Uncomfortable.

"Huh?"

"Someone to show me how to do things like this."

Matt grunted in response.

"It must have been nice."

"Guess so."

"Obviously so. You still do it. And you're amazing at it."

Matt sighed again.

Still, Cat pushed. It was too weird, the otherwise hush of the room. To not speak, let him sit there and help her paint her apartment in silence…it was just too bizarre.

"You know what?"

Matt growled. "*What?*"

The impatience and frustration lining the single word convinced Cat as nothing else had up to that point. "Sorry," she mumbled, her cheeks pinkening, her heart thudding in her chest. Nothing was going as planned. "Never mind."

Either unaware or uncaring of the sulkiness in her voice, Matt resumed painting.

"You know what, no," Cat amended. She hadn't planned to say that, hadn't expected to be so vehement, but she didn't exactly regret the statement either. Descending the small stepladder, she reached the hardwood floor on those static words. With the toe of her shoe, she scooted the stool a little farther down the kitchen but she didn't ascend the steps, her eyes intent on Matt. "I mean, I just don't get it."

"Get what?"

"Why you're here? Why you're *really* helping me. I mean, we hardly know each other, and it's clearly not because of the company," she added dryly. "You say it's not because of Birdie, but I'm not buying the whole, 'I just love to paint' concept." Cat frowned, her arms moving now, gesturing with the words. "Certainly, you don't seem all that jazzed to be here so what gives—!" Cat hadn't seen Matt move until he was suddenly standing in front of her, the paintbrush she'd been holding seconds go now firmly in his hand.

Eyes wide, she wasn't able to finish that sentence.

"Keep this up," he said, holding the painting tool up to her face, "and it won't just be kitchen cabinets we'll be painting today." With a pointed look at the wall behind her, which even she could see was dangerously close to the paintbrush she'd been wielding so wildly in her hand, he let that sink in.

Cat felt her face flame. She hadn't realized...

"Paint gets everywhere, Cat." This was said gently, the recrimination almost soft.

"I know."

"*This*," he said, indicating the brush he still held up before her face, "is why I'm here, since you seem to curious to know."

Cat's face paled. "I see." And she did truly see. A scratchy laugh emanated out of her throat. "Sacrifice one weekend for the greater good, am I right?" Trying to cover her mounting mortification, Cat managed a feeble smile.

Matt's eyes narrowed.

"What's one Saturday if it means I won't be tromping in and out of your store over and over again trailing broken household items in my wake."

"Hell," Matt muttered, clearly seeing through her forced humor to the hurt buried beneath the words. "That wasn't what I meant—"

"Of course it was," Cat argued, her voice conversational. "I've done everything wrong up to now. Come on, we both know that."

"Well," Matt conceded with a smile: "you do kind of excel at doing things in the most complicated way possible."

Cat grinned but her eyes gave her away. Skipping away from his gaze, they shifted to take in her feet. A few splatters of paint dotted the tops of her shoes. With a flick of her hand, she gestured blindly toward the wall. "Well, thanks for saving me from my hysterical ways."

"Hey, that's not—"

"No, you're right," she continued. Her voice abandoned its cheap caricature of humor, replaced now with a tone of confession. "I should have asked you that first day about the cabinet hinge. But I was too embarrassed. And then, when I busted the door, I let Birdie talk you into helping me. And now today?" She shook her head. "What the hell was I thinking, trying to repaint my entire kitchen? You must think I'm an absolute idi— —oh!"

In a flash, Matt moved. Thrusting the paintbrush in his back pocket, his hands moved with an economy of motion: coming up to cup the sides of her face at the same moment his head dipped low, his lips pushing down against her own.

For the second time in as many minutes, Cat wasn't allowed to finish her thought.

This time, she didn't mind.

Feeling the wall crash up against her back with the force of Matt's sudden movement, Cat caught her breath. That would be her last coherent thought, however, when his hands slid from her jawline down to her throat, his fingers caressing the skin there before traveling lower—over her shoulders and down her sides to her waist, her body reacting visibly to every skimming touch. Contracting at her hips, his hands brought her impossibly closer as his mouth ravished her opening lips.

Blindly, Cat lifted her arms, twining them up and around his shoulders as she sank into the sensations pulsating within that kiss—the electric zip running up and down her stomach, the trembling quiver in her legs as her lips answered the heat and longing of his embrace, her mouth shaking as his tongue penetrated the darkness there, lashing against her teeth, parrying with her own tongue.

"Dammit," Matt muttered, drawing back just far enough to stare down at her misty expression. Gone was the frustration of moments before, the stark irritation that had led them to this moment. In its place was a mix of both affection and desire.

Cat couldn't form words. She was still trying to process what had just happened. Her breasts were crushed up against his chest, her legs tangled with his as she leaned between his solid frame and the wall behind her.

"I lied," he breathed down into her parted mouth. His eyes were staring fixedly at the contours of her lips. There was a storminess in the depth of that gaze.

"What?" Cat breathed.

"This is why I came." His grinned wolfishly. "Well, both reasons are why I came."

Unconsciously, Cat licked her lower lip, delighting in his reaction—his brown eyes following the action. "Oh." Then she frowned. "Then why...?"

"Why?"

"You were acting like I was annoying you."

HIs head bent closer to hers again...but not quite close enough to touch. "I was merely waiting for you to take a breath."

Cat grinned. "Next time, just tell me to shut up."

Matt chuckled.

"I won't even—"

"Shut up, Cat." Lowering his mouth to hers, Matt kissed her again.

She responded instinctively at the contact: their lips clinging hotly to one another, his head shifting, her body arching as his hands moved to her back, a current of need bowing between them.

"Hello? Cat? Are you home?"

The static echo of a disembodied voice boomed suddenly throughout the whispered hush of the apartment. Jerking apart at the sound, Cat stumbled against the drop cloth at her feet at the same moment Matt whipped around, his hands running unconsciously through his disheveled hair. His eyes roamed the room. There was no one there.

CHAPTER SIXTEEN

"The intercom," Cat realized, her voice coming out in a croak of surprise. Through the haze of her confusion—from both the kiss and the sound of her friend Ashley's voice—she fought for composure. Bracing a hand against the wall, Cat took a moment to steady herself, to lower her breathing, her heartbeat, before moving. Her legs felt like jelly as she deftly skipped around Matt, past the doors littered on the floor, her hands reaching for the backs of her chairs as she skirted by them and rounded the hallway.

She wasn't sure if she was running away from Matt or running toward Ashley.

She only knew she needed to move.

The intercom sounded again. "Cat? Are you there?"

"Coming," Cat called uselessly, her legs picking up the pace as she sprinted down the length of her hall toward the front door. Reaching her destination, her fingers flew to the keypad. Pressing down against the ANSWER button, she forced a note of coolness to her voice.

"Hey! Ashley?"

"Thank goodness! You *are* home."

"Yeah, sorry—"

"Explain later. Let me in," her friend complained good-naturedly. "It's cold out here."

Biting her lip, Cat cast a worried look behind her. From where she stood, she couldn't see Matt's expression, though she knew he'd heard Ashley's request. But what else could she do? With a resignation she'd never encountered before, Cat admitted her best friend into the building. Unlocking her door, she pushed it open in welcome before turning back around, her feet taking her toward Matt. She'd better at least warn him...

Walking into the kitchen, Cat saw that she'd been right; Matt had, indeed, heard Ashley. Dismayed, she spied him packing up his toolbelt which was now off his waist.

Glancing up as she gained the room, he paused momentarily before returning to his task.

"I'm sorry," Cat said, unsure of what else to say. She lifted her arms in a feeble gesture. "I-I didn't know she was coming. I'll just set her up with a movie or something in the living room while we finish—"

"No, don't worry about it," Matt assured her as he tossed his toolbelt over one shoulder. "I should get going anyway." He hesitated, his eyes sweeping over the room—the two-by-fours holding the doors, the drop cloths covering the floors, the random bits of supplies he'd brought with him. Cat noticed he hadn't looked her in the eyes since she'd come back in the room. "I'll leave the rest of this here for you, huh?"

Cat blinked at his swift change in demeanor, at the distance she could practically feel separating them with Ashley's unexpected intrusion. Nodding absently, she felt her throat bob with the action. "O-okay. Yeah, that-that's...um, sure, that's nice of you," she concluded. "Thank you. For everything."

Matt grunted noncommittally.

Biting her lip, Cat's hands fell limply down to her sides. Her heart was slowly rocking back to its normal beat and in place of the hot rush from minutes ago, a cool pit of anxiety was billowing in her stomach.

What had happened?

Did he regret kissing her?

Was he planning to come back tomorrow and help her finish painting?

Was he planning to see her again, period?

Without outright asking these questions, Cat knew the answers lay out of reach. At least, for the moment. Still, she hoped that maybe, if she kept him talking long enough, he'd make some suggestion, say something...

"Really though..." Running a hand through her loosened ponytail as her eyes traveled the length of her kitchen, Cat smiled. "Despite this interruption, we got a lot done here today."

Matt's eyes followed the direction of her gaze. "Yeah." Then he nodded toward the doors laying wetly on the floor. "I'd leave them there for at least twenty-four hours. You want them to be completely dry before you paint the other sides."

Cat hardly glanced toward the littered space, her body reacting almost physically to his dismissive, cool redirection.

"And I didn't get to those two over there," Matt said, pointing toward the doors in question.

Reaching down, Cat picked them up. She smiled too brightly as she hugged them against her chest. "I should probably put them on the table," she said. "Otherwise, knowing me, I'm likely to get them confused and..."

Matt's lips twitched. Cat's heart lurched when she saw it. "Yeah," he agreed knowingly, teasingly. "I wouldn't put it past you."

Opening her mouth in rebuttal to this, Cat was almost pleased with the return of his familiar mockery, the humor darkening his eyes. Only, before she could expand on it, before she could force a sense of normalcy back to the conversation, the sound of approaching feet, and the inclusion of a new voice in the apartment, silenced her.

"My good Lord," Ashley hollered as she swung Cat's apartment door open wide. Cat winced as she heard the crash of the door banging shut again and the quiet thuds of two shoes being flung off feet. "Can I just tell you how crazy my week has been? You won't even believe—oh!" Stuttering to a stop as she rounded the corner of the hallway, her tall, leggy frame following the sound of her voice, Cat wasn't sure if it was the sight Matt or the disaster zone that had once been her kitchen, but her best friend's hazel eyes rounded as she entered that room, her mouth freezing mid-sentence.

"Oh!" Ashley managed again. Then, her gaze swinging inquiringly up to Matt's, she smiled in recovery. "Uh, hello?"

He lifted a hand. "Hey. Matt McBoy."

"From the hardware store?"

Matt raised an eyebrow. "You know it?"

Ashley smiled. "Well, I can't say that I ever frequented the place much but...my dad is a devoted customer."

Matt inclined his head.

Cat watched this exchange in nonplussed silence. Holding the cabinet doors up against her chest as though they were a shield, she wasn't sure what to say next, what to do.

Ashely, however, didn't seem to share that problem. "And clearly," she said, laughing softly. "I'm interrupting something. Well, shit. I guess a surprise visit wasn't such a good idea..."

Cat opened her mouth.

But Matt beat her to the punch. "No," he assured her. "It was good timing."

Ashley raised disbelieving brows. Cat's eyelids flinched.

"I have someplace I need to be," Matt said evasively.

Cat's stomach coiled, congealed at the deliberate brushoff.

With a dry glance, Matt took in Cat's stiff posture. "In fact," he continued, "I almost completely lost track of time."

At the quiet intimation, a small flicker of hope reinstated itself. The half-smile on his face, the playful mischievousness of it, helped as well.

"Yeah?" Cat murmured inanely.

His grin lengthened. "Yeah." Hoisting his toolbelt a little higher on his shoulder, Matt nodded toward the kitchen. "Sorry to leave you with this mess though—"

"Not at all. It's not a problem. I really appreciate all your help. Thanks again."

He didn't respond directly to her gratitude, but then again, he never did. Cat waited for half a beat. Waited for him to say something.

"Okay," Matt said, scratching his chin. "Well...try not to paint the walls when I go."

Cat smiled at the words, at the reminder of what had happened the last time he'd accused her of being sloppy. "I'll do my best."

"And no rush on returning anything," he said as he stepped out into the hallway, his body narrowly squeezing past her and Ashley. "Keep 'em for as long as you need."

So, he wasn't coming back. Cat swallowed. It was only what she expected, wasn't it? It would have been hardly fair to expect him to give up his entire weekend. She would have outright re-fused if he'd suggested coming back anyway.

"Okay. But I think I can knock out the last of this tomorrow anyway, so..."

"Sounds good." Letting his eyes settle on Ashley's una-bashed, if quiet curiosity to the undercurrents swirling around the room, he nodded. "Nice to meet you."

"Yes, you too."

"Cat," he murmured by way of goodbye, his eyes swiveling back to her one last time as he inclined his head in farewell.

"Matt," she returned dryly. Bemusedly, she watched him turn and walk away then, the fall of his feet reverberating softly with his exit.

Ashley had the decency to at least wait until he was com-pletely out of Cat's apartment before she turned her large hazel eyes on Cat. Her full lips split into a large, twinkling smile as she pointed an accusing finger. "Okay. Spill!"

Cat rolled her eyes. Finally relinquishing her hold on the doors, she set them down on her kitchen table. Running her palms unobtrusively against the sides of her pants, she refused to meet her friend's penetrating gaze. Instead, grabbing the brushes she and Matt had been using she brought them to her sink and began to clean them out.

Tapping one stockinged foot on the floor, Ashley refused to be put off. Following behind Cat, she insisted: "Seriously. Who the hell was that gorgeous man?"

"Enough."

Ashley laughed. "Why don't you try saying that without blushing?"

"Oh!" With a snap, Cat banged the side of one brush against the sink, dropping the act. Turning to face her friend, who was leaning against one wall, Cat grinned. "God, isn't he some-thing?"

"I'm still trying to get my heart rate under control."

Cat wagged a finger at her friend. "Hey now, remember that you have a boyfriend."

Ashley held up both hands, laughing delightedly. "Ohh, you *really* like him."

"Excuse me?"

"Ready to bust your best friend's nose just for looking at him?"

Cat rolled her eyes again. Then, as her amusement ebbed, she held her arms open belatedly. "By the way, get over here," she commanded even as she stepped toward Ashley. "Hi!" she squealed when Ashley lunged forward, her arms coming to wrap around Cat's waist.

"Hi!" Ashley returned, squeezing a little harder. "And I truly am sorry if I interrupted something..."

"Seeing you is worth it," Cat lied.

"I sincerely doubt that, but thanks." Stepping back, Ashley nodded toward the kitchen. "So. Want to explain what's going on here?"

Cat looked around her, sighing with exhaustion. Now that Matt was gone, she realized how tired she was with the whole thing. Glancing back at Ashley, she rubbed the side of her neck. "It's kind of a long story."

"I hear that Mick's Bar serves beer at this hour."

Cat didn't need to think twice. "Let me get my coat."

"That's my girl."

CHAPTER SEVENTEEN

Over a frosty pale ale, Cat regaled Ashley with the woes of her kitchen cabinet renovation. True to her status as Cat's best friend, Ashley presented herself as being equal parts interested and entertained by the rollercoaster of events that had followed.

Arching her eyebrows as Cat caught her up to speed, Ashley pursed her lips. "So, you decided to repaint the entire kitchen?"

Cat made a face into her beer. "Yeah, that was pretty much Matt's reaction too."

Ashley leaned back in her chair, a knowing smile settling on her face. "Matt again?"

"What do you mean?" But even Cat wasn't fooled by the innocent question. He'd played a pretty prominent role in her story. Perhaps too prominent.

"His name has popped up with unparalleled popularity this afternoon."

"Well," Cat reminded her, trying to tone down the instinctive defensiveness that branded her words, "he is kind of a big part of it all."

"But he didn't need to be."

Now Ashley sounded distinctly like Birdie. Squashing the thought, Cat shook her head. "I mean, you heard what happened when I tried to strike out on my own."

Reaching over, Ashley covered Cat's hand on the high-top table. "Fair enough. But what about today? He didn't need to be there to help you today. Painting is pretty self-explanatory. Even for you."

Cat lifted one shoulder uncomfortably. "I mean, no..."

"I'm not making fun of you," Ashley insisted, reading the look on Cat's face easily. "It was *his* choice to be there. From everything you told me, you gave him numerous opportunities to back out."

"I think he just didn't want me to screw anything up."

"Could be," Ashley conceded, hiding behind her pint glass as she brought it to her lips. "But unlikely."

"Ashley, don't."

"Don't what?" Ashley placed her glass back down on her coaster. "Now you're telling me you're not interested? Didn't seem to be the case an hour earlier..."

Cat swirled her own glass on the table, her fingers feeling the wet condescension on the side of it coating her fingers. "No, I'm interested."

"Okay."

"But he's never..." choosing her words deliberately, forcing her face to remain neutral, Cat plowed ahead. She hadn't told Ashley about the kiss. Guilt nagged at her stomach. She told Ashley everything. That was part of the best friend code. And she knew she would tell her...eventually. Only, despite the yearning to spill, to relive again those unexpected moments in Matt's arms, to feel again the touch of his fingers against her chin—for now, Cat didn't want to talk about it. She didn't want to analyze it for meaning and purpose. She didn't want to defend her feelings or wonder over his. She was afraid to put too much stock behind it. She was afraid to jinx what had happened. Which was stupid and yet... all the same, she kept her mouth shut.

"Sometimes he seems so, I don't know, *whatever* when we're together. Like I'm just this mildly amusing but irritating girl he's helping out—and only to appease his grandmother no less. Like it's a kindness he'd do for anyone in a similar situation."

Ashley's smile faltered a little. "I see."

"And then, every now and then he'll say something that's just playful enough that I wonder..." Cat flicked her gaze over the bar absently.

"If he's flirting?"

"And if he is, how serious it is."

"I see."

"I can't quite read his expressions. Or intentions."

Ashley nodded thoughtfully. Crossing her arms over the table, she leaned on them, her gaze narrowing. "That sucks."

"Yeah, tell me about it," Cat said, blowing out a breath. "I just don't want to get any more confused about the situation."

"You don't want to get your hopes up."

Cat lifted one eyebrow in confession. "That either."

Ashley was silent.

"I think he knows how I feel though." The words felt sticky leaving Cat's mouth. She didn't like admitting to that probability, but neither could she convince herself otherwise. It left her vulnerable to his whims. It left her waiting for him. Or, at least, that's how it felt.

Ashley opened her mouth in instant denial, but on second thought, merely stated: "You've never been very good at hiding your feelings."

"Nope."

"Hey," Ashley said insistently. "That's a good thing."

"Sometimes he looks at me like I'm just a customer. And then...sometimes, like I'm someone special. But then I wonder if that's wishful thinking, you know?"

"Yeah, I do—"

"Well, hello there, Cat!"

At the interruption, the second one that day for Cat, Ashley paused. Turning at the exclamative greeting, both women were surprised by the toothy grin of an unusually tall, blonde woman standing in front of their table. Neither had heard her approach.

Ashley's mouth turned down the slightest bit.

Cat smiled. "Hey, Sam!"

"Sam?" Ashley asked no one in particular.

"Hi," Sam said, turning to introduce herself to Ashley.

Taking the proffered hand, Ashley shook it. "Hello." With a speaking sidelong glance at Cat, Ashley wondered aloud: "How long have I been gone? Years? Why don't I know anyone in this town anymore?"

Not taking offense, Sam grinned wider. "If it helps, I'm not from around here."

"Please excuse my friend," Cat said, shooting Ashley a scathing look. "She usually doesn't talk about people as though they aren't currently standing in front of her."

Ashley had the grace to blush. "Yes, I'm sorry. I didn't mean to be rude..."

Sam waved her hand. "Nah. No worries."

"Whatcha got there?" Cat asked, jerking her chin toward the binder Sam held against one hip. Her intention was more deliberate than curious: she wanted to change the subject.

"This?" Sam asked, looking down as though she'd almost forgotten about it. Grinning almost sheepishly, she shifted it a little higher against her side. "I, ah, I took your advice. Went to the gardens and did a bit of sketching this afternoon."

Ashley's eyebrows rose archly but otherwise, she remained quiet.

"Sam here is a painter," Cat offered helpfully. "And she's rather fallen in love with our hometown."

Turning toward Ashley, Sam made a face. "Moved here for a boy, stayed despite him. This place, it's got something, you know?"

"Hmm." Ashley's response was noncommittal.

Sam snapped her fingers together. "Character."

Cat nodded toward the sketch pad. "I can't wait to see the finished product."

"Give me a couple weeks and some liquid courage and you've got a deal."

Ashley laughed politely. Cat shook her head.

Grinning broadly, Sam glanced between the girls. "Well, anyway, I won't keep you. I just wanted to stop over and say hi..."

"Would you like to join us?" The invitation came from Ashley. She smiled charmingly. "Unless, of course, you're here with other people?"

Sam shook her head. "Party of one, I'm afraid."

"Then please," with a graceful sweep of her hand, Ashley motioned toward an empty seat at their table. Cat could have kissed her for the generosity of welcome. For one thing, Ashley didn't even know Sam and for another, she'd driven a long way to see Cat and would now be consigned to converse with a relative stranger...

"Are you sure? I don't want to intrude on anything...?"

Cat smiled wryly. It was the second time that day that some-one had said that to her. Unlike with Ashley, however, she shook her head genuinely when she assured Sam: "Not a bit of it. Please, join us. Ashley here only beat me to the punch in of-fering the invitation." Which wasn't quite true—but only be-cause Cat wouldn't have felt comfortable inviting anyone to join them, not on Ashley's time.

"Yeah? Okay. Let me go and grab myself a drink—be right back…" and with that, the blonde skipped off toward the wait-ing bartender.

Taking the moment of reprieve, Ashley lowered her voice as she leaned toward Cat. "Who's that?"

"Sam. She lives in my building. You'll like her. She's nice."

"I'm sure I will," Ashley said, but her voice held a funny note. Her gaze leveled on her friend. "I thought you didn't have any friends here, anymore?" There was no accusation in the words, only inquiry. Clearly, that statement was no longer true.

"Is that why you came home?"

"Of course."

Cat grabbed Ashley's hands. "You're the best."

"Obviously. Stop evading my question."

Cat smiled. "I didn't have friends. At least, not a week ago."

"What changed."

"Honestly? I think it was that damned kitchen door."

Ashley grinned. "You think?"

Cat shrugged. "I don't know. It forced me out of the apart-ment, out of my comfort zone."

"What, were you one weekend staycation away from becom-ing a hermit?" Ashley teased her.

"No, of course not. But it was like…I never went anywhere new, I never did anything at *all*."

"Okay," Ashley conceded, and this time there was no teasing in her voice.

"Walking into that hardware store…" Cat couldn't quite meet Ashley's eyes. "Well, it sounds kind of cheesy but it—"

"No, it doesn't sound cheesy."

Cat's wary eyes swung back to her friend. "No?"

"I've been home for a little over an hour and I've already met two people you didn't know mere days ago."

"And you haven't even heard about my canasta team."

Ashley sputtered over her drink of beer. "Your what?"

Before Cat could respond, Sam returned. In the veritable nick of time. Setting a margarita on the high tabletop, she smiled obliviously at both Ashley and Cat. "So, what are you girls up to today?"

"Girls weekend," Cat said.

"How fun!"

"I surprised her," Ashley inserted with an almost apologetic tone. "Then again, I have some regrets about that decision now."

"What? Why?" But Cat had a feeling she knew what Ashley meant.

"I think I may have scared Matt away."

"Matt?" Turning her attention to Cat, Sam lifted her eyebrows curiously. "Who's Matt?"

"Just a guy."

"Hardly." At Sam's frank confusion, Ashley added: "He's gorgeous. Tall, broad-shouldered, dark complexion, if you catch my drift."

"Mmm! Tell me more."

"He was helping me paint some cupboards in my apartment," Cat grumbled. "Nothing to it."

"Painting?"

"Yeah. Well, he thought I'd strike disaster if left with a paintbrush and no supervision," Cat muttered, picking up her beer. Letting her eyes gaze across the room—dim-lighting with scattered round tables beside a long intricately designed wooden bar replete with a mirror-back, and a few Saturday afternoon drinkers and families—Cat refused to meet her friends' eyes. Focusing on the aesthetics, she forced herself not to show her mounting excitement at Matt's continued presence in their conversation.

Matt.

Her body reacted at the mention of his name.

"And bumbling fool that I am, I showed up while they were the in middle of things," Ashley said, finishing the story when Cat stalled out. She lifted her hands. "So now *half* her kitchen is sporting fresh paint."

"He pull the skedaddle at the sight of you?"

Ashley raised her eyebrows incredulously at the phrasing, but she nodded in a serious enough fashion. "That's about the size of it."

Sam elbowed Cat playfully, the action effectively bringing her back into the conversation. "That's curious, huh?"

Cat smiled tightly.

"Sounds like a man who needed some fresh air."

Cat refused to play along. "Paint fumes?"

"Sexual tension," Ashley confirmed. She nodded at Sam. "It was damn near palpable."

"Enough guys," Cat insisted. At the slight edge in that statement, both women were quick to wipe the teasing grins off their faces. Straightening up in her chair, Ashley let it go.

Sam merely switched tracts. "Does this have anything to do with your search in the basement storage the other day?"

"Basement storage?" This came from Ashley.

"Long story."

"You're racking up a lot of those lately," Ashley murmured, and Cat thought she heard the slightest tenure of displeasure in her friend's voice.

"It's how we met," Cat explained, pointing at Sam. "I was looking for some leftover paint to, well you know, paint the kitchen."

"Ah."

"I was looking for paint, too," Sam said. She chuckled, "but of a different kind."

"For different reasons."

At the words, Sam furrowed her brows. "Wait. So, you and Matt weren't able to finish painting?"

"Nah," Cat said. "But there's not much left to do."

Ashley seemed ready to disagree with that statement. "That's a bit of a stretch."

Sam nodded. "Want some help?"

"No, no. I couldn't ask you to do that."

"But she could ask Matt?" Ashley sidelined to Sam.

Sam winked back at her. "Very curious indeed."

"Okay," Cat cried, throwing her arms up. "I would love the help. That would be great. Fabulous actually."

Sam grinned slowly, rubbing her hands together. "Great."

"It's hardly worth that level of excitement," Cat assured her.

Sam shrugged. "Painting is painting."

"I'm not so sure…"

"Plus, I've still got a bit of residual resentment leftover from my ex," Sam said. "What better way to exercise some of that rage—brushstroke up, brushstroke down. I'm already feeling the cathartic effects."

"And she won't have to worry about ruining a perfectly good piece of canvas," Ashley interjected.

"It was a mistake," Cat realized, her finger pointing between Ashley and Sam, "letting the two of you meet."

… °●°● …

Of course, this prophecy proved to be only the beginning for, an hour later, Cat received a text message from Amelia—she'd had a last-minute cancelation which had rather succinctly freed up her evening and what was Cat up to? Beyond another eyebrow-raising grin from Ashley, who was secretly marveling at how much her friend had changed in so short a span of time, it was quickly agreed on by everyone that she should, of course, join them.

As Sam was quick to say, if they were going to enjoy an impromptu girlfriends' weekend, the more the merrier.

As Cat had quietly hoped, when the four of them sat down together, the night turned into a comedy special.

"I've been dying to get a new business portrait taken," Ashley had squealed upon first meeting Amelia.

"Well, I'm not technically set up yet, but I suppose I could be persuaded…"

"Bartender," Ashley had cried playfully. "Get this girl another drink. On my tab!"

….

"How gorgeous! You painted this?" Amelia had asked Sam, looking up from a picture on Sam's phone of some of her previous pieces of work.

"Yeah." It was the first time that Cat had ever seen the tall, blonde look…well, almost petite as she'd shrunk into her seat. It had been at Cat's insistent cajoling that the artist had shown off some of her art.

"It's brilliant."

"Thanks."

"No, seriously," putting the phone down, Amelia fixed Sam with her steady gaze. "I've been toying with the idea of matching some of my photos alongside some local artists' work. I would love to see more…if you're interested."

"Bartender," Sam had cried, winking at Ashley. "Get this girl another drink…."

....

"How'd the door turn out?" Amelia asked, taking a healthy swallow of wine. It was later in the evening, and the girls had moved from that first taproom to a small bar and grill to grab dinner.

Ashley made a face.

Sam made exaggerated hand gestures.

Amelia only looked confused. "What's happening here?"

"We're not allowed to talk about Matt."

"I didn't say that—"

"You didn't have to," Ashley told Cat dryly.

"I knew it!" Pumping her fist in the air, Amelia giggled. "And you told me you guys were only kinda-not-really friends."

"We are!"

"Oh God, we can't go round and round on this again," Ashley groaned. "I'm dizzy enough already."

....

Opening the door to her apartment in the delinquent hours of the night, her head fuzzy and her footsteps not quite steady, Cat smiled crookedly. It had been a good night. A great night. Throwing an arm around Ashley's dangerously leaning frame, Cat steered her friend down the hallway and into her bedroom.

Dumping her unceremoniously on the bed, Cat took herself into the adjoining bathroom to get changed.

Staring back at her hollowed-out expression, her mascara gunky and her eyes red-rimmed from exhaustion and over-indulgence, she grinned as she considered that tomorrow she'd pay for the afternoon of laughter and alcohol.

Shuffling to her bed, Cat wasn't surprised to see that Ashley was laying on top of covers, completely passed out. Shaking her head ruefully, Cat just managed to tug off her friend's boots and jacket before struggling to relinquish the comforter from underneath her.

Closing her eyes as she clambered in beside Ashley, Cat felt the first bite of rising nausea invade her senses. Clenching her teeth, she squeezed her eyes shut even tighter, breathing past the urge to vomit.

Whatever. It had been worth it.

CHAPTER EIGHTEEN

Grinning over at Sam the next morning, Cat couldn't quite keep the smirk off her face. Leaning back against one of her kitchen chairs, her new friend looked quite the thing: her blonde hair was scraped ruthlessly back into a small ponytail, but despite this, speckles of white paint still managed to dot her hairline. As to that, splatters of paint also coated her thin, long fingers and drab sweatpants.

Catching the look, Sam raised her eyebrows. "What's so funny?"

"Nothing," Cat assured her on a laugh. "You just look real fancy right now."

"Yeah, yeah," Sam said teasingly. Her eyes traveled up and down Cat's own tattered pair of blue jeans which she'd paired with a long-sleeved shirt broadcasting a marathon Cat had not personally run in. "You're looking pretty hot yourself over there."

Bowing with a flourish, Cat waved in acknowledgment of this. Straightening up, she met Sam's giggle with a smile.

"Seriously, though, thank you so much for helping me."

Especially considering how hungover everyone had been that morning, Cat's sincerity was as genuine as it was exasperated. After a rough awakening, in which Ashley had firmly stated her intention to never touch an ounce of alcohol ever again in her life, Cat had drug her friend's protesting body out of bed and made them a greasy breakfast of eggs and hash browns. Walking Ashley out to her car an hour later, Cat's head beating a steady tempo of dehydration, the girls had barely reached the front entrance of the building than Sam's door had cracked open.

Beaky-eyed and pale, Sam had nonetheless informed Cat that she'd be over around noon to help finish up painting.

"As in, today?" Cat had croaked.

"No better cure for a hangover than sweat," Sam had assured her.

Laughing weakly, Ashley had poked Cat in the ribs. "That makes me feel a whole lot better."

Cat had blinked.

"It makes a long, terrible car ride more enjoyable, knowing I won't be the only person suffering."

"Cute," Cat had remarked.

"Bye, Sam," Ashley had said then, turning to wave at the blonde.

"Bye girl. See you soon."

"Count on it" and with a last glance at Cat, Ashley had left.

Though she'd been loath to admit it, Sam had been right. Within half an hour of setting up the paint supplies and finishing on the last of the framing and the doors, not to mention copious glasses of water, Cat had started to feel better. Two hours in and she almost felt human again. Now, semi-wet paint glinting off the fluorescent bulbs of the room, newspapers and rags scattered about over every available space, she sighed in exhausted appreciation of those facts. "I'd have left this for tomorrow but for your insistence otherwise."

"And to think, I had to practically twist your arm to get you to agree to my help at all."

Cat rolled her eyes. "I know, I know."

"Usually, it's the other way around."

"Rub it in."

"You mean, how amazing I am?" Sam batted her eyes at Cat innocently. She even brought one hand up to her chest. "I wouldn't dream of it."

"Beer and pizza?"

Sam grinned. "Now you're talking my language." With a frown, she glanced back at the floor, which still held the cabinet doors, all but two now flipped over on their other sides. She flicked her hand toward them. "Let me know when they dry and I'll help you hang them back up."

"No, no. You've done more than enough." Cat's voice was as firm as her head shake. "Plus, those two doors still need a coat of paint on their inside panels," she reminded Sam, her reference aimed at the cabinets that Matt hadn't been able to start on yesterday. It would be another couple of days before she'd be able to officially complete the project.

"I don't mind, whenever you need..." Sam hedged.

"Nah. Besides, that part'll be super quick," Cat reasserted. But that wasn't the only reason she was reluctant to accept Sam's help. Maybe it was because Cat already felt she'd assumed too much of Sam's generosity. Maybe she was overly protective concerning the doors safety. But probably, it was because Cat wanted to celebrate the conclusion of this project—a project that was once supposed to be an evening activity that had ended up stretching through the days—by herself. To fully enjoy the euphoric feeling she knew would rush through her system when she screwed in the last hinge...

Taking Cat at her word, Sam said nothing more on the matter, instead settling comfortably on Cat's couch with her beer as the other woman phoned up the pizza parlor to place their order.

It was three days later, after having assured herself that the paint was good and dry, that Cat set to work, picking up one door after another until at last, she was living the long-awaited reality of screwing the last door (not coincidentally, the one that Matt had had to resurrect) into place. Feeling the screw tighten, watching the hinge set securely against the wooden panel, Cat stilled. It was done. Taking a careful step backward, her drill hanging in one hand, Cat surveyed the finished product.

Her kitchen looked like a kitchen again. The paint gleamed freshly under the lights, and though she knew it was probably her imagination, Cat thought the new coat *did* made the room look brighter. Happier.

Smiling at the compilation of every seeming change in her life of recent, Cat waited for the rush of satisfaction, the onslaught of pure, unadulterated excitement at the realization that all the hiccups had been taken care of there, there was nothing else to worry about going wrong, no anxieties of the unknown. She was done.

She was done.

No missing doors, no paint mishmashes, no detours or unexpected roadblocks. Letting her eyes roam over the gleaming cabinet doors, across the straight cupboards, their hinges secured and polished, Cat waited.

The culmination of new gray hairs, of stress eating, but finally, it was over. There was nothing else to worry about...

Cat frowned at the void of sensation following this assessment.

She felt nothing but tired as she stared at the accomplishment before her. "What in the world is wrong with you?" she scolded herself as a wash of discontent settled over her shoulders. "This is what you wanted." Swinging her arms out wide, she took in the room at large.

Instead of a rush of adrenaline, she felt only a mild letdown.

And dammit, she knew why.

Her kitchen was in perfect order. Nothing more needed to be done. Which meant she had no further business at McBoy's Hardware Store. Which meant that she had no more reason for seeing Matt.

No sooner had the thought taken root than Cat's eyes seemed to move of their own accord toward the drop cloths she'd neatly stacked on one of her kitchen chairs and the two-by-fours lined against the far wall. The smallest smile tugged into place. "Okay," she said, refusing to admit to the charge of warmth that spread through her body at the sight. "I guess there's still one thing left to do."

There was only one problem: Matt wasn't working.

Half an hour later, her hair carefully piled into a messy bun on top of her head and her body artfully draped in leggings with a long denim shirt, Cat came to a stumbling halt as she stepped inside the hardware store and came face-to-face with an employee she'd never seen before.

His nametag read Kyle.

Uneasily, her eyes flickering down the aisle to one side of the building, her stomach dropping at the lack of another presence discernable in the building.

It had never occurred to her that Matt wouldn't be there. Which was entirely ridiculous when she thought about it, only...only he'd *always* been at the store before. Every time.

Swallowing past the urge to turn and leave, the drop cloths and clunky two-by-fours still in hand, and simply return another day, Cat marched determinedly toward the cashier.

That would have been too obvious.

Too desperate.

And really, maybe this was the sign that she needed. It really *was* done.

With a tight smile, Cat handed the equipment over to the young clerk behind the counter. "Hello, could you please give these to Matt. Tell him...tell him they're from Cat. Cat Cryer. He lent them to me for a project..." Slowing to a close, Cat didn't bother finishing her story as Kyle nodded disinterestedly.

Offering her a professional smile, Kyle opened his mouth only long enough to ask if there was anything else she needed?

Though she was tempted to inquire about Matt's whereabouts, pride killed the question dead on Cat's lips. The very last thing she needed was to come across like some clingy woman. Instead, she shook her head no, told him to have a goodnight, and left.

Still, hope prevailed as Cat drove herself home. She figured that he'd call her, text her at the least once he saw the return of his supplies, once Kyle informed him who they were from (though she doubted Matt usually lent out painting supplies, but still...). He'd want to know how it all went. Frowning as ash parked her car in front of her apartment building, Cat's fingers drummed against the steering wheel.

"Either that or I'm a bigger dope than I realized," she said as she alit from her vehicle.

Yet, no matter how many times she checked it that evening, no matter how hard she willed it otherwise, her phone remained stubbornly silent. Despite the pit that started to form in her stomach, the pit that seemed to reconcile her to a place of anonymity, Cat tried to shrug it off.

"This is silly," she repeated to herself as she headed for bed that night. "He wasn't there when I returned the items. It's highly doubtful he dropped by afterward."

He wouldn't know anything about her visit until at least the following day, when he arrived at work—and maybe not for a few hours after that, too. It made sense. And really, how pathetic that she'd spent the larger part of her evening on tenterhooks waiting for a measly phone call, a few lines of text.

A coil turning cold in her stomach, Cat tried not to think of the alternative. That Matt was so grateful to be done with the whole fiasco that he'd all but written her off. After all, it wasn't like he'd volunteered to help with her little 'project'…in fact, he'd been all but forced into it.

But if that were the case, why'd he kiss her?

She frowned. Of course, he'd been quick to make his exit after doing so.

"This is getting you nowhere," she assured herself as she settled into bed. Still, her mind refused to listen to reason. Her thoughts roamed, spinning chaotically as bits and pieces of the last few weeks flittered through her consciousness. Laying there, she felt once again the almost uncontrollable rage that had stolen over her body when she'd heard the cracking hiss of her cabinet door as it had splintered in two—how her hands had shaken, her eyes biting back tears as she'd stared down at it: "No good, rotten piece of—!"

The resounding thwack! after she'd thrown the fractured pieces of it on the floor.

She remembered all over, the touch of Birdie's powder-fine hand coming to rest on her shoulder inside McBoy's Hardware Store, as though the simple contact would offer Cat a lifeline. (And it had!) The warmth in that woman's blue-eyed gaze when she'd smiled. *"Matthew here actually does some wood-working."*

Smiling almost involuntarily now, she could still see the look on Matt's face—the compressed lips and narrowed eyes. His oft-repeated motto: *"…I'm not a professional."*

She heard again the clink of wine glasses as Cat sat, her legs crisscrossed on the floor of Amelia's studio, her eyes raking over the mirrored wall, that hideous wardrobe as they'd cheers to Cat's broken door, to everything that had transpired because of it.

The friends she'd made—even the kinda-not-really ones.

In the darkness of her bedroom, Cat's eyes shifted to the right, mentally gazing out past the wall separating her from the rest of her apartment and toward her kitchen. Even though Cat couldn't see it from behind her closed door, she saw the room clearly in her mind's eye.

It had certainly shaken up her life. And not just hers, either...

"This is good practice for him," Birdie had assured Cat, the sound of her voice clear even in memory. *"You're good for him."*

"And she'd been right," Cat said aloud to herself now. "He *had* enjoyed custom-making my kitchen door." She could still hear the confident sound of his voice when she'd called him after the door was finished.

"It looks good."

"Will it, you know—?"

"They'll never suspect a thing."

There had been no denying the smile in those words.

Whirling, her mind returned to Birdie, leaning in close, like a co-conspirator, to confide this simple sentiment: *"...despite his growling, he's tickled to be working on this project...This business,"* she'd said, waving toward the hardware store, *"It's not his dream."*

"What about that?" Cat had asked Amelia, her chin jutting toward the mammoth wardrobe snuggled up against the back wall. She felt her lips twist. *It looked like something straight out of the seventies....* "I've got to be honest. It's hideous."

"Matthew here actually does some wood-working..."

The memories swirled frantically past her ears now, coming to her in no particular order:

"You mean, you'll make me a door?"

"Yeah. I'll make you a door."

"...He did my bathroom remodel last year."

"It wasn't exactly a difficult design."

"It's an exact match. Perfect." Cat staring down at the door unblinkingly, unbelievingly. *"No one will ever now."*

"Still, I've got to be honest. The wardrobe is hideous."

Somewhere between these spinning thoughts, Cat finally tumbled into a restless sleep. But they were still there the following morning. Despite an incredibly hectic day at work, she heard the clatter of those words, repeating, repeating...

It didn't help that, though her office phone rang almost off the hook, her cell phone remained quiet. At least, concerning Matt.

No call. No text message. Nothing.

Her eyes glanced toward her office wall clock. It was a little past three in the afternoon. There was almost no way he hadn't seen or been notified of the return of his painting supplies.

Cat wasn't about to call him. She wasn't about to beg him to take an interest in her. She wouldn't seek out his attention.

Her stomach tightened. Her brows furrowed. She had her pride.

"I guess that's that," she muttered to herself, bending over her keyboard, her nails tap-tapping in tempo. Ironically, his damning silence only made her mind spin all the harder. Granted, Matt wasn't an easy man to read at the best of times, but she couldn't believe, refused to believe it was that simple for him to just, to just—

To just, what? Go about his life like normal? The thought struck Cat profoundly. Well, of course that's what he'd do.

"That's what you need to do, as well. That's normal," she scolded herself.

"You mean, you'll make me a door?"

"Yeah. I'll make you a door."

"Still, I've got to be honest. The wardrobe is hideous."

"...He did my bathroom remodel last year."

"It's an exact match. Perfect."

"...he's tickled to be working on this project..."

That damn ugly wardrobe in Amelia's studio....

And suddenly, like the snap of a finger, Cat realized where her thoughts were headed. She knew why they'd taken up so much space in her mind. Taking her fingers off her keyboard, she felt them drumming quickly, rapidly on her desk as the nebulous idea started to fully take root.

"Of course, it's none of my business," she assured herself. Still, her heart rate sped up. "I probably shouldn't mettle," she continued, but the image of Birdie kept popping back into her mind:

"Matthew here actually does some wood-working."

If it hadn't been for Birdie's insistence, her refusal to accept Matthew's initial rejection of it, Cat would still be missing a cabinet door. And Matt would have successfully continued to hide his amazing gift away, sight unseen from the world....

These rationales were mere excuses, of course. Cat wasn't being altruistic in her aim. But they comforted her all the same, gave her a believable backdrop of deniability.

A smile slowly reached her mouth as this loophole presented itself. Cat *wouldn't* seek Matt out. Not in so many words.

"Well, hell." Reaching for her phone before she could think herself out of the perfectly half-baked plan, Cat felt her fingers dialing. Pressing the phone up close to her ear, she heard her feet keeping time with her fingers: tap-tap-tapping as the phone rang once, twice.

"...Hello?"

"Amelia?" Springing up from her chair, Cat bounded from one end of her desk to the other.

"Girl, I owe you a bottle of wine for the impeccable timing of this phone call," came the harassed response. In the background, Cat could just make out the sound of a high-pitch scream.

"New clients?"

"Mother-daughter photo shoot. The daughter's five and she missed her nap," Amelia said. Her tone was dry, but Cat could hear the irritation lining the words.

"Oh—"

"And mom's quite the perfectionist and indifferent to her child's wailing ways. So, yup, this call was a much-needed break."

Cat laughed. "Gotcha." Her teeth nibbled on her lower lip. "Any chance I can collect on that bottle of wine tonight?"

The was a slight pause. "Uh. Sure."

"Great."

"My place or yours?"

"Yours." Cat cleared her throat. "Actually, it'd probably be best if we met at your studio. Is that okay?"

There was another pause. "Okay." The word was sounded out slowly, cautiously.

"What time are you done tonight?"

"Officially? Five o'clock."

Cat smiled. "Unofficially?"

"Be here by seven."

"Got it." Smiling now as she'd been scowling earlier, Cat felt an immediate release of the tension that had been building in her stomach since she'd arrived home last night. Motivated into action, she lost the despondency of earlier, felt a rush of excitement, of anticipation steal through her body.

"...oh, but you'll have to buy the wine," Amelia said, her voice bringing Cat's attention back to their conversation. "I'll repay you once you're here though."

"I'm so sure."

"...Amelia? Amelia?! We're ready!"

"Ah, shit," Amelia whispered. Cat couldn't blame her. Even over the phone, the woman's voice was loud, pettish, and high-strung.

"Good luck," Cat offered.

"I'll need it."

CHAPTER NINETEEN

At seven o'clock precisely, Cat opened the darkened door to Amelia's studio. Breathing a sigh of relief that she'd avoided meeting Amelia's mother-daughter duo from earlier, she breezed into the back room. The lights were on in there, but the room was empty. Unlike the last time she'd entered the building, Cat felt no reserve as to her welcome, felt no pressure expanding in her chest when she didn't immediately spot Amelia.

Setting the bottles of wine down on the floor, her eyes surveyed the room curiously. Much as she'd predicted, the floor-to-ceiling mirrors that had once graced an entire wall of Amelia's studio had been removed. The hardwood floors were now covered here and there with oriental rugs, giving the room an unexpected warmth in the otherwise bare settings. Pivoting slowly, her curiosity to see what Amelia had changed distracted Cat momentarily.

Her heart rocked for a second as her eyes swiveled quickly to the object of her visit...

Ah. Her eyes lit eagerly upon the scattering of props, the extra blocks and towers and pillars lined neatly against the far wall...and butted up against that wardrobe.

Thankfully, that hadn't been replaced.

She'd been counting on it.

"Two bottles?" Amelia asked, her voice shaking Cat out of her reverie. Turning at the sound of her friend's voice, Cat watched the willowy brunette enter the studio floor from one of the back rooms. Peering over Amelia's shoulder and past the now slightly ajar door, Cat could just make out a desk and lamp shining from within its depths.

Ah. So Amelia had turned one of them into an office.

"There you are," Cat said in greeting. Her eyebrows lifted quizzically. "Finish with the edits?"

Amelia pulled a face. "Not even close, and after one afternoon with Mrs. Marsden, nothing but absolute perfection will do… still, I'm calling it for the night."

Tough customer, huh?"

"I'll say." Grinning almost sheepishly, Amelia seemed compelled to add. "Then again, she tipped rather generously."

Cat smiled absently. Running her hands up and down the jeans she'd changed into after work, Cat considered her words. Her eyes flickered nervously back to the wardrobe and then, just as quickly, they dropped down to her feet.

"Shall I do the honors?" Amelia asked. Holding up one hand, she indicated the wine key dangling between her fingers; clutched precariously in the other, Amelia held two wine glasses. Cat blinked. She hadn't even noticed them until now. Amelia must have brought them from her office….

"Umm. No." At Amelia's frank look, Cat shrugged. "At least, not yet." It would probably be better that her faculties stay clear for this conversation.

Narrowing one eye, Amelia waited patiently. But when Cat didn't immediately explain that cryptic remark, she demanded: "Okay, what's up?"

"Up?" Cat cringed at the octave of her voice. Clearing her throat, she shook her head. "N-nothing."

"You're a terrible liar."

"Okay, okay." Holding both of her hands up in surrender, Cat capitulated. "The thing is…I don't want you to take this the wrong way or anything—" Now that she was at Amelia's studio, Cat was having some serious reservations. Never mind how Matt might react, she didn't want to offend her new friend. With each passing minute, the spark of this idea, now cooling with time, was starting to look rather…um, pitiable.

"Conversations don't tend to end well that start that way," Amelia confided to her, but she was still sporting the same easy grin. Crouching down beside the bottles of alcohol, she deposited the paraphernalia in her hands before standing back up.

"Well, I was thinking about your wardrobe—"

That knocked Amelia for a loop. "My what?"

Pointing toward the bulky wooden structure, Cat shrugged. "Your wardrobe," she reiterated. The top of her shoe toed the polished floor nervously. "It's an eyesore."

"As you've said before," Amelia returned dryly.

"And you agreed," Cat returned breathlessly. This was probably not the most tactful way to go about this conversation, but now that she'd started...well, now that she'd started, she couldn't seem to stop.

Amelia nodded. "And?"

"And?"

"Is that all you were thinking? That my wardrobe is ugly?" There was a laugh threading Amelia's words, for which Cat was entirely grateful.

"No, I just—" Cat shook her head. Her eyes moved toward it frantically, her gaze taking in the jumble of blocks and towers beside it. "I remember you said you used it for props."

"Mm-hmm."

"Well, wouldn't you rather have a custom-designed piece for the studio? You know, something that actually fit all your stuff, something that was specially designed for everything, even the odd-shaped things?" Cat's hand flickered pointedly toward the excess items leaning against the bulky structure. "And, you know, something that wasn't so, well, hideous?"

Amelia was silent for a moment, her large eyes taking in the item in question. Her lips pulled up a little. "You really have been thinking about this."

Cat dug in a deep breath. "Yes, I have—"

"Okay. Yeah, and now it's my turn to tell you what I'm thinking."

Cat swallowed thickly.

"I'm thinking we need to get you laid."

At the words, Cat sputtered. "Wait. What?"

"You've been sitting at home thinking about my wardrobe? My *wardrobe*, Cat? I think that says it all."

"No, no..."

Snapping her fingers together, the sound reverberating off the walls, Amelia laughed. Throwing her head back, she let the sound flow effortlessly out of her mouth. "Aha!"

"Aha?" Cat's voice was weak, nervous.

"This *is* about getting you laid, isn't it?"

"Would you stop saying that?" Flustered, Cat let her eyes shift away from Amelia's penetrating gaze.

"Come off it already. You were on the verge of oh-so-innocently offering Matt up to the task, weren't you?" But it was clear Amelia wasn't expecting a response. She already knew the answer.

Cat's hands balled into fists at her sides. "You told me you wanted to get a new wardrobe."

"Yeah. Maybe someday," Amelia reminded her. "It's far and away a low priority right now."

Cat made a face. "But it's godawful."

Amelia only grinned, her lips splitting open to show her straight, white teeth. "True, true."

"And it obviously doesn't hold all of the equipment you have."

Amelia nodded thoughtfully. "That's also true. And convenient."

"How so?"

"Because before walking in here, you didn't know that."

Cat blinked. "Well. Still."

"But let's be honest—you weren't really thinking about my wardrobe. You were thinking about Matt."

"I wasn't." Feeling her face flame, Cat balked at the accusation in her friend's voice. It was all rather humiliating. Here she was, despite her best cover story, obviously chasing after him and he was…what? Interested when she happened to be around, within easy access?

"I won't agree to your little scheme until you say so," Amelia sang.

Cat considered the words. Feeling her fingernails biting into her palms, she hitched up one shoulder defensively. "It's not *only* about him."

And that was true. Okay, it was partly true. All that Cat knew was that she'd felt better the moment she'd jumped up and called Amelia, the moment she'd found the motivation to move, to act, to do something—anything but return to the same old staid existence she'd known only days ago. She was done letting life just happen to her. Now she wanted to make moves, to make waves.

Hell, even if that meant making a fool out of herself.

"No, no." Amelia pursed her lips amusedly. "Admit it."

"Fine!" Cat cried. "Okay, I *was* thinking about Matt. But...but, I was also thinking about you." Which was the partly true aspect of this whole thing. "Because yes, I do think he'd do wonders for your wardrobe."

"Guess it's a better idea than breaking a window in your apartment."

Cat's eyes narrowed.

"Or, I don't know, deciding to re-tile the bathroom by yourself."

"Hardy har."

"All right," Amelia said, reading the look on Cat's face accurately. "I'm officially done teasing you."

"I appreciate that."

"And you think Matt'll do this?"

Cat hesitated. Matt had been blatantly reluctant to work on *her* cabinet door. Then again, she'd also seen with her own eyes how much pleasure he'd taken in the project... So yes, maybe it *was* time to take a page out of Birdie's book and give him a right proper shove.

"There's only one way to find out."

Groaning, Amelia eyed the wine. "So, you haven't even asked him yet?"

"No, I thought I'd wait to make sure you were on board."

"And if he says no?"

"Well," Cat shrugged, a smile playing at the corners of her mouth. "It's far and away a low priority for you right now, anyway."

"Brat."

"But you'll consider it?"

"Depending on the price..." Amelia hedged, "yes, I'll consider it."

"That's all I needed to hear," Cat insisted. Clapping her hands together, she nodded toward Amelia's office. "Now, go grab your coat."

"My what?"

But Cat was already heading for the front door. "It's a bit chilly outside."

"You're going to ask him now?"

At the words, Cat stopped. Looking over her shoulder, she smiled sweetly. "No. *We're* going to ask him now. Hurry up."

"I knew it," Amelia muttered, trailing after her. "I should have insisted on opening that bottle of wine when I had the chance."

"We'll have it in celebration."

... °●°● ...

Within minutes, Cat and Amelia arrived at the hardware store. Though her stomach knotted instinctively—what if he wasn't there again?—Cat quickly staunched the rise of panic. Because she hadn't wanted to sound like a total nutcase, she hadn't admitted to Amelia that she'd driven past the hardware store on her way to that woman's studio and, as she'd crawled oh-so-slowly by, she'd spied Matt's dark blue truck parked in the back alleyway.

The odds that he'd have left seemed slim to none.

And if he had? Well, there was always tomorrow.

Luckily, the short worry was swiftly put to rest. Amelia and Cat had no sooner stepped through the doorway when they spotted him, standing as usual at the front register, his hands shuffling through receipt paper as he organized the cash drawer.

Lifting his head automatically at the sound of their approach, Matt's professional mask of mingled welcome and interest eclipsed at the sight of Cat. Instead, a flash of amusement settled across his lips, his right eyebrow arching richly. Crossing his arms as he leaned over the counter, he stared her down good-naturedly. "All right," he drawled, "what'd you break this time?"

Cat smirked. "Funny man," she returned dryly.

"Hi, you must be Matt," Amelia said, stepping forward. Stretching out one slim hand, she smiled with warmth as she approached him.

"Guilty," he assured her. As his hand engulfed hers, Cat watched a slow smile break across his face. "Nice to meet you...?"

"Amelia Kelley." Laughing softly, Amelia complimented these words by effortlessly tossing her long wealth of hair over one shoulder.

Cat watched enviously as Matt's eyes followed the artless yet graceful motion.

"And," Amelia admitted, slanting her body toward the cash register as she lowered her voice in confession: "I'm very much afraid that the reason we're here has to do with me."

"I see." Dropping his hand back down to the counter, Matt switched his gaze back to Cat. Unlike Amelia, she was still standing beside the doorway. His lips twitched when his eyes glanced off hers. "Still, Cat's with you so I'm guessing she has *something* to do with your visit tonight."

Amelia laughed. Again. The sound held the slightest tinkle; Cat scowled at the delightful tone. "Something all right."

Blowing out a breath, Cat realized that this was probably the opening she needed. She should have been grateful to Amelia for so easily steering the conversation in this tract. Letting her gaze settle over her friend—one hip leaning against the counter now, her arms folded elegantly across her waist—Cat couldn't muster up the genuine rush of gratitude for the offering.

"Yes, actually..." at the sudden inclusion of Cat's voice, Matt's gaze riveted to her once more. "Well, see the thing is..." her lips mashing together, the words clogged in Cat's throat.

In retaliation, Matt's eyebrows only rose. He nodded. "Spit it out."

"Well...then don't get mad."

Matt's eyes narrowed. Standing upright, he pursed his lips. "That's hardly an inviting introduction."

"I told you, you need to work on that," Amelia commented, turning her head toward Cat too.

"Amelia is new to our town."

"Welcome," Matt said, glancing back toward Amelia.

Cat raised her voice, urging his attention back on her. Amelia had had more than her share of it up to now. "And she just opened up a new photography studio."

Matt nodded. Cat was pleased to see the indifference in his response. "Congratulations."

"But...but, well, she has this clunky old wardrobe that she uses for some of her equipment. And, well, you know how it is when you first start out. It's very costly—"

Matt was fully focused on Cat now. It was almost a relief, despite the overt suspicion staring back at her. "Yeah?" The word was said softly. Too softly.

Cat's fingers fidgeted tellingly down at her sides. "Yeah. And she needs a custom-made cabinet. Something that can hold all of her...stuff." Her voice petered out on the last word of her admittedly lame pitch. She wasn't explaining this with much pomp and circumstance.

"Which means I have excess props currently cluttering my floor space," Amelia finished gamely.

With her gaze cast down at her shoes, Cat couldn't see the expression on her friend's face, but she could practically hear the beseeching look in her large, almond-shaped eyes.

It was becoming all too clear to Cat that she should have left Amelia at the studio.

Matt's voice was polished, ready with an answer. "I've got some great catalogs for custom woodworkers. I can grab them for you."

"I saw what you did with Cat's door."

Matt stopped mid-motion. Cat's eyes snapped wide at the words. It was a lie. Amelia hadn't yet seen Cat's newly-finished cabinet.

Matt cleared his throat. Cat could feel the heat of his gaze settling on her averted features. "That was a one-time thing."

"That's a shame," Amelia said. "It was beautiful craftsmanship."

Matt made a sound in his throat. "Hardly."

Without meaning to, Cat's head rose, her eyes clashing with the muted anger in Matt's. Before she could offer a rebuttal to this piece of flippancy, however, Amelia's voice rang out again.

"Simple, elegant lines," the brunette amended. Cat had to hand it to her, the woman could lie like a professional. Those had been the words Cat had used when she'd described the completed project to Amelia.

"Yeah, well, as I said to Cat, it was an easy design."

"So is mine." Another lie. On the drive over, Amelia had admitted to Cat she didn't even know what she wanted in a wardrobe.

Standing back, watching them, Cat felt like an unnecessary addition to this conversation. Amelia didn't need her help cajoling Matt. She was doing all the work by herself.

"I don't know what Cat told you, but I don't actually—"

"No, no, Cat was very clear about that. That you'd done her a special favor, that it wasn't something you did on the regular. Still, I was hoping..." sighing a bit dramatically for Cat's taste, Amelia gestured emptily. When Matt didn't immediately respond, she dropped her eyelids, peeking up out from under her lashes in mock-defeat. "Well, it was worth asking anyway. You are very talented. And, as a photog, I have an eye for art."

Matt glanced toward Cat. "Laying it on a bit thick," he mused. "Wonder where she got that from?"

Cat's cheeks felt stiff. "Oh, fooey."

"Fooey?"

"Stand there and glower at me for all your worth," Cat snapped, tilting her head at a royal angle. "But you liked working on my cabinet door. I know you did." Thrusting a finger at his skeptical expression, she nodded. "I saw you. You were having fun."

"So, this *was* your idea," Matt concluded, his fingers gesturing between the two of them.

Amelia grimaced.

Cat only stood up straighter. "Of course it was my idea!"

Matt shook his head. "I knew you and Birdie were spending too much time together."

"Shove it, Matt. You know you love this kind of stuff."

"I never denied that."

"Actions over words, bud."

"I'm not even sure what that means," Matt returned with exasperation. Rounding the counter, he advanced toward her.

Cat refused to back down. If she'd thought she'd look half as good as Amelia had when she'd done it, she'd have whipped her own head of hair over her shoulder. Instead, she smiled icily. "If you love it, then why say no?"

Out of the corner of her eye, she saw Amelia looking at her—her head cocked a little confusedly to the side, her eyes wary.

Okay, sure. Cat was kind of being an ass. It probably wasn't a recommended negotiating tactic—especially when you're on the wrong side of the power exchange. But hell, what did it matter, anyway? Amelia didn't require Cat for her charm. Amelia was handling that perfectly on her own.

"For one thing, because I already have a full-time job. No, scratch that," Matt said, taking another step nearer Cat. "I own this place. Full-time hardly covers the sixty-odd hours that I work each week."

Cat let out a weary breath. "No, I know, I know—"

"And I've already told you, I'm not a professional."

"Amelia knows that. She's still here—"

"Yeah, to commission a piece for her very *professional* business," Matt returned.

"Oh, please," Cat said because she couldn't think of anything wittier to say. "You're just looking for excuses now."

"And as for your free time," Amelia said, her voice piping in to distract them from their arguing. Startled, Matt stopped to look back at her. "I don't have any set deadline for completing this." She smiled readily. "I already have one right now. It works for the interim. You could complete this project on your timeline."

"Aha!" Cat cried, mostly because she wanted Matt's eyes back on her. Or more aptly, she just wanted them off Amelia. Part of her hated the jealous hole spewing in her stomach, chewing away at all her rational parts, which were assuring her that Amelia would never try to catch Matt's eye, that she knew how Cat felt…but the insecure voice in her head kept noticing how Amelia's eyes flirted with Matt, how her body seemed to be ever-leaning in his direction, how her voice had shifted, catching a huskier tone than normal.

Turning back to Cat, Matt raised his eyebrow.

"So really? What's stopping you now?"

Matt sighed slowly, hesitantly.

Cat bit back a smile at the telling sound, at the look stamped across his face now. He was waffling. She could see it in the clench and release of the muscles in his jaw. She spotted it in the tiny shift of his posture, the loosening of his shoulders.

As if on cue, Matt angled his body back toward Amelia. Lifting his hands, he only proceeded to drop them back down at his sides. He sighed. Again. "You have a design in mind?"

"Well, I'm sure I'd love your input on that," she returned breezily.

"And if you hate the finished product?" he challenged her.

Cat's eyelids flinched at the words. An eruption of irritation bit at her. Why was he always so damned concerned about that question? She knew him well enough to know that that was what really held him back. The fear of failure.

"I sincerely doubt things will come to that," Amelia assured him. "Not from what I've seen. But, if it does, I'll buy it anyway."

"Okay."

"Okay?" This came from Cat. She smiled teasingly. His reticent agreement was almost becoming predicable. "Okay *what*?"

Matt shoved his hands into the front pockets of his jeans. Rocking back on his heels, he took his time answering. "Yeah. I'll do it."

"Well, hot damn!" Looking down at her wrist as if she wore a watch, Cat nodded in mock solemnity. "And right on time too."

"Stuff it, Cryer."

"Thank you," Amelia said. Stepping forward, she touched Matt lightly on his forearm. "I really appreciate this."

"Yeah, no sweat."

Tilting her head to one side, Amelia pursed her lips. "If you say so."

Taking his right hand out of his pocket, Matt flicked his eyes to the wristwatch he actually wore. "Okay. Let me lock the doors and we can discuss some details."

"Lock the…" Cat ate the rest of her words at Matt's sardonic look. Walking past her, he produced a key she hadn't seen in his hand earlier and turned the crash-bar on the door, locking customers out.

"We're closed," he announced to no one in particular.

"Right. Of course."

"Listen," Amelia said, shooting Cat a warning glance. "We don't have to do this now. We never meant to keep you…"

Matt lifted an eyebrow, his gaze shifting from Amelia to Cat. "I was planning to do some paperwork anyway. It's as good a time as any."

"Great," Cat said, overriding Amelia's obvious anxiety at their newfound situation. "Now is good for us too." With an empathic look, Cat silenced Amelia when it was clear that woman was on the verge of speaking.

"Okay. Let's go." Spinning on his heels, Matt didn't wait for further confirmation. He simply marched down one of the aisles and toward the back of the building, his boots ringing sharply against the vinyl tiling.

CHAPTER TWENTY

Sharing slightly bemused glances, the women moved to follow after Matt's quickly receding form. Just as he had with Cat, his stride led them to the Employees Only door located on the rear wall of the main store. As he pulled it open, Amelia's fingernails bit viciously into Cat's arms. "We don't have a design, Cat," she hissed into her ear as they exited the front of the hardware store.

"Thank you," Cat returned, tugging her arm free. "I'm well aware of that fact."

"Matt's going to back out if we bumble around like idiots," Amelia insisted.

"Umm, when have we stopped doing that?" Cat volleyed as they walked down the cold cement flooring of the back storage space. She threw Amelia a confident smile that she was far from feeling. Amelia was right. If Matt caught one whiff of duplicity, he'd probably nix the whole thing. And there went her last chance. "Listen, it's all good. We'll wing it."

"You mean *I'll* wing it?"

"What was that?" Half turning in their direction, Matt looked over his shoulder at them.

Amelia. "Nothing!"

Cat. "Actually," she sighed. "Amelia's having a design meltdown over here."

"I am not!"

"Changing your mind?" Matt's voice was silky, carefully disguised to show no trace of emotion as he came to a halt, stalling halfway down the row of household appliances stacked up on either side of the walkway.

"Not about hiring you," Amelia assured him. "I just, I want to make sure the design is perfect." She pouted prettily up at him. "I'm one of those obnoxious people who can never make up their mind."

Cat's eyes narrowed. Amelia was good on her feet.

"That's where we come in," Cat said with an edge in her voice. Her eyes raked over Matt's expression. It was unbelievable that he wouldn't respond to beautiful, playful Amelia. In comparison, Cat felt like a wet blanket.

Still, with a shooing motion, she urged Matt forward. "Lead on."

Nodding slowly, Matt did as Cat requested. Bringing them out to the loading dock, he gestured toward his small woodworking space. "Okay," he said, shifting toward Amelia. "Why don't you start with what you're thinking?"

Going to lean up against the utility sink set up on the far wall, Cat crossed her arms over her chest as Amelia obliged him, her voice quick and impulsive as she pretended to possess a list of demands.

It was a terrible thing she'd asked Amelia to do, and yet, watching Amelia's face flush with animation, Cat didn't feel particularly apologetic. For one thing, Amelia didn't appear to be having too tough of a time. Nor did her conversational skills seem to be lacking.

Narrowing her eyes, Cat watched as the other woman talked— her long, elegant fingers at once splaying wide and then shifting to show parallel lines, and then fluttering out to her sides with indecision and guile. Her full lips, a natural red color which Cat had never thought to envy before, were on full display: they pouted, smirked, and laughed up at Matthew's absorbed face.

And he *was* absorbed. Shifting to take in his expression, Cat watched him standing beside his table saw, his hands blindly writing down keywords from Amelia's implausible description, his eyes frequently glancing up to survey her movements, his head nodding now and then, his voice interrupting her occasionally for clarification or to laugh at something particularly funny that she'd said.

He chuckled a lot.

"...and I have a couple of large, bulky props," Amelia was saying, her voice pulling Cat out of her reverie when she added: "About how large are those, would you say, Cat?"

Cat shrugged indifferently. She pretended not to notice Matt's arched eyebrows at her response.

Amelia, however, didn't seem the least put-off. Tapping a finger against her chin, she seemed to be imaging the items in her mind's eye. Then her hands spread apart again. "The block is about this wide and this tall...I suppose I should have taken measurements, huh?"

Matt grunted. "No big deal. You can do that later. Send them to me when you get 'em. Right now, I'm looking for a general idea."

Cat zoned out again. Her eyes roamed shrewdly over Matt. With his ball cap pulled low over his eyes, she couldn't quite gauge his expression. Standing a little to one side of her, his attention was focused on Amelia.

Fucking Amelia.

Catching herself short on the furious thought, Cat felt vaguely nauseated at the direction of her musings. Okay. Jealousy was one thing and yes, okay, she wasn't sure she'd ever be entirely convinced that Amelia wasn't, indeed, flirting with Matt—not after the show she'd been watching the last fifteen minutes—but still, still...letting that turn her against her friend, well that simply wasn't acceptable.

And it was a little mortifying. To think she'd sunk that low in feminine competition and masculine appreciation. As if she was so shallow and desperate for some man's attention that she'd allow herself to become a walking-talking cliché of catty insecurity?

Blushing at the realization of these baser feelings, Cat lowered her head, her eyes traveling down to her shoes which were crossed at the ankles as she tried to swallow the crazed side of herself that seemed to have taken over her identity ever since she'd walked into the hardware store.

"...Cat? Ah, Cat?"

At the sound of Matt's voice calling out her name, Cat's eyes jerked up...directly into two pairs of amused faces.

Amelia was biting back a smile.

Matt was once again raising that infernal eyebrow.

Well, great.

"Fall asleep over there?" Amelia teased.

"Sorry," Cat mumbled, but her eyes avoided Amelia's playful gaze. Guilt refused to allow her the option of friendly banter. Instead, she cleared her throat, her fingers drumming a quiet tattoo against the sides of her jean-clad thighs. "Zoning out a bit."

"Woodworking isn't her thing," Matt assured Amelia.

She giggled. "Color me surprised."

"Why, because you love it so much?" Cat snapped. She regretted the words immediately. For one thing, they sounded bitchy and for another, Amelia's head flew back in hot reaction.

But really, did the woman *have* to giggle at every damn word Matt said?

"Ah, okay," Matt said, jumping into the fray of fissured silence. His voice was smooth in its redirection: "I think I've got everything I need tonight." He tapped his pencil against the notepad in his hand. "I'll, uh, I'll draw up a quick sketch and email it to you in the next couple of days, and we'll go from there. In the meantime, get those measurements for me, huh?"

Amelia nodded distractedly her eyes steady on Cat. "Okay. Yeah, that sounds good." Holding out her hand, but a bit more stiffly this time, she smiled. "Again, thank you. I'm so grateful for this—and so excited."

Matt took her hand. "Yeah," he said, "no problem." But there was a heaviness, a stiltedness to every party in the room now.

"Okay." Pulling at the ends of her coat, Amelia made an odd movement. "Well, we should probably get going, huh?" Without waiting for a response from Cat, however, Amelia spun around her feet taking her determinedly back down the long warehouse toward the door which led to the storefront. Her shoulders were set at a stiff, harsh angle. The length of her strides bespoke of her rush and insistent urge to leave.

Well, fine. Cat didn't personally care if Amelia was in a flying rage. Pushing herself off the table, she mumbled a quick goodbye to Matt, her chin tucked under the collar of her jacket, her eyes hard when they glinted over his, her smile little more than a gnash of teeth as she uttered a dry: "See ya later" before shifting in the direction of Amelia's quickly retreating shadow.

She'd barely taken two steps when his voice called out.

"Whoa. Cat, wait up a minute."

"Can't," she called over her shoulder, not even bothering to glance behind her. Amelia had already slipped through the doorway and out onto the main floor. "Amelia's waiting for—oh!" Swinging forcefully, almost roughly, back around by the sudden grip of fingers against her wrist, Cat found herself staring up into Matt's shadowed face. Towering over her, he stared down into her shocked countenance, his eyes falling to her slightly parted lips.

Then he smiled, his gaze flicking back up to her guarded eyes. His own held a look of something predatory and dangerous.

"Jealous, Cat?"

It was having it put out there like that, so blatant and clear. Opening her mouth in embarrassed surprise (because, even though she was well-aware that she had been jealous, she hadn't expected him to call her out on it), Cat choked on her reply: "What? N-no, of course not."

"No?" Matt asked, clicking his tongue. "Want to try that again?"

"God. Get over yourself," Cat muttered, tugging at her arm. In response, he only tightened his hold.

"I should stop teasing you, I know," Matt said, but whatever response Cat might have had to that blatant form of conceitedness, he forestalled when his head bent suddenly over hers, his mouth coming down to whisper over her trembling lips. Almost but not quite touching.... "But you make it so damn tempting."

"I don't know what you're talking about," Cat breathed back, her words uneven, her mouth quivering the tiniest bit, lost somewhere between disbelief and utter anticipation; his lips still hovered over hers, tantalizingly close. So close she could almost feel the impression of them...just one last breath away.

"Pouting in the corner," he said, his fingers releasing her wrist. Raising his other hand, both came up to skim over her arms.

Denial was a waste of time. And besides, though Cat wasn't particularly proud of her behavior from minutes ago, she was also unwilling to rewrite history for the sake of her vanity. "I didn't think you'd notice," she confessed, her chest rising sharply when the pads of his thumbs pressed down against the inside juncture of her elbows.

"Life's a lot easier when you stop overthinking everything," Matt assured her, his lips brushing—just barely—over hers with the words.

"So they say," Cat managed back.

"Yeah, I'm getting the feeling that nothing is ever the easy way with you. Nothing is ever uncontrolled," he challenged, the last words passing into her mouth as his lips pressed fully over hers, the action effectively swallowing back any answer she may have come up with.

At the first touch, Cat felt herself surrender, her lips falling open, welcoming, inviting the entrance of his tongue. Responsive now as she'd been stoic minutes earlier, Cat let her head fall back at the thrust and insistence of his ministrations, her hands coming to rest against his upper arms, her fingers curling over the bunched muscles coiled there, her legs tangling inside the length of his.

Her senses were alive to the slight buzz of the fluorescent bulbs overhead, her skin smothered by the soft cotton of his shirt, the scrap of his calloused fingers as he brought his hands upward to cup the sides of her face. She shivered.

"Matt..." she breathed when his teeth found her lips, nibbling against them.

"Yes?"

She moaned. "Don't-don't stop."

"'Atta girl," he whispered back before his lips claimed hers again, swallowing the whimpered sigh of her satisfaction.

The minty taste of his mouth overwhelmed her, his lips forming to the contours of hers in a devouring kiss that knocked her breathless. Clutching at his shoulders with the last of her strength, Cat allowed herself to sink into the hot, searing sensations clamoring for attention as his hands moved again, this time to press against her back, bringing her closer into the curve of his body.

"Cat? Cat, are you still back here...?" At the sudden sound of Amelia's voice, Cat felt the shattering return of reality. She hadn't heard the back door reopen, but the echo of Amelia's booted feet against cement flooring was not be ignored.

"Dammit," she heard herself whisper when Matt lifted his head, his brown eyes dark as they stared down at her flushed face.

Pressing her legs straight even as Matt gently set her away from his body, Cat tried to infuse a bit of levity into her voice as she called out: "Ah, yeah. Over here." Her sense were reeling, racing though, her body swaying unconsciously toward Matt as she stared blankly up at him.

"Steady as she goes," he said, chuckling softly.

But before Cat could respond Amelia's voice called out again. "Oh, thank goodness," she said, her slim form finally coming into view as she advanced into the back area of the warehouse again.

By now, Cat had pulled herself up to her tallest height, her body free from the tantalizing proximity of Matt, who'd taken a half-step backward in anticipation of Amelia's entrance.

That woman, apparently finding nothing amiss about Cat's ruffled appearance or Matt's arms-crossed posture, only laid a hand on her chest when her wary eyes connected with Cat. "I thought I'd lost you," she joked, laughing weakly.

"N-not. No." Cat's brain was too sluggish, her lips too delightfully stunned to summon any further response.

"Sorry we kept you waiting," Matt said, inserting himself in the curt silence following Cat's response. "I was asking Cat how the kitchen turned out."

Cat peeked up at him. A little of the hurt she'd tried to bury resurfaced at the words, the lie. "A little late in the game to be asking though."

Matt only shrugged, his usual mask of indifference settling casually over his person. "I figured it must have gone well," he argued, "otherwise I'd have known."

Cat glowered, but she couldn't deny the truth in those words. "It looks great. Better than before." Still, she felt the slight sting of his lacking interest.

"I'm not surprised," Matt said. Glancing over at Amelia, he smiled charmingly. "I've never met a woman who took the adage to return things to their owner in better condition than before they found them more seriously than our Cat."

Our Cat. Mentally throttling the rise of reaction those words inspired, Cat outright refused to read anything in that statement. Regardless of that, her body hummed at the quiet admission.

Amelia shook her head, her gaze also on Cat—and there was a hesitant, almost guilty expression on her face. "Yeah. I'm learning that."

Cat didn't respond to either of them.

"Well, all right," Amelia said as the return of the earlier stiltedness settled once more upon the group. "Are we ready to go?"

"Yes. Yeah." Cat nodded quickly, her eyes skimming up at Matt as she uttered her last note of thanks.

"Yes," Amelia seconded, taking this as her cue. "Thanks again." Offering him a slight wave, she turned around once more, her steps again leading her toward the doorway separating them from the hardware store—in seconds, they heard the unmistakable sound of her exit as Amelia passed over the threshold, the door banging resoundingly closed behind her.

"Well, I should probably," hitching a thumb over her shoulder, Cat took a pointed step backward, "follow after her this time."

Still, there was a hesitation in her retreat.

Matt nodded. "Yeah, I suppose so."

Cat turned around. "Bye."

"Cat?"

Pausing, her stomach twisting, pinching at the casual call, Cat forced herself not to overreact. As such, she didn't turn around, merely lobbed over one shoulder. "Yeah?"

"What are you doing tomorrow?"

Much as he'd known she would, at that, Cat whirled to face him. "To-tomorrow?"

Matt smirked. "I'm going to work on the design for Amelia's cabinet."

"Okay?"

"Want to help?"

"Me?" Cat stuttered. "Shouldn't you be asking Amelia that question?" She hated the very thought of that idea.

"I already did," he said, his lips curving upward at some private joke. "'Bout five minutes ago." He gestured toward the table saw. "That's sort of what we were talking about."

"Oh, right."

His lips twitched, his arms uncrossing to dive into the front pockets of his jeans. "Besides, I got the impression she didn't know what she wanted."

That was true enough. "Well, yeah, I guess…"

"And isn't that why you're *really* here?" Matt asked, that hateful grin spreading across his face.

Cat drew in a breath. "Excuse me?"

"Oh, it was an excuse, all right."

Cat stared at him, bereft of words.

Matt took a single step toward her. "I know a bluff when I hear one. The design concept Amelia described to me was nothing short of utter nonsense."

"Well, she's not a carpenter…"

But Matt wasn't buying it. Worse, he'd obviously seen right through their subterfuge. "She *does* need a new wardrobe," Cat confessed, giving up the game both swiftly and baldly.

Matt inclined his head. "So, I'll see you tomorrow?"

"You really want my help?"

He grinned. "Wasn't that part of the plan, all along?"

Cat frowned. "You can be quite conceited, you know that?"

"I'd like to get started on the early side" was all he said in answer.

Despite herself, Cat heard the beginnings of a laugh bubble up inside her throat. "What time?"

"Eight."

"Anything I should bring with me?"

Matt's eyes darkened, his gaze sweeping up and down her body, assessing, gauging. "Nothing you don't mind getting some sawdust on."

Before Cat could stutter out a response, he winked.

CHAPTER TWENTY-ONE

Walking the length of the hardware store, her steps hurried, Cat thought only of her impending exit. She needed a breath; she needed to escape from this place to unpack what had just happened with Matt. Additionally, she was aware that, for the second time in as many attempts, Amelia had been left waiting for Cat. Then again, Cat wasn't sure she cared that much about the latter consideration.

Brushing through the front door of McBoy's Hardware Store and outside, Cat felt another nip of guilt squeeze rebelliously past her defenses. Huddled against the wind, Amelia was bouncing from foot to foot, her arms crossed snugly over her chest to ward off the chill of the night as she stood beside Cat's locked car.

"Sorry about that," Cat said, her voice clipped as she scurried over. With a quick click of her finger on the key fob, she unlocked both doors.

Amelia brushed her words aside. "No, that's fine. It's totally…" stalling out when she realized that Cat wasn't listening to her, that she hadn't even waited for her to finish speaking before getting into the driver's seat, Amelia swallowed the last of her words. Clamoring inside, she barely snapped her seatbelt in place when Cat was pulling off the curb.

For a moment, silence descended. A thick, harsh silence filled with all the words left unsaid.

"I'm sorry," Amelia said pleadingly, her eyes raking over the taut lines of Cat's face. "Look, I'm so sorry." Throwing out her arms in surrender, she shook her head. "I went too far. I see that now. Well, actually, I saw that inside the hardware store," she muttered inanely, laughing humorlessly to herself.

"Went too far?" Cat asked despite herself, her gaze shifting quickly to Amelia's contrite countenance. "What does that mean?"

"Flirting with Matt—"

"You *were* flirting with him then?" Cat cried incredulously, her hands thumping against the steering wheel. "What the hell, Amelia!"

"No, wait," she insisted, "let me explain."

"Explain? Explain what, how you were going to slide right in and throw your gorgeous face and rocking bod in his face, even though you *knew…*"

"Well, at least I got a reaction out of you." Amelia wiggled her eyebrows.

"No, no. Don't be cute," Cat warned, throwing her left blinker on with enough force to break the switch.

"Fine," Amelia returned, sinking into her seat. "But at least understand that I did it for you."

Cat laughed. "For me?"

"Yes. From the moment we walked into the hardware store, you got all weird."

"I did not," Cat returned, slowing the car as they came upon Amelia's street.

"Yes, you did. You were stilted and stiff and kind of…I don't know, you acted like you didn't even want to be there. You just stood by the door. And when you bothered to join the conversation, you were snappish."

"Hah!"

"It's true," Amelia maintained, reaching out to lay a hand on Cat's shoulder. "And so, I thought…maybe a little competition would, I don't know, make you try a little harder." Amelia laughed gently. "Only, I went too far."

Cat felt her stomach loosen. "Really?"

"Come on Cat, you honestly think I'd do something like that? Compete for the guy you like?"

Cat heard the hurt in Amelia's voice. Shame snipped at her sides. "No, I don't think you'd do that. That's why I was so surprised earlier…"

"Surprised? Try homicidal."

"Oh, whatever."

"I promise, I thought it'd help. And if that doesn't assure you, perhaps this will." Amelia took a deep breath. "I'm gay."

Cat's head whipped around. "You're—"

"Gay."

"Gay." Cat chewed on the side of her lip. "I didn't know that."

Amelia laughed but there was a shakiness to the quality. "Yeah, well, it's not something I tend to broadcast."

"Clearly."

"And, you know, when you become friends with a gorgeous single woman it can become sort of…difficult to navigate that conversation."

Cat chuckled. "You think I'm gorgeous?"

"Not the point."

Cat sobered up. "You thought I'd worry that you would hit on me?"

"It's happened before."

"I'm sorry."

Amelia shrugged. "I promise, when it comes to Matt you have nothing to worry about." She wrinkled her nose. "You too. Lesbians can be just friends with other women. I hope that doesn't change—"

"My God, don't be ridiculous," Cat swore, cutting Amelia off at the pass. "Of course, I know that! And it changes nothing between us."

"Okay. Good."

Cat chuckled. "If only I'd known this information half an hour ago."

"Yeah," Amelia agreed. "Then again, that knowledge would have surely loosened the effect of what I was trying to achieve in there." She smiled ruefully across the center console. "I just wanted you to stop acting like…"

"Like a freak?"

"You need to believe in your ability to attract him."

"Easier said than done."

"Yeah, I saw that. It was like you gave up before you even tried."

Cat nodded grimly.

Amelia grinned. "Although…" she let her teeth raze over her bottom lip as Cat pulled up to Amelia's studio. "Then again, maybe it's a good thing I went too far. It worked."

Cat cleared her throat, averted her gaze.

Amelia pressed. "What kept you and Matt so long when I left you two alone?"

"Matt told you…"

"He told me a pack of lies."

Cat blushed. "Yeah, okay. It worked."

"I'm glad." Once again, Amelia let her hand reach out to touch Cat's shoulder. It was considerably less tense than minutes ago. "Are *we* good?"

Cat placed her left hand on top of Amelia's. "We're good. And…I'm sorry. I acted like a jealous child."

"You thought I was being a bad friend."

"I should have known better."

Amelia didn't comment on this directly. "Look, since you don't hate me anymore, there's still a couple bottles of wine inside…?"

Unbuckling her seatbelt, Cat grinned. "I could use a glass."

"Agreed." Reaching for the door handle, Amelia flashed Cat a naughty grin. "I could also use a few details."

Cat forced herself not to react.

In retaliation, Amelia wiggled her eyebrows again. "You and Matt?"

Cat laughed then. "Wine first."

"Then spill."

"Deal."

… °•°• …

"Knock, knock." Poking her head inside the back door of the hardware store the next morning, Cat squinted into the dim lighting. Biting back the eagerness zipping up and down her spine, she was relatively pleased with the casual tone of her voice.

"Over here," she heard from the general direction of Matt's workshop.

Opening the door fully, she walked inside. The heels of her short brown boots clipped a pleasant echo in the large building. As she approached Matt, Cat took a moment to silently congratulate herself on her outfit: wearing a pair of tight-fitting blue jeans with a red chambray shirt, the latter both feminine but also loose-fitting and offering just a tease of the curves underneath, she looked both stylish but laid-back. Even better, she nicely complimented his long-sleeved cotton shirt and khaki pants.

"Okay, boss," she said, rubbing her hands together as she reached Matt's woodworking table, a smile lighting up the whole of her face. Her expression was as telling as it was artless.

Matt, on the other hand, wore an expression of intense concentration. Sitting on an old barstool, he stared down at a piece of drafting paper spread out on the table before him, a pencil in his mouth. Pulled up beside him was another chair—this one advertising a local brewery. Dropping her purse on the short counter running alongside the utility sink on the back wall, Cat plopped down on the open stool.

"Is this it?" she asked as she stared down at the large scroll of paper laid out on the table, her eyes taking in the intricate lines he'd already sketched into place. She'd never thought to consider the amount of work that went into designing and building a piece of furniture, but as she glanced down at the blueprint, she swallowed uneasily. She'd never considered what she'd been asking him to do—and all so that she'd have an excuse to see him again.

Which seemed all the more pathetic given the realization that he had done nothing to orchestra seeing *her* again.

Thrusting the thought away, Cat reminded herself that, in his own way, Matt had made his interest in her known too.

Just. You know....

After she made the effort to be available.

Frowning, she brought her attention back to the task at hand. Leaning over the table, she looked at the design. Her eyes widened. "Wow. You're a beautiful drawer."

Once the words had been spoken, Cat felt her nose crinkle. It seemed like a kind of stupid thing to say. Shifting her gaze to Matt's, she saw that he thought so too.

"Yeah, well, it sort of goes with the territory."

"To be good with wood it's only natural that someone is good with a pencil?" Cat wasn't sure she was buying that.

Matt shrugged. "Well, maybe not natural, but like any muscle, the more you use it..."

Cat let it go. He wasn't interested in being complimented. Still, she was smart enough to know, and bad enough an artist to realize that at least part of what he possessed was innate, raw talent. "How long did this take?"

Matt shrugged. "Not that long."

Strumming her fingers against the tops of her thighs, Cat waited for Matt to expand on that. When he didn't, his eyes instead going back to the drawing in front of him, his mouth tightening at what he saw, she rolled her eyes. "Has anyone ever told you you're a fantastic conversationalist?"

"Huh?"

"I mean, really Matt, we're here to work and if you don't shut up this very instant..." Cat continued, smiling gently at him when he raised his head with slight impatience.

"Bored already?"

"Well," Cat considered, dropping her eyes back down to the drafting paper. "I'm not sure what I'm looking at here, exactly. Care to explain what I'm supposed to be doing?"

Matt made a sound in his throat. Then his finger lifted, gesturing toward the image. "I'm mapping this out. What are your thoughts?"

"Is it to size?" Cat asked inanely, turning her head this way and that. "And this is the top, correct?"

"I'd hardly be looking at it upside down, would I?"

Cat pursed her lips in a prissy fashion. "Well, I don't suppose I'd know."

"Yes, Cat, this is the top."

She ran her finger over the detailing of the arched door, with its grooved lines. "It's very...pretty." Acknowledging that this was perhaps not all that helpful, she shrugged: "I mean, honestly, it looks almost old, with the scrolled lines and the curved dimensions in the wood."

Matt squinted. "Is it too much?"

"No!" At the quick response, Cat only shook her head vehemently. "I love it. I mean...it looks beautiful. A conversation piece."

"How about the size?" he asked, his hands gesturing toward a line in the floor plan representing the back wall of Amelia's studio. "She sent me measurements of the studio this morning. This wardrobe is considerably bigger than the piece that's currently in there..."

Bending to the task, Cat considered the image. "I'm not sure. Probably, this would be a better question to ask Amelia."

"I intend to."

Cat raised her head confusedly. "Then why ask me...?"

Matt smiled. "You asked for something to do. All input is helpful at this stage."

"And you think I'm the person to offer it? I know next to nothing about photography," Cat returned, lifting her head to look at him. For the first time since they'd met, Cat felt like she had the upper hand. The excuse was weak. If he wanted input, he'd ask someone who knew something about this kind of thing.

"I think this whole thing was *your* idea," Matt reminded her.

"Well, sure, I already owned that..."

"As I said yesterday, I think you wanted to be here."

"So I could be on the design team?"

"No," Matt returned, his hand reaching up to turn Cat's head toward him. "For this," he whispered, leaning forward until his lips brushed against hers. Feeling her stomach muscles clench at the surprising speed of his movement, Cat's lips trembled under the weight of his.

Pulling back a hair, Matt's brown eyes looked into hers. "Or am I wrong?"

"No," Cat admitted, her breath coming in soft gasps. He was so close to her. Right there. "No, you aren't wrong...."

Sitting in her apartment later that evening, Cat's stomach was still knotting up in memory of that afternoon. Throwing her pajama-clad legs up on top of her coffee table, she let her eyes wander down to her lap. They hadn't managed to get in much more work in on Amelia's wardrobe that morning. As she recalled, by the time she'd left, the drafting paper had floated unnoticed down onto the floor.

What had started as a simple kiss of exploration had quickly ignited. Flooded with the newfound confidence that despite his sometimes-deadpan expression, Matt felt something for her too, Cat had sunk into their second kiss, her arms winding around his neck, her fingers playing with the short hairs there.

Hearing his muffled groan, she'd slipped off her barstool, her feet bringing her inside his splayed legs. Letting one hand move from his neck to the side of his face, her fingers had rubbed against the stubble of his unshaven face.

"God, Cat," he'd groaned, and that's when she had been lifted unceremoniously off the floor. In one smooth movement, Matt stood up, his hands grabbing the backs of her upper thighs to twine them around his waist.

Moaning at the sensation—the rough feel of his jeans, the soft cotton of his shirt pressed tightly against her chest, Cat didn't stop to think. She only opened her mouth wider, her lips melding with his.

When he'd moved, she hadn't thought to wonder where he was going, had only accepted the feel of the Formica countertop when she'd been set upon it, her right thigh nudged up beside the industrial sink. When she'd felt his fingers on her waist, Cat only leaned farther into the sensations crowding her senses, the heat pooling low in her belly. Her body reacted visibly to the feel of his hands sliding up and down her ribcage, her breath shaking when they finally lifted just a little bit higher.

"Cat?" Matt asked, his voice questioning, his thumb toying meaningfully with the top button of her shirt.

In answer, Cat offered a whispered plea: "Yes."

Moving confidently, those long-tapered fingers quickly flicked first one and then another of the fastenings free. Moaning, Cat felt the cool air of the warehouse settled over her shoulders and chest—after that, she forgot to notice anything else, her body blindly following his lead.

"Well, he'd been right about one thing," Cat giggled to herself now, her voice breathy even in the memory of it. "I definitely got a little sawdust on me."

She supposed she probably should be over-thinking every detailed moment that had transpired that afternoon, taking apart each and every second, analyzing her response, questioning his, perhaps even worrying over her headlong reactions but instead she was only excited. For tomorrow.

She'd been all but bared to the waist, the only remaining clothing her bra, when Cat had felt Matt slowly end the kiss. Breaking contact, breathing heavily, he'd taken a half-step backward.

Lifting misty eyes in his direction, her mouth parted, Cat had watched him run a shaking hand through his hair. "Matt?"

A rueful smile graced his lips. "Your dangerous."

"You too."

"Yeah." Reaching out, his fingers clamped down against her waist and with an economy owing to his strength, he'd hoisted her up and off the counter and back on her feet. "That's why I think it's time for you to go."

"Go?" Even through the haze of desire, Cat's hands scabbed furiously for her shirt, which he'd grabbed off the counter and was currently holding out for her. Tugging her arm ruthlessly through one sleeve, she felt hot humiliation settle over her skin.

What the hell? He wanted her to leave? *Leave?*

Watching her with patent amusement, and more than just a hint of desire (though she'd been too mortified at the moment to realize it), Matt seemed to sense the direction of her thoughts. "Cat. I'm not about to seduce you in my warehouse."

That had effectively slowed down her hurried, prideful pace. Pausing over a button, Cat had lifted her eyes up to his. "But you do *want* to seduce me?"

Reaching down, Matt's fingers quickly did up the rest of the buttons on her shirt, his pace almost frenzied. "I think that's pretty obvious."

She caught her breath. "When?"

But Matt had only laughed—it had been a big sound, a rough release of pent-up longing. Leaning down, he placed his hands on either side of her upturned face, giving her a quick kiss. "How about dinner first?"

Staring up into his eyes, Cat found herself nodding stupidly. The most contrary feelings bubbled up to vie for attention: regret and frustration that he'd ended things when he had, appreciation that he hadn't let things go too far (and in a warehouse of all places), and pure and unadulterated excitement over his proposal.

He could have done anything he'd wanted to her moments before. She'd not only have let him she'd have eagerly helped him. But he hadn't wanted to do that. Not there. Not so soon. That had to mean something. That had to mean that *she* meant something.

"When?" Cat had asked again, her voice a little husky, a little breathless.

"Tomorrow?"

"Do I really have to go?"

In response, Matt had let his gaze sweep over her disheveled appearance, her hair wild where his fingers had delved into its depths. There had been something so complimentary in the tautening of his features when he'd nodded in affirmative. "If I want to get any work done today."

CHAPTER TWENTY-TWO

Sitting across from Matt the following evening in a trendy bar and grill, Cat settled back against the plush leather back of her chair as the server enquired over Matt's meal. High, arched windows danced around two of the four walls in the otherwise exposed brick building. Dim, amber-lighting set off a quiet, affluent glow against a backdrop of black-tie servers, polished mahogany tables, and an impressive wine and beer list.

Reveling in the moment, Cat recognized an intense desire to slow down time; it had been worth it, all her fumbling, bumbling attempts to get to this point. Even better, the anticipation for it was beginning to fall far shy from the reality.

"...steak, prepared med-rare, please," Cat heard Matt say. Snapping back to attention, she watched idly as the server made a smiling gesture before taking his leave.

Alone for the first time that evening (since they'd driven there separately and the hostess had only just seated them before the server arrived with wine list in hand), Cat tried to swallow past an entirely expected attack of nerves.

"So, how's the—"

"Did you get any—"

At the simultaneously poised questions, both Matt and Cat stopped speaking. Blushing a little, Cat waved Matt onward. "I'm sorry. Go ahead."

"I was just going to ask...we never did get a chance to talk about what happened with the kitchen after last Saturday?"

Cat flapped her wrist dismissively. "It went great. My friend Sam came over to help me finish."

"Sam?"

Cat rather enjoyed the predatory note that slipped into Matt's question. She hadn't done it on purpose, but she relished the split second of victory she received upon acknowledging the very gender-neutral quality of the name.

"*She's* one of my neighbors," Cat said with enough emphasis to show Matt that she'd read his jealously quite well. "We finished up the painting and when everything was dry, bam-boom I threw the doors up together."

Matt chuckled, leaning back in his chair as the server returned with both of their drinks. "Bam-boom, huh?"

Swirling her glass of wine, Cat refused to acknowledge that teasing tone of voice. She shrugged. "Well, it's pretty bam-boom to me now."

"Fair enough."

Taking a healthy drink, Cat mirrored Matt's pose. Lounging into the barrel-chair, she let her arms lay loosely on the curved, wooden rests. "Did you get much done on Amelia's project yesterday?"

A crack of tension spilled across the table at the words. Over the rim of his beer, Matt's eyes crinkled. Then, with slow precision, he took a drink of his dark beer. "You mean after I'd taken care of my biggest distraction?"

Cat giggled. "Is that what I was?"

"Yes. As you well know."

She smirked down at her glass of chardonnay. "Yes, Matt. *After* I left."

"I got through three different mock-ups."

"Three?" She whistled.

Matt shrugged. "Well, since she didn't know what she wanted, I thought it might be best to give her some ideas to play around with."

"Still." Cat whistled. "That must have taken a while."

"Yeah, I suppose."

"How long where you at it?"

Matt seemed somewhat reluctant to answer the question. "I don't know. Eight o'clock maybe."

"Eight o'clock? God, that was…almost twelve hours."

Matt shrugged again. His shoulders seemed a little tense with the action now. "Yeah, well, I sort of lost track of time."

Cat eyes gleamed with amusement.

"What?"

"I don't know," she confessed, her finger playing with the stem of her wine glass. "It just seems…odd."

"That I'd do a thorough job?"

"Oh, of course not," Cat returned, her eyes sparkling at the remark. "Don't be ridiculous. It's just, for a man so staunchly opposed to doing this kind of work, you sure get sucked into it."

Matt shook his head, but there was a gesture of impatience in the action. "It's not that I don't love doing it."

"Well, obviously." Cat's voice couldn't have been drier.

"But, as I've said to you on more than one occasion, I already have a full-time job. More than a full-time job. I can't afford to spread myself too thin. To make a go of something like this I'd need to—"

Raising her hands up in surrender, reading the growl edging into his voice as a signal for retreat, Cat was quick to change tactics. "Okay, okay, I'll shut up now. Still, I don't see why you couldn't pick up a few gigs on the side, when you had the time. Or make a few pieces to sell in your store."

Matt didn't respond directly, instead, all he said was: "I could. Or I could be spending the evening out with a beautiful woman. I think I made a wise choice."

And really, what girl didn't want to hear that? Smirking into her drink, Cat felt her pulse speed up. "The first round goes to you, sir."

Chuckling softly, Matt lifted his drink in salute. "I thought as much."

… °•°• …

"I heard a certain someone went on a date with my grandson yesterday," Birdie announced on Monday evening. Staring with an unusual fixation on her cards, she let the words travel across the Canasta table. Ignite. Settle.

"What? Who?" Erna asked. Leaning so far forward that everyone had a view of her cards, she waited for Birdie to continue.

Groaning silently, Cat prayed the older woman would show some tact. Pulling her own cards up to just under her eyes, she watched as Birdie slowly laid down a meld on her team's board. Then her eyes flicked over to Cat.

"Care to comment, Ms. Cat?"

"You?" Pointing a gnarled finger at Cat, Mary practically shouted the word—which felt a little more like an accusation than a declaration.

Sighing, Cat set her cards down on the table. Unlike Erna, she had the forethought to turn them face-down. Keeping her features composed, Cat wasn't about to spend the evening under interrogation. "We had dinner."

But dammit! Despite her determination otherwise, Cat's mouth moved of its own accord, the shape shifting, melting into a dreamy smile. And her eyes dropped their coolness, falling shyly to the table.

"And?" Harriet asked, elbowing Cat none-to-gently. "How'd it go?"

"It's pretty obvious by her mucky face," Mary said on a snort. "Look at the girl, she's ready to fall off her chair."

"I am not!" Cat said, but the vehemence in her voice gave her away.

"Was he a gentleman, my dear?" Birdie asked, laying a soft hand over Cat's. "Now mind, I don't want the details or anything but..."

"He was a perfect gentleman," Cat assured her, and it was true. After dinner, he'd walked her to her car. Wrapping his arms around her, he'd given her a sweet, soft kiss before asking her if she had any plans for Wednesday evening.

"N-no," she'd told him.

"Good," he'd winked, letting his arms break away from around her shoulders. "Spend it with me?"

"What did you have in mind?"

"I'm not telling yet," he'd whispered. Bending down, he'd given her one final kiss before whispering goodnight.

"See—the girl's gone officially loopy," Mary said, gesturing to Cat's admittedly distracted face. "That's it!" She gave Cat a dark look. "This is the last week I'm going to partner with her."

"*Mary.*"

"At least until she can manage to mention his name without getting that stupid look on her face," Mary said, but there was the smallest inkling of a smile on her face. "She's useless to me now."

"Cut the girl a break," Harriet said, shooting Mary a frown. "Have you seen the boy, lately?" Waving her fingers like a pretend fan in front of her face, Harriet cooed. "My God, he's a hunk."

Cat giggled.

Erna blushed.

Birdie looked smug. "Takes after his grandfather."

"I'd be falling off my chair if that man took me as far as across the street, that's all I'm saying."

"Jesus, Harriet. Keep it in your pants."

"Hush. You know you'd be making googly eyes too."

"I am not making googly eyes," Cat insisted weakly.

"Oh, honey, even a woman with cataracts couldn't mistake that gleam," Harriet assured her.

"Can we just play?"

"*We* can," Mary muttered, "It's you we're worried about."

"And just who brought our team such high scores in the last round when she picked up the pile?" Cat mused.

"Lucky," Mary muttered.

"My foot," Cat returned. But Mary was right. She was holding at least one card in her hand that should have been laid out on their board. She was losing her focus.

"Okay, okay. Another conversation?" Birdie offered, taking pity on Cat. Turning pointedly to Erna, she asked: "Speaking of grandsons, isn't yours in town this week?"

Relieved when Erna promptly responded and the attention was whisked to a new tract, Cat took a steadying breath. She really needed to get her nerves under control.

"Yes. Sweet boy. Lovely to have him here." Erna frowned then. "Though I've hardly been able to see him."

"Grandmothers aren't exactly a high priority on a young man's social calendar."

"It's not that. He's here for work. And his company sure keeps him busy!" Erna shook her head. "Running here and there for one project and then another."

Using the much-needed distraction to reign in her instincts, Cat studied the cards in her hands, strategizing her next move.

"...he was saying something about needing to find a good local printer." Erna laughed. "I told him that the library had a printer for public use, but apparently that's not what he meant. It's for a business conference or something."

"Have him use Paper Makers," Cat murmured absently as she watched Harriet lay down a new meld. Her turn was next.

"What's that, my dear?"

Lifting her head, Cat looked at Erna. "Paper Makers. It's a copy and print shop in town. They do binding, as well. I'm not sure what your grandson needs, of course..."

"Oh." Erna brightened. "I'll let him know about it."

"How do you always know this stuff? All the best people and places to go to for any kind of question or assistance," Birdie mused with a wide-eyed glance. She held up one finger. "There was Jerry Briggs who worked miracles on my car." She lifted another finger. "Then there was that woman you told Harriet about..."

"Donna Larson," Harriet supplied. "Thought I'd never find a good seamstress again. Dying profession."

Cat shrugged. "I don't know. I mean, I have lived here my whole life and—"

Harriet snorted. "Us too, ducks. And we've got a few years on you."

"More than a few," Mary yapped.

"It sort of goes with my job, I guess," Cat amended on a laugh. "Knowing the community, the people."

"You could be a phone operator," Birdie insisted. "Or the yellow pages."

"Now you're just needlessly aging us," Mary muttered.

"I don't know about tha—oh, wait." Turning back to Erna as a new thought occurred to her, Cat interrupted herself. "Is he looking for graphic work too? If so, I'd actually recommend SkyArt. It's down on third avenue. Their team is amazing."

Erna's forehead crinkled. This time, however, her voice carried a hesitant, unknowing tune. "Well, yes...I'm not sure what he's looking for exactly." She chuckled. "Honestly, when he talks about his work it usually goes right over my head."

Cat nodded vaguely, her eyes straying back down to her cards. It was her turn to play.

"Would you...do you think maybe I could give him your number and you could help him?"

"What?" Glancing up, Cat found herself staring into Erna's watery eyes, a glint of tentative hope in that woman's look. "Yeah. Sure."

"Really? I wouldn't want to bother you."

"No problem," Cat assured her. And it wasn't. "Won't take me but a minute to point him in the right direction." And really, anything to keep the conversation off her and Matt (though, while she wouldn't admit to anything so contrary, Cat almost missed hearing the sound of his voice being tossed around, back and forth between the women, missed the tingle of awareness that shot down her spine every time she felt the shape of it trip off her own tongue).

"Thank you, dear."

Mary grunted. "Gets the guy and she's nice to boot. Almost enough to spoil my dinner."

"You say the nicest things," Cat fired back, batting her eyelashes for good measure.

"And I'm only getting warmed up..."

... °•°• ...

Cat exactly wasn't sure when the idea first took root. Perhaps it had been right at the very beginning. In the way Birdie had talked about Matt's passion for woodworking, or maybe it had been in the reluctant but nonetheless genuine enthusiasm he'd shown once he'd started on her cabinet door, or perhaps it was even in the squeal of excitement she'd heard in Amelia's voice when she'd called her office on Tuesday afternoon.

"Goodness but the man's a genius," Amelia cried upon hearing Cat's professional, "Good afternoon, Fireside Credit Union Lending and Loans Department—"

Cat had felt her breath freeze in her chest. "Matt?" Just saying his name was enough to turn her stomach in a frenzy of anticipation.

"Of course, Matt."

"The wardrobe?"

Amelia sighed. "I mean, I was blown away when I got the mock-ups on Sunday. The originality in those designs, I was breathless."

"Probably not speechless though," Cat intoned.

"Never! But girl, I had a time just picking out which one I liked best. I wanted all of them," Amelia continued, her voice picking up pace as her excitement grew. "And then, today, he asked me to stop by and get a look at what he's done so far—to make sure the concept is matching what I had in mind."

"Which would be hard to argue since you never had anything in mind."

"It was gorgeous, Cat," Amelia continued, not paying her friend any notice. "The artwork, the detail. My God—he'd only started on the top rest but…it floored me."

"What were you expecting?" Cat asked. "Utter crap?"

"Honestly? I don't know," Amelia admitted. Through the phone, Cat could just make out the low sound of Amelia's radio playing in the background. "I thought they'd be good and all, but these…"

Cat leaned forward. "Yes?"

"He's got a gift. You were right." Amelia laughed. "Honestly, I only agreed to this so that you could get closer to Matt but now…" she whistled off-pitch, "I'm reaping some serious rewards myself."

"You did that for me?" Cat asked, slightly taken aback though she supposed that she shouldn't have been.

"Well, of course. I got your back, girl."

"And if he had sucked at woodworking?"

Amelia was quiet for a moment. "I doubt it could have been much worse than what's already here. And anyway, you had confidence in him. I trusted you."

Cat felt a peculiar pull on her stomach, a tingling in her nose. Sniffing, she pressed the phone more tightly to her ear. "God, I love you."

"'Bout time you admitted it."

Then again, Cat knew her scheme *definitely* had something to do with the obvious love Matt couldn't hope to disguise when it came to the few projects he begrudgingly took on, almost all of his free time spent in the back of that warehouse, his attention so focused he'd simply lose track of time.

Case in point: when he'd taken her out on Wednesday, he'd stopped in to show her how far he'd come on the wardrobe. Standing beside him, she'd felt his swell of pride when his hand had swept over the sawhorses displaying individual pieces that, when even while indistinguishable as a whole, Cat could see were fabulous. Walking forward, she'd let her finger run across the deep grooves and the swirls and whirls at the edges of the doors and head piece.

Looking up at Matt, she'd felt bereft of words. "These are beautiful."

Staring down at the intricately carved doors, Matt hadn't been able to disguise a smile. "Yeah, these were interesting to work on..."

It was probably the longest she'd ever heard Matt speak at one given time. Staring raptly up at him as he explained some of the frustrations he'd encountered trying to line everything up, she'd experienced something akin to pride herself; she'd been part of this and watching the effect it had on him, her toes had curled in her shoes, her hand reaching out to grab his fingers. When he'd squeezed back, she'd felt a rush of pure happiness. She hadn't understood most anything that he said but she'd nodded mutely alongside him, taking a deep sort of pleasure in this unusual moment—where the usually taciturn Matthew McBoy couldn't seem to shut up, when the usually private Matthew McBoy had opened up, allowed her to see inside his reserved nature.

Because he loved what he was doing so much. Wednesday had been the only day he'd taken off working on Amelia's project.

"Well, don't work yourself to the bone," Cat had teased as they'd walked, still hand-in-hand, through the small park at the edge of town on their way to an outside music festival. The abrasive feel of his thumb rubbing against her knuckle had sent a thrill down her spine, and the sight of the tree-lined path ahead of them—a path she'd all but forgotten to notice, had walked down so many times that she'd stopped seeing it—reminded her how lovely her hometown was. Maybe it was because she was walking down it with someone new, someone who made possibilities sprout up like the tiny buds shooting out of the soil. "Amelia meant what she said. She doesn't have a deadline."

"Yeah, I know. I just..."

He didn't need to finish that sentence. She knew what he just. He just couldn't help himself.

The only question that haunted her, sitting in her office that Thursday morning, her eyes staring absently at the report on her computer screen that she should have started on half an hour ago, was his initial, seemingly reflexive reluctance at the onset of these projects. But then, once he'd start, Matt was completely enthralled. He'd all but itch to get back to the wood, to ground himself in the whirling white-noise of his machinery, in the concept of creativity and art. The inconsistency between these two reactions was as startling as it was challenging. Intriguing.

Chewing on the end of her pen, Cat considered that perhaps he was scared. The thought felt disloyal even if she was his staunchest believer.

But Matt *was* scared. Scared he'd fail. Scared the reality of his passion wouldn't live up to the idea in his mind. She supposed that was fair. The only thing worse than not chasing a dream was finding out that it didn't hold up in the stark light of day.

"And then there's his grandfather's hardware store," she muttered, remembering what Birdie had told her: that it wasn't Matt's dream, rather familial obligation that had him running and operating the store.

"But Birdie would understand," she mused, pushing her chair backward. "If he wanted to sell the place, she'd understand." Getting up, Cat stalked the small space of her office, her hand brushing against the edge of her desk, the thin back of the client chair facing it, her eyes bouncing off the pictures and books...

And then, suddenly, almost without thought, Cat found herself back at her computer. Closing down the screen on her desktop, she pulled up her internet browser, her fingers moving of their own accord.

At least, that's what she'd tell herself later.

She wasn't sure exactly that prompted her to do it. Certainly, she had work to get accomplished that day, but pushing all that to the back of her inbox, Cat bent to the task of research.

She knew she was overstepping.

She knew it was none of her business.

Then again, she knew it was business that needed to be conducted.

She also knew that what Matt needed was a little push. It had sort of been the pattern of their experiences together. Scooting a cooling cup of coffee to one side of her desk, Cat closed her mind to further arguments as she read one document after another. Within minutes, she was printing off state guidelines. Following that, time slipped by as she read up on the industry by experienced bloggers, perused a few government and municipal websites... By the time Cat left the office that evening, far later than usual thanks to the work she belatedly finished up after closing time, Cat's arms were loaded down with information, graphics, a few doodles and scribbles.

But she wasn't done yet. There was one last stop—the office supply store. Stopping in, Cat eagerly purchased copy paper, card stock, a cartridge of ink and some markers and pens. Checking out, she felt her stomach clench as the clerk bagged up her supplies. There was a bottle of wine waiting for her at home, and a pair of scissors. She'd undoubtedly need both.

CHAPTER TWENTY-THREE

"McBoy Hardware, how can I help you?"

"Matt?"

"Hey Cat."

Licking her lips, Cat stared down at the black portfolio she held in her grasp. It was a little after two in the afternoon on Friday and she should have been eyeballs deep in work—especially considering the amount she hadn't quite completed the night before. With a dismissive flick of her shoulder, she supposed it was bound to be another long day at the office.

Whatever. This was going to be worth it.

"What, eh, what are you doing tonight?" She hated the pitchy quality of her voice, the insecurity that oozed out despite her best efforts.

"Well, I was going to do a little more work on Amelia's closet."

Cat felt a smile tug at the corners of her mouth. That might just play to her advantage. "Mind if I stop over for a quick minute after work? I won't interrupt you for long, I promise."

"Sure."

Cat felt her breath catch, her excitement morphing as she glanced up at the overhead clock. "Okay. I should be there about seven."

"Sounds good."

Cat was, as usual, punctual. The clock in her car had ticked over to the hour when she pulled into the back parking lot of the McBoy's Hardware Store. Crossing her fingers, she hoped that Birdie didn't have plans in town that afternoon since her small sedan was now snugly taking up residence in that ladies' designated spot. Hopping out, her arms crossed around the binder, Cat marched up the rutted driveway and into the dingy warehouse.

At the sound of the door opening, Matt lifted his head. Smiling in muted greeting, he set down a carving tool on the workbench beside him. Brushing his hands on his jeans, he stood up. "Cat," he offered warmly as he walked toward her.

Cat was hardly allowed time to open her mouth before she felt his fingers come to rest at her waist, his lips pulling into a wolfish grin as he bent down and pressed his lips against hers.

For a moment, she allowed herself to forget the purpose of her visit, to sink into the wonder of being in Matt's arms. One hand coming to rest against the side of his jaw, her skin warming, her breath catching somewhere in his throat as the tip of his tongue slipped inside her mouth, Cat savored every second.

"What's up?" Matt finally asked a moment later, his head lifting upward, laughter in his eyes when he glanced down at her misty expression.

"Hi," Cat whispered back, a goofy grin stamped across her face, her feet moving on tiptoe, her body trying to entice his mouth back down to hers.

"What you got there?" Matt asked instead, his gaze switching to catch the binder she still held in her right hand.

Like a splash of cold water, Cat blinked. Dropping back down on the flats of her feet, she dropped her eyes, a shiver of nerves running down her spine. A shiver of nerves and expectation. Without preamble, she thrust out toward him. "It's, uh, it's something for you."

Tilting his head to one side, a quizzical smile transforming his face, Matt took the binder. His eyes lifted once more to her flushed features. "Yeah?"

"Just." Waving her hand, Cat squirmed. "Take a look." Holding her breath, she watched as Matt slowly flipped it open, his eyes narrowing curiously as he started reading, his lips moving silently as he turned over one page…then another.

Unable to take her eyes off of him, Cat waited for his expression to clear, waited for understanding to dawn. When it finally did, she had to admit, it didn't look the way she'd imagined. "What the hell is this?" Matt finally asked, snapping the binder closed. His brown eyes shot up to her face, catching her smile and devouring it.

"It's, it's a business plan," Cat stuttered, her fingers pointing to the now-condemned thing in his hand. Grabbing for it, she re-opened the first page. "Now, obviously I don't know much about this industry—"

"Obviously."

Ignoring his sarcasm, Cat sailed ahead. "And this is only a mock-up example, but I threw together a quick business proposal. Oh, and here," she said, flicking over a couple of pages. "These are some of the worksheets you'd need to fill out to get yourself incorporated, if you wanted... plus I added a directory for locating any licenses or permits..." A little breathless now, she lifted her head only to see an angry slash of color rising in his cheeks.

Dropping her eyes frantically, her movements more out of desperation now than demonstration, her fingers turned to another page. "And here—well, I sort of organized a list of local professionals who could be of aid to you," Cat said, her finger coming down to settle against one of the names listed. "This guy, he's an amazing graphic designer. Our office used him when we updated our logo a couple of years ago. He's fabulous and very affordable...and this lady," she said, talking too quickly, almost breathlessly. If she could make him see, if she could get him to lower his guard long enough to *listen* to her... "She sets up vendor accounts at craft fairs and whatnot." Another co-worker at the credit union, Janice had mentioned her work a few weeks ago after she'd mentioned needing extra time off so she could finish knitting some items for an upcoming event. "And I mean, these are just ideas, of course. Sort of a-a compass if you will but...but—"

"But what, Cat?" Matt's voice was starkly quiet. Still, he might as well have shouted for the venom, the shattering quality of that question.

"Well," but Cat wasn't sure what to say anymore. She'd exhausted her false gaiety. She'd failed to make him understand. She could no longer deny the bile of anxiety biting at her as she chanced another glance at Matt's shuttered expression, his narrow-eyed gaze, the tight line of his compressed lips. This was not how she'd planned this to go. She wasn't sure what she'd expected really, but... Her throat burned. "I wanted to show you how easy it would be to—"

"To what? To start a business?" Matt barked with laughter, his arms spanning out wide. "Yeah, I'm well aware of what it takes to start a business."

"But you didn't start *this* business."

Too late, Cat realized she'd made a mistake. Another mistake.

Matt's eyes widened and then narrowed again. His lips compressed so tightly that a thin white line appeared around the edges. "Are you kidding me?"

"I'm just saying..."

"And you think that the hard work is only involved in the beginning? That taxes and renewals and licensing—that those are all one-shot deals?"

"I'm sorry, I didn't mean—"

"I don't know how many times we have to have this conversation," Matt growled. "I already have a business, Cat. I'm not in the market for another one."

"No, I know."

"Do you?"

"But you don't love this place," Cat protested, her own arms sweeping wide to mirror Matt's earlier movement. "Not the way you love woodworking."

"Woodworking is a hobby, Cat. For Christ's sake."

"It doesn't have to be," she returned, her voice almost pleading now. Her eyes skipped over to the piece he'd been working on when she arrived. "You love doing this. I know you do."

Matt ran an irritated hand through his hair. "That doesn't mean—"

"And you're brilliant at it. I think so, Amelia clearly thinks so too. I could barely get her off the phone she was so pleased with your work."

"If I wanted to make this a business, I would have done so."

"I don't think so." Pulling her shoulders back, Cat waited for the explosion. She knew she was going too far, saying things she had no right saying, and yet...

"Excuse me?"

"You're so afraid of failing. Of failing Birdie by selling this place, afraid of starting a business only to lose it, afraid of not being good enough. You're terrified that it won't work, but if you never start, well…that's safe then."

Matt's jaw clenched at the words.

"That's why you made such a fuss over fixing my door and, and working on Amelia's wardrobe," Cat continued, her voice growing in volume. She'd already said too much, what was a little bit more? "At first I thought it was because it was an inconvenience to you. That you didn't want to spend what little free time you had working out here, but that's not it."

"Christ."

"It's because you were afraid of how much you'd love it, how intoxicating it would be. I think you knew it would lead you here, wanting something desperately but unwilling to go after it. If no one knew, if you could pretend that tinkering was enough, if no one could witness the energy and genius behind your work, then you could tuck it away, unseen and unrealized."

"I'm afraid?" Matt scoffed. "*I* am?"

Cat lifted her wobbling chin. Matt was looking at her in a way that seemed to determine the course of their future. "Yes, I think so."

"I think you've got it backward, lady." Matt leered down at her. "You're so busy pushing your nose into other people's lives, have you ever thought to ask why?"

"I don't—"

Matt flapped a hand toward the binder she still held in one hand. "I mean, who the hell asked you to do that?"

"Certainly you didn't!"

"You're damn right. And who's idea was it to meddle in Amelia's closet reconstruction?"

Cat felt her cheeks suck in. "But, you know why…"

"Do I?" Matt countered. "I used to think you were just dramatic, but now I think maybe you're the one who's running away."

"What?"

"You accuse me of hiding behind the comfort of my grandfather's business? Why did you make such an ordeal out of fixing that damn door—why'd you stretch it out, fretting and fretting over nothing?"

"Really? This again?"

"Because," Matt said, talking over her, "you needed the distraction. Just like now."

"Oh?" Cat challenged, though a part of her recognized the truth in those words. At least, a little bit. "From what?"

"I don't know," Matt shouted. "Unlike you, I don't think it's any of my business to go poking into your life."

Cat shuddered. "That's not fair. I was only trying to help."

"No, you weren't. If that were the case, you would have dropped this whole damn subject when you first brought it up to me. When I first told you no."

"I get it that you're upset," Cat said through stiff lips, "but I'm not sure your reaction is entirely appropriate."

"That's why you worked so hard to convince Amelia she needed a new closet," Matt considered. "Just another way to prove yourself right. Another thing to fixate on."

"You make it sound diabolical," Cat protested, the smallest of smiles edging out on her lips.

That was mistake number three.

"I'm done explaining myself to you," Matt said, his voice clipped. Re-crossing his arms over his chest, he swore softly.

"I'm sorry," Cat said. "Please." Throwing up her arms, the book unintentionally waving in front of Matt's face, she cringed. "I never meant to go behind your back."

"There's no other definition," Matt insisted. Snatching the book out of her hands, he tossed it on the floor. Empathetically. "Let me be clear. I'm *done* with this."

"Matt, please, I—" Feeling her lips trembling, Cat's eyes switched from his face to the binder and back again. There was something so final, so accusatory in the space between them.

"Look, I need to get back to Amelia's project," Matt said, cutting her off. Running a hand through his hair with checked-violence, he glanced pointedly behind him toward his workbench.

Before now, Cat hadn't thought Matt possessed the emotional range to get this upset.

She'd been wrong.

She'd been wrong on so many counts.

Three hours ago, Cat had been brimming over with excitement, her eyes checking and double-checking her facts and research, adding and eliminating pages at the last minute, her lips pulling into an irrepressible grin as she'd envisioned Matt's reaction.

Ten minutes ago, she'd been eagerly tossing the book in his hands...

She probably should have known it would go over a little like this.

But after all the work he'd done for Amelia—his undeniable excitement even after he'd labored late into the evenings, his conversation veering toward that subject matter on more than one occasion on their nights out...

Evenings that would come to an abrupt end after this.

Cat had figured she'd have to do a little cajoling, a little convincing to get him on board but she'd thought...laid out in those simple terms, she'd thought he'd find comfort in the neatly arranged information, that he'd find confidence in the breakdown of paperwork, the forms and facts he'd need to compile. She'd thought she'd finally used that overactive, overthinking brain to good use by locating everything he'd need and then organizing it in an easy, step-by-step system.

Now she stood in the burnt ashes of it all. She'd been a fool. And not just because he'd thrown her offer back in her face. He'd also stopped looking at her.

Cat sucked in a breath, her hand wiping the bottom of her nose. "Please, don't be mad at me."

With a flick of his eyes, Matt's feelings went into eclipse. The emotion was replaced now, smoothed out in a cool mask of indifference. "It's fine, Cat." He gave her a level look. "Now you know."

"Yeah. Now I know."

A moment of silence passed.

Matt hitched a thumb over his shoulder, indicating his workbench again. "I, ah, I really should get back to it."

"Yes, of course." Swallowing, Cat bent down to retrieve the binder. "I'll just get rid of this for you," she mumbled unevenly. Glancing up, Cat tried to smile. Despite his easy words, she could still feel the force of Matt's anger. "It was a stupid idea, anyway."

Matt held up a hand. "Stop. Leave it alone, Cat. Let's be done with the whole thing, okay?"

Cat tensed. "The whole thing?"

Matt sighed. His eyes stared at her without expression. And suddenly, she was terrified of what he'd say in response.

Holding up a hand to ward him off, she pulled her lips into a grotesque smile. "Okay." Taking a step backward, the binder clutched to her chest, her eyes traveled no higher than his broad shoulders. "I'll let you get back to it."

"Cat?"

"Yes?"

Out of her peripheral vision, Cat saw Matt's chin jut forward. "Throw that thing away, huh?"

"I'll do that very thing," she whispered, her free hand already reaching behind her for the doorknob.

CHAPTER TWENTY-FOUR

Cat was standing in her kitchen uncorking a bottle of wine when she heard the telltale sound of a knock on her door, followed almost immediately by the quiet swish of it opening; this was unsurprising since she'd left it deliberately unlocked and cracked slightly ajar.

"Hello?" At the sound of Amelia's voice, Cat almost smiled. As well as her apartment, she'd also propped the building's exterior door open with a rock...she hadn't wanted the bother of standing in the entryway just so she could admit her inside.

"Hey, Amelia!"

"I'm here too." Sam.

"Good timing," Cat hollered back, her voice carrying down the hallway separating them. "In the kitchen!"

Amelia. "I've got the pizza."

"And it smells delicious."

A small laugh followed this and Cat could just make out Amelia's muffled voice exclaiming. "Wait. What is that—did you bring chocolates?"

"As per requested," Sam replied, her conversation floating along with the sounds of their nearing footsteps.

Pouring three glasses of cabernet, Cat found herself soothed by their bantering.

Amelia. "I dibs the one with almonds in the center."

Sam. "Fine because I want the coconut one."

"Ew. Take it."

"I always knew you were a generous person…and without taste, of course."

Amelia laughed as the women finally rounded the corner of the kitchen.

Smiling tremulously, Cat forced herself to keep her composure. It wouldn't do to break down the moment they walked in. "So," she asked instead, her voice a little higher than usual as she spared them both a quick glance. "What kind of pizza did you get?" Her attempt to join their lighthearted talk may not have been exactly believable, but they were too kind to let on.

Instead, Amelia wiggled her eyebrows with a flourish. "Only the best kind," she assured her as she popped the top off the box and tipped the pizza toward both girls for their inspection.

Sam licked her lips. "Green peppers," she moaned. "Onions, sausage—"

Cat rubbed her hands together. "And mushrooms."

"Delicious."

Grinning wolfishly, Amelia set the opened pizza on the table. Following suit, Sam mirrored her movements, depositing the chocolates beside it.

"Hi there, honey," Amelia offered belatedly, her attention shifting from the food to the pale pallor of Cat's countenance. Amelia's voice gentled as she moved to embrace her. "Bad day, huh, pumpkin?"

"Not very good." Then Cat felt Sam's arms come up, around, and over Amelia's. Leaning into her friends, she felt the first true smile of the afternoon drift across her lips. "Thanks for coming over."

"Hey," Sam murmured. "When you get a mayday text, you take care of business."

"Absolutely," Amelia agreed. "Now, where's that wine?"

Laughing in unison—not because Amelia's words had been particularly witty, but because none of the girls wanted to start the evening off with tears—they separated at the words. Moving with economy, they filled up their plates and grabbed their wine before settling in Cat's living room.

"Want to tell us what happened?" Amelia asked, taking a nibble of her pizza.

Cat sighed. Setting her untouched dinner down on her lap, she leaned forward, her hands searching underneath the coffee table in front of her.

"You okay?" Sam asked.

"This is what happened," Cat said, retrieving that damned black binder. Looking at it, she grimaced. She'd told Matt that she'd destroy it, and she would, but first—tossing it to Amelia, she grabbed for her pizza again. Shifting on her cushion, she watched while Amelia bent her head over first one page and then another; anxious, Sam leaned forward to read over Amelia's shoulder.

Much the same as Matt, Cat was forced to wait while their crinkled brows smoothed out, as understanding flitted across their puckered lips. And, as with Matt, neither of them were smiling when their wide eyes lifted to Cat's.

"What is this?" Amelia asked skeptically. Setting the binder down on the coffee table, she took a bite of pizza.

"I, uh, well, you know how good Matt is at woodworking," Cat said, sputtering to a start. She looked up at Sam. "He really is—tell her."

"He's amazing," Amelia said, but there was still skepticism clinging to her tone.

"But he, well, he's so afraid to do anything with this gift, so he hides it away. Keeping it safe from the unknowns of a reality that might not match up with his dreams," Cat said, repeating the mantra she'd been playing on a loop for the better part of a week now. "Even though he loves doing it," she muttered down to her pizza. "I mean, honestly, I've never met a man more content to spend hours on end with the whirl of table saws and whatnot ringing in his ears."

"Wait a minute," Amelia said, lifting up a hand. "*You* made that thing?" she asked, her hand pointing toward the binder.

Cat's lips pursed. "Yeah."

"Did Matt ask you to do it?"

"No."

"Oh," Amelia and Sam said together.

Cat picked up her pizza, then she set it back down again. "I thought it would help."

Setting her empty plate down at her feet, Sam reached forward to rifle through the binder again.

"Sweetheart," Amelia sighed, shaking her head. "I wish you would have talked to us about this first."

Cat's eyes filled with tears. "Yeah—Matt hated it, too."

"I didn't say I hated it," Amelia said, reaching forward to squeeze Cat's knee. "It's just a little…"

"Insane," Sam supplied. Lifting her head, she smiled her toothy grin. "But in that great Cat Cryer kind of way—everyone's best, most loyal supporter."

Cat sniffled. "It was insane."

"Your heart was in the right place," Amelia said.

"And it's brilliantly laid-out," Sam said.

"Will you please?" Amelia bit out, her head turning dangerously in Sam's direction.

"What?" Sam asked with big eyes. "This is fantastic. If I wanted to start a business, I would want this puppy." For added effect, she patted her hand against the hard-plastic cover.

"But Matt doesn't want to start a business," Cat said, shaking her head. "He told me so repeatedly today." And, yes, he'd probably made that point clear even before that…

"Oh, hon."

Cat felt the first tear fall from her eyes. It was shortly followed by another. "I know it's stupid to be this upset," she cried, wiping her eyes, "but I was so excited to show him. I thought he'd love it." Well, that was maybe a stretch.

Amelia and Sam exchanged eloquent glances. Nonetheless, both girls abandoned their spots to squeeze in on either side of Cat.

"Well, okay, I didn't think he'd love it," Cat stressed, looking down at her knees. "But I thought…I had all the data, I'd researched all the facts and figures and, you know, they aren't nearly as terrifying as he'd like to believe. I had examples of profit and loss sheets from other woodworkers and…I thought it would steady him, make him realize that it was possible. More than possible. I included a feasibility study and—"

"Damn girl. That is impressive."

"Not according to Matt. He looked at me like…" Cat batted the words away. "I ruined everything."

"I'm sure that's not true."

Cat nodded. She wasn't sure she believed Sam's strong defense, but she also knew she didn't want to think about the alternative.

"I worked so hard on that," she said. "Which is totally selfish, isn't it?"

"Well, a little. Ow!" Sam cried, jumping from the slight pinch of Amelia's fingers. "But hey, who isn't a little selfish?"

"And Sam was right," Amelia admitted. "The binder is amazing. You have every right to be proud of the work you did."

Cat sniffed. "Yeah?"

Amelia smiled gently, her eyes traveling back to the object at hand. "Yeah. I mean, you included business cards for a local website designer, and a graphic artist...everything that someone would need to start-up." She grinned when she saw her own name listed under the heading, *professional headshot*: Amelia Kelly Studio.

Cat shrugged. "I have a lot of connections in this town. Through my work. Having grown up here."

"And your generosity is brilliant. Help them by helping someone else. A real community approach to entrepreneurship."

Cat shrugged again. "Yeah, I figured...I don't know, that maybe..."

"I would have loved one of these when I got the crazy idea to start my studio."

"Yeah?"

"Yeah. But..." Amelia took a deep breath. "Only after *I* decided to start it. Myself."

... °•°• ...

Though they tried, in the end, Sam and Amelia were little more than a few hours of distraction for Cat. Her thoughts wouldn't be ignored forever. Her self-recrimination could only be denied for so long. Lingering after the girls left, Cat remained on her couch, sitting cross-legged as she stared mindlessly at the binder on her lap, her eyes stuck on its stiff backing.

What the hell had she been thinking?

"And really, why did you think he'd welcome the invasion?" she asked herself. It truly had been an invasion. Only, she'd been so sure the result would justify the means. Shrugging her shoulders, Cat sank deeper into the green couch cushions. She'd just wanted to do something for him. After everything he'd done for her.

"...and I *do* think he's wasting this amazing gift," she muttered, her eyebrows pulling low. "But it's not the comfortable, safe road to travel so he'll be content to pretend he'd rather work at a hardware store that his *grandfather* loved." She stuck out her tongue. "Well, whatev—"

At the sudden buzz of her apartment intercom, Cat broke off mid-word. Perching forward, she caught the tail-end of a voice echoing out of the loudspeaker, the sound hardly carrying down the length of her hallway. Added to that, there was a slight scratchiness to the words which made it impossible to identify the caller.

Shoving off the couch, Cat drug herself over to the intercom. Pushing down on the TALK button she said: "I'm sorry? Who's there?"

"Matt."

Her stomach twisted at the one-word response. Without bothering to respond, her fingers slipping against the keys in her rush, Cat admitted him inside. Her hands moved in a frenzy of chaos as she unlocked her front door. She could hear him coming down the hallway even as she swung it open.

Her large green eyes skittered nervously up to his as Matt came fully into view. Stopping just outside her door, a lightweight sheepskin jacket thrown over his shirt, he didn't speak for a moment. His brown eyes were slightly shadowed beneath the brim of his hat.

Cat licked her lips. "Hi."

Matt inclined his head. His lips kicked up at the corners of his mouth. "Been drinking?"

"Huh?"

Without waiting for an invitation, he shouldered his way through the door. Bewildered, Cat stepped backward to allow him easier entrance.

"I thought as much," Matt muttered, one hand coming up to take his hat off his head. Then she could see his eyes. They glanced down at her with undeniable mirth.

"I'm-I'm—" Cat's eyes rounded, her feet back-pedaling as Matt continued moving forward, his steps calculated as they swallowed up the space between them.

"I can smell it on your breath, Cat," he murmured, his head bending down at the same time as one hand came up to cradle the side of her face. It was then that she felt the strength of the wall behind her. She'd come to the end of the hall. She had no place else to go.

Not that she wanted to go anywhere.

She pinkened. "Yes, well..."

"I wonder what's been spinning through that head of yours all day," Matt mused.

Cat pouted up at him. Her heart was rocking against her chest. He was there. In her apartment. But... "You were so mad at me earlier."

Matt nodded solemnly, but his eyes were focused on her lips. "Yeah. I was."

"I wasn't sure—" Cat slithered to a pause, her large eyes peeking up at him cautiously. She wasn't sure she could say the words. Standing there now, cocooned in his arms, she felt rather...foolish. "I wasn't sure you even wanted to see me again."

He titled his head a little to one side. "Really?" The incredulity in his voice only seemed to confirm the notion that she'd perhaps overreacted. Yet again.

She squirmed.

"That seems a bit extreme," Matt informed her, but the smile never left his voice. Instead, he leaned even closer, his lips hovering, teasing hers when they stopped just a breath away from her mouth. "Then again, I wouldn't have expected anything else from you." His lips brushed against hers with the words. Cat mewed quietly, piteously. "That's why I'm here."

"Saving me from myself, again?" She asked, her mouth following after his.

"Looks like I'm just in time, too."

"Maybe," she conceded, her arms reaching up, her fingers trailing over his arms and across his shoulders. "But you should have seen your face earlier."

"That was then," he whispered, "and this is now."

"Hmm—"

"And for the record," he said, his lips nibbling against hers in chaste, biting kisses. "They are mutually exclusive, okay?"

"I'm starting to get that."

"Yeah, but I think the reminder will come in handy."

Cat smirked up at him. "For the next time I piss you off, you mean?"

"Did I say that?" Matt whispered before finally, *finally* cutting off further communication and taking full possession of her lips with his own.

Cat's back arched as his hands trailed a lazy line up and down her sides, his lower body coming to press down against her hips.

"Matt?" Cat's chest rose and fell heavily with the word.

"Yes?"

She was moderately satisfied to hear the same hoarse, uneven quality to his voice.

"Are you staying the night?"

"God, is that an invitation?"

In answer, Cat stretched her left arm out to the side and, grabbing for the doorknob to her bedroom, she gave it a quick, firm twist. With a groan of feeling, Matt brought his mouth crashing down against hers once more. Then, suddenly, Cat was no longer pushed up against the wall. In a swift sweep of motion, she found herself hoisted up in Matt's arms, her legs swinging around his hips as he shouldered the door to her room fully open.

The next thing Cat knew, the world tilted as he set her down on the bed, his legs straddling her hips as he bent down at the waist to trail kisses down the side of her neck....

CHAPTER TWENTY-FIVE

Try as she might, Cat couldn't quite focus. Staring down at the deck of cards in her hand, she felt her lips pull down in wanting-concentration, her fingers grazing over the cards tips as she considered her next move. Reaching forward, she picked up the stack.

"No!"

Jerking at the sound, Cat almost dropped the deck. Startled, her eyes met Mary's across the table. There was no disguising the immediate guilt, the recognition in Cat's expression that she didn't understand...

With disgust, Mary dropped her cards down in her lap. Running her gnarled hands through her messy hair, she glared at her partner. "Do you have any idea how many black threes are in that thing?" she moaned to no one in particular.

Eleanor tisk-tisked, shooting Cat a sidelong glance. "I'll pray for you, dearie."

"That's it," Mary muttered, shooting her gaze around the table. "That's *it*. Next week, she's somebody else's problem."

"Mary."

"Nope. No way," that woman insisted, her thin lips pulling into a wrinkled line. "I'm out. Girl's even worse than she was last week."

"Mary—"

"Except last weeks she was all grins and goopy smiles," Mary said, her gaze settling on Cat finally. She leaned across the table. "But not today."

Watching this almost as though she were merely an audience member at a play, Cat didn't bother to comment. She wasn't interested. Mary had a right to be irritated. She wasn't paying attention. She should have called-off for the evening.

Yeah, that's what she should have done.

"Her lips are all smushy."

"Yeah, but not daydreamy," Mary said as if this was an important distinction.

"That's true," Erna considered.

"You know, now that you mention it, Matt was a bit...grumpy this afternoon at the store," Birdie said, her eyes swiveling to Cat's in a searching gaze.

Fanning out her cards in a deliberate show of indifference, Cat took a glance at the deck she'd stupidly decided to pick up. Scratch her earlier thought. Mary not only had a right to be irritated—she had the right to be throwing an all-out temper tantrum. There wasn't one card in the pile that she could use. Sighing without quite meaning to, Cat laid down a black three.

"See?" Mary said, waving her hand in front of Cat's face. "Nothing. Last week, the girl darn near passed out at the mention of his name. This week? Nothing."

"Cat?"

Lifting her head, Cat smiled weakly. "I have no idea why Matt might have been grumpy—other than the fact that it's one of his favorite moods." She said this last bit with a lighthearted tinge to her voice. "And Mary is right. I'm off my game today. I'm sorry."

Perhaps it was the too-conversational tone of her voice, but three pairs of eyes looked at her, nonplussed at the words.

"Everything okay?"

"Yes," Cat said, and she meant it. She smiled. It came naturally to her face. But still—something must have looked off. The other women almost recoiled at the turn of her mouth. "Everything's fine."

And everything was fine. Staring down at her cards, Cat tried to compose her features. Friday night had been...special. Especially the night part. And, yes, all right, the start of Friday evening had kind of sucked but—Cat mentally shrugged, at least she'd learned some things about Matt.

He didn't like to be pushed, and he didn't like to be surprised, and he most certainly did not want to start a woodworking shop.

Then again, she'd also learned he didn't hold a grudge.

That's where the latter part of Friday night had come into play. Crossing her legs in reaction to the thought, Cat settled into her chair. If Matt's appearance had been a revelation, the rest of the night had been…a marathon. Biting her lip at the stray thought, Cat felt the tip of her finger playing with the edge of the cards in her hand again.

So everything was fine.

Really.

Except.

Except something was missing. In only the span of a weekend, Cat could feel it. Certain subjects had become off-limits. By silent mutual agreement, neither of them uttered so much as a word about woodworking. The subject was too raw; Cat couldn't bring it up without feeling conspicuous—like Matt would assume she was only trying to elbow in one more pointed comment. Hell, she hadn't even felt comfortable asking him about Amelia's project. And he'd never offered up any information on that front either.

Even talk about the hardware store felt slightly taboo now. Almost queasy. Cat had avoided any mention of his working life or his one great hobby, which was okay, she supposed, because it left a lot of time to talk about other things—

Cat frowned. The conversation hadn't lacked over the weekend. In fact, it had held an almost frenetic quality to it as they'd swapped stories concerning everything from childhood shenanigans to first dates to most their embarrassing moments…. It had been enlightening, entertaining, a way to fill the silence with white-noise. Then again, when they eventually did run out of small-talk, well, that left the hours open for other activities.

So yeah, it was good.

Everything was fine.

This time, she wasn't going to overthink things.

She wasn't.

Get a grip, she scolded herself. With a forceful shake of her head, Cat brought her mind back to the present. She was sitting at Julie's Café, playing Canasta with her eighty-year-old friends. Not an appropriate time for daydreaming.

Still, a stubborn part of her brain persisted: Cat just wished Matt had listened to her. About the woodworking. She knew what she was talking about—mere weeks ago Cat had felt like a completely different person than she knew herself to be today. She'd felt vaguely restless. Her friends had moved away. She hadn't been sure why she hadn't done more with her life. She'd suddenly realized her job wasn't as fulfilling as she'd once imagined it would be.

And yet, all of those worries, those questions, one on top of another, had been so overwhelming she'd been paralyzed by indecision.

And then—one broken door and so many things had changed in her life. It'd forced her into the hardware store, broken her out of her safe, boring little routine. It had filled her with anxiety, sure, but also with a sense of purpose and interest, which had expanded into other areas of her life. She had friends. Great friends. And, thanks to Sam's obvious infatuation with it, thanks to that woman's fresh perspective on things Cat had stopped seeing, she was finding herself falling in love with this town all over again. Falling in love with the life she was cultivating within it.

She could see the same rut wrapping itself around Matt.

"...Cat? Cat, it's your turn."

Snapping back to reality, Cat looked up at Mary apologetically. Then she picked up a card. Biting her lip, she carefully scrutinized her hand, then her team's board before discarding another worthless black three.

Then again, maybe Matt had been right. That she'd been using him as a distraction. She certainly felt that way lately. Distracted. And she was starting to realize why, too. It all came back to that damned black binder. Which made it another thing on an alarmingly growing list of them she wasn't sure she felt comfortable talking about with Matt.

Canasta had just finished for the evening, with Harriet gathering up the cards. Standing at one corner of the table, hugging Erna in goodbye, Cat's softly uttered: "Well, it was too kind and the pleasure has always been mine…" was cut short when she suddenly felt a hand settle against her shoulder.

Breaking away from the older woman before her, Cat turned in blinking surprise when she encountered Mary's frowning face. In the bustle of movement, she hadn't seen the older woman rise to her feet.

"Walk me to my car," Mary said. It wasn't a request.

"Uh, sure," Cat replied, a questioning note in her voice. All the same, she quickly vacated her spot, shooting Birdie a nervous glance as she said a hurried goodbye to the group. Turning around, she saw that Mary was already at the door, her rubber-soled shoe tapping impatiently. Paying for her coffee, when they gained the outside walkway, Cat hunched her shoulders up in preparation for the scolding she knew she deserved.

"About tonight. I'm sorry—"

Waving off the words, Mary huffed into the chilly evening air. The sun was hanging low in the sky now, with only a weak light of warmth. "He's a good one."

"Huh?"

"Matthew McBoy. He's a good catch."

Opening her mouth, Cat caught a breath of cold air against her teeth. Slowing to a stop, she looked at Mary. "I'm not sure I'm following you."

"Last week you were practically dancing on the table. It was nice to see."

"It was?"

Mary shrugged. "Of course it was. Don't screw it up now."

"Me?"

Mary gave her a searching look. "Why else would he be grumpy to his grandmother on the same day you look like a deflated ragdoll."

Cat grinned into the biting wind. "You've got a real way with words."

"Don't try to butter an old lady up," Mary said with a small chuckle. Slipping her arm through Cat's, they resumed walking. "And don't pretend that nothing's wrong. You don't have a good poker face."

"Guess it's a good thing we don't play that card game."

Mary harrumphed. "Don't know about that, you couldn't get much worse at the one we are playing."

"Nothing's wrong," Cat said, continuing her newfound mantra. "We just...we got into a bit of a fight last weekend." Hearing the words with something of a shock, Cat shut her mouth promptly. She couldn't begin to understand why she felt the need to explain herself to this woman.

"Resolve it then."

"We did," Cat assured her but her eyes stared straight ahead as they neared Mary's car.

"Doesn't seem like it."

"And how would you know?"

"Don't you get smart with me," Mary said, her fingers curly a bit viciously around Cat's forearm. "I was happily married for thirty years. I know when emotions get the better of things."

Cat was quiet for a moment.

"It's easy to get caught up in the feelings at the start," Mary continued as they reached the end of the block. Crossing the street, she continued: "Everything seems so big. The first time you realize you have feelings for someone, the moment you realize it's reciprocated. The first kiss..."

Cat tried not to cringe at the intimate talk.

"And the same goes for the first fight. It all seems so...intense."

Cat frowned. She wasn't sure what was more troubling, her own preoccupation with Matt or the fact that Mary had somehow become a love expert.

"Yeah, I guess."

"It can be overwhelming, starting something new. There are so many expectations and hopes. Sometimes that's good, and sometimes it's not."

Cat nodded silently.

"Don't let it get the best of you. Don't let it get the best of what's happening *between* you two, that's all I'm saying."

Pulling up to Mary's small blue sedan, Cat waited while the older woman fished her keys out of her pants pocket. "Look, I know I was a bit distracted today..."

"Not just distracted," Mary argued. "You seemed sad. Quietly sad, I'll give you that and I'll thank you for not sniveling all over the card table."

"Ah..."

"You didn't seem any too surprised to hear Birdie say that Matt was grumpy today." Cat wasn't confused. Mary was not asking her a question.

Cat shrugged one shoulder. "He kind of always is."

"Not with her."

"No." Cat sighed. Mary had a point. "I guess not."

"Nor did you seem altogether interested in the subject."

"Well, someone was already blasting me about my level of attention on the game."

"Well, hell," Mary grumbled. "That's not it. You didn't want to ask any leading questions."

"No?" Cat knew she was acting like a snot, but she wasn't all-together sure she appreciated Mary's sudden nosiness.

"No, and you didn't want anyone else to ask any either."

Cat clenched her teeth.

"Listen, it's none of my business, and I'm sure I don't care much one way or another," Mary said, sounding a bit like her usual self once more. "But I like you."

"Thank you?"

"And I love that boy. Figure yourself out and then let this, whatever it is, let it go." Cracking open her car door, Mary carefully lowered herself in the seat. Looking up at Cat, she offered one final piece of advice. "I don't know you well, but you play cards like you're always imaging the worst-case scenario—so focused on what the other teams' strategies might be that you don't take time to figure out your own. And once you do figure it out, you always go for the biggest extreme. The move that'll make it or break it for your team." Mary nodded to herself. "It's got promise, but it's also got pitfalls."

Cat's mouth was open in response but she never got the option to speak. With those words hanging in the air, Mary shut her door in Cat's face. With a quick twist of her wrist, she started up her car and, without even waving goodbye, pulled out onto the street.

"Well, hell," Cat said, unintentionally repeating Mary's own words.

... °•°• ...

The credit union was officially closed when Cat finally replaced her work phone in its cradle the following afternoon. Glancing up from her desk, her eyes lit upon the bright vase of yellow roses gracing one side of her desk. Erna had had them delivered to Cat's office early Monday morning.

Cat wouldn't admit for the whole world that when she'd first viewed the delivery man arrive at her office holding the beautiful floral display that she'd felt an overwhelming surge of excitement followed by a quick swallow of deflated surprise when they hadn't been from Matt.

Thank you so much for helping, Jeff! He was truly grateful. As am I. (I'm also so glad you've joined us for Canasta. You're a true blessing, my dear.)

> *Yours,*
> *Erna B.*

Blinking in surprise when she'd received the flowers, Cat had been almost embarrassingly bemused by the action. Much as she'd predicted, her and Jeff's conversation last week had hardly taken more than a few minutes—nothing which had deserved such a generous response. All the same, Cat had given Erna an extra-long hug at the end of Canasta the Monday evening to whisper her heartfelt appreciation in that lady's ear, all to which Erna had batted away with a graceful swipe of her hand.

"You should have seen the difference. He was so stressed the day before he called her. And the next? Poof. He had enough free time to take his Grandma out to lunch."

Which had been all the thanks that Cat could have wanted.

Then again, she supposed she was now the one who was grateful for the flowers, for the reminder of them. Because her last phone call that afternoon had come from none other than Jeff, himself—someone who, without those flowers, she'd have more than likely filed away as nothing more than another anonymous name in the overflowing number of them that Cat handled in her workday.

It had been five minutes to the close of the afternoon when her office phone had started ringing. Looking at it with resignation lining her face, Cat had reached over to grab it.

"Hey, Cat. This is Jeff. Jeff Barns. I'm not sure if you remember me…"

Glancing over at the floral bouquet, Cat had nodded. "Sure, I do. Hey Jeff." Frowning a little, because she hadn't expected to hear from him again, Cat had leaned forward. "Did you get the pamphlets back? Everything turn out okay—?"

"Yes, and they're great."

"Okay. Well, great."

"I was hoping you'd lend me your expertise again," Jeff had said, chuckling over the line. "You clearly have some connections in this town."

"Oh, I don't know about that..."

"When I mentioned to Dan at SkyArt that you recommended his business he offered us a twenty-percent discount."

Cat smiled. "That's great."

"Yes. Even better, you were right. They're geniuses over there. My boss loved the design."

"I'm not surprised."

"So, if you have a minute, I'd love to pick your brain concerning some local vendors..."

Cat smiled. "Of course. Shoot."

As with the time before, Cat and his conversation took little more than a few minutes. Nodding along as he outlined what he wanted, Cat had little difficulty helping steer him down the right track. As she'd already known, Jeff wasn't from the area. He was there temporarily helping set-up a new client his company had recently acquired. "...and please," she insisted at the conclusion of their call, "don't hesitate to call me with any future questions. It's no trouble. I promise."

"I appreciate it."

"Nah. It's one of the perks of the job. I get to know people." There was a slight pause. "And they like you."

"That's always the hope."

"It's a valuable commodity."

"I guess."

"I know."

"Well, as I said, I enjoy helping out when I can. So, sing out if you come up against anything else."

His response had left her mildly curious. "I have a feeling I'll be calling you again. Though, perhaps not for the reason you're thinking. But I hope when I do, you'll at least hear me out."

Which had inevitably turned her thoughts back to Matt. Sitting silently in her office now, the quiet sound of tellers closing up for the night drifting through her closed door, Cat frowned at the flowers.

Much though she hated to admit it, she couldn't quite manage to get Mary's words out of her head. Or Matt's for that matter. In their way, each had told her the same thing. She was so focused on other people that she didn't seem to be seeing herself or playing for her *own* win.

Which meant that her conversation with Jeff would best be relegated to the list of things she couldn't talk to Matt about. More than likely, he'd accuse her of using Jeff to distract herself, of helping him because she was running away from something missing in her own life.

Poppycock, really.

At the thought, her eyelids jerked. Set guiltily beside the vase of flowers was the black binder. Yes, *that* black binder. The one Matt had heatedly handed back to her, the one she'd sworn she'd destroy. The one that should have been empty, all contents sitting on the wrong side of the shredder. But there it remained, perfectly intact.

It wasn't stubbornness that kept her from tossing it in the garbage heap. It was…something different, something harder to describe. And weirdly enough, it had nothing to do with Matt. Gaze narrowing, Cat felt her teeth scrape against her bottom lip. As she considered the hours she'd put into it, the wealth of knowledge she'd handed to him, something inside her kept seizing. Years of experience, years of community involvement through her work, years of market research and analysis… People would pay for that kind of leg-up in the start-up world.

Hell, Jeff had proved that, hadn't he?

Shaking her head, Cat bounded to her feet. Okay, so she wouldn't talk to Matt about her admittedly mundane conversation with Jeff. That was hardly a fracture in their budding relationship. She probably wouldn't have told him about it regardless. Because there were a lot of other things to talk about.

More interesting things.

She was overthinking it all.

It was oddly comforting to hear the lies—even as she knew them for what they were.

CHAPTER TWENTY-SIX

Waiting, her hands pushed deep into the front pockets of her jeans, Cat watched as the superintendent of her building checked out her newly painted kitchen.

Grant had called that morning and inquired over the project. After she'd assured him that everything was done had his true intentions been known. He needed to stop by to do some inspections for a unit that had recently been vacated—he figured it wouldn't hurt to check out the kitchen at the same time.

Cat hadn't been fooled by his words. Translation: he wanted to make sure that when she inevitably moved out, he wasn't going to be stuck with an apartment colored an unrented shade of paint.

Holding her breath when he entered the room, Cat waited for him to notice the door. Her eyes twitched to keep from looking directly at it. Instead, she leaned up against the table and kept up a steady flow of small-talk, anything to keep him just distracted enough...

"I don't remember the last time I've painted," she said, her voice coming out a little too quick, a little too high. Luckily for her, Grant had never stuck around long enough to engage in unnecessary small talk with his tenants so he didn't notice. Cat watched as he slowly circled the room, his double chins wobbling with the movement as he took in the fresh-looking space. "But I'll tell you what, I sure didn't need to go to the gym for arm day afterward."

Other than a grunt of disinterest, Grant hardly seemed to be listening. Even as she spoke, Grant shifted, his eyes traveling the length of the kitchen. And then, suddenly, he was looking right at the newly constructed door. Cat held her breath, the words dying on her lips. Then his eyes moved on to the next door.

He nodded. "It looks good, Ms. Cryer," he said, using her last name because he probably couldn't be bothered to remember her first. Cat didn't mind.

Clapping her hands together, Cat smiled demurely, her eyes glancing down at the floor. "Thank you. I'm pretty happy with it myself."

"Good, good. Well, I won't keep you any longer—that is, if there's nothing you need from me?" But it was clear from the haunted look on his face he wasn't interested in any forthcoming complaints.

"No, no," she rushed to assure him. "I'm good. And, um, thank you for letting me, uh, make this place a little more my own."

He grunted again. That was literally as socially polite as the man could make himself out to be. Again, Cat didn't mind.

When he left moments later, the heavy door shutting behind his bulky frame, Cat reached instinctively for her phone. Calling Matt, she waited impatiently for him to answer. *This.* This was something they could talk about...

"McBoy's Hardware Store—"

"Matt," Cat rushed to say, her stomach tightening instinctively at the timbre of his voice, even over the line. "Grant just left my apartment."

"Who?"

She took a deep, steadying breath. "The landlord, er, the super."

"Yeah?"

Cat's lips twisted at the lack of recognition in his voice. Still, she ploughed ahead, silently pleading with him to care. "And he loved the kitchen."

"Yeah? Well, that's good."

Okay, so it was probably unfair to expect him to do verbal cartwheels over the news, Cat told herself. All the same, there was the smallest crack of hurt at his unmoved response, his lack of feedback.

"It's official," she pressed on nonetheless. "He didn't notice a thing."

"Not even the new paint?"

"Well, of course he noticed that," Cat grumbled. "That's why he came."

"Hmm."

"But the door—Matt, he didn't notice the door."

"I thought that was the whole point?"

She rolled her eyes. "Don't tease me, Matt."

The unexpected sound of a warm chuckle over the line warmed the insides of her stomach; the block in her airways opened. He was a hard person to read, Cat reminded herself, wishing suddenly that she could at least see his face.

"How'd it feel? Taking your first real deep breath since it happened?"

"Amazing. So amazing that I was hoping to celebrate tonight."

"Yeah? What are you going to do?"

And just like that, Cat felt a hollowness envelope her. At his polite refusal to understand that she meant she wanted to celebrate with him.

Don't overthink it. Don't overthink it. "Well, I was hoping something with you?"

"Oh. Well…"

There was a heavy implication in those pregnant words.

"Tonight's not good?"

"It's," Matt coughed a little as he hesitated. "I'm about finished with Amelia's wardrobe and I was planning—"

Cat's mouth jumped to a start, cutting him off before he could say more. "Of course!" she cried out, her voice taking on a pitchy quality. Here it was again, that thing that they didn't speak about. Since last Friday, she had yet to set foot in Matt's workshop. She hadn't even gone to the hardware store.

"That makes sense," she hurried to explain, her voice shoveling the words out of her mouth. "Another night this week then."

"You're sure?" Still, there was no denying the relief in his voice.

"Yeah. Of course." There was no way she was touching that subject. There was no way she was pitting herself against it again. "Have, have fun."

Hanging up minutes later, she told herself that she really *was* okay. It didn't matter that Matt hadn't invited her to come and hang out with him while he finished the project. It didn't matter that there was this whole part of his life that she felt singularly excluded from.

And that it was eeking out into other areas. At the thought, her mind flashed back to the phone call she'd received that afternoon at work. From Jeff. Again. Good as his word, he *had* called her back. And much like he'd foretold, she'd been left fairly dazed by the end of it. By the purpose behind it.

"...Just, promise me you'll think about it," he'd said before ringing off.

Cat tried to convince herself that she hadn't told Matt about the very telling exchange between her and Jeff simply because she'd made quick work of getting him off the phone, getting him back to that damn table saw.

It was fine.

Mary was right. She was probably making it more than it was.

This time, however, the lie didn't sit so well in her stomach.

... °•°• ...

"...Just, promise me you'll think about it."

Jeff's words played like a broken record throughout Cat's mind the following days. Silently spinning, whirling. And, as she'd promised, Cat had thought about them. She'd hardly been able to think of anything else.

Only. Well, she still hadn't discussed the matter with Matt. To be fair, it wasn't like she needed to talk to him about it. But it was the natural cycle of things when you were dating someone, right? You talked about the big moments. The small ones too. You talked about your life. You shared and you asked for input.

If it hadn't been for that damned black binder. Not for the first time, Cat deeply regretted that she'd ever been stupid enough to create it. That she'd been naïve enough to show it to him.

So she didn't talk to him. Not about that, not about Jeff. Instead, she kept her conversation casual when he showed up the following evening, entertaining him with anecdotes, like the world's longest scarf Janice had spent the better part of the week working on. And how Sam had somehow talked her into doing a portrait.

Which made her feel guilty.

She'd *almost* told him Saturday morning. They'd been lounging in her living room, watching a news report that hardly captured their attention. It had been the perfect opportunity.... Only, as she'd opened her mouth, the words trembling on the tip of her tongue—well, Matt had taken a different tact. Shifting toward her on the couch, his mouth brushing against the hairs on the side of her neck, just above her ear, he'd knocked her plan sideways. Shivery at the almost-contact, the words had fled from her thoughts almost as quickly as they'd come.

Any chance of talk had evaporated when she'd felt his tongue swirl a small circle against the sensitive skin there. The only thing that escaped from her lips had been a low, quiet moan of need. Shifting back against his shoulder, her mouth had tipped upward and that'd been all the invitation he'd needed.

It had waited until Sunday for the guilt to return. Matt had left early Saturday afternoon, claiming work at the shop to finish up. Though she'd expected him to return that evening, she hadn't been altogether surprised when he hadn't—sometimes he got so sucked into paperwork or customer interactions or stocking that everything else fled from his mind. Sitting at her kitchen table, sipping a cup of coffee as her mind whirled back and forth, she knew what she wanted to do. Ask for Matt's advice. Gauge some of his wisdom on the matter with Jeff.

As it happened, she was reaching for her phone when it started ringing, cutting her off at the pass.

Only, it wasn't Matt who phoned.

It was Amelia.

"My God," that woman squealed over the phone without preamble. "It's here and it's…I'm so in love I'm considering moving in."

Cat's brow furrowed. "What?"

"The wardrobe. God, Cat I can't believe you didn't tell me."

"The wardrobe?" Cat's voice was mechanical, tense.

"Matt just dropped it off and, oh Cat, you minx. It's, it's even more than I hoped for!"

Cat swallowed down the growing pit enveloping her, crawling up her throat. Matt had finished Amelia's wardrobe. And Amelia thought that Cat had known about it. And why shouldn't she?

Composing her voice, Cat said: "Yeah?" It was weak, but it was the best she could do.

"He customized the shelves so that—"

But Cat wasn't listening anymore. Chewing on her bottom lip, she felt her eyes glaze over. He'd finished Amelia's piece, and he hadn't even bothered to tell Cat about it.

All that time he'd spent working on.

And to think, she'd felt guilty all weekend for not talking to him about...well, about *that*.

Hell, she was the one who'd set the whole thing up. And he knew that.

It was mortifying. It was telling.

"...seriously, I can't believe it."

"I'm glad you like it." Cat heard her voice as though through a fog.

"Like is not the word."

Cat felt tears prick at her eyes. "Um, listen, Amelia, I have to go. My mom just got here and..." she lied.

"Sure, sure! Didn't mean to interrupt but I couldn't *not* call you."

"Yeah, of course." Cat cringed at the toneless sound of her voice. "I'm so glad you did."

Her pride was suffocating.

"Okay, well I'll let you get back to family time."

"Thanks girl," Cat said, her voice coming out thick. "Talk later."

"Bye!"

Setting her phone down on the table, her movements automatic, almost absent, Cat sat staring blindly at the cooling coffee before her. For several long minutes, she sat there, hardly daring to breathe, to move.

And then the first stirrings of anger began to churn to life.

Turns out, Mary had been wrong. Cat wasn't making a mountain out of a molehill. She wasn't letting her emotions get the best of her. Matt was shutting her out of areas of his life. Big areas. Areas that a couple weeks ago she'd held a pivotal role inside.

Scooting her chair back roughly, Cat was on her feet and headed for her bedroom in a flash. Within minutes, she re-emerged wearing a pair of loose-fitting jeans, a plain cotton t-shirt, and a look of almost fanatical determination.

... °•°• ...

Walking inside McBoy's Hardware Store minutes later, her head was empty of all but one thought: that she needed to find Matt, and she needed to find him *now*.

Smiling up from the cash register, as she'd known he would be, was Kyle Harris, the teenager that Matt hired on a part-time basis. Clearly, Matt wasn't working or he wouldn't have had time to drop the wardrobe off at Amelia's.

"Matt here?" Cat asked, her voice clipped. She was playing a hunch, but Matt frequently caught up on bookwork when he had Kyle working the front. She bit back a frown. It was what she'd assumed he'd been doing the night before. Then again, she'd been wrong on that front.

"Yup. In the back..." But Cat was already walking in that direction before he could finish speaking, her feet smacking against the tiling as she headed toward the rear of the building. Entering the back warehouse, she didn't even slow down to let her eyes adjust to the low lighting. With each step, her temper pricked, rising higher and higher.

"Kyle, is that you?"

"Nope."

At the sound of her voice, Matt's head jerked up. Emerging from the stacks of storage boxes, Cat had the small victory of watching the shocked surprise cross his face. Getting up from behind his workbench, Matt met her halfway.

"Hey, what's up?"

"Look," Holding her hand, Cat cleared her throat. "I get it. This part of your life is off-limits now, right?" Looking around, her gaze took in the entire warehouse, skipping over the pile of wood leaning against his table saw, the smell of fresh-cut cedar permeating the air. "Probably, that's my fault."

Matt's brows crinkled. "Cat..."

"But I mean, come *on*? You finished Amelia's cupboard and didn't even think to tell me?" Cat straightened her shoulders. "Dammit, I was instrumental in this whole project but instead of hearing it from you, I had to sit and pretend not to be astonished when Amelia called to talk to me about it."

"Wait a minute."

"I kept thinking to myself, well, this will blow over and when it does—" Cat paused, shaking her head, her arms spreading wide. "How's this going to work, Matt?"

"What?"

"I mean, we can't talk about this stuff anymore?" Her voice rose to an unnatural level. "I get it. I do. This is just a hobby. But it's still a big part of your life and now I'm just...cut off."

"Cat."

"And don't you dare tell me I'm being dramatic. I'm not," she insisted, stomping her foot. "I've felt the distance. You stopped talking to me, so I gave you your space because I knew I screwed up with that whole staring a business idea, and I waited for you to...to let me back in. I bided my time and I told myself it didn't matter. That it was fine. But it's not. I don't want there to be walls up."

"Whoa. Hey, I'm sorry I didn't tell you but I only finished it yesterday evening—"

"Plenty of time between then and now," she reminded him.

Matt grinned wolfishly. "When it comes to you, I tend to get distracted..."

"No, don't make jokes."

Matt let his head tilt a little to one side. She hated that particular look on his face, the one he wore when he thought she was being difficult.

"Tell me you didn't deliberately keep this from me?"

"You're making it sound bigger than it is. It was a wardrobe, not some secret identity."

"Tell me," Cat persisted, her arms clutching her hips.

Matt sighed. Running his fingers across the brim of his hat, he dislodged some specks of sawdust.

"I said I was sorry about the business thing," Cat reminded him, her lower lip trembling. "And you said it was over, done with."

"It is."

"Obviously not."

Matt sighed again.

"There's this whole part of your life that I can't reach anymore."

"You keep saying that, but you're forgetting—as I think you've always forgotten—that it's not all of who I am," Matt said. "I'm more than just a guy who loves woodworking."

"I know that."

"Really? Then why aren't you upset that I've never told you about the time I broke my wrist racing bicycles with my friends in the third grade? Or the fact that I've never told you I hate chocolate or that I love professional baseball?"

Cat blustered. "That's—that's..."

"That's also part of who I am," Matt finished for her. "I hate bikes because of the memory of that fall. Won't even get on one. And chocolate gives me migraines, which is why I won't eat them. And—"

"Okay. Fine, you've made your point," Cat considered, but her lips were in a thin, angry line across her flushed face. "But just because you haven't told me about those things doesn't mean you were hiding them from me."

Matt opened his mouth and then closed it again.

"I won't push you, Matt. I told you that. I apologized."

"Yeah, but you haven't let it go."

Cat gaped at him.

He made a rough sound. "It clearly consumes your thoughts. You're second-guessing everything I tell you and everything I don't, but only as it concerns this one goddamn subject."

Cat sucked in a tough breath. "You know what?"

"What?"

"I'm leaving."

"Dammit, Cat," he said, throwing his arms out wide. His eyes implored her. "Don't be like this."

Spinning on her heel, Cat only stopped long enough to toss over one shoulder. "And this time, don't bother coming over after you're done here." Stomping back up the long hall, Cat could barely see the door by the time she reached it.

CHAPTER TWENTY-SEVEN

Crying in her car helped a little. Though she'd told him not to, Cat remained parked outside the hardware store a few minutes longer than strictly necessary; Matt didn't follow after her. No pretense, nothing. He hadn't so much as chased her to the door.

Evidently, her departure proved to be of little matter to him.

On that sobering thought, Cat pulled away from the curb. She made it all the way to her apartment before her fingers reached treacherously for her phone. Picking it up, she told herself, demanded to herself, that she wasn't upset nor was she surprised to see that Matt hadn't tried to reach her. Not even a text message.

That was rather par for the course, wasn't it?

Her lips twisting, Cat felt her spirits sink, if possible, even lower. It was true. She and Matt would have long since stopped talking if she hadn't kept showing up, if she hadn't kept pushing and picking and making herself available.

When her eyesight misted again, Cat shook her head. Bringing the back of her hand up to her nose, she sniffed. "Well. I guess…" Slinking out of her car, Cat let herself into her apartment, her steps silent as she snuck past Sam's door.

She wasn't in the mood for company.

Not tonight.

... °•°• ...

Taking a deep breath, Cat's foot tap-tapped anxiously as she brought her cellphone up to her ear. All last night, to distract herself from the ache settling deep in her stomach, from the fear that she'd picked the fight that would end everything between her and Matt, the absolute dread that he wouldn't even try to fight for their relationship, she'd bent her mind to other matters—(correction: to that one other matter: incidentally the black binder, Jeff's latest phone call, that proposal)... her thoughts forming into a buzzing hive of manageable diversion, her fingers flying across her laptop as she filled in forms, searched specific websites, her printer zip-zipping merrily as she composed her findings into meticulously arranged categories and tabs. It held a distinct quality of déjà vu.

It was almost three o'clock in the morning when her exhausted body finally slumped over on the edge of her couch, scattered bits and pieces of paper strewn around her sleeping form. Sometimes, distraction was the only possible solution.

"Pick up, pick up, pick up," she muttered aloud now, her hair still mussed from sleep, her shirt from yesterday wrinkled where it hung off her shoulders, her eyes sporting thick smudges of unrest.

As if they'd heard Cat's pleading, there was a quiet click as the call was answered. "Hello?"

"Amelia. Hey."

"What's up?"

"Are you, do you...are you free?"

Unbeknownst to Cat, Amelia's forehead furrowed at the thin, tinny sound of her friend's voice. "Everything okay? You sound...stuffy?"

"Me? I'm fine. I'm fine," Cat assured her, pushing the sleeve of her crumbled shirt up a little on her forearm. Her movements were as aimless as they were pointless. "I wanted to talk to you about, um, well...it sort of has to do with your business."

"Thinking about getting new professional headshots?"

Cat blew out her breath. "Well, yes. Though that's not actually why—"

"Really?" And then: "That's awesome, Cat!" There was the sound of papers rustling in the background. "Let me see—I'm guessing you'll want to take them at your office."

"The credit union? No. Definitely not."

"No?"

"It'd be dated before I even got them."

"What? What are you talking about?"

"Plus, I always thought that space was so…beige. Plastic plants and bland prints on the walls." Cat shook her head. "No, no, I want something more aesthetic than that, something that'll showcase my personality more. God, that is, I hope *I'm* not beige. Thoughts?"

"Cat, what the hell are you talking about?"

Cat reached up to scratch the side of her head. "Do you, uh, do you want to get lunch?"

"Now?"

Cat considered her appearance. She made a face. "Well…how about half an hour from now."

"Uh, sure."

"Meet me at Mick's?"

"Cat? Is everything okay?"

"Yup."

"Is this about Matt?"

"Nope."

If Amelia heard the warning in the stark response, she heeded it wisely. With a quick nod, she said: "Half an hour then."

Hanging up, Cat was up and off the couch in seconds, her fingers already reaching for the hem of her shirt as she pulled it over her head. A quick shower, time to gather her addled wits, half an hour should just about cover it…

Forty minutes later, her still-damp hair pulled into a ponytail, a dash of eyeshadow and lipstick applied to her pale countenance, Cat nipped inside Mick's. Surveying the half-full restaurant, she let out a sigh of relief when she realized that she'd beaten Amelia there. Nabbing a seat at a high-top table, she shucked off the large shoulder-bag she'd brought with her. She no sooner hung the shoulder strap on the edge of her chair when Cat spotted Amelia.

Plunking down in her own seat, Amelia's initial smile of greeting faltered when she saw Cat unearth that most condemned of items, the black binder, from her bag.

Her eyes narrowed as they meet the gleam of excitement in her friend's gaze. "Cat..." There was a loaded note in that tone. "Come on."

"No." Laying her hand protectively over the cover, Cat shook her head. "No, it's not what you're thinking."

Amelia pursed her lips. "Good, because what I'm thinking right now doesn't look good for you."

"It's not about Matt."

Amelia nodded slowly. "Proceed."

Cat's lips pulled apart in a tremulous smile. "You started your own business."

"Yes." Amelia cocked her head a little to one side. "As you well know."

"So, well..." with a touch of her hand, Cat pushed the binder across the table toward Amelia. "I was hoping, you'd take a look at this. It's just a mock-up example—"

"Something I well know," Amelia couldn't help reminding her.

"Not quite." Cat looked down at the binder. "This is new. Something I whipped together last night. It's still a bit rough..."

That got Amelia's attention. Lifting one eyebrow she paused. "New?"

"I mean, it's a different mock-up this time. It's one...it's one I would have done for you, if you'd needed help when you first wanted to start a business." Cat heard the breathless quality of her voice. Nodding toward the binder, she pleaded. "Would you just...would you look it over? Knowing now what you know, did I forget anything vital? Would you have found the information helpful? Informative? Did I get it correct? Do you agree with some of my thoughts and business connections?" Waving her hands, Cat chanced a look at Amelia.

"Okay," that girl said readily enough. Leaning forward, her gaze dipping low, Amelia flipped open the first page. Then the second.

Intent, Cat studied Amelia's face—her lips moving silently as she read and scanned over the papers inside, her eyes widening at one point, her lips pulling into a smile, a small line of concentration appearing between her eyes...

Finally, Amelia reached the end of the binder. Closing it, she crossed her arms over its top before bringing her gaze back up to Cat.

"So," she said slowly. "Want to fill me in here?"

Cat shrugged. "I mean…is it any good?"

"Yeah." Blowing out a breath, Amelia smiled. "It's actually amazing."

"Really? And the businesses I would have recommended…?"

"I use most of them." Amelia's smile widened. "And, after reading this, I'll probably inquire after a few others you mentioned."

"Yeah?"

"Yeah, Cat. Now, you finally want to tell me what's going on?"

CHAPTER TWENTY-EIGHT

Matt didn't call the next day. Or the one after that. Soon an entire week passed...and then some. Still no word. Though her thoughts strayed to him far more frequently than she wanted to admit, though she'd completely lost her appetite after the third day of deafening silence, though she felt an ache in her chest that felt almost physical, Cat didn't try to reach out to him either. Even if she'd wanted to (and she did—good Lord did she want to talk to him, hear his voice), Cat resolutely kept her days and evenings full to bursting:

It started with a pregnant pause outside the office door of the president of the credit union that first Monday morning after their blow-up. A quick knock and then a long, heavy conversation. The hitch in her voice, the sweat coating her palms had focused her attention, blocked everything else out. After all, what she had said was monumental, life-altering...

The whispered rumors circling from the mouths of her co-workers had kept her preoccupied during her work hours. These chats had oddly steadied her, reminded her of what she was doing and why.

Then, the most ferocious and silent game of Canasta she'd ever played. She and Mary won by a landslide. (No one asked questions. Then or later. No one mentioned her sudden mean streak of aggressive playing. They knew enough to keep quiet about answers that weren't forthcoming.)

After that, multiple days spent over long conversations with Jeff. And a woman named Pamela. Forms to be completed. More calls to make, meetings to set-up and then finally: "Is there anything else you need from me?"

"Just your signature."

A terrifying leap. "Okay."

A shopping spree soon followed. She bought a new coffee table. And a living room lamp. The thrill of the purchases, of what they symbolized, kept her spirits buoyed, gave her the false hope of new beginnings. They also helped erase the images of Matt stamped across her home.

Yet still, despite all of this, she thought about him. She couldn't escape thinking about him. This nagging pull was unduly helped along by Sam who swung over late last Wednesday evening to hang out.

Whistling at the paperwork before Cat on the kitchen table, Sam had tucked an errant strand of hair behind her ear as she'd smiled hugely at her friend. "Wow. What does Matt think of all this? I mean…shoot, he was kind of the catalyst to it all."

Cat shrugged, her eyes dropping down to where her fingers were playing on the edge of her tabletop. "I, uh, I haven't told him."

Sam didn't bother to misunderstand. Instead, her smile dimmed. "Ah, well that explains it then."

Cat gave her a narrowed look.

"The almost fanatical look about you." Sam arched a pointed eyebrow. "And how much you've been able to accomplish in such a short period of time."

"Sam."

But that girl only raised up a hand at Cat's warning tone. "Look, I get it. When Tony and I broke up, I needed something to occupy my time, to keep my thoughts from thinking too much. Only," she shrugged almost apologetically. "Only, Tony and I were no longer good for each other. We needed to break up. But you…girl, you were happy with Matt."

Cat made a sound low in her throat.

"I'm just saying, don't let pride get in the way of what you want."

"I'm not. This," Cat said and using the sharp edge of her fingernail, stabbing at the paperwork spread out before them. "I want *this*."

"Right. But you also want him. And unlike me, you can have both."

Sam was smart enough to end her argument there.

So yes, Cat thought about Matt but that's as far as she would allow herself to go. In between the calls she made, when her fingers would suddenly pause over the keyboard as her treacherous mind wandered, she'd find herself wondering about him. Wondering what he was doing. Wondering if he was missing her too.

And yes, she thought up a ridiculous number of reasons to call or text him. She thought up perfectly excusable scenarios in which she'd be forced to run down to the hardware store, all of them seemingly innocent.

But at the last, she'd scratch the thought, throttle the urge.

She was done being the only one invested in this relationship…that was, if they even still had one. She was done being the only one willing to show her cards, to put her vulnerabilities out on display.

Not to mention, she felt a bit silly. Missing him so much. For all intents and purposes, she'd only just met him. She'd only recently become aware of the timbre of his voice, of that sweet cedar smell that seemed to cling to his skin, only just become accustomed to the taste of his lips, the feel of his breath against her skin.

But she did miss him. His dry sense of humor, the tingle of sensation that always accompanied his touch, the way he'd poke fun at her until she found herself laughing along with him. Okay yes, Cat wanted to reach out to Matt, but she wasn't sure if he'd even care enough to make himself available. Just the idea had her pride shriveling up. Certainly, he hadn't tracked her down after she'd walked out of his warehouse. He hadn't come up with myriad reasons to reach out to her. She wanted him to make the first move, to answer her insecurities with his own.

This time she wanted to be chased. And if she was cutting off her nose to spite her face, then so be it.

"Anyway, he was right," she murmured up at her ceiling two long nights later. "It's time that I focus my attention on me."

Easier said than done and by the following Thursday, she was forced to admit defeat. She'd lost. He wasn't coming for her. She hadn't meant that much to him after all. No matter how many times she told herself that it was useless if it wasn't reciprocal, she kept circling back to the same hope. Until it finally died.

Biting back a harsh film of tears, Cat waited endlessly for the work day to come and go. She should have been excited. This should have been a day of bittersweet reminiscing and cake with her co-workers. One last, final day to go.

Instead, she felt hollow, like a limp ragdoll as she envisioned another lonely night ahead of her.

And another after that.

Pretty soon, they'd consume her. When all the distractions would come to an end. When she'd be forced with her thoughts, with everything that might have been. By four o'clock, punching in some last-minute data reports, Cat could hardly think past the hard, dull beat of her heart, of her shattered senses.

He hadn't come for her. She would go home alone tonight. Again. It was a routine she'd have to get used to once more.

These damning fortunes swirling about her, Cat felt a hot surge of irritation lick at her throat when someone knocked on the other side of her office door. The last thing, the very last thing, Cat wanted was another meeting, another round of conversation held across her desk. She had one more day. Was it too much to ask that she manage to leave on time just this once, slip effortlessly out the door?

Apparently, it was.

"Cat?" Poking her head around the door, Marge, one of the front tellers, smiled tentatively. "Got a spare minute?"

Cat swallowed back her instinctive reply. "Uh. Yeah. What's—?" but before she could finish her sentence, Marge's head disappeared, only to reemerge sections later, followed closely behind by the tall length of a mirage.

It must have been.

She'd become delusional. That was the only thing that explained it.

Because the man who followed Marge into Cat's office was none other than Matthew McBoy.

Cat's mouth dropped open the tiniest bit, a soft gasp half-smothered in her throat. Blinking, she wondered again if she hadn't lost her mind—if she hadn't envisioned this moment one too many times in her daydreams and now she'd officially conjured him out of thin air. But when Cat reopened her eyes, he remained in front of her.

She had to force her body to stay seated, to not react.

"Here you go, sir," Marge said, motioning him forward. With a quick smile at Cat, she retreated back into the hallway, shutting the door behind her.

A beat of silence spread across the office. By now Cat had pressed her lips back together. But her hands, clenched against the side of her desk, gave her nerves away.

"Matt?" she croaked out. "What, ah, what are you doing here?" She felt her eyes grow larger in her face when, in response, he casually pulled out on the chairs across her desk and took a seat.

Okay, she hadn't dreamt him up. He was there, in her office, sitting opposite of her, those whiskey brown eyes half-obscured beneath his baseball hat.

"Well," he said, crossing one ankle over his thigh. "You came barging into my place of work often enough, I figured it was only fair that I returned the favor."

The words would have been mocking had it not been for the gentle amusement in his voice. Cat felt her hands pressing more sharply against the faux-wood of her desk. She nodded. "Okay."

Another beat of silence passed. His habitual baseball cap was slung especially low over his forehead, shadowing his eyes. Still, Cat waited.

If he wanted to come barging in then fine, but he was going to be the one doing the talking too!

"You were right."

Cat leaned forward when the words, softly said, floated across the expanse separating them. "I was?"

Matt smiled, his gaze flicking up to catch hers. "Going to make this hard on me?"

"Not deliberately." Cat licked her lips. It was the shock of seeing him, especially after radio silence. She'd thought for sure...well, no matter about that now. Fighting to keep her composure, to keep the upswing of hope from rising up only to be caught in a fall, she inclined her head questioningly.

"I did shut you out," Matt admitted on a deep, gentle sigh of regret. "With Amelia's closet, with the woodworking. But dammit, sometimes you make things impossible." Shoving a hand up underneath his hat, Matt sighed before readjusting the brim. "You overreact and... I was tired of fighting that look that enters your eyes every time the subject of woodworking gets brought up."

Cat swallowed an instinctive urge to argue that point. He was right. She knew that. Instead, she nodded in slow acquiescence. "I know. I felt it too. The tension."

But Matt wasn't finished talking. "But I didn't mean to—wait." Shifting his gaze, Matt's eyes narrowed.

At the sudden redirection, Cat blinked, following his line of sight. "Huh?"

"Is that the binder?" Reaching forward, Matt's fingers slid toward where it now habitually rested to one side of her desk.

"God," Cat grumbled, "I should really switch it over to a blue folder or something. Just to make everyone shut up."

"What?"

Blushing at the hot tone of her voice, Cat shrugged. "Yes. Yeah, it's the binder. But I promise—" holding up both hands, she stared Matt down. "I promise, it's not what you're thinking."

He was still leaning forward, his fingers splayed across the front of it. "What am I thinking?"

"That I should have destroyed it already. I promised to do that and it seems like I didn't but, I swear I'm not...I'm not about to..."

"To attack me with it again?" Mat supplied helpfully when it seemed that Cat lost the momentum of her words.

"Something like that." Taken aback by the evident humor in his voice, she wasn't sure how to respond. "But I'm not. I learned my lesson."

Nabbing the binder up, Matt settled back with it on his lap. "Then why do you still have it."

"It's for me."

"You?" Glancing up at her, his eyes twinkled. "Thinking of getting into woodworking? Am I going to have some competition?"

"Don't be ridiculous," Cat muttered. "Besides, how could I possibly compete with someone who doesn't *do* woodworking?"

Matt pursed his lips. "I was actually hoping you still had it," he said as his fingers flipped open to the first page.

"That's not—" but Cat didn't need to finish her statement.

Matt's eyes clouded momentarily before he lifted his gaze.

"That's, that's for Amelia."

Matt raised an eyebrow. "She's starting up another business?"

"No—" Cat shrugged, dropping her eyes down to the top of her desk. "No, it was just…I was running through a, a test, I guess."

Matt's head tilted a little to one side, not surprisingly more confused than clarified at her words.

Cat took a deep breath, her eyes staring guardedly at her computer screen. "Because, well, as it happens you were also a little right."

"Come again?"

There was no attempt to hide the amusement in those loaded words.

With an exaggerated move, Cat hitched up her shoulders. "I *was* focusing on you because something was missing in my life. But you were wrong about why. It wasn't because I was running away from something, rather I was running toward it." She pulled a self-deprecating face. "I just didn't know it then."

Matt nodded. "Okay."

"Still. I shouldn't have, you know, pressured you. About the woodworking," Cat admitted begrudgingly, her gaze lowering demurely. "I truly am sorry about that."

She heard his heavy sigh. "I know, Cat. I know."

"But, well, what I did—the researching and the forms and applications, and all of the background work…I liked doing it." One finger played absently with the mouse beside her desktop computer. "And I'm good at it. I always have been. For years, I've been the person that people came to for advice about which company to use for this, or which product works best for that.

"Okay."

"The idea of inter-business collaborating, of gathering a team of people to help one another out—throwing website designers and accountants and photographers and whatnot together to aid

mutual business growth and economic development..." She
lifted her hands. "It's, well, I never realized that it was a workable, valuable skill set. Fitting the pieces together, realizing
what someone needs, knowing the lingo and the analysis studies
and..." she nodded toward the binder. "As I said, I'm good at
it."

"I know."

Cat's lips widened into a smile. "And just so you know, the
set-up I did for you. It was excellent."

Matt smiled. "I should have appreciated it."

"Helping you, it was really like helping *me*. I—you know, I
like what I do here at the credit union," she said, her words coming out quickly. "But it's not my passion. And I guess, harping
at you about that very subject made me realize..."

"Realize you want a career change?"

"No. That's just it...I sort of fell into the idea of a career
change."

Cat still hadn't managed to chance a look at his face, but she
could hear the smile in his voice when he spoke next. "Doing
what?"

Cat looked down at her desk. Her fingers were now chipping
at the edges. "Basically, I'll be a business consultant." Clearing
her throat, she gave him the condensed version. How she'd met
Jeff and helped him with a client and how that had, in turn, re-
sulted in a job offer from his company—a business to business
networking firm. "...they're expanding and, with a growing cli-
entele in town here, they're opening up a satellite office. And,
anyway, with my financial background and connections
they...well, they asked me to step in as a sort of liaison. Bro-
kering introductions and helping navigate business integration."

"Ah."

"Don't laugh," Cat muttered. She could feel the stiffness of
her features, the uncomfortable weight of vulnerability as it
cloaked her person.

"I wouldn't."

"So that's what I was doing with the binder. I wanted Amelia's opinion to see, well, to see if I was any good at this sort of
thing."

"So, you took the job?"

"My last day at the credit union is tomorrow."

Matt didn't hesitate. "Good for you, Cat. I'm impressed but not surprised."

At that, her eyes lifted, catching the sincerity in his own. "No?"

"No." Matt shook his head ruefully. "Once you set your mind to something—"

"I can be a bit stubborn, I know."

"That's not always a bad thing."

"Or always a good thing."

Matt merely shrugged.

"But none of that," Cat took a deep breath. "None of that explains…"

"Explains?" Matt helped.

"What *you're* doing here." Cat ducked her head. She prayed her voice would keep neutral, would withhold any undue expectation. "What you're really doing here."

Matt smiled down at his lap. "Got a bit sidetracked, huh?"

"Then let's return to the point at hand."

"It's kind of hard to explain," Matt muttered, the words coming slowly, haltingly. "I'd rather show you."

"I'm not following."

Matt glanced up at the wall clock. "I didn't come in here at closing time on accident."

Cat's stomach pitched at the words. Still, she waited him out. She wasn't sure she trusted herself to speak.

"I was hoping that, after you've finished up here, that you'd maybe come back with me to the hardware store?"

For the briefest moment, Cat saw the mask slip on his face. And with it, all the fight went out of her. In that flash of time, where, moments ago, a man had sat looking as though this was all too easy for him, the truth revealed itself. Matt was good at hiding his emotions. Though he hadn't seemed the least bit nervous or anxious since he'd entered her office, though he hadn't seemed as though he were containing any feelings at all, any of the emotions she'd found herself racked with pretty much since she'd met him, Cat finally saw underneath all that subterfuge.

To a man whose fingers thrummed a frantic beat against the denim of his jeans, whose jaw had twitched just the tiniest bit at the invitation, whose eyes had almost imperceptibly shifted away from her gaze at the words.

He cared too. He was just better at pretending otherwise.

She couldn't help but ask. "Why?"

Matt's eyes swiveled back to her. "I'm not a quick study," he admitted. "And you're not the only person who could be accused of stubbornness."

At that Cat smiled.

"But I'm here now. I hope that counts for something."

CHAPTER TWENTY-NINE

Parking beside Matt's rig in the back lot of the hardware store, Cat took a deep breath before alighting from her vehicle. Though she'd gotten the impression that he'd meant to drive her over, Cat had beaten him to the punch, insisting that she'd meet him there—there had been no misunderstanding her point.

She would be driving herself, thank you very much.

She wasn't going to expect too much.

And she most definitely wasn't going to get stuck inside a vehicle with a man who kindly but firmly let it be known that everything they'd had, everything she'd dared to want with him, had come to an end.

Walking over to where he waited beside the long, rutted path before the loading docks, Cat spared Matt a fleeting smile.

"Thanks for coming," he offered quietly.

Cat nodded mutely. She didn't want to come across as cold. Or indifferent. Then again, she didn't want to have it all dashed away again. That pitiful swell of hope. It was a tough balancing act. She only prayed she was walking the line straight.

"Want to tell me what we're doing here?"

"You'll see," Matt promised before leading her forward. Coming up to the side door, she watched with mounting curiosity as Matt's wrist sprang forward, his fingers gripping the knob before twisting and pushing it open.

With a sweep of his hand, he gestured her inside. "After you."

Tilting her head, Cat did as he requested. "Where am I going?"

"My workstation."

Cat nodded as her feet took her seamlessly in that direction. She knew the building well by now. Only, halfway there, she jerked to a stop at the unfamiliar sight before her.

Fetching up beside her, Matt stopped too, his eyes wary, guarded as they searched her face.

"Wait," Cat said, her voice little more than a whisper as she took in the unpolished, untreated mission-style desk sitting a little left of the workbench, the narrow bookcase with a curlicue top standing beside it, the gorgeous nightstand... Slowly, she turned her head, her eyes catching his. "What is all this?"

Matt's gaze flickered from her rapt expression to the objects in question and then back to her. He hefted one shoulder. "It's a start."

"A start?"

In answer, Matt reached out a hand. Settling it on her shoulder, he half-turned Cat in his direction. "If you're still interested, I'd love some of that business advice now." His lips tugged upward. "You know, the advice I was too pig-headed to take before."

"You would?"

His fingers squeezed slightly. "For a small, a very small, side business."

"But..." Cat could feel the creases of confusion spreading across her forehead, her eyes clashing with his. "But you said that—?"

"And I meant it," Matt said. "At least, I meant some of it. I'm not closing down the hardware store."

"Okay."

"Despite what you and my grandmother think," Matt continued pointedly, "because I know she had a part to play in all of this, I love this store. Yes, I was my Grandfather's passion first, but I love it too."

Smiling falteringly, Cat nodded before saying again: "Okay."

"You were right about another thing too," Matt said as though he disliked the taste of the admission. "I didn't think I could juggle both woodworking and running the store." His left hand came up to grasp her other shoulder. "And I wasn't sure I had the talent to make something of this."

"You do."

"Thank you," Matt replied, his eyes drifting momentarily to the collection of work in question. "I'm going to start small— build a couple of pieces and set them out in the store for sale and see how they do."

"And custom work?"

"If and when I get requests, I'll schedule them as my calendar allows."

"Okay."

Matt's hands tightened on hers. "Is that all you're going to say?"

Cat sucked her lips inside her mouth. "I mean, I'm sur- prised." Gently pulling free of his hold, Cat found her feet mov- ing toward the workbench, her fingers spreading out to run across the top of the bookcase. "When, when did you do all of this?"

"When did you storm out of here last?"

Cat half-turned back toward him, a begrudging smile on her face. "Week and a half ago. Give or take."

Matt's lips tugged upward. "Well, that's when."

"I see."

"I had a lot of free time on my hands suddenly." Matt stepped up beside her. "And I needed something to distract me."

"Yeah, I know what you mean," Cat murmured.

"And somewhere between me tossing that black binder on the floor," Matt added, gesturing sheepishly toward the spot now, "and finishing Amelia's wardrobe...I don't know, I couldn't shake the idea to planted in my head. I found myself hearing what you said..."

"Told you so," Cat mouthed.

Matt ignored her. "I found myself resentful that these pro- jects—your cupboard, her wardrobe—were over. That they were the exception. And I realized that I wanted more. That maybe I could actually do more."

Cat made a noncommittal sound. She felt sick to her stom- ach. She had been right to drive herself over to the hardware store. It hadn't been what she'd thought—his invitation. "So that's why you came to my office today," she concluded, shifting her gaze away. "You were hoping I still had that binder."

"What? No." Matt's voice rose in warning. "No!" And just like that, his hands shot out again, gripping both of her arms. Turning her abruptly toward him, Cat's gasp of surprise only seeming to spur him on, Matt growled, "But it was as good a reason as any that I could come up with."

"I don't—"

"This is why I came to your office." Swooping down, his lips captured the questions still clinging to her own.

Moaning a little under the pressure, the tumultuous shift that her emotions were still processing, Cat's mouth conformed eagerly to his.

When his lips finally broke off from hers, his forehead coming to rest against hers, Cat caught her breath at the look in those chocolate eyes so close to her own.

"Well," she breathed, a rush of confidence entering her voice at the undisguised vulnerability, of longing staring back at her. "What the hell took you so long?"

"You, sitting so poker-straight in that office chair, hardly a smile of greeting on your face," he confessed. "I wasn't sure…"

Cat's eyebrows furrowed. "No, I don't just mean today. Why'd you wait to…to…"

"To?"

To come after her. "To tell me. To see me."

Matt smirked. "Other than the fact that you more or less demanded space?"

"Like that would have really stopped you. Yes, other than that."

"I guess because I wanted to see if it was even possible. If I'd still love it as much. Outside of a hobby." He shrugged. "And, I suppose, I needed a little time to cool off myself."

"Anyone ever tell you that you're incredibly hard-headed," Cat mused but there was a smile in her voice.

"Or that you can be a bit…much?"

Cat scoffed. "I've never heard of such nonsense."

Matt grinned. Loosening his grip around her upper arms, he dropped a quick kiss on her lips. "But at least you try. You're always trying."

Cat felt her lips jerking upward. It was hard to deny the pleasure in that compliment. "Sometimes to no avail," she said graciously.

"Sometimes. But at least you do something. You get an answer."

"You may be giving me far too much credit," Cat said. "Before I met you, I was entirely bored with my life."

"Did you know that? That you were bored?"

"Yes." Her lips twisted. "Well, no. Not at first."

"And what did you do when you figured that out?"

Cat smiled slowly. "I broke my kitchen door."

"Yeah, that's about what I figured."

"It definitely had a big effect on my life."

"And mine."

Leaning against his bulk, Cat's own hands went up and around Matt's waist. "Yeah. Sorry about that."

Matt chuckled. "Was I complaining?"

"Hard to tell with you sometimes."

Matt sighed. "I know I didn't react well when you first brought up the idea of starting a woodworking business."

"That's an understatement."

"You really destroyed the business plan you made for me?"

"As requested."

"I'm sorry to hear that."

"Yeah?" Cat couldn't help the note of incredulity that eeked into her voice.

"Yeah."

Cat's eyebrows rose. "My, my. How you've changed, sir. I hardly recognize you."

Tugging her closer, Matt's head descended, his voice rasping over her parted lips. "And this is only the beginning."

Cat grinned.

"So, how 'bout it? Will you take me on as a client?"

Cat paused. "Actually," she confessed, "I'm not sure that's such a good idea after all."

Matt stilled. The smile on his face froze the tiniest bit. "Oh. Uh, okay."

"I have a code of professional ethics," Cat hurried to say, her voice dropping to a huskier tone. For added effect, she wiggled her eyebrows. "And really, romantic relationships with clients is probably against company policy anyway. Conflict of interest. I'm sure you understand…"

A muscle in Matt's jaw tremble in dawning amusement. "Yeah," he murmured, his hands lowering to her hips. "I could see how that might be a problem."

Tangling her fingers in the short hairs at the nape of his neck, Cat grinned as she slowly pulled his head down to meet the upward thrust of hers. "But. I suppose if it were pro bono…?"

"You think?" Matt's lips nibbled against hers.

Cat made a low sound in her throat. "Yeah," she whispered, "I think we might be able to work something out." Those were the last words she managed before his mouth took full possession of hers.

Cat didn't mind the disruption.

 … °•°• …

A Contemporary Women's Fiction Novel,
by
Amber Laura

*She swore she'd never give into her feelings for him,
swore he'd never know how much she loved him. A fall
from grace years ago had left its terrible, lacerated mark—
—she wasn't willing to put her heart at risk a second time.
That's what she promised herself. And then, one fateful
night, she slipped…*

A Contemporary Women's Fiction Novel,
by
Amber Laura

Planning her sister's wedding will require humor and imagination, a dash of sibling animosity, and a few white lies…but hey, at least there will be cake. Twenty-Seven Tiered Almond Cake is a light-hearted women's fiction story about relationships, self-reflection, and redemption (there's even a little romance…and a whole lot of cake!)

A Contemporary (Western) Romance Novel
by
Amber Laura

She wasn't supposed to stay.
But after him, how could she leave?

topaz
and
lace

A NOVEL

Amber Laura

Cassie wasn't supposed to stay. Her move to Pantula, Texas, working as a student veterinarian in a small animal hospital, was only supposed to be temporary. She wasn't supposed to fall in love. Then she met him. Brannt McDowell, owner of the most prosperous ranch in town. Well, some much for supposed to.

Made in the USA
Monee, IL
30 January 2022